THE COURAGE TREE

DIANE CHAMBERLAIN

THE COURAGE TREE

MIRA®

ISBN 1-55166-799-1

THE COURAGE TREE

Visit us at www.mirabooks.com

Printed in Canada.

Many people helped me in the creation of *The Courage Tree*.
I spoke with Search and Rescue experts, medical personnel, real
patients and their families, and fellow writers who kept me on
track. I would like to thank Ann Allman, Tim Arthur, Mary Alice Kruesi,
Gretchen Lacharite, Kathleen Lawton, Char LeFleur, John Nelson,
Alice Soto and Monica Walton for generously sharing their expertise
and knowledge with me.

I am especially grateful to my editor, Amy Moore-Benson, for
her incredible patience; to readers Beth Joyce and Esther Jagielski,
who created a one-of-a kind basket for me in gratitude for my
previous books, as well as to encourage my future efforts, and to
Craig MacBean, for helping me thrive in the midst of chaos.

You cannot be a hero without being a coward.
—George Bernard Shaw

PROLOGUE

She would have no music where she was going.

Zoe stood in the center of her living room, with its vaulted ceilings, white carpeting and glassed-wall view of the Pacific Ocean, and stared, transfixed by the huge speaker in the corner of the room. She'd come to terms with the fact that she would lose the beach and the smell of the sea. She knew she could live without television—*gladly* without television and its bevy of new, young talent—and she could live without newspapers and magazines. But no music? It suddenly seemed like a deal breaker. But then her eyes drifted to the picture of Marti, where it rested on the top of the baby grand piano. Marti had been twenty in that picture, standing next to Max on the beach. She was *near* Max, but not touching him, and there was no sense of connection between father and daughter, as though each of their pictures had been taken separately and then spliced together. It disturbed Zoe to see that distance between them. If the picture had been of herself and Marti, would they look equally as detached from one another? she wondered. She feared that they would. It was time to change that.

In her boyish way, Marti looked beautiful in the picture. Zoe studied the short cap of blond hair, the compact, small-breasted body, huge blue eyes and long dark lashes that gave away Marti's identity as a female, and Zoe knew she was making the right decision. In a choice between music and Marti, there was no contest. Everything else in the universe paled in comparison to Zoe's need to save her daughter.

She turned away from the wall of stereo equipment and began climbing the broad spiral staircase to the second story, her resolve once again intact. It was quite simple, really, leaving forever. She had planned well ahead and now had no need even to pack a suitcase. What could she possibly put in a suitcase that would last her the rest of her life? Besides, someone might realize a suitcase was missing. Unlikely, since she had an entire room on the third story filled with luggage; but still, it was possible, and she couldn't take that chance.

She walked into Max's bedroom. She and Max had slept together for the forty years of their marriage, but they'd each had their own bedroom in addition to the master suite they'd shared. Their separate rooms had been for times alone, times of renewal and refreshment, for reading without disturbing one another, for making phone calls late into the night when one of them was working on a project. It was in Max's room where she knew she would find exactly what she needed.

Opening the door to Max's walk-in closet, she was startled by the spicy aroma that enveloped her. Max's aftershave still filled this room, four full months after his death. She had not touched the clothes that hung in neat rows along the walls of the closet since that miserable day in November, and they slowly took on a blurred, surrealistic shape before her eyes. How was it that scent could instantly evoke so much pain? So many memories? But no time for them now. She brushed her hand across her eyes as she pulled the step stool from the corner of the closet toward the shelves in the rear. Climbing onto the stool, she reached toward the back of the top shelf.

Her hand felt the soft-sided rifle case, and she wrapped her fingers around it and drew it down from the shelf. Climbing off the stool, she rested the green case containing Max's rifle carefully, gingerly, on the carpeted floor of the closet, then returned to her perch on the stool. Reaching onto the shelf once again, she found the box of bullets, then the Beretta pistol and a few loose clips. Never before had she touched these guns, and she hadn't approved of Max having them. Probably the only thing they'd ever disagreed about.

"Max Garson's death marks the end of one of the longest running and, by all accounts, most harmonious marriages in Hollywood," *People* magazine had written.

For the most part, that had been a highly accurate assessment. And right now, Zoe was glad Max had defied her when it came to the guns. She was doubly glad she had told her friends about the rifle and the pistol and where they were hidden. They would tell the police, and the police would discover the guns were missing. *Perfect.*

The police would no doubt talk to Bonita, the therapist Zoe had seen for "grief counseling," as well. Zoe had not needed to employ her acting skills to fake her symptoms of depression.

"Do you think about suicide?" Bonita had asked her on one recent visit, when Zoe had been particularly tearful.

"Yes," she had nodded truthfully.

"Do you have a plan?" Bonita asked.

The question had shaken Zoe for an instant. How could Bonita possibly know? But then she realized Bonita was asking her if she had considered how she would end her life. Nothing more than that.

"No," she had answered, knowing full well that if she said she had a plan, Bonita would arrange to have her locked up someplace, and wouldn't the tabloids have a field day with *that*. Zoe most certainly *did* have a plan. Just not the sort of plan to which Bonita was alluding.

She carried the guns into the bedroom and caught sight of herself in the mirror above the dresser. The image horrified her. She looked completely ridiculous. Her long blond hair fell across the rifle case, her deep bangs hung all the way to her eyelashes, and there was something about the lighting in the room that made her skin look sallow, her eyes sunken. She was a large woman. She'd always been tall and full-figured, and back in her James Bond days, she'd been considered voluptuous, but now she was simply big. Amazonian. *An aging sex goddess.* She had bristled when she'd read those words about herself somewhere, but suddenly, she understood them to be the truth. Who had she been trying to kid, still wearing her hair the way she had when she was twenty-five, coloring the heck out of it to mask the gray? She looked away from the mirror and headed for the stairs. There would be no more two-hundred-dollar trips to the beauty salon in her future, and the thought was rather liberating.

Downstairs, she walked through the kitchen and out into the garage, where she rested the guns on the back seat of her silver Mercedes. Returning to the house, she sat down at the dining room table and gave her attention to what would be her final—and most difficult—task in this home she had cherished for so many years.

Staring down at the sheet of cream-colored parchment on the table in front of her, she picked up the Pelikan fountain pen Marti had given her several Christmases ago, on a day when the world had still seemed benevolent and the future still held promise. She rested the nib of the pen on the paper.

I see no choice but to end my life, on this, the eve of my six-tieth birthday, she wrote. Leaning away from the paper, cocking her head to the side, she noted that her penmanship looked like that of an old woman. Her hand quivered above the page.

"Pathetic old cow," she muttered to herself, then continued writing.

My life is not worth much anymore. My beloved husband is dead; my daughter has been wrongly, cruelly imprisoned for the murder of Tara Ashton; the tabloids persist in noting each new wrinkle on my face, and I'm losing my singing voice. Although my acting skills are at their peak, they go unrecognized these days. Parts that once would have come to me are now given to actresses much younger than myself.

Zoe stopped writing for a moment and looked out the window toward the ocean. That last sentence made her sound small and bitter. She could leave it out, but then she would have to start the letter all over again. And what did she care what anyone thought of her at this point? She laughed at the bruised ego, the irritating narcissism that had dogged her these past few years and that seemed intent on following her to her counterfeit grave.

What do I have left to live for? she began writing again. *I hope to take my life somewhere where I won't be found. I don't want to be seen in that condition. Marti, I'm sorry, darling. I'm so sorry I failed you. I tried every possible avenue I could to help you prove your innocence, but the system has failed both of us.* The tears were quick to come this time. One fell on the paper, and she blotted it from the word *innocence* with the side of her hand.

She *had* failed Marti—in far too many ways—choosing the demands of her career over the needs of her daughter at every turn, placing Marti's day-to-day care in the hands of nannies, sending her off to boarding school to let someone else deal with her moods and her mischief.

Suspicion would never have fallen on you had you not been my daughter, she wrote. *Zoe's daughter. I love you, dearest.* Zoe's breath caught in her throat, and she stared out the window at the sea for a long moment before continuing. *Be strong,* she wrote. *All my love, Mother.*

Moving the sheet of paper to the center of the table, she stood up, blotting her damp palms on her khaki-covered thighs. Her knees barely held her upright as she walked toward the garage, and her entire body trembled now, from the gravity of the lies she had just committed to writing, and from the fear of the journey she was about to make.

CHAPTER ONE

The guest cottage seemed stuffy, its four small rooms over-flowing with sunlight. At two-thirty, Janine turned off the air-conditioning and opened all the windows, starting in her bedroom and Sophie's room, then the kitchen and finally the living room. Although it became instantly warmer in the cottage, the air was arid, a remarkable phenomenon for June in northern Virginia, and the faint breeze carried the scent of magnolia and lavender into the rooms.

Janine sat sideways on the sofa in the living room, her back against the overstuffed arm, bare feet up on the cushions, gazing out the window at Ayr Creek's gardens. In fifteen minutes she could leave, she told herself. That would make her early, but there was no way she could wait here any longer.

The view of the gardens was spectacular from this window. Bands of red and violet, yellow and pink dipped and swirled over more than two acres of rolling landscape before losing themselves in the deep woods between the cottage and the mansion. The nineteenth century, yellow frame, black-shuttered mansion could barely be seen at this time of year due to the lush growth on the trees, allowing Janine to imagine that she was master of her own life and not living on her parents' property. Not that Ayr

Creek truly belonged to her parents, who were little more than caretakers. The house was owned by the Ayr Creek Foundation, which was operated by the descendants of the estate's original owner, Angus Campbell. The Foundation had deeded enough money to the county to keep the garden and a few of the mansion's rooms open to the public on weekends. And through some quiet arrangement, Janine's mother, Donna Campbell Snyder, had been given the right to live in the mansion until her death, although she did not otherwise have a cent of her family's fortune. This, Janine had always thought, was the source of her mother's bitterness.

Nevertheless, Donna and Frank Snyder adored the Ayr Creek estate. Retired history teachers, they relished the task of overseeing the upkeep of the house and gardens. And they willingly allowed Janine and her daughter, Sophie, to live rent-free in the "guest cottage," a euphemism designed to masquerade the true history of the diminutive structure: it had once been home to Ayr Creek's slaves.

There was a tear in the window screen. Just a small one, and if Janine closed one eye and leaned nearer to the screen, she could see one perfect, blue-blossomed hydrangea captured in the opening. If she leaned a little farther to the left, she could see the roses Lucas had planted near the wishing well. She should get up and repair the hole instead of playing games with it, she thought briefly, but shifted positions on the sofa and returned her attention to the gardens instead.

This restlessness, this stuffy, claustrophobic feeling, had been with her all weekend and she knew it was of her own creation. She had not drawn a full breath of air since Friday evening, when she'd watched her daughter ride away in the van with the rest of her Brownie troop. Sophie had grinned and giggled with her friends, looking for all the world like a perfectly healthy eight-year-old girl—except, perhaps, for the pallor and the delicate, willowy, white arms and legs. Janine had waved after the van until she could no longer make out Sophie's red hair against the tinted window. Then she offered a quick smile to the two other mothers in the parking lot of Meadowlark Gardens and got into her car quickly, hoping that the worry hadn't shown in her face. There hadn't been a day in the last five years that she had not worried.

She'd planned to use this weekend alone to clean the cottage from top to bottom, but she'd gotten little done. She'd spent time on Saturday with her mother in the mansion, helping her research historically accurate wallpaper patterns on the Internet for one of the mansion's bedrooms, and listening to her complain yet again about Lucas, the horticulturist in charge of the gardens. Janine knew, though, that she and her mother were both preoccupied with thoughts of Sophie. Was she all right? Eight years old seemed far too young to be spending the weekend at a Girl Scout camp nearly two hours away, even to Janine, and she knew her mother was furious with her for allowing Sophie to go. Sitting in the office, which was part of the mansion's twentieth-century addition, Janine had tried to concentrate on the computer monitor while her mother leaned over her shoulder.

"It's hot out and she'll drink too much water," her mother said. "She'll forget to take her pills. She'll eat the wrong things. You know how kids are."

"She'll be fine, Mom," Janine had said through gritted teeth, although she couldn't help but share her mother's concerns. If Sophie came back from this trip sicker than when she went, the criticism from her parents would never end. Joe would be furious, as well. He had called last night, wanting to know if he could come over to see Sophie after she got home tonight, and Janine knew he was feeling what she did: the deep love and concern for the child they both treasured. Like Janine's mother, Joe had expressed strong disapproval over Sophie's going on this trip. One of many things Joe was angry with her about. Joe's anger was hard for Janine to ignore, because she knew it came from a place of caring, not only about Sophie, but about herself, as well. Even in the ugliest moments of their separation and divorce, she'd been aware that Joe still loved her.

At two-forty-five, Janine left the cottage and got into her car. She drove down the long gravel driveway, banked on both sides by boxwood as old as the estate itself, and looked toward the mansion as she passed it. Her parents would be inside, waiting anxiously for her to bring their granddaughter home. She hoped she'd have some time alone with Sophie before she had to share her with them and Joe.

Meadowlark Gardens was less than half a mile from the Ayr Creek estate, and the parking lot of the public gardens was as full as she'd ever seen it. As Janine turned into the lot from Beulah Road, people dressed in wedding regalia spilled out of one of the brick buildings, probably getting ready to pose for pictures. In the distance, Janine could see another wedding taking place in the gazebo by the pond. A beautiful day for a wedding, she thought, as she drove toward the southeastern corner of the lot, where she was to meet the returning Brownie troop, but her mind quickly slipped back to her daughter. Suddenly, all she could think about was scooping Sophie into her arms. She pressed her foot harder on the gas pedal, cruising far too fast through the lot, and parked her car near the corner.

Although Janine was early, one other mother was already there, leaning against a station wagon, reading a paperback. Janine knew the woman, whose name was Suzanne, vaguely. She was pretty, a bit older than most mothers of children Sophie's age, and it was hard to tell if her chin-length hair was a pale blond or actually gray. Janine smiled as she walked toward her.

"They certainly had great weather, didn't they?" Suzanne asked, shading her eyes from the sun.

"They did." Janine joined her in leaning against the car. "I'm glad it wasn't too humid."

Suzanne tossed her paperback through the open window of

her car. "Oh, that wouldn't have bothered them," she said with a wave of her hand. "Kids don't care whether it's humid or not."

Sophie would have cared, Janine thought, but she kept the words to herself. She tried unsuccessfully to remember what Suzanne's daughter looked like. In truth, she'd paid little attention to the other girls in Sophie's troop. It was so rare that Sophie could take part in any of their activities that Janine had had no opportunity to get to know any of them or their mothers. She looked at Suzanne. "Has your daughter..." she began. "I'm sorry, I don't remember her name."

"Emily."

"Has Emily been on one of these camp-outs before?" Janine asked.

"Yes, she has," Suzanne said. "But none this far away. And I know this is a real first for Sophie, isn't it?"

"Yes." She felt somehow touched that Suzanne knew Sophie's name. But, then, the other mothers probably talked about her.

"It's wonderful she could go," Suzanne said. "I guess she's feeling better, huh?"

"Much better," Janine admitted. So much better it was scary.

"I heard she's receiving some sort of experimental treatment."

"Yes." Janine nodded, then hesitated a moment before adding, "She's in a study of an alternative medicine. She's only been in the study a couple of months, but she's had some dramatic improvement. I'm just praying it will last." It was hard for Janine to give words to Sophie's improvement, to actually hear herself say those words out loud. She lived in terror that it might not last. Since being in the study, Sophie had not only remained out of the hospital, but had finally learned to ride a bike, had eaten almost anything she wanted, and had even attended the last of week of school. For most of the year, she'd been tutored at home or in the hospital, and last year had been equally as bad. Most indicative of Sophie's improvement, though, was the fact that she no longer needed to spend every night attached to her dialysis machine. For the last couple of weeks, she'd required treatments only two nights a week. That had given her the freedom to do something she'd never before been able to do: spend the night away from home with her friends.

Sophie's astonishing improvement seemed miraculous, although Dr. Schaefer, the researcher behind the study, had warned Janine that her daughter still had a long road ahead of her. She would need to receive twice-weekly intravenous infusions of Herbalina, the name he had given his herbal remedy to make it more appealing to the pediatric population of the study, for at least another year. Despite the ground Sophie had gained, her own nephrologist, the doctor she'd been seeing for the past three years, scoffed at the study, as did every other specialist with whom Janine had spoken. They'd pleaded with Janine to enroll Sophie in a different, more conventional study of yet another experimental drug, but Sophie had already participated in several of those studies, and Janine could no longer bear to see her daughter suffer the side effects of the toxic drugs they gave her. With Herbalina, Sophie had only gotten better. No rashes. No cramps. No bloating. No sleepiness.

The positive results were merely a temporary reduction in symptoms, Sophie's regular doctor and his colleagues had argued. Beneath the surface, the disease still raged. They claimed Schaefer offered false hope to the hopeless, but stopped just short of calling the small, wiry, soft-spoken doctor a charlatan. Janine could easily see the situation from their perspective. After all, the medical profession had been grappling with Sophie's form of kidney disease for decades, searching for a way to turn the tide of its destruction. Then along comes some alternative medicine doctor, with his combination of tree bark and herbs, and he thinks he can do what no one else has been able to do: cure the incurable. Sophie's regular doctor said Schaefer's treatment was nothing more than a Band-Aid, and it terrified Janine that he might be right. She was just getting her daughter back. She could not bear to lose her again.

"Where are the other parents?" Janine looked behind her toward the parking lot entrance. It was nearly three.

"Oh, I think it's just you and me. I'm going to drive a couple of the girls home. Gloria and Alison will take the rest, but we figured you'd probably be anxious to be with Sophie, so we didn't think to ask if you wanted one of us to give her a ride."

"You're right," she said. "I can't wait to see how she made out."

"She looked so excited when she got into the van Friday evening," Suzanne said.

"She was." Janine was glad she was wearing sunglasses, because her eyes suddenly burned with tears. *Her baby girl.* How rare it was to have seen such unfettered joy in Sophie's face rather than the usual lines of pain and fear. The sort of fear no child should have to endure.

"She's so cute," Suzanne said. "Where'd she get that red hair?"

"It's a combination of mine and her dad's, I guess," she said, touching her hand to her own strawberry-blond hair. Joe's hair was dark, his eyes blue, like Sophie's.

"It's her kidneys that are the problem, right?" Suzanne probed.

"Yes." Janine didn't mind the questions. The only time she was bothered by them was when they were asked in front of her daughter, as though Sophie were deaf and blind as well as very, very ill.

"Would a transplant help?"

"She already has one of mine." Janine smiled ruefully. "Her body rejected it." Joe had offered one of his, as well, but he was not a good match. And now, Sophie was beyond being helped by a transplant.

"Oh, I'm so sorry," Suzanne said kindly. "She seems to handle everything very well, though. I was so surprised when I met her, because she's so tiny. I thought she was about six. But then this eight-year-old voice comes out of her, with a ten-year-old vocabulary. It's such a surprise."

Janine smiled. "Kids with kidney disease tend to be small."

"What a lot you must have been through with her," Suzanne said. "And to think of how much I worry when Emily has the sniffles. I really admire you."

Janine didn't feel admirable. She was coping the only way a desperate mother could—searching for solutions, doing all she could to make Sophie's time on earth as happy and carefree as possible...and crying only when she was alone at night.

"Emily told me you're a helicopter pilot," Suzanne said.

"Oh." Janine was surprised. "I was, a long time ago. Before Sophie got sick." She had learned to fly a helicopter in the army and had flown for an aircraft leasing company after getting out of the reserves. Was Sophie telling people she still flew? Maybe it embarrassed her that Janine had turned from an adventurous pilot into a stay-at-home mom. But with a chronically ill child, she could imagine no other course of action.

"Emily has a secret hope that, when the girls in the troop get a little older, you might give them flying lessons."

She had thought of that herself, in those rare, optimistic moments when she could picture Sophie reaching her teenage years. "Maybe one day," she said. "That would be fun." She turned to look at the parking lot entrance again.

"You must worry about Sophie when she's away," Suzanne said suddenly, and Janine knew that the worry was evident in her eyes, or maybe in the way she was knotting and unknotting her hands.

"Well," she said, "this is new to me. Sophie's never been away from home without me or her father by her side." She'd also never been so far from emergency care, which was why Joe had said the trip was out of the question. But Sophie had begged to go. There was so little she ever asked for, and so little Janine could do for her. She said yes, after getting permission from Dr. Schaefer, who even called Joe to assure him that Sophie would be fine, as long as she watched her fluid intake and was home for dialysis on Sunday night and back at Schaefer's office for Herbalina on Monday. Joe, who lost his temper too easily and too often, had hung up on him.

Like Sophie's regular doctors, Joe thought Schaefer's study was a sham, and he had argued with Janine about making Sophie into a guinea pig. Although Janine and Joe had been divorced since Sophie was five, they usually were in agreement on how to handle their daughter's treatment. This study had driven a wedge between them and was unraveling the already frayed edges of Janine's relationship with her parents, as well. They hadn't wanted Sophie to take part in such an unconventional treatment, either. It wasn't like Janine to stand up to any disapproval from Joe or her parents, at least not in recent years. But Sophie was terminally ill. Even dialysis was failing her, and she'd been given mere months to live. There was little to lose.

"I don't think you need to worry," Suzanne said. "Gloria seems like a very caring and responsible leader."

"I wonder about Alison, though," Janine said. Alison was the younger of the two troop leaders. Only twenty-five and single, Alison had no children of her own. She'd been a volunteer leader in Sophie's troop for the past two years, and all the girls loved her. She was fun-loving, comical and had a spirit of adventure that the girls adored and the parents feared. Alison had made a few errors in judgment over the past couple of years. Very minor. Nothing life-threatening. But then, she hadn't had a child as frail and needy as Sophie under her care before.

"Oh, I think Alison's super," Suzanne said. "How many young women do you know who are childless themselves but still volunteer to work with kids? And the girls love her. She's a good role model for them."

Janine felt mildly chastened and wished she had thought before she'd spoken.

She was about to apologize, when she spotted a white van pulling into the parking lot.

"Is that them?" she asked.

"Looks like it," Suzanne said.

The van was heading toward them, and Janine waved.

Stepping away from Suzanne's station wagon, she wished she could make out the faces behind the van's tinted windows. *Patience,* she told herself. If she charged the van, or God forbid, started crying when she saw Sophie, she would only embarrass her.

The van came to a stop next to the station wagon, and Gloria stepped out of the driver's side, giving them a quick wave as she walked around the front of the car to slide open the side door. Five grimy, tired little Brownies began tumbling out. Suzanne stepped forward to give her daughter, Emily, a hug, and Janine looked past them, watching for a sixth girl to emerge. She walked toward the van, trying to see through the dark windows, but there appeared to be no movement inside.

"Janine," Gloria said. "How come you're still here?"

"I'm waiting for Sophie," Janine said, confused. "Isn't she with you?"

"Didn't Alison get here yet?" Gloria asked.

Janine frowned. Alison? Gloria had let Sophie ride with *Alison?*

"No." She tried to keep her voice calm. "I've been here since ten of. I haven't seen her."

"That's strange," Gloria said, reaching into the van to pull out one of the girls' knapsacks. "Sophie and Holly wanted to ride with Alison," she said, "and they had a good ten-minutes' head start on us."

Suzanne must have caught Janine's look of panic. "Maybe Alison drove Sophie straight home?" she suggested.

"She knew she was supposed to come here first," Gloria said, reaching for another knapsack.

"But maybe Sophie or Holly persuaded her to take them straight home," Suzanne said.

Gloria shook her head. "She knew Janine would be waiting here for Sophie."

Janine turned her head between the women as if following a Ping-Pong game. "I'll call home," she said, heading for her car. "I'll see if they showed up there."

Her hands shook as she opened her car door and reached inside for her cell phone. She dialed the number for the mansion, and her mother answered.

"I'm at Meadowlark Gardens, Mom, waiting for Sophie to get back, and I just wanted to check to see if her troop leader might have dropped her off there."

"I haven't seen her," her mother said. "Could she be in the cottage?"

"Possibly." Although if Sophie had been dropped off at the cottage and found that Janine wasn't there, she probably would have walked up the driveway to the mansion. "Could you check, please?"

Janine heard some movement of the phone. "Frank?" her mother called, her voice obviously directed away from the receiver. Janine pictured her father sitting in the leather recliner in the Ayr Creek library, his favorite perch, either reading or working on his laptop. "Go over to the cottage and see if Sophie's inside. She might have been dropped off there."

"Thanks, Mom," Janine said, once her mother was back on the phone.

"Why would they bring her home if they were supposed to meet you at Meadowlark Gardens?"

Janine tensed. *Here we go,* she thought. "There might have been a misunderstanding," she said.

"Well, if they could get something as simple as that wrong, what else could they get wrong?"

"Mom, please."

"She's only eight years old, and a very fragile little girl," her mother said. "I wouldn't have sent you off to camp when you were eight, and you were healthy as a horse."

It was true that her parents had never sent her to camp. She'd had to create her own adventures, and create them she did.

"I think this was a terrific experience for Sophie," Janine said, although she'd argued about this with her mother and father and Joe so much over the past few weeks that she knew anything she said now was pointless.

Janine heard her father's voice in the background, but she couldn't make out what he was saying.

"She's not there," her mother said into the phone.

"All right. Please call me on my cell phone if she shows up there instead of here, okay?"

"How late is she?"

"Not really late at all, Mom. I was just checking in case they took her home. I've got to go now." She hung up and walked back to the van, where Gloria and Suzanne were talking. Emily leaned tiredly against her mother, and Janine felt a pang of envy witnessing the simple, uncomplicated warmth between them. She wanted Sophie here with her, *now.*

Gloria and Suzanne were looking toward the entrance to the parking lot. Janine followed their gaze, but there were few cars pulling into the lot this late in the day.

"What color is Alison's car?" she asked.

"Blue Honda," Gloria said. "Sophie's not at home?"

Janine shook her head.

"They probably took a bathroom break," Suzanne suggested.

"We had to take three of them," Emily groaned. "Tiffany had to pee twice."

"Shh," said her mother.

Janine turned to look toward the far corner of the parking lot, searching for a blue Honda. Maybe Alison had her southeast and northeast confused, but this was the same spot from which the troop had taken off. Besides, she surely would have noticed the van by now.

"I'm sure they'll be here any minute." Gloria touched her arm. "They probably got stuck in a traffic jam."

"You would have gotten stuck in it, too, then," Janine said. "Does Alison have a cell phone with her?" Her voice sounded remarkably calm despite the fact that she was furious with Gloria for allowing Sophie to ride with the young troop leader.

"*Yes,* she does." Gloria sounded relieved at that realization. "I have her number in the van. Hold on." She walked quickly toward her van, stopping only a second to talk to her daughter.

"Sophie's just fine," Suzanne said in a reassuring voice.

Janine tried to nod, but her neck felt as if it were made of wood.

"She had a really good time, Mrs. Donohue," Emily said, somehow picking up her mother's cue that Janine was in desperate need of reassurance.

"What sorts of things did you do?" Janine tried to smile at Emily, one eye on the van where Gloria was making the call.

"We rode horses," Emily said. "That was my favorite part."

"Really?" Janine asked. "Did Sophie ride a horse?"

"Yup." Emily told her some of the other things they'd done, but Janine was stuck on the image of her daughter astride a horse for the first time in her life.

Gloria moved the phone from her ear and started walking toward them.

"Did you reach her?" Janine asked.

"No answer," Gloria said. "She probably has it turned off."

Brilliant, Janine thought.

The other girls were getting grumpy. They slumped wearily against the van, begging to leave. Their cheeks were pink from the sun, their arms blotchy with mosquito bites.

"Be patient," Gloria said to them. "As soon as Alison gets here, we can divide up and start for home."

Gloria and Suzanne chatted calmly as they waited, but Janine could not follow, much less participate in, their conversation. Minutes passed, and her hand became slick with perspiration around the phone locked in her fist, while the world in the parking lot took on a dreamlike quality. Janine was only vaguely aware of the movement of the cars and the people and the tired Brownies, who now sprawled on the stretch of grass between the parking lot and Beulah Road. She glanced repeatedly at her watch as the minute hand made its steady fall toward three-thirty, and her mind raced with explanations for Alison's tardiness. Maybe Sophie had gotten ill and they'd needed to stop. Or maybe they were simply caught in a traffic jam that Gloria had somehow circumvented. Or maybe Alison had decided to take them on some new, unplanned adventure. Janine wanted to ask Gloria what she had been thinking, putting Sophie in Alison's car for the ride home. Did Alison have with her the three pages of instructions Janine had written outlining Sophie's special needs? Did these women understand how sick Sophie was? She suddenly wondered if Joe had been right in not wanting Sophie go on this camping trip. Maybe it had been a foolish decision, after all. Thanks to Dr. Schaefer's treatment, Sophie looked quite well right now. It would have been easy for the troop leaders to have forgotten how seriously ill she was.

Gloria tried several more times to reach Alison's cell phone, without success, and at four o'clock, Janine could take it no longer.

"What's Alison's home phone number?" she asked Gloria. Her voice sounded curt, but she felt herself soften as she saw the look of concern in Gloria's face.

Gloria knew the number by heart, and Janine dialed it on her own phone.

"Hello?" A woman's voice answered.

Janine gripped the phone. "Alison?" she asked.

"No, this is Charlotte. Alison's not here."

"Are you her...housemate?"

"Yes."

"I'm waiting for her at Meadowlark Gardens," Janine said. "She's supposed to be bringing my daughter and another girl back from West Virginia. Have you heard from her?"

"No," Charlotte said. "I was wondering where she was, actually. She should have been home an hour ago. We're supposed to go to Polyester's tonight."

Janine had no idea what Polyester's was, nor did she care. "Look, if you hear from her, tell her to call this number immediately." Janine gave the woman her number.

"You could call her, if you want," Charlotte said. "I can give you the number for her cell."

"We've tried calling her. She must be out of range."

"I doubt that. She has the same phone plan I do. We're never out of range."

"Well, I guess she has it turned off, then."

Charlotte laughed. "She never turns her phone off. She's terrified of missing a call."

Janine said goodbye, then hung up her phone. She looked toward the entrance of the parking lot, where a short line of cars was waiting to exit, and none were waiting to come in.

For whatever reason, Alison had turned her phone off now.

CHAPTER TWO

They waited until nearly four-thirty before calling Holly's parents, and by that time the muscles in Janine's face ached from trying not to cry. She wondered how another mother might react in a situation like this. The mother of a healthy child would take tardiness in stride. She wanted to behave like the typical mom of a typical child, but she'd had so little practice with that.

Gloria stood next to Janine as she placed the call to Holly's parents, but it was apparent from her end of the conversation that they were not home.

"Are you Holly's sister?" Gloria asked into the phone. "Will you have them give me a call as soon as they get home? It's important...no, now don't worry them. I'm sure everything's fine." Her voice was tight but upbeat. "Holly's just a little late getting back from camp, and I wanted to let them know, that's all." She gave the girl her number, then hung up the phone and smiled at Janine.

"They have seven children," she said. "Can you imagine?"

They could lose one and still have six left, Janine thought, although she knew such thinking was both irrational and callous.

"Holly falls smack in the middle," Gloria continued.

Suzanne glanced over at Emily, lying on the lawn with the

four other girls. "Em's the middle child, too," she said. "Though she doesn't have that middle kid syndrome. Not yet, at least."

"Jason has it, that's for sure," Gloria said, referring to her son. "Of course he's stuck in the middle between two girls, so it's not just the middle child syndrome he's coping with."

Janine had nothing to add to this conversation. How could Gloria and Suzanne stand there chatting about birth order when Sophie and Holly were over an hour and a half late? She stepped away from the two women and dialed Alison's cell phone number again. Still no answer. She thought of what Alison's housemate, Charlotte, had said about Alison never turning off her cell phone out of fear of missing a call. Had she had the phone glued to her ear on this trip? Might she have been concentrating on a conversation rather than on her driving and smashed into a tree? But then, wouldn't Gloria have seen the accident, since she had been behind her? Maybe Alison had taken a different route. Then Gloria wouldn't have been able to see the accident, and...

"Why don't I take the girls home?" Suzanne interrupted her ruminating with a question to Gloria. "I've got the station wagon. I can fit them all in. Randi, too," she said, referring to Gloria's daughter.

Gloria looked at her watch, then nodded. "That would be great," she said. "No sense in all of us waiting here."

Suzanne gave Janine a quick, one-armed hug. "I'm sure everything's fine," she said. "This is just one of those crazy misunderstandings. You'll see."

"I hope so." Janine tried to smile.

She leaned against the van, watching Gloria and Suzanne help the girls load their gear into the station wagon. She supposed she should help, but felt unable to move from the side of the van, dazed by the sight of all those healthy brown arms and legs, as the girls climbed into the station wagon with their sleeping bags and knapsacks. From the other end of the parking lot came a cacophony of whistles and applause, and she turned to see a car drive out of the lot onto Beulah Road, streamers sailing in the air from the rear bumper. Her mind was so heavy with worry that it took her a moment to realize it was a bride and groom making their getaway.

Gloria came to stand next to her as they watched the station wagon pull out of the parking lot. She looked at her watch again.

"I think we should call the police," she said. "We should make sure there haven't been any accidents."

"Yes," Janine agreed. She thought they should have called the police an hour ago.

Again, she listened to Gloria make a call in that tight, even voice, describing the problem in terms Janine deemed far too mild. She wanted to grab the phone from Gloria's hand to tell the dispatcher her view of the situation, but she kept her hands knotted firmly around her own phone.

"They're sending someone over here to talk with us," Gloria told her as she clicked off her phone. "Though I hope by the time they get here, we won't need them." She looked toward Beulah Road as if hoping to see the blue Honda.

"I can't believe this is happening," Janine said. "The one time I let her go someplace alone, and now she's... Who knows where she is?"

Gloria put a gentle arm around Janine's shoulders. "I'm sure she's fine," she said. "And Sophie had the best time, Janine. I was so glad she was finally able to do something fun with the rest of the girls. I just can't get over how well she seems."

"I know," Janine said. "But she still needs to be careful. To watch her fluid intake and her—"

"And her diet," Gloria finished the sentence for her. "We were careful with her, Janine. We were vigilant. Although she knows what she's supposed to do to take care of herself. She's very sophisticated about her condition."

"Yes, she is," Janine admitted. "But it's gotten more complicated because of the study she's in. Her fluid needs are always changing."

"She told me about Herbalina."

"What did she say about it?" Janine asked, curious.

"That she hated getting it at first. The needle was painful and all. But she knows it's made her feel so much better. And it's given her more freedom at night from being hooked up to that machine."

"It has." She remembered how Sophie had cried the first time that fat needle had pierced her vein. The last couple of weeks or so, though, she'd been so brave, sticking her arm out for Dr. Schaefer's attack. Janine owed that change to Lucas and his courage tree.

"Is it a cure?" Gloria asked. "Or just a treatment."

Janine sighed. "Depends on who you ask," she said. "The doctor in charge of the study believes it can ultimately cure her. But Sophie's regular doctor thinks it just buys a little time, and not much of it at that." She looked away from Gloria, toward the road, tears burning her eyes again.

Gloria squeezed her shoulders. "Even if that's the case, at least she's able to enjoy herself right now."

"Exactly my thought," Janine said. Although she knew she was lying. Deep inside, she could not settle for mere temporary relief for Sophie. She wanted Sophie to have the chance at a normal life, the same chance Gloria's daughter had.

"She's such a sensitive little girl," Gloria commented. "I don't mean that the way it sounds," she added quickly. "It's not like she's overly sensitive to what people say to her, or anything like that. But she's very sensitive to the needs of the other girls. Brianna was homesick that first night, and Sophie told her jokes to take her mind off it."

"That's my girl." Janine smiled. Sophie would always talk about the other kids in the hospital with sympathy. She felt sorry for them for being sick, as though she didn't recognize that she was one of them herself.

"She said she was worried about you," Gloria said.

"About *me?*"

"That you'd be lonely without her over the weekend."

Janine shook her head, pressing a fist to her mouth. "I don't want her to worry about me," she said. Yet she knew that Sophie always did. More than once, Janine had stood in a hospital corridor, peeking unnoticed into Sophie's room. Sophie's pale, freckled face would be contorted with pain and misery, but her features would shift instantly into a devil-may-care smile once she realized her mother could see her. What about right now? she wondered. Wherever Sophie was, she had to know that Janine was worried about her. And that would upset her. Sophie had always taken on too much responsibility for the feelings of others.

A police car pulled into the parking lot, turning toward the southeast corner, slowing as it neared them. The car came to a stop next to Gloria's van, and Janine felt her hope pour into the young officer who stepped out from behind the wheel. He looked little more than a child himself, though, as he walked toward them. She could see the sunburn on his nose and the gawky way he carried himself, as if he'd suddenly found himself in his father's police uniform and didn't know quite how to wear it.

"Are you the two ladies with the late Girl Scouts?"

"That's right," Gloria replied, but Janine was struck by the insensitivity of his words. *The* late *Girl Scouts.* She supposed it was her own sensitivity that was putting her on edge.

"They were due here at three." Gloria told him about the trip back from the camp and gave him the names of Alison and the two girls. He wrote the information down slowly, in neat block letters, on a small notepad.

"Are you sure she took the same route as you?" he asked Gloria. He pronounced the word *rowt.*

"I assumed so. I mean, we followed each other going up there. I imagine she would have taken the same route back."

"But you don't know that for sure."

"No."

"Did you notice anything unusual when you were driving back? Any construction or anything going on along the side of the road—maybe a crafts fair or something—that they might have stopped for?"

"No. But I wasn't really looking, either."

The young man studied the words on his notepad as though he wasn't sure what to make of them. "Okay, first of all, let's get everyone down here. The troop leader's roommate, your husband." He nodded toward Janine, and she thought of correcting him, but there was little point in doing so just then. "The other girl's parents," he continued. "And I'm going to call in my supervisor. He has a phone and can check with the dispatchers along the route to see if any accidents have been reported. Unfortunately, only a small part of the route is in Fairfax County, so we'll have to coordinate with the other police barracks between here and the camp. Of course, we've got a recent change of shift, so whatever dispatchers are on duty now might not know about any accidents that occurred on the other shifts." He tapped the end of his pen against his chin as he stared at the notepad, and Janine grew impatient.

"Wouldn't they have a record of any accidents, though?" she asked.

"Oh, sure, of course. I was just thinking out loud. Shouldn't do that." He grinned at her, and she looked away from him. He was too young to have any children of his own, she thought. He had no idea what this felt like. She watched him stride over to his car just as Gloria's phone rang.

Gloria quickly brought her phone to her ear, but the caller was only Holly's mother, and Janine wanted to scream out loud with her disappointment.

"Right," Gloria said into the phone. "She's riding in the car with Alison and one other Brownie, Sophie Donohue, and they haven't shown up here yet. I'm sure everything's okay, but we've contacted the police just in case...yes, you should come over. The police want everyone to be here."

Somehow, knowing that the police wanted everyone together at Meadowlark Gardens made the gravity of the situation even more real.

"I'll call my ex-husband," Janine said, dialing his number on her own phone.

There was no answer on Joe's end, just his taped message about being unable to come to the phone right then.

Yet another cell phone turned off, she thought. But at least with Joe, she could be reasonably sure where to find him...and who would be there with him.

CHAPTER THREE

Joe had never seen Paula quite so vicious on the tennis court. He dove to return her serve, missing the ball and nearly tripping over his own feet in the process.

Paula must finally be pulling out of her period of mourning, he thought, as he sent the ball back over the net to her. Six weeks ago, he'd accompanied her to Florida for her mother's funeral, staying with her in her childhood home, trying to comfort her when she seemed inconsolable. Her mother had been her last living relative, and Paula's pain over her death had been fierce and was only now beginning to lift. It was a particular sort of pain Joe knew and understood all too well.

Or maybe Paula just seemed more aggressive today because *his* heart was not on this tennis court in Reston, but rather at Ayr Creek, where Sophie would be babbling excitedly to Janine about her weekend at camp. He wanted to hear all about it. Despite the fact that he had strongly objected to her going, he hoped she'd had a wonderful, healthy time. He had no desire to have his grave misgivings about the trip proven correct.

Paula let out a whoop as she sent the final ball over the net, far out of his reach. He didn't even bother attempting to return it. Instead, he bent over, his hands on his knees, trying to catch his breath from the wild ride she'd just taken him on.

"Congratulations," he called across the net. This was the first time she had beaten him so decisively. He straightened up, walked toward the net, and shook her hand.

"A hollow victory," Paula said, pulling the clasp out of her dark hair and letting it fall across her shoulders. She tossed it back from her face with a shake of her head.

"Why do you say that?" he asked, as they walked on opposite sides of the net toward the benches.

"Because you weren't paying a bit of attention to the game."

"Well, my focus might have been a little off, but you won fair and square."

Paula sat down on the bench and mopped her face with a towel. "You're still worried about Sophie, huh?"

"Not worried, really." He slipped his racquet into its case. "If anything had gone wrong at the camp, we would have heard. I'm just really curious to see how she made out. This is the first time she's ever done anything like this."

"The first time she's been able to," Paula reminded him, and he knew where she was headed with her train of thought.

"Right," he said. He sat down and took a long drink from his water bottle.

"But you still can't admit that it's that herbal treatment that's made the difference, can you?"

"Oh, I'm willing to concede that it might be," he said. "But everyone says—everyone except the doctor in charge of the study—"

"Schaefer," she said. "And I know what you're going to say. That everyone else thinks her improvement is just a temporary effect of the herbs."

He guessed he was beginning to sound like a broken record. "Right. So who would you believe?" he asked. "Sophie's type of kidney disease has been around a long time, with bona fide researchers looking at it from every angle. Should I believe them, or some alternative doctor who appeared out of nowhere with his bag of weeds?"

"But she's doing so much better," Paula argued.

"I'll admit that those IVs she gets have made her *feel* better. That doesn't mean she *is* better."

"Are you going over to Ayr Creek to see her tonight?"

"Uh-huh. Want to come?"

Paula nodded. "If that's okay with you," she said. "Unless you want to spend the time alone with her and Janine."

He appreciated her consideration, but he also knew how much she cared about Sophie.

"No, I'd like you to—"

They both turned toward the small parking lot at the sound of a car door slamming shut. The tennis court was surrounded by trees, and Joe stood up to try to peer through the branches. A woman was running from the parking lot toward the tennis court.

He frowned. "That looks like Janine," he said.

"Joe!" the woman shouted as she pulled open the chain-link door of the court, and he could see her clearly then—clearly enough to see the fear in her face.

He froze where he was standing. *Sophie.* Something was very wrong. Paula stood up next to him, clutching his arm as Janine ran toward them.

"What's the matter?" he asked, finding his voice as he took a step toward her. "Is Sophie all right?"

Janine glanced at Paula, then back at Joe again. "She's late returning from camp." Janine was winded. "She's riding with another girl and one of the leaders. I've been waiting at Meadowlark Gardens for her, but she hasn't shown up yet."

"What time was she supposed to get back?" he asked.

"Three."

Joe looked at his watch. It was six-thirty. "She's three and a half hours late?"

"Yes."

"We need to call the police and—"

"They already know," Janine said. Tendrils of her strawberry-blond hair were matted to her damp forehead. "They want everyone to come to Meadowlark Gardens to try to sort out what might have happened."

"Damn it!" Joe punched the fence with the side of his fist, and he saw Janine flinch. "I knew she shouldn't have gone on this trip!"

Paula rested her hand on his arm. "Not now, Joe," she said softly. "We'll follow you," she said to Janine. "Where in the parking lot should we meet?"

"In the front, close to Beulah Road," Janine said. She turned away from them and headed back to the gate at a run. "You'll see the leader's white van."

Scooping their equipment into their arms, Joe and Paula ran down the court after her.

"Maybe she'll have arrived by the time we get there," Paula said as they got into Joe's car. Paula was always like that—rational and optimistic. She'd been Joe's co-worker at the accounting firm for the past four years. Co-worker and closest friend. Sometimes he didn't know what he'd do without her to keep him sane. Right now, though, even Paula could not quiet his anger.

He pounded the steering wheel with both hands. "I should have taken Janine to court over this idiotic study," he muttered. "I never should have allowed my daughter to be a guinea pig."

"The study really doesn't have anything to do with Sophie returning late from—"

"It has *everything* to do with it," he snapped. "If she hadn't been feeling better, she never would have gone."

"That doesn't make sense, Joey." Paula's voice was calm. "Don't you think it's even a little bit terrific that she's feeling so much better?"

"The disease is still there, Paula," he said. "It's still raging. Still killing her."

Those words shut her up as she fell silent next to him. This had been the major area of disagreement between them in recent weeks, and he knew she was tired of the argument.

Sophie'd had an entire cadre of nationally renowned physicians treating her over the last three years. When Janine had told him that she planned to enroll Sophie in the alternative medicine study, Joe had asked those doctors to dissuade her. One of them told Joe, far too bluntly, that Sophie was going to die, anyway, so it mattered little what sort of treatment she received now. The other doctors, however, spent hours talking with Janine, on the phone and in person, but she wouldn't budge on her plan to subject Sophie to Schaefer's snake oil.

Joe had even gone to see Schaefer himself, determined to try to understand exactly how he thought his Herbalina could help. Schaefer was a nerdy little man, unable to make eye contact, and seeing him had done nothing to ease Joe's discomfort about the study. Even Schaefer's voice was weak and hesitant. But he told Joe he was "almost certain" that he was onto something that would help children like Sophie. That was his reply to each one of Joe's questions. Johnny One-note.

In early April, Sophie's primary nephrologist contacted Janine to tell her about a new study at Johns Hopkins, one using a more conventional approach to treat Sophie's illness. Joe had pleaded with Janine to allow Sophie that chance, but she seemed positively driven in this. She refused to let Sophie suffer any longer if she could find a way to give her some relief, she'd said, and she'd found support for her intentions from an unlikely source.

"It's the gardener's fault," he muttered, as he turned the car onto Route 7.

"What?" Paula asked.

"The gardener at Ayr Creek. You know, Lucas Trowell. The guy Janine's parents think is a pedophile?" He could picture the thin, bespectacled gardener pruning the azaleas or mulching the trees at Ayr Creek. The few times Joe had seen him there, Lucas had looked up from his task to stare at him. Not *glance* at him, but literally stare, as though Joe were a member of a species the gardener had never seen before. There was definitely something odd about that man.

"How on earth is this his fault?" Paula asked.

"He told her the study sounded like a great idea. He told Janine it made sense to him. He's a *gardener,* for Pete's sake. And probably certifiable, too. He lives in a damned tree house. I can't believe she would listen to him instead of to Sophie's doctors."

He and Janine's parents had joined forces to try to dissuade Janine from putting Sophie in the study, and again from sending her away this weekend, but they had failed on both counts. Janine seemed to be under the spell of a lunatic doctor and a persuasive gardener.

"I can relate to how Janine must feel, though," Paula said, in her most careful, not-wanting-to-upset-him voice. "She's concerned about quality of life for Sophie right now. The way I was about my mom before she died."

"Well, I think she's lost her mind." He honked his horn at a driver who pulled in front of him, cutting him off from Janine. "She never had most of her mind to begin with."

"Look, Joey." Paula adjusted the chest strap of her seat belt so that she could turn to face him. "You're angry and upset, and it makes sense that you're trying to find someone to blame, but the truth is, if Sophie is late getting back from camp, it isn't the fault of the study, or Schaefer, or the pedophile gardener, or Janine, or—"

"It *is* Janine's fault," Joe interrupted as he passed the car ahead of him, pulling up behind Janine again. "Sophie should never have gone on this trip. She's never been away from us. Even during all her hospital stays, she's had one of us with her. Janine completely disregarded my wishes. I don't get it, either. For the past few years, we've agreed on how to handle things with Sophie. And now..."

"You mean, she's gone along with everything you wanted to do."

He glanced at her. "What are you saying?" he asked.

"I'm saying that Janine hasn't dared to think for herself since Sophie got sick, when you and her parents pinned the blame on her."

"I never overtly blamed her for it," he said, although he knew the argument was weak and that Paula could see through him. "Even though I *do* think there's a good chance that Sophie's problem was the result of Janine's stint as GI Jane."

"Oh, Joe, there's no record of other Desert Storm soldiers producing kids with kidney disease. Just because Janine—"

"Let's not talk about this, okay?"

"You always say that when you're about to lose an argument, you know that?"

He barely heard her. They were parked at a too long stoplight on Route 7, and he could see the back of Janine's head in the car in front of him. She was brushing the hair from her face...or maybe wiping tears from her eyes, and he softened. If he was in her car right now, he would touch her. Hold her hand, perhaps. It had been a long time since they'd had any physical contact. But that didn't mean he didn't want it.

"How can I be so angry with her and want to jump her bones at the same time?" Joe asked.

Paula was quiet for a moment. "You're still in love with her," she stated.

He kept his eyes on the road. How did Paula know that? He'd never told her. Except for this last comment, which he knew to be inappropriate in both content and timing, he'd said nothing positive about Janine in months. How did women always manage to know what you were thinking?

"What makes you say that?" He turned off Route 7 onto Beulah Road, following closely on Janine's bumper.

"Jumping her bones is just guy talk for the fact that you love her."

"I can't love her. I'm too angry with her."

"Love and anger can exist at the same time," Paula said. "I

should know." Paula had been divorced for five years from a man who had swindled her out of her savings. Only recently had she stopped talking about him with longing.

"I don't know how I feel about her anymore," he said. "I just think...we used to be a team. We used to be in sync—at least when it came to Sophie."

He knew it was his fault that their marriage ended. He'd been stupid and angry, and if he could make it up to Janine somehow, he would. He wanted her back. The three of them were meant to be a family.

"Look, Joe," Paula interrupted his thoughts. "Janine needs support right now. You guys need each other. So put the anger aside and just be a dad for now. Okay?"

She was right, and he nodded. "I'll try," he said.

The parking lot at Meadowlark Gardens was nearly empty, except for the bustle of activity in the corner nearest the road. Joe followed Janine's car across the lot and parked between the white van and a police car. Scanning the small group of people, he tried to find a skinny, little red-haired girl among them, hoping Sophie had arrived safely during Janine's trip to Reston.

But Sophie was not there, and Joe and Paula got out of the car and followed Janine into the circle of people.

"Any news?" Janine asked a tall woman, who shook her head, then looked at Joe.

"You're Sophie's dad?" The woman reached her hand toward him and he shook it quickly, as if he didn't want to touch her for too long. He was angry with her, too. Angry with anyone even remotely responsible for putting Sophie in harm's way.

"Yes," he said.

"I'm Gloria Moss. Sophie's troop leader."

"What's going on?" He heard the impatient, officious tone to his voice and felt Paula's steadying hand on his arm once again.

"Sergeant Loomis just arrived," Gloria said, pointing in the direction of a large black man in uniform. He was talking with a young male officer, who used his hands as he spoke, cutting the air with them, while the big man listened.

Gloria introduced Joe, Paula and Janine to Holly's parents, Rebecca and Steve Kraft, who had apparently arrived only minutes earlier in a large, midnight-blue Suburban. Everyone had questions for one another, but no one had the answers, and they stood waiting uncertainly by the white van, while the sergeant spoke to someone on the phone. Joe wanted to walk over to him and tell him to hurry up and do something, but he knew that was not going to help.

A Honda sped into the parking lot, giving all of them a hope-filled start until they realized that the car was silver. It came to a stop near the fence, and a young woman jumped out.

"I'm Charlotte," she called as she ran toward them. "Alison's roommate. Did anyone hear from her yet?"

"No," Janine said. "You haven't heard anything, either?"

Charlotte shook her head. She looked about twenty years old, with shoulder-length blond hair and tiny glasses perched atop her button nose. Within seconds, Joe knew she was the sort of young woman who could make any event into a disaster.

"This is *terrible,*" she said repeatedly. "Alison would never be this late without a good reason. We're supposed to go out tonight."

"Well, the police are working on it," Gloria said, although she looked uncertain as she glanced in the direction of the sergeant and young officer. Gloria wore her tension and worry in her face. She couldn't have been more than his and Janine's age, thirty-five, Joe thought, yet her forehead was creased with deep horizontal lines and her mouth was tight, her lips narrow.

Janine, on the other hand, carried her worry as she always did, with a calm resolve that made her face impassive and hard to read. How often he'd seen that face across Sophie's hospital bed or while waiting for news from one doctor or another. She would fall apart later, he knew, when she was alone. But for now, there was little outward sign of the anguish he knew she was feeling.

Holly's parents were another matter altogether. Steve and Rebecca Kraft wore wide, optimistic smiles, as though they dealt with this sort of thing all the time and refused to let it get them down. They were an older couple, somewhere in their mid-forties, he guessed, with the look of well-aged hippies. Steve wore his graying hair in a pony tail; Rebecca's mousy-brown hair fell to her shoulders from a center part. Two of their seven children were with them—one a young boy, barely a toddler, the other a sour-looking six-year-old named Treat. "Everything will work out all right," Rebecca said to Joe and Janine as she bounced the toddler in her arms. "It always does. We've been through this sort of thing so many times, we're used to it."

Their optimism was catching. Or at least Joe *tried* to catch it as he listened to them tell tales about their older children's misadventures. He felt like the young, green father next to Steve's and Rebecca's soothing voices of experience.

Finally, Sergeant Loomis approached them, gathering them together with a sweep of his big arms. Joe stood between Janine and Paula in front of the white van, listening to Loomis's deep, booming voice.

"The police agencies between here and the Scout camp have been alerted to notify us of any accidents along that route," he said. "So far, there are no reports of any accidents involving a car like Ms. Dunn's. Of course, it's possible that they are simply lost."

"She has the best sense of direction," Charlotte offered. "Whenever we're in Georgetown or D.C., she's the one who can find her way around when the rest of us are totally lost. Except she also likes to take shortcuts, and sometimes they turn out to be more like longcuts."

"They're four hours late," Joe said. The words gave reality to the facts, and he licked his dry lips. "That's pretty damned lost if that's what happened."

"Now, it's possible they just stopped to rest or to eat somewhere," Sergeant Loomis suggested. "Maybe they got sidetracked by an event or an attraction of some sort and didn't realize everyone would be worried by their late arrival."

"Alison would've called me if she was going to be late," Charlotte said. She was literally wringing her hands, and Joe couldn't take his eyes off the way her knuckles whitened, then pinked up again, each time she passed one hand over the other. "Something is very, very wrong."

"I'm guessing it's one of those two options," Sergeant Loomis seemed deaf to Charlotte's remarks. "But we do need to entertain other possibilities."

"Weren't some hikers murdered in that area recently?" Charlotte asked, and everyone turned to look at her in a horrified silence.

"Let's not expect the worst, okay?" Loomis said, in a firm, kind voice.

"Is she right, though?" Gloria asked. "Was someone recently murdered near the camp?"

"Not recently, and not really near the camp," Loomis said. "It was last fall on the Appalachian Trail. A couple of women were found. And it's not worth thinking about."

At least not yet. Joe could hear the unspoken phrase at the end of the sergeant's sentence.

"Is there a chance Alison Dunn might have taken off with the two girls?" Loomis looked from Gloria to Charlotte and back again. "I'm not saying that's what happened, but we need to look at every possibility."

"That's crazy," Charlotte actually laughed. "Why would she? Alison would never do anything like that."

"Was she acting at all out of the ordinary as she was getting ready to give the two girls a ride?" Loomis asked Gloria.

Gloria shook her head. "No, and that just wouldn't make sense, Officer. Alison's very responsible. I know she has the reputation of being a little bit...ditzy...but that's just her fun-loving side. She would never do what you're suggesting."

Joe could hear Janine breathing next to him. Long, ragged-sounding breaths, and every few seconds or so, her gaze would leave the sergeant and turn in the direction of the parking lot entrance. He didn't blame her. He, too, expected Alison and his daughter to arrive any moment and put an end to this silly exercise in worry. The light was just beginning to fade, edging toward dusk. Soon it would be dark.

"You know," Rebecca said slowly, and Joe noticed for the first time that she had a slight drawl to her speech. She was leaning against the van, her toddler in her arms and a look of amusement on her face. "That Alison is quite a character," she said. "I wouldn't put it past her just to decide Holly and Sophie didn't have enough fun at camp and take them off to some amusement park or something. What amusement parks are there between here and there?" She looked at her husband. "Where's that Water World place?"

"She wouldn't do that," Gloria insisted before Steve could respond. "Even if she wanted to, she'd know better than that."

"That's right," Charlotte added. "I mean, Alison can be crazy and everything, but she knew we were going out tonight, and she would have come straight home. Plus, it doesn't make any sense at all that we can't get her on her phone. That's what's really freaking me out. No matter where she is, she has that phone on."

"Well, batteries run out and phones break," Sergeant Loomis said calmly. Charlotte was annoying him, Joe thought, but to the man's credit, he was doing his best not to let it show.

"Could they have been kidnapped?" Janine spoke up, and only then did Joe realize how quiet she had become during this whole discussion. "I mean, by someone other than Alison?

"If they're not back in a few hours, and if we have no reports of an accident, that's something we'll need to consider," Loomis said. "Whether it be by Alison Dunn or someone else."

"Please consider it now," Janine said, a tremor in her voice. "Just in case that's what happened. We can't waste any time."

"Right now," the sergeant said, "I want to talk with each of you individually." He pointed to Janine. "You first, Mrs. Donohue."

"Are we suspects?" Steve asked, and only then did that thought occur to Joe. The parents were the first to fall under suspicion when a child disappeared. And too much of the time, they were guilty. He suddenly saw Steve and Rebecca Kraft with new eyes. They were a little too cheerful about this whole thing. A little too cavalier.

"I just want to see what information each of you has," Loomis said. "Separately, you might remember something...be able to think of something that's evading you now. And I'll need to get more identifying information from you on the missing girls."

Janine looked flustered. "Could you start with someone else?" she asked. "I need to call my parents first. I spoke to them earlier. They must really be worried by now."

Joe touched her arm. "I'll call them," he said. She would hate dealing with Donna and Frank about this, and he didn't blame her.

"Thanks." Janine nodded, looking away from him. She was having trouble meeting his eyes tonight, he thought. She knew he blamed her for this, no matter how kindly he acted toward her now.

He watched her walk over to one of the police cars with Sergeant Loomis, then turned to Paula. "Be right back," he said.

In the front seat of his car, he dialed the number for the Ayr Creek mansion on his cell phone, hoping Frank would answer. Neither of Janine's parents would handle this news well, but Frank would be the calmer of the two.

"Hello?" It was Donna's voice on the line.

"It's Joe, Mom," he said. He could see Janine sitting in the police car, the doors open to catch the faint breeze.

"Joe! I just tried to call you," Donna said. "Do you know where Sophie and Janine are? Janine called hours ago to see if Sophie got dropped off here, but she hadn't, and then I figured maybe they stopped at your house. Although I thought you were coming over—"

"Hold on, Mom," he interrupted, then hesitated, not sure how to tell her. "I'm with Janine at the parking lot where Sophie and her Brownie troop were due to arrive. Some of the girls are back, but the car Sophie was riding in hasn't shown up yet."

Donna didn't speak for a moment. "I thought they were supposed to arrive at three. That's what Janine said."

"Yes."

"And they haven't gotten there yet? It's nearly seven-thirty!"

"I know, Mom." He'd never stopped calling Donna "Mom." When he and Janine split up, he'd tried to go back to addressing his ex-in-laws as Donna and Frank, but they had pleaded with him to continue calling them Mom and Dad. He'd been relieved. They were the only parents he had.

"We've contacted the police," he informed her. "They're looking for the car. They think maybe it had a breakdown or something." It was a lie, but what else could he say?

"I told Janine not to send her." Donna was already in tears, and Joe could hear Frank's deep voice in the background asking her what was wrong. "Sophie hasn't ever been away for an afternoon, much less at a camp a thousand miles away."

"It wasn't that far," Joe said, although he certainly shared her concern. "I can hear Frank there," he said. "Can you put him on?"

There was some fumbling with the phone, then Frank's voice came on the line.

"What's going on?" he asked, and Joe repeated what he'd told Donna.

"Janine isn't a clear thinker these days," Frank said. "She's gone back to that crazy girl she used to be, all of a sudden. After this, I want you to go to court and get more say over what happens to Sophie, all right? Get veto power."

Joe was already thinking of taking that step. "Well, for right now, we just need to get through this situation," he said.

"Do you think this has to do with the gardener?" Donna had gotten on the extension.

Joe was confused, but only for a moment. "Lucas Trowell?" he asked. "What do you mean?"

"I mean, maybe he knew Sophie was due back, and he kidnapped her and the other girl, or—"

"No, Mom, I don't think he'd go to those lengths."

"You don't really know him," Donna asserted. "You don't see how he's always looking at the cottage, watching for Sophie to come out. He hardly does any work, just bosses the fellas under him around. He tries to get close to Janine to get her to trust him, and—"

"I know you don't like him, Mom, but let's not get into this now, okay?" Joe was no fan of Lucas's, either, but it seemed unlikely that he'd had anything to do with Sophie's disappearance.

"I'm always afraid that Janine will turn her back one day," Donna continued, "just for a second, and Lucas Trowell will make off with Sophie. You hear about that happening all the time. It's always the gardener or the handyman or someone who works nearby."

It seemed far-fetched, but maybe Donna had a point. "I'll ask one of the cops to take a drive by Lucas's house just to make sure he's there and that there's nothing fishy going on, okay?" he offered.

He saw Janine step out of the police car. Although it was not yet dark out, the parking lot lights came on, and Janine stood uncertainly in the glow of one of them for a moment before walking toward the white van. There was a fragility about her that Joe had never noticed before. Not even during all those days and nights in the hospital, standing at Sophie's bedside, wondering if she would live or die. A moment later, Sergeant Loomis got out of the car himself and waved to Joe.

"I've got to go," he said to Donna.

"Should we come over there?" Donna asked.

"No, you sit tight. We'll call the second we know anything."
He passed Janine as he walked toward the police car.

"You okay?" he asked her.

She nodded, unsmiling, and he knew she was anything but okay.

"Too hot in there," Loomis said, as Joe approached the police car. He wiped his damp forehead with a handkerchief. "Let's stand out here and talk."

Joe leaned against the closed door of the car, while Loomis asked him the predictable questions. Where had Joe been that day? What was his relationship with Sophie like? With Janine?

"Your ex-wife says you strongly disapprove of the medical treatment your daughter is receiving."

"Yes, I do," Joe said. "But I haven't kidnapped her and taken her to the Mayo Clinic, if that's what you're getting at."

"And you didn't want her to go to this camp, either," Loomis continued. "How badly do you want to prove your ex-wife wrong about her decision to send your daughter there?"

Joe's temper was rising, and he wondered if that was Loomis's intent. "I would never use my daughter that way," he said, working to keep his voice calm.

Loomis asked him a few more questions, about where he worked, about his relationship with Paula. Finally, he sighed and looked toward the clot of people a dozen yards or so away from where he was standing with Joe.

"Do you have any gut feeling about this?" he asked, once he'd seem to run out of questions. "Any instinctive sense of what's going on here?"

Joe thought for a moment. "Well," he said, "I just spoke with my in-laws. Sophie's grandparents. They have some concerns about their gardener. Sophie and Janine live on their property, so the gardener knows them. My in-laws think he's a little too interested in Sophie, and they're worried he might have something to do with this. I told them I'd pass that along to you, in case you wanted to swing by his house and just make sure he's there...and that Sophie isn't."

"What do you think?"

"I think the guy's maybe a bit more interested in little girls than he should be, but I frankly doubt he has anything to do with this."

"Do you know his address?"

"It's on Canter Trail. Over near Wolf Trap. I'm not sure of the number, though. It's a small ranch sort of house. A rambler. Brick. But he actually lives in the wooded lot behind the house, up in a tree house, and—"

"Are you talking about that Trowell fellow?" Loomis looked interested.

"You know him?" Joe felt a flash of fear. Why would the police know Lucas? Could he really be the pedophile Donna and Frank feared him to be?

"No, not personally," Loomis said. "I just know that he lives there. Everyone knows about the guy in the tree house."

"Can you check to see if he has a record?" Joe asked. "His first name is Lucas."

"Will do. And I'll have someone swing by there."

"Thanks."

It was dark by the time Sergeant Loomis had finished his questioning of everyone in the group. He stood beneath one of the parking lot lights and drew them all together again with a wave of his arms.

"All right," he said. "That's it for tonight. You—"

"That's it?" Joe asked. "What are you going to do? Who's out looking for them?"

"Look, Mr. Donohue," Loomis said. "We're not miracle workers. We've got a situation here of some travelers not reaching their destination. They've covered about a hundred miles, through several counties, in a blue Honda Accord, not exactly the rarest car on the road, and we don't have a clue if they might have taken off in another direction altogether or if they stopped at a rest stop and took naps on a picnic table or if they were kidnapped by someone or decided to stop to eat, or who knows? So there's not much for us to go on right now. We'll do all we can. We'll have the patrol cars along the route keep a lookout for them. Not much else we can do tonight."

"What about talking to people in shops or restaurants along the way?" Paula asked.

"Most departments don't have the manpower to do that, ma'am. At least not at this point in the investigation. So for now, you should all go home and stick close to your phones tonight."

Go home? Joe could not imagine being able to go home. He looked at Janine and knew she was thinking the same thing.

He moved next to her. "Let's drive up to the camp," he said. "Follow the route they would have taken."

"We've already got that covered." Loomis had heard him. "There's no need for you to—"

"I want to," Janine insisted.

"And we're staying right here," Rebecca said. "In case they've just been delayed somehow and are on their way back."

The police officer sighed. "Most of you have cell phones. I've got all your numbers. Let's make sure you've all got each other's."

Holly's parents had no cell phone, but Paula said she would stay with them so that they could use hers. Joe was grateful to Paula for not suggesting she join Janine and himself on their drive. She knew he'd want this time alone with Janine.

They exchanged phone numbers with everyone, and he and Janine got into his car. Once they were on the road, Janine began to cry. She wept softly, her face toward the window, and he pulled the car to the side of Beulah Road and turned off the ignition.

"It'll be all right," he said, his hand on her shoulder.

She turned to him. The light from the street lamp lit her hazel eyes and settled in one tear that slipped down her cheek. "I'm sorry, Joe," she said. "I'm so sorry I sent her."

He bit his tongue against an angry retort. "You couldn't have known this would happen," he managed to say instead. He reached over and pulled her into his arms, felt her melt there in the comfort of his touch, and he knew without a doubt that he wanted her to be his wife again.

CHAPTER FOUR

Lucas turned his head from his computer and listened. Far below the tree house, something was moving. It was not unusual to hear sounds at night on this deeply wooded lot. There was the steady June buzz of cicadas and crickets, and the leaf rustling of raccoons and possums and an occasional deer. But this was the unmistakable heavy crunching footsteps of a man. Lucas held very still, listening.

"Mr. Trowell?" A male voice called to him from somewhere below.

Lucas quickly logged off the Internet. He left his small study, reaching in his pocket for the key to the room, and he carefully locked the door and pocketed the key before walking through the living room to the front door. Opening the door, he stepped onto the deck and leaned over the railing, slipping into the blinding glare from a flashlight.

"Yes?" he called, lifting his hand to block the glare.

The flashlight was instantly turned off. "Sorry," the man said. He was now illuminated by the deck light, which fell in a soft glow over the trees and cast shadows through the woods. The light bounced off the badge on the man's uniform, sending an icicle of fear up Lucas's spine.

Damn.

"Are you Lucas Trowell?" the man asked.

"Yes," Lucas said, wondering if the county would send a policeman on a Sunday evening to tell him his house was out of code in yet another way. The county was never quite sure what to do about his tree house.

"Can I come up there for a minute?" the officer asked.

"Sure." Lucas leaned over the railing again to point to the broad trunk of the oak tree beneath his house. "Can you see the steps? They're around the back of the oak."

"Right. I see them."

Lucas listened as the man climbed the stairs, cringing at the squeaking sound a couple of them made. They were not rotted or anything like that, but he knew he should fix them, anyway. He had so little time these days to get work done on the house, though.

He didn't like the anxiety he felt as the policeman neared the top of the stairs. Did everyone feel a pang of guilt when a cop wanted to see them? Did everyone's mind race, searching for the reason for the visit? Or did that happen only to a person with something to hide?

The policeman joined Lucas on the deck. He was a young guy—*very* young—blond and blue-eyed, and he was grinning. Lucas's anxiety dropped a notch.

"Totally cool," the cop said. "I've always wanted to see this place. Everyone talks about it, but I don't know anyone who's seen it up close."

"What can I do for you?" Lucas asked.

"Do you actually live up here?" The cop was not ready to get down to business, and Lucas wondered if his banter was intentional. Was he trying to throw him off guard? "Or do you just come up to get away from the house every once in while?" He looked toward the small, nondescript brick rambler, dark at the edge of the woods.

"I live up here as much as is reasonable," Lucas said. "I store things in the house, and I cook in the house. I don't like to keep food up here. I think I'd have a bug problem. The trees go through the house, and I have a steady stream of ants and spiders as it is. We're living harmoniously at the moment, but I wouldn't want to encourage any more of them to visit."

"Any chance I can see inside?" the officer asked.

"In a minute," Lucas said. He'd had enough of the game playing. "First, though, tell me why you're here."

"Yes. Sure." The young man looked embarrassed, and Lucas relaxed to see that the cop's interest had, in all likelihood, been genuine and not some ruse to get him to open up. He'd been seduced by the trees. It was usually that way. People lost themselves up here. They forgot about everything else in the world, at least for a moment. "I'm Officer Russo," he said. "You work over at the Ayr Creek estate, right?"

"That's right."

"Well, the little girl who lives there..."

"Sophie." He felt his heartbeat quicken, but carefully kept his face impassive.

"Sophie. Right. She was away at a camp this weekend and she was due back at Meadowlark Gardens at three, but she and one of the other girls and their leader never showed up. So I'm talking to people who know her to see if they might have any information."

"I don't understand," he said. "Are you saying the rest of the girls are back?"

"Right. They showed up on time, but they were riding in a separate vehicle."

"Maybe Sophie's ride got a late start?" Lucas offered.

"No. The other leader saw them take off ahead of her."

He felt a sort of panic rise up in his chest. "Could they have been in an accident or—"

"We're checking on all of that," Russo said. "So far, they've just fallen off the map."

"Well, I was aware that Sophie was going away for the weekend," Lucas said. "I don't know any more than that. I'm not even sure where she went." That was a lie—and probably an unnecessary one—but he felt the need to play dumb to this cop when it came to Sophie.

"Have you been here all day?" Russo asked.

"Most of it," he said.

"And when you weren't here, where were you?"

"What are you getting at?" Lucas asked.

"Just routine questions," Russo assured him.

"I took a drive to Great Falls to see a friend around one or so. I was back here by three-thirty."

"Could your friend verify that information for me?"

Lucas sighed. He should have lied. "Do you think I have something to do with this?" he asked. "With Sophie being late?"

"We're just checking out everyone who has any relationship to Ayr Creek," Russo said easily.

Everyone with a relationship to Ayr Creek, Lucas wondered, or just the gardener Frank and Donna Snyder distrusted around their granddaughter?

"My friend could verify it, but I'd rather not put him in that position," he said. That would make things *very* messy.

"All right, I think we can hold off on that for the moment," Russo said. "Now can I have that tour?" He looked up at the second tier of the house. "How many trees is this thing resting on?" he asked.

"It's built between four, actually," Lucas said. "This one's a white oak." He pointed to the tree supporting the deck. "That second level is built on a shag bark hickory, and, it's hard to see from here, but there's another oak and a tulip poplar doing the rest of the work."

Russo stomped his foot on the deck. "Feels sturdy enough," he observed.

"Oh, sure," Lucas said, as he opened the front door and led the officer inside. "On a really windy day, though, the whole contraption sways in the wind, and I start to wonder if I'm out of my mind to live up here. Other than that, it's pretty secure."

"Holy..." Russo exclaimed, as they walked into the living room.

It was the usual reaction Lucas got when he brought someone inside. The trunk of the hickory cut through the room. The floor was tongue-and-groove fir, the walls, shiplap paneling. Huge windows and healthy houseplants were everywhere. A sofa was built in along one side of the room, and three captain's chairs provided the rest of the seating.

"This is something else," Russo said. "I wish my wife would let me do something like this in our backyard. We have the trees for it, I think."

Lucas switched on the light for the back deck, so that Russo could see the treetops through the windows.

"Unreal," Russo said. "And you even have electricity. What do you do in the winter?"

Lucas pointed to the baseboard heaters. "I have heat," he said, "and everything's insulated."

"Man, oh man." Russo shook his head. "So, show me the rest. Where's the bedroom?"

"Up here." Lucas pointed to the covered stairway leading to the second tier. He climbed up ahead of Russo and opened the door to the bedroom.

Russo walked past him into the room. He glanced at the double platform bed and the dresser. An air-conditioning unit, unattractive but necessary, was in the bedroom window. "It must be great to sleep up here," he said, opening the small closet at one end of the room and peering inside, and Lucas knew this was not merely a tour to satisfy Russo's curiosity about his house.

"Ready to go down again?" Lucas was getting impatient.

"Sure." Russo pointed to the blue splint on Lucas's left wrist. "You must have carpal tunnel syndrome, huh?"

"That's right." Lucas said. He'd blamed the splint on carpal tunnel so often that it was beginning to feel like the truth.

"My wife has that," Russo said, as Lucas led him down the stairs and into the living room again. "She got it from her computer job."

Lucas tried to usher Russo toward the front door again, but the officer had noticed the locked door at the rear of the living room.

"What's in there?" he asked.

"My study," Lucas said.

"I'd like to see it."

"It just has my computer and printer and some books," Lucas said, walking toward the door. He reached in his pocket for the key. "I keep it locked in case any kids decide to come up here. I don't want them to make off with my equipment."

His heart thudded in his throat as he tried to remember how he'd left the study. Was there anything in clear view that might tweak the cop's suspicions? He couldn't remember. Thank God he'd thought to log off the Internet.

He opened the door about ten inches, enough so that Russo could see inside without actually stepping into the room.

"Nice," Russo said, peering in, nodding. "Hey, I like that screen saver."

Lucas followed his gaze to the baobab tree on the screen of his monitor. "Thanks," he said.

Russo drew back from the door, showing no interest in the narrow closet with the louvered doors, and Lucas felt the muscles in his neck release. He was home free now—at least as far as the tree house tour went.

But Sophie was missing. He wanted to ask if they had any clues as to what might have happened to her, but he didn't dare appear too interested. "Sophie's mother must be very upset," he said, hoping that would prompt Russo to tell him where Janine was.

"Yes. Everyone's pretty shaken up."

"Maybe they just got lost coming back," Lucas suggested.

"Not five and a half hours worth of getting lost," Russo said. "Highly unlikely."

"I know she's been sick. Could that have something to do with it?"

"We don't know," the officer admitted.

"Well, I sure hope she's okay." Lucas worked at the indifference in his voice as he walked Russo out the front door and onto the deck again. "Good luck trying to find her."

"Right," Russo said. "I have your phone number. I'll be in touch if we need to talk with that friend of yours."

Lucas listened as the officer descended the stairs and watched as he disappeared into the darkening woods. Then he looked through the treetops toward Ayr Creek, a couple of miles from his house. What was going on over there right now? Was Janine there, waiting and upset? Was Joe with her?

Sophie didn't like the dark. He recalled the evening she'd been up here in the tree house, playing a game with him and Janine in the living room, when the power went out. It had gone out all over the neighborhood, and the still darkness was a glorious wonder up here in the trees. But Sophie had been panic-stricken, clinging to Janine until he'd lit several candles, enough to let them see one another's faces. Wherever Sophie was now, he hoped she had light, and for the first time the seriousness of the situation sunk in. Sophie had been due to arrive at three. It was now nearly nine. There could be no simple reason for that much of a delay.

He looked toward Ayr Creek again, wondering if he could come up with some excuse to go over there. Not much need for a gardener in the dark, though, and they would know. They'd know it was his interest in Sophie that brought him there.

And they would be entirely right.

CHAPTER FIVE

Janine's eyes burned from trying to pierce the darkness. For hours, she and Joe had been driving along the route Alison and the girls should have followed from the camp. Joe was at the wheel, and he drove as slowly as safety would allow, while they searched the side of the road for a disabled car hidden by the darkness. They stopped at every restaurant and gas station that was still open at that hour, asking if anyone had seen the missing Scouts. Several sheriff's cars had passed them along the way, reassuring them that they were not alone in their search. Still, their cell phones didn't ring. They'd kept in touch with everyone who had remained behind at the parking lot, hoping for good news, but nothing had changed. Nothing except the fear which grew inside all of them as the minutes ticked by.

When they'd reached the camp, they'd spent some time talking with the sheriff who was questioning the supervisor and counselors there, then started to retrace their route back to Virginia. Joe suggested they get a hotel room—actually, he wisely suggested they get two—but Janine couldn't lock herself, safe and secure, into a hotel room when she had no idea where Sophie was.

Leaning her head against the window of Joe's car, Janine

closed her eyes. Instantly, a familiar, unwanted image slipped into her mind, as it often did when she was in a moving vehicle and slightly disoriented. She was suddenly flying her helicopter through the smoke above the Saudi Arabian desert. The smell was acrid, filled with the chemicals that she, in her darkest moments, feared had altered something inside her and caused her to produce a child whose kidneys did not work correctly.

If it had been Lucas with her in the car, rather than Joe, she would have told him about those memories, but she had no energy to recount them to her ex-husband. He would have no sympathy for her, anyway.

"Tell me more about this Alison," Joe said grimly, bringing her back to the present.

Janine opened her eyes to see that they were driving slowly past a restaurant, while Joe tried to determine if it was still open. It was not, and he sped up again.

"Is there a real chance that Alison might have taken off with them?" he asked.

"She's a free spirit," she said, only half aware that those were the same words Joe had often used to describe her in their early years together. "She's made a few mistakes working with the girls, but I just can't believe she'd do anything that extreme."

"What do you mean, a few mistakes?"

"Oh, she talked to them about the birds and the bees without getting parental permission, that sort of thing."

"Well." Joe let out a sigh. "Let's face it, Jan. They never got back from this trip, and I know it's dark, but we've scoured this route, and her car is not anywhere along it. Wouldn't you agree?"

She nodded.

"That has to mean that she and the car and the girls are somewhere we're not looking. Somewhere they're not supposed to be."

The thought was strangely reassuring. "Maybe Holly's mother...Rebecca...was right and Alison decided it would be fun for them to go to an amusement park or something, and she'll bring them back tomorrow. She can probably get by without the dialysis tonight, but she *has* to be back tomorrow to get her—" She stopped herself, but Joe knew what she was about to say.

"To get that damned herbal crap," he said.

Janine turned her face to the window again. "It's made her feel so much better," she said weakly. Tears burned her eyes. "I just wanted to see a real smile on her face again."

"At what cost, Jan?" Joe glanced at her. "Maybe she'll get a few weeks or a couple of months of feeling good before the disease catches up with her again and kills her."

"Shh!" She didn't want to hear him say those words.

"What are you shushing me for?" he asked. "It isn't news that she's going to die. The only real remaining chance she had was the legitimate study at Hopkins, but you were determined to do this no matter what I wanted." He braked the car abruptly. The driver behind them honked, swerving sharply to avoid hitting them, and with a yelp, Janine grabbed the dashboard.

She saw what had caught his attention—a car parked on the side of the road. Her heart still pounded from the near accident as she opened her car window to get a better look. The parked car was huge and looked deserted, a white paper stuck to its antenna.

"It's a...I don't know, some big car," Janine said. "Not a Honda, anyway."

"Sorry." Joe apologized for his erratic driving. He reached across the gear shift to touch her hand, a surprising gesture. "Are you all right?"

"Fine," she said. She would have braked with equal force had she been the one driving.

Joe sighed again. "So," he said. "Back to Sophie. Here's what I don't get. You and I have always talked to each other about how to deal with her, whether we were communicating about her medical care or her behavior or anything. Isn't that right?"

She nodded. Joe sounded genuinely perplexed, and she felt guilty. She *had* always consulted with him in the past and taken his feelings to heart. Decisions about Sophie had, in every instance, been mutually made.

"I loved that about us," Joe continued. "I was proud of us. We might have been divorced, but we were still a team when it came to her. Then you go off and do something half-assed like enrolling her in that study. Something that goes completely against what I want."

"I'm sorry," she whispered. "I thought it was the right thing. I still think it was the right—"

"What possessed you?" He looked at her. "You're usually smarter than that. Whatever made you think Schaefer's herbs could fix what no one else has ever been able to fix?"

"I didn't go into it blindly," she said. She heard the weakness in her voice. She always felt weak around Joe, as though being near him sucked the strength and self-esteem right out of her. "Lucas Trowell knows a lot about herbs and he researched the ingredients in Herbalina for me. He really felt it might have a chance of—"

"You know, Jan." Joe shook his head. The muscles in his cheeks contracted, and she knew he was trying to control his anger. "Lucas Trowell is a *gardener.* He's not a doctor."

"He knows a lot about herbs, though," she said.

"How do you know that? Because he told you so? I think he'd tell you anything to get close to Sophie."

There it was again. That Lucas-Trowell-is-a-pedophile paranoia.

"That's crazy, Joe," she said. "He's been very kind to Sophie. She adores him."

Big mistake. Joe nearly lost control of the car, sending it over the line into the middle lane, and again, a driver honked his horn at them. "You keep him away from her, Janine," Joe shouted as he steered the car back into the slow lane. "I mean it! I am damn serious. I don't want that guy anywhere near her."

She hated it when he yelled. Joe had never laid a hand on her, but he didn't need to. He was big and muscular, and his anger could be so powerful that it alone was enough to frighten her into submission. She lowered herself farther into the seat and shut her eyes.

"What does it matter to him if the treatment works or not?" Joe continued his argument. "Sophie's not his daughter. She's nothing to him. Your judgment is all screwed up."

Eyes still shut, Janine pressed her temple to the window. She was not wrong about Lucas, although she'd twisted the facts of Sophie's enrollment in the study a bit. It was actually through Lucas that she'd learned of the study; she probably never would have known about it had he not told her.

Lucas had heard a short ad on the radio about a researcher who was looking for pediatric subjects to be in a study of an alternative treatment for pediatric kidney disease. Janine had called about the study and learned it involved an herbal remedy, delivered intravenously. When she told her parents and Joe that she wanted Sophie to participate in the study, they refused to even discuss the matter with her. Instead, they wanted Sophie to participate in a Johns Hopkins study of one more horrid, toxic medication—that if it didn't kill her—might help her.

The herbal approach had no such side effects, Dr. Schaefer had told her. As a matter of fact, Sophie would feel much better very quickly. Even so, Janine did not enroll her right away. Schaefer was a bit strange, a mousy man of few words who seemed remarkably unsure of himself to be leading a study of any kind, but she checked into his background and learned he had conducted some research of minor importance in the past, in which his hypotheses had been proven correct. She assumed he was one of those cerebral types who was brilliant despite a nerdish exterior.

Lucas researched the herbs for her, telling her he thought Schaefer might actually be on to something. She'd sat with him in his tree house, studying the computer screen as he pulled up information about each herb from the Internet and translated the scientific descriptions of them into language she could easily understand. Lucas was the only person with whom she could speak rationally about the study, who didn't scoff at the idea or belittle her for considering it. Her parents and Joe simply wouldn't discuss Schaefer's approach as an option.

Still, it wasn't until Sophie suffered another crisis, one her doctors felt certain spelled the end of her short life, that Janine did something she hadn't done in many years: she rebelled against Joe and her parents, that mighty, controlling threesome, and enrolled Sophie in the study behind their backs. Their fury had been quick to flare, and Janine would have backed down had it not been for Lucas. He'd lifted her guilt and rebuilt her backbone. But look where that backbone had gotten her now. Look where it had gotten *Sophie.*

Long, long ago, Joe had appreciated Janine's independence and daring. They'd known each other since their first year of junior high school, and back then, Joe had often expressed an admiration of her tomboyishness, her competitiveness and her spirit. Something shifted in their relationship during their junior year of high school, though, when Joe became attracted to her as something more than just the girl who could win any race and would accept any dare. They began to date, very quickly becoming a steady item in the halls of their high school. He grew less tolerant of her rebellious side, as he began to long for her to be more like the calm, faithful, feminine young women who dated his closest friends. One bonus of that wild streak, though, was Janine's uninhibited sexuality. She'd wanted to lose her virginity, and Joe had been more than pleased to oblige—after first making certain she was on the pill.

She *had* been on the Pill, but as in most areas of her life, she was not terribly careful about taking it. Still, it wasn't until the spring of their senior year that she became pregnant.

Her parents blamed her, not Joe, for the pregnancy, and they were quick to encourage Janine to marry him. The wedding took place the day after their graduation, in the garden at Ayr Creek, and Janine, a bit overwhelmed by all that was happening, allowed her parents to plan the event. The wedding was traditional in every detail, except, perhaps, for the bloated stomach of the bride, which pressed firmly against the fabric of her wedding gown.

Her parents adored Joe. He was the son they'd never had, and for Joe, the Snyders filled the lonely, empty space only an orphan could know. His mother had abused drugs and alcohol, deserting Joe and his father when Joe was only a year old. His father abandoned him in his own way, by dying in a plane crash when Joe was ten. Joe was then raised by his elderly aunt and uncle. Janine couldn't blame him for being thrilled by her welcoming parents, even if she had never found them welcoming herself.

Her parents, who taught history in two different high schools at the time of the wedding, helped them out financially so that Joe and Janine were able to rent a small apartment in Chantilly. Janine's mother bought them things they would need for the baby, and her father built them a crib from a kit. But all during that pregnancy, Janine had a sense of unreality. Her body grew rounder, yet she couldn't quite grasp the fact that, in a few months, she would be a mother. She was barely eighteen, and not ready, not willing, to settle down.

She was good, at least as good as she could be. She didn't swallow an ounce of alcohol once she learned she was pregnant, and she stopped smoking. But the physical risks she loved—climbing the cliffs at Great Falls, kayaking in the white water of the Potomac, canoeing the Shenandoah River—she did not give up. She wanted to learn how to fly, she told Joe. Maybe she would even be a stunt pilot or a wing walker. Joe told her to "grow up." They had no money for her to take flying lessons, he said. He was working at a grocery store, trying to keep food on their table, and Janine thought he'd become remarkably stodgy overnight. It would be years before she understood that Joe's quiet commitment to his job was a sign of his maturity, and that her wild streak was the hallmark of a self-indulgent, self-centered girl who had no business being married, much less a mother.

It was during one of her canoe trips that her baby decided to be born. Joe was not with her; he was working and would have been upset if he'd known she had gone off with her friends for a day on the Shenandoah. It was a weekend, and she didn't see why she should have to stay home just because Joe had to work. Yet she knew better than to ask him if he minded. She simply went. She never would have gone if she'd known the baby would come six weeks early.

She was with three of her friends from high school: her best friend, Ellie, and two male friends who were simply that— friends. They were in two canoes, deep in the forest, battling a patch of white water, when the pains started. Quickly, Janine was bleeding, her terror mounting with each stab of pain.

They paddled to the riverbank, and Ellie stayed with her on a bed of leaves and moss, while the guys went for help. Ellie had no idea what to do, of course, and looking back on the event later, Janine barely remembered her friend's presence. Instead, she remembered feeling completely alone, the trees a canopy of gold above her as she gasped from the pain and shivered in the October chill.

By the time the paramedics found her, she had delivered a stillborn baby boy, which Ellie had wrapped in her windbreaker.

The paramedics lifted Janine onto a stretcher and covered her with blankets.

"What the hell are you doing out here when you're nearly eight months pregnant?" one of them asked her, as he rested a blanket on top of her.

She couldn't answer, but she knew she deserved the hostile tone of the question. Once in the ambulance, she stared at the un-moving bundle where it rested in a clear plastic bassinet, and it was as if she were acknowledging for the first time that there had truly been a life inside her that she had taken for granted. A life she had, in effect, abused and neglected. She didn't cry, at least not aloud, but tears washed over her cheek onto the stretcher.

Joe had been furious. He didn't talk to her for weeks, and she'd felt alone and completely deserving of the isolation. She would mourn for that baby for the rest of her life. That had been her first true taste of guilt—a bitter, vile taste that was unfamiliar in her mouth. But it was not to be her last.

"Are you awake?"

She heard Joe's voice in the darkness and drew herself back to the present.

"Yes." She sat up straight, brushing tears from her cheeks. They were still in the car, somewhere on Beulah Road, and she saw the lights of the Meadowlark Gardens parking lot ahead of them. Leaning forward, she tried to make out the vehicles in the far corner of the lot.

"Looks like Gloria's van," Joe said. "And Rebecca and Steve's Suburban. Your car. That's it."

They pulled into the lot, vast and dark in its emptiness, and drove to the corner. The four of them—Paula, Gloria, Rebecca and Steve—were sitting on small beach chairs set on the macadam. The Krafts' two sons were no longer with them, and Charlotte had apparently gone home. Crushed bags and empty cups from Taco Bell littered the ground near the chairs.

Everyone stood up as Joe parked the car next to the Suburban.

"Any news?" Janine asked, as she got out of the car.

"Nothing," Gloria said. "How about on your end? Did you see anything?"

"No clues," Joe said. "But it was so dark up there, and the people working at the gas stations and restaurants are not the same people who were there this afternoon. So it was a little frustrating."

"Plus, a lot of the shops and restaurants are closed," Janine added.

"The police told us to go home and stay close to the phone," Gloria said. "But we didn't want to leave until you two got back."

"Your parents called us a million times," Rebecca said to Janine. "They're so worried. You might want to give them a call."

Rebecca and Steve no longer wore their wide, optimistic smiles. They looked a little ragged around the edges now, with dark shadows around their eyes, and Janine wanted to pull Rebecca into a hug. But there was still some distance in Rebecca, as if she were intentionally holding herself apart from the scene, and Janine did not feel that they were sharing the same frightening experience at all.

Joe touched Janine's arm. "I'll take Paula home, then meet you over at Ayr Creek, okay?" he asked.

She nodded, uncertain if it would help or hurt to have Joe there when she spoke to her parents.

She walked toward her car. It seemed like weeks had passed since she'd driven into the lot, full of excitement at seeing her daughter. Inside the car, she felt the emptiness in the back seat where Sophie should have been, and she kept turning to glance behind her, as though Sophie might pop up, yelling "Surprise!" and telling her this had been some silly kind of trick, some crazy scheme of Alison's. But Sophie was not in the car, and as Janine drove through the dark, winding back roads on the outskirts of Vienna, she said a prayer that, wherever Sophie was, she would be alive and healthy and, somehow, unafraid.

CHAPTER SIX

Janine didn't drive directly home. She pulled out of the parking lot at Meadowlark Gardens and onto Beulah Road, glancing in her rearview mirror as if she still expected the blue Honda to turn into the lot any moment, then drove as quickly as she could toward Lucas's property. He lived at the end of a cul-de-sac on an acre of mostly wooded land bordering Wolf Trap National Park. She parked in the driveway near the small, rambler and walked along the darkened, familiar path through the woods to reach the tree house. She was relieved to see that the lights were on in his living room; she would hate to wake him.

Gripping the banister, she climbed the stairs that circled the oak tree. He must have heard her, because he was waiting for her on the deck by the time she reached it. Wordlessly, he pulled her into his arms. She breathed in the soap-and-earth scent of him, feeling enclosed, but not truly comforted; sheltered, but not safe. Nowhere would she feel safe right now.

"You must know Sophie's missing," she whispered.

"Yes." His breath was warm on her neck.

"How?"

"Cop came to ask me some questions."

She pressed her hands against his back. "Oh, no," she said.
"I'm sorry."

"It's all right. Is there any news?"

She pulled away from him, running her hands through her
hair. "Nothing," she said. "Joe and I drove all the way up to the
camp and back again, trying to cover the route she would have
followed back to Vienna. There was no sign of Alison's—the
troop leader's—car anywhere. And we must have talked to every
gas station attendant and waitress between here and there.
They've just disappeared."

"Come in," he said. He guided her into his small living room,
an arm around her shoulders. "Have you eaten anything?"

"I can't."

"Iced tea? Soda?"

She shook her head. The thought of trying to get anything
down her throat nearly made her gag.

Lowering herself onto the built-in sofa in his living room, she
suddenly began to cry. "I feel so helpless," she said, accepting
the handkerchief he handed her and blotting it to her eyes.

He pulled one of the captain's chairs in front of her and sat
down, taking her right hand in both of his. "Tell me everything,"
he said. "What do the cops think?"

She ran her fingers over the blue splint on his wrist as she
wearily answered his questions, and Lucas suggested the same
possible explanations for the disappearance of the girls that she
had gone over with Joe and the police and Gloria. They were
lost. They'd fallen asleep somewhere and forgotten the time.
They'd taken a recreational detour. The explanations sounded
weaker now, in the middle of the night, and for the first time,
Janine allowed the worst to enter her mind.

"What if she's dead?" she asked Lucas. "Children disappear
all the time. They're always found dead somewhere."

"Children don't disappear all the time, and they are rarely

found dead," he said softly. "They're simply the ones you hear about. It doesn't do any good to start thinking that way, Jan."

"She's supposed to have dialysis tonight," she said, "and she needs her Herbalina IV tomorrow."

Lucas nodded. "I know. I was thinking about that. Have you ever asked her doctor what would happen if she missed an IV?"

She shook her head. "I would never allow that to happen."

"You should call him right now."

"Schaefer? It's the middle of the night."

"Yes, but I think the police should have a very clear picture of her illness. Did you tell them?"

"Yes. But not in great detail. Not anything about what would happen if she misses that IV."

"They should know, Jan, don't you think?" Lucas asked. "They can get the information to the media, and the media can get it out on the airwaves. They need to know how urgent this is. If—and this is only an if—Sophie's been kidnapped, by the Scout leader or someone else, and the kidnapper hears that Sophie needs treatment right away...well, maybe he or she has a soft spot in his heart and would drop her off at a hospital or something."

She nodded. He was right, and making the call would give her something to do to ease the helplessness. "His number's stored in my cell, but can I use your phone?" she asked. "I don't want to tie mine up."

He handed her his phone and she dialed the number. It was after one in the morning, and the woman at Schaefer's answering service sounded annoyed at being disturbed.

"I need to speak with Dr. Schaefer," Janine said. "It's an emergency."

"If this is an emergency, you should hang up and call 911," the woman said.

"No. Not that sort of emergency. Please...just get in touch with him and ask him to call Janine Donohue right away. Only not at my usual number." She gave the woman Lucas's number, then hung up the phone. Her hand was shaking.

The doctor called within five minutes. He sounded wide-awake, although his usually faint New England accent was more pronounced than she'd ever heard it before.

"Is Sophie all right?" he asked, and Janine was grateful for the genuine concern in his voice.

"I don't know," she said. "She went to a Girl Scout camp this weekend and she hasn't come home. She and another girl and their leader are all...missing. They were due back at three. The police are involved, but there's no trace of them. And I'm worried she won't be found in time to get her IV tomorrow. Will she...will she be all right without it?"

There was a long silence on Schaefer's end of the phone line.

"Dr. Schaefer?" she prodded, wondering if he had fallen asleep.

Finally he spoke. "This sounds very serious," he said.

"Yes, it is, but right now I'm just worried about her physical condition. What will happen if she's not back in time for her appointment tomorrow? And she's supposed to have dialysis tonight."

He hesitated again. She would have chalked it up to sleepiness on his part had it not been for the fact that this slow reaction time was his usual style. "As soon as she arrives tomorrow, bring her in," he said. "Don't worry about the appointment time."

"What if she doesn't arrive, though? I mean, tomorrow. What happens if she misses tomorrow's IV altogether? And what if she misses Thursday's, too?" She looked at Lucas, who was leaning toward her, his arms on his knees.

"The obvious," Schaefer said.

"What do you mean, 'the obvious'?" she asked.

Lucas scowled, apparently annoyed with the doctor as he listened to Janine's frustrated side of the conversation. He reached for the phone, asking her permission with his eyes. She nodded, relinquishing the phone to him gladly.

"Dr. Schaefer?" he said. "This is Lucas Trowell. I'm a friend of Janine's. Maybe you could tell me precisely what you think will happen if Sophie misses her IV and her dialysis. And if you could also give me the details of her illness, we can give them to the police."

He reached behind him to grab an envelope from the coffee table, then motioned to Janine for a pen. She found one in her purse and handed it to him, watching as he began to take notes, the phone nestled between his shoulder and his ear.

Apparently Schaefer had found his voice, and Lucas filled the entire back of the envelope with his small, neat script. When he hung up the phone, he gave Janine a sympathetic smile.

"Thanks," she said. "He was driving me crazy. What did he say?"

"It's what you would expect. Without the dialysis, she'll have a buildup of fluid and toxins, but that will happen much more slowly than if she'd never had the Herbalina. And she'll get gradually worse with each Herbalina IV she misses, until she's back where she started."

"How many can she miss before that happens? And will it work again for her if she starts it up again after missing it for a while?"

"He didn't seem to know how long it would take to be out of her system, but he does think it will work just as well as it did before, if she needs to start it all over again. He gave me some general information about her condition you can pass on to the police so they can get the word out, although I really think you know at least as much about it as he does." He often told her how much he admired her tireless research into Sophie's condition and the few treatment options that were available.

"Would you mind calling the police?" she asked. "You can read your own notes better than I can. Besides, I seem to be screwing things up tonight." She picked up his phone again and dialed the number Sergeant Loomis had given her.

"I'll do it," he said, taking the phone from her hand, "but

only if you promise to cool it with the self-deprecating comments, all right?"

She nodded. "Okay."

She listened while he spoke with the sergeant, explaining who he was and why he, rather than Janine, was calling. It reassured her that Loomis was still working on the case, even though it was the middle of the night. He hadn't sloughed it off onto someone else's shoulders.

Lucas was so calm. A rock. As he spoke to the officer, he reached for her hand again and held it on her knee. He could talk to anyone, she thought: the gardeners he supervised, a medical specialist, a cop. An eight-year-old girl. She remembered how he'd ceremoniously presented Sophie with a small, black penknife before she left on this trip, her first camping adventure.

Janine's love for Lucas brought easy tears to her eyes as she watched him on the phone. His body was lean, yet tight—an odd mix of physical laborer and computer geek. His brown hair was frosted by the sun and beginning to thin at the temples, and he wore wire-rimmed glasses. His gray eyes looked cloudy now, inside at night, but in the daylight, they were translucent. Sometimes she thought she could see straight through them to his soul.

"I assume they don't know anything new?" she asked, once he had hung up the phone.

"Nothing. But he was grateful for the information and said they'd send out a press release right away."

"Thanks for calling." She looked at her watch and shuddered. "I have to go to Ayr Creek and see my parents. Joe should be there by now, and I'm sure they're furious I haven't gotten over there yet."

"Don't let them blame you for this, Janine," Lucas said, standing up. "You haven't done anything wrong."

"Haven't I?" she asked. "Then why do I feel like I have? Why do I feel as though every time I make a decision that flies in the face of what they think I should do, something terrible happens?

I canoe while I'm pregnant, I kill my baby. I join the army, I kill my daughter. I—"

"You haven't killed anyone." He ran his hands down her arms, drawing her into an embrace.

"I enrolled her in a study no one wanted her to be in except me," she said into his shoulder, "and she felt so well that I let her go to camp, even though everyone told me I shouldn't. But I did, and now she's probably lying in a ditch somewhere, dead and—"

"Stop it!" His voice was so loud and so uncharacteristically harsh that she did stop. He held her shoulders. "I don't want to hear this, Jan," he said. "It's irrational. You love Sophie as much as any mother could love a child, and you've let your parents—and Joe—do a number on your head all these years. She's not dead. Don't start thinking that way, all right?"

She pressed her forehead to his. "I'll try," she said, her gaze on the floor. On the Berber carpet, his feet were bare, hers in sandals. She felt his hand circle the back of her neck.

"Good." He kissed her forehead. "I love you, Jan," he said. "And all I want is for you to start loving yourself."

CHAPTER SEVEN

Darkness gave the Ayr Creek estate an otherworldly feel, and on this night, with the half-moon masked by the trees, Janine felt as though she were slipping into a dream as she drove up the long driveway. The broad, meandering gardens slept, and beyond the boxwood, the willow trees drooped low to the ground in their lacy, moon-speckled shrouds. The forest surrounding the house and gardens on three sides was so thick and deep, that the moonlight could not penetrate it. Only where the trees parted to make room for her little cottage at the rear of the property would the light truly fall, the play of moonglow and shadow making the building look as though it had been lifted straight out of a spooky fairy tale.

Friends often asked her if she was afraid out here at night, hidden away in the woods in a cottage which, according to historians with the most vibrant imaginations, was still haunted by the spirits of those slaves who once lived within its walls. Janine rarely thought of Ayr Creek as foreboding, but tonight the estate, the entire *world,* seemed malevolent.

In the daylight, the gardens of the Ayr Creek estate held none of their nighttime mystery. They were meticulously cared for, and several acres of the plants, trees and flowers were dedicated to reflecting historical accuracy. That was the reason Lucas had been hired to oversee the grounds and the gardeners at Ayr Creek. He had excellent references, having worked at historic Monticello, making sure that nothing was planted that would not have grown in the time of Thomas Jefferson. He never would have been hired at Ayr Creek if Janine's parents had had their way, however, the decision had not been up to them.

Her father had been the one to take Lucas on his initial tour of the grounds. He'd reported that the gardener had seemed disinterested and distracted until Frank mentioned that Janine and her little girl, Sophie, lived in the cottage on the property. Lucas had brightened at that fact. He'd asked questions about Sophie, raising Frank's suspicions about his intent. Frank had reported his concerns to the Ayr Creek Foundation, but the Foundation was thrilled by the opportunity to have a former Monticello gardener work at Ayr Creek, and they were the ones to make the final decision. Frank and Donna's concerns were disregarded. They had warned Janine to keep an eye on Sophie when Lucas was around and never to leave her alone with him. In the beginning, Janine had heeded their warning. Now she knew they had misinterpreted any interest Lucas might have shown in her daughter.

As she neared the rear of the mansion, she saw that Joe's car was parked in front of the freestanding, three-car garage, which had at one time served as the stable for the estate. She pulled her car next to his, her mouth set in a grim line. She was about to face the formidable Anti-Jan Triad. That's what Lucas called her parents and Joe. He'd tell her to put on her suit of armor. But tonight she had no armor, and despite Lucas's words of encouragement, she felt as though she didn't deserve to possess any.

Bracing herself, Janine walked in the unlocked side door of the mansion, passed through the mudroom and into the kitchen.

All three of them were there. Her mother sat at the mahogany table, while Joe and her father leaned against the counters, and they all turned to look at her when she walked in.

"Janine!" Her mother jumped to her feet. "Where on earth have you been? We don't need you disappearing, too. Joe said you should have been here by now." Her face was red from crying, and her blond hair, which she usually wore tied back, hung loose around her face. She was a worrier under the best of circumstances, but tonight, the lines in her tanned face looked as if they'd been carved there with a cleaver.

Janine set her purse down on the table. "I stayed a little while at the parking lot," she lied, glancing at Joe. He looked tired. His dark hair was askew, and he rubbed his eyes with the palms of his hands.

"Any news?" Her father walked toward her and gave her shoulder the slightest of squeezes, his awkward way of comforting her, or, she supposed, the kindest gesture he could manage while being furious at her. And he *was* furious. All three of them were. That she knew for certain. The air of the kitchen was filled with blame.

"Nothing," she said, taking a seat at the table. She looked again at Joe. "You haven't heard anything, either?"

He shook his head.

"Joe said the woman Sophie was riding with was very young and irresponsible," her mother said. "Why you would ever let her go away with someone like that, I just don't know."

"She's not irresponsible, Mom," she said, annoyed with Joe. "Just young. Plus there was another leader with them." If only Gloria had been the one to drive her home.

"*Why* did you send her to camp?" her mother asked. "Didn't I tell you she's just too young? Even a healthy eight-year-old has no business going two hours away for an overnight in the woods."

"Mom," Joe said. "What's done is done. It's not going to help to go over that argument again."

Janine was surprised and gratified by his sudden support.

"I just..." Her mother shook her head. "I'm just appalled,

that's all." She sat down at the table again, facing away from Janine as though she couldn't bear to look at her. "Has anybody thought that maybe Lucas Trowell has something to do with this?" she asked the men, who leaned against the counter on opposite sides of the refrigerator, like bookends. "You know how he's always got his eye on Sophie. They should go see if he's up in his tree house or if he's somehow gotten hold of Sophie and the other little girl." She turned to Janine. "Did you mention to him that she was going to Girl Scout camp this weekend?" she asked. "I hate how you're always talking to him."

"Lucas had nothing to do with this," Janine said.

"How can you know that?" her mother asked. "He's just the sort you'd suspect of something like this. You know how you always hear about those men after the fact. They were quiet. A little odd. Kept to themselves. That fits Lucas to a tee. The only time you see a glimmer in his eye is when you mention Sophie to him."

Janine didn't bother to respond. She had seen a glimmer in Lucas's eyes any number of times.

"I asked the police to go by the tree house and make sure Lucas was there," Joe said.

So, it had been Joe who'd instigated the visit from the police. He certainly knew how to win her parents' favor.

Joe took his cell phone from his back pocket. "I'll give them a call to make sure they did," he said.

"The police already interviewed him," she said, surprising herself with the admission, and the three of them turned to look at her.

"How do you know?" Joe said.

She drew in a long breath and folded her hands on the table in front of her. "Because I was just there," she said. "At his tree house. The police were there hours ago."

"You went to his house alone?" her mother asked. "Are you out of your mind?"

"Why did you go there, hon?" her father asked. "Did you think you'd find Sophie there?"

"No, Dad, I never suspected Lucas. I just stopped by to tell him what happened."

"Why?" Her mother's blue eyes were wild with disbelief. "What possible business is it of his?"

"It was foolish to go there alone, Janine," her father said. "What if—"

"Please stop!" Janine rose to her feet, sending her chair thumping against the wall. "Please stop all this crazy paranoid talk about Lucas."

They stared at her.

"He had nothing to do with this whole mess," she said. "He cares about Sophie."

"He has you fooled," her mother said. "Don't you see—"

"No, I don't see any such thing." Janine walked around the table toward the door. She considered escape, but turned instead and leaned against the door frame, her arms folded across her chest. "I may have made some mistakes in my life," she said, "but my judgment is not so screwed up that I couldn't tell if Lucas was the type to hurt Sophie. I would never put Sophie in danger."

Her mother let out a cynical laugh. "Do you hear yourself, Janine?" she asked. "You *have* put Sophie in danger. *Repeatedly.* What do you call this weekend away? What do you call putting Sophie in a harebrained study to use herbs to cure—" she used her hands to put quotes around the word *cure* "—end stage kidney disease? You've gone out of your way to put Sophie in danger."

"Mom," Joe said. "Maybe that's going too far."

Maybe? Janine's eyes burned from the assault.

"It's insane that you stopped doing her nightly dialysis." Her mother wasn't quite finished.

"She doesn't need it every night anymore," Janine said.

"Your mother might be exaggerating a bit," her father said, in his even, controlled voice, "but we *do* need to talk about this. About what's been going on the past few months."

"What do you mean?" She tightened her arms across her chest. How much did they know?

"We've been talking with Joe about what to do when Sophie gets back," her father continued. He was tall and gangly and always looked like a little kid whose body had grown too quickly for him to handle with grace. "We really think Joe should have custody of her," he said. "I mean, you could still have her live with you much of the time, the way you do now, but when it comes to making the medical decisions and...decisions like this one, about the Scout camp and all, we think Joe should be the one to make them." Her father's calm disappointment in her cut even deeper than her mother's shrill accusations.

Joe moved next to her, touching her hand where it gripped her elbow.

"Let's not talk about it now," he said to her parents. "Don't even think about it tonight, Janine. Right now, let's just focus on getting Sophie back."

He was the voice of reason, and his kindness seemed genuine, but she knew better than to trust him. Behind her back, he was conspiring with her parents. She took a step away from him to pick up her purse from the table. "I'm going to the cottage," she said, heading for the door.

"*What?*" her mother said. "We need to stay right here until we hear some news."

"I can be reached just as easily in the cottage," she said.

Joe rested his hand on her shoulder. "Do you want me to come with you?" he asked.

She shook her head without looking at him, then walked through the mudroom and out to the driveway.

Walking through the darkness toward her cottage, she bristled from the encounter with her family, and she was glad Joe hadn't tried to follow her. Having Joe with her was the last thing she wanted. She didn't need to hear any more about his plans to assume custody of Sophie. She didn't need any more blame. It had been this way her entire adult life: her parents and Joe against her. Over the years, their disapproval of her had crystallized into something hard and unmovable. Even now, when they should be pulling together with her, fighting on the same side of this war, she felt like their enemy.

Once in the cottage, though, she would call Lucas. That's where she would find her advocate. That's where she would find her strength.

CHAPTER EIGHT

Zoe held a match to the kindling at the bottom of the fire and watched as the wood began to flame. She was getting good at this. Very good, actually. For someone who had never built a fire in her life—in spite of having had four fireplaces in her Malibu house and six on Max's dream ranch in Montana—she could now call herself an expert.

Resting near her on the ground was a pot filled with water, uncooked rice and chunks of the rabbit she'd killed that morning. She moved the pot to the small grill she'd laid over the fire pit and sat down on one of the flat rocks to wait for the water to boil.

She could not yet claim to be comfortable with the whole meat preparation process, but she was getting there. As of today, she had killed six animals: two rabbits, three squirrels and, amazingly, a porcupine. She had shot at many more, and she felt worse about those she'd merely terrorized with her bullets than those she had killed with one clean, quick shot. Still, this slaughtering and eating did not come easily to someone who had been a vegetarian for a dozen years. She'd been such a champion of animal rights that she'd refused to wear leather shoes, and she'd even been arrested for protesting in front of stores that sold fur.

Ah, yes, if only PETA could see her now, she thought, boiling a rabbit she had killed, skinned and gutted herself.

She'd left the lid to the pot inside—the tiny, rundown cabin she had quickly come to think of as her home, so she got to her feet and walked inside. When she returned to the small clearing carrying the lid, she spotted a large dog standing a couple of yards from the fire, and she froze. It was the dirty yellow dog this time, as opposed to the huge black bear of a dog who had visited her a few days earlier. Both of them had temperaments as nasty as their matted and unkempt coats. When she'd first seen the dogs, she'd feared they belonged to someone living nearby and that she was not alone in these West Virginia woods. But their hungry, neglected appearance made her think they were probably wild.

The yellow dog looked in her direction, silently baring his teeth.

"Scram!" she shouted at him. "Get lost!" She banged the lid against the flat rock, and that seemed to work. The dog turned around and trotted off into the woods.

It was her fault the dogs hung around the shanty. She'd made a tactical error with them in her early days out here. She had killed her first animal, another rabbit, and she'd had to force herself to go through the motions of preparing it to eat. Following the instructions in one of the wilderness survival books she'd brought with her, she told herself she had no choice: she would need protein to be able to live out here. Despite the fact that she'd fashioned an impressive spit above the fire and that the aroma of the cooked rabbit had actually made her mouth water, she had not been able to make herself chew and swallow the meat. Instead, she'd tossed it into the woods. That night, she'd lain awake, weeping quietly over the life she'd taken for no good reason, and listened to animals—wild dogs, she knew now—fighting over the carcass in the darkness.

The next time, though, she was hungrier and more determined. Marti was a meat eater, and Zoe knew she would have to be able to kill and cook meat to feed her. On that day, she killed and ate her first squirrel. She'd also caught a small, dark-scaled fish in a net she'd brought with her, and she'd managed to get that down despite the fact that it bore no resemblance to any other fish she'd ever eaten and could have been poisonous for all she knew.

The water was boiling, and she leaned forward to stir the stew before covering it with the lid. The fire pit was in the exact center of the small clearing, just a few yards in front of her shanty. That was what she called the dilapidated cabin, finding *shanty* a far prettier word than *hovel* or *shack,* which would have been a more accurate description of the building. Her little shanty was hidden so deeply in the forest that Zoe was certain no one would find it unless they actually knew it was there.

She herself had found the structure through a painstaking search of these wooded West Virginia mountains back in early April, when she and Marti first agreed on their plan. She'd actually discovered several abandoned cabins, but this one had appealed to her most, both practically and aesthetically. On the practical side, it was far from the nearest road, a good five miles, and even that road was barely paved and rarely traveled. The nearest main road was a couple of miles beyond that one. This cabin was as far from civilization as Zoe had ever been, and she was frankly thrilled by the distance between her and the rest of the world. That world thought she was dead. It held nothing for her any longer.

Her shanty would never appear in *Better Homes and Gardens,* but it was still more appealing than some of the other shacks she'd seen. Some of them were little more than decrepit piles of rotting wood, while this one had a little character. It was a log cabin and looked as old as the mountains themselves. The logs were separated by a mortar that had once been white, but was now green with moss on two adjacent sides of the house, dirty and crumbling on the others. The roof was rotting, and she'd initially covered the decaying wood and scraps of tin with the tarp she'd brought along with her. But then she realized that, if anyone *should* find his way to her little clearing, the bright-blue tarp would give away the fact that someone was living in the shanty, so she took it down. Now, when it rained, she put a couple of buckets beneath the worst spots in the roof and let it go at that.

Inside the front door of the shanty was, what she called for want of a better term, the living room, which ran the width of the building. Behind that, an identical room served as a bedroom. And that was it. A two-room log cabin, both rooms together nearly equaling the size of her Malibu bathroom.

But the shanty had what she was coming to think of as amenities. Remarkably clear water ran from a rusty old pump in the overgrown yard. A wood-burning stove in surprisingly good shape sat on the floor in the main room, its chimney pipe winding its way through a leaking hole in her roof. The pipe was round, the hole square, and that about summed up the care that had been taken by whomever constructed this place. She'd used the stove only once to cook on, but it heated the entire shanty, and she knew she would have to do her cooking outside until the cooler months. At least she and Marti would not freeze here in the winter.

There was a sofa in the living room, and once she'd gotten over the revolting, disintegrating fabric and protruding tufts of stuffing, she was grateful for a place to sit. She'd brought a dozen or so sheets with her, and she threw a cream-colored one over the sofa and thought that it looked like it came straight out of some campy catalogue—as long as no one noticed the splintery wooden floor beneath it and the lack of glass in the window behind it.

Not far from the house, but hidden behind a shield of brambles and vines, was an outhouse. It tilted to one side, giving her vertigo when she sat inside it. The outhouse had smelled nearly as fresh as the forest when she'd first arrived, a testimony to how long it had been since anyone had called this place home.

When she'd first stepped inside the cabin, the floor had been covered with debris—branches and twigs and rotting leaves that had fallen or blown through the gaping holes in the roof. Mice skittered away from her broom, and she remembered reading something about mice droppings causing that flesh-eating virus, so she'd covered her nose and mouth with a kerchief, unsure if that would help. Unsure if it really mattered. She just needed to live long enough to save her daughter. After that, death could come anytime, and she truly wouldn't mind.

Once she'd emptied the back room of its tree branches and leaves, she discovered four sleeping palettes on the floor, one in each corner. She'd brought two air mattresses with her, which she inflated on the palettes against the far wall. Then she tore one of the king-size sheets and made the palettes and mattresses up as best she could. She'd stepped back to look at them and was amazed at how much the simple sight of those two low beds, dressed in Egyptian cotton, pleased her. She was glad she'd thought to bring these lavender sheets; they were the only ones that did not remind her of Max, since he'd always hated the color and she had used them only on the guest beds. She hadn't wanted to bring any tangible traces of her grief with her. Living here would be hard enough without adding mourning to her list of things to do. Once she'd left Malibu, once she'd pulled the car out of the driveway and headed for the mountains, she knew she was leaving Max behind forever. She was leaving *everything* behind—except her duty as a mother.

She'd been in the shanty for over a month now, but she'd been planning this trip, this new life, for weeks prior to her "suicide." She'd been planning it ever since Marti had written her, telling her she was being transferred to the prison at Chowchilla. It had been unbearable to picture Marti in prison *anywhere,* but Chowchilla, with its reputation for abusive guards, toughened prisoners and intolerable living conditions, was out of the question. Zoe had lain awake all that night, Marti's letter in her hand, a bizarre plot taking shape in her mind.

She'd gotten out of bed to walk downstairs to the study, a room she'd been avoiding ever since Max's death. Sure enough, the Persian rug and the burgundy walls lined with books and awards still held his scent, that musky scent of cigars, as though he'd just left the room for a moment. Standing stock-still in the doorway of the room, she'd had to shut her eyes and remind herself that he was dead. This was the room where she'd found him, crumpled on the floor near the hearth, the way a blanket would crumple if you dropped it, limp and folded in on itself. She'd known instantly that he was dead, and yet she'd screamed his name over and over as if he could hear her. It had been his third and final heart attack. The cigars were to blame, she'd thought. Or maybe the pace he'd insisted on holding himself to. He'd been seventy years old and still producing a movie a year, still insisting on having his hand in every aspect of it, from the casting to the final cut. She did not, however, blame herself, except for not checking on him sooner when he hadn't come up to bed that evening. She had been a good wife to him, and he had been the finest of husbands. A forty-year-old marriage in Hollywood was something to point to with pride. Yet, she'd hoped to see fifty years with him, and maybe more.

She could not be the single woman again, not at sixty. Not with the paparazzi following her every move, noting each new wrinkle, each gray root marking the birth of every dark-blond hair on her head. She'd been known for that long, thick, shimmery blond hair since she was a little girl, and she had not been able to let go of it. She'd had three surgeries on her face already, and she was sick of the doctors and the recovery time and the fact that she no longer looked like herself. And now the wrinkles were starting again and the tabloids were taunting her. They criticized the extra pounds she'd put on. Last year, one of them had described her as a mountain. A *mountain!* Only Max had still seemed to think she was beautiful and desirable and valuable, and when he died, there was no one to tell her the tabloids were simply wrong and mean-spirited. She'd been an actress and a singer since she was three years old, well-known enough to go by her first name alone, like Cher and Madonna and Ann-Margret. Only those women were aging far better than she was. Escape began to sound marvelous. She would not have to endure growing old in the unforgiving spotlight.

In Max's study, she'd found an atlas. She'd taken it with her down to the first level of the house, where the floor was covered with Italian tiles the color of eggshells. Small changing rooms, where people could slip into their bathing suits in the summer months before heading out to the beach, lined one side of the broad hallway. One of the rooms on the other side of the hall was used for storage, and that was her destination.

She had a goal, but it took her much of the night to find what she was looking for, because she could not stop herself from sorting through the old reviews in the scrapbooks piled on the shelves. There were the sparkling reviews of her as a child star, and critical acclaim of her as an adult. "Zoe possesses a voice like torn satin," one of them read. "*The Kiss,* an otherwise lackluster film, glows due to a phenomenal performance by Zoe," read another. Reading the reviews pulled her down into a deep well of pain. She'd had a past few could point to with such pride, a past so joyful and full that her present sense of loss—of her husband, her beauty, her fans—was beyond bearing. There was only one thing left worth living for, and that was Marti.

After finally forcing herself to reshelve the scrapbooks, she began rummaging through the cardboard boxes stacked on the other side of the room. She found the brochures of West Virginia and the Sweetwater Spa in one of the boxes marked Travel on the side. She and Max had visited the spa several years ago, selecting it because of Max's old family roots in that state. People had stared at them while they were there, of course, and cameras had flashed, but for the most part, they were left alone.

She and Max had taken a break from the spa activities one afternoon to visit some of Max's elderly relatives, and while driving back to the spa, they became extremely lost. *Intentionally* lost, laughing with abandon at the sudden freedom they felt as they wandered, unconcerned, away from everyone and everything, down the deserted country roads that twisted through green mountains on the outskirts of the George Washington National Forest. The only signs that anyone had ever been in those parts were the occasional little cabins, abandoned, boarded up or simply left to rot. She had thought then how someone might hide out in one of those cabins. A fugitive could probably stay there for years, undetected. She'd spoken this aloud, and Max had asked her how the fugitive would eat. He would have to know in advance what he was going to do, she'd said, and before going on the run, he would have to bring supplies to the cabin. Her imagination had been on fire, thinking about it. He could bring everything he would need ahead of time so that he could sustain himself there for long periods. And he could learn to eat squirrel or rabbit. He could fish in a stream.

"What about electricity?" Max had asked her.

"Candles," she'd replied. "Lanterns." He would bring a lot of books to read for entertainment. He'd need to find a cabin with a fireplace for warmth.

Max had commented that she sounded almost wistful, and she supposed she had. Their life had grown too complicated. There were the two houses to take care of, in Malibu and Montana. There was too much money to oversee. Too much of everything in their lives, she'd said, and he'd looked at her with some concern. She'd reassured him she was very happy and grateful for all they had, and turned away from the thick forest and its abandoned homes. Never would she have guessed that she would one day be the fugitive in her imagination.

She was better at living a life on the run than she ever would have guessed. She'd become a real master at hiding cars, for instance. It was remarkably easy. There was a lot of empty space in this country, and if you were willing to walk a bit after leaving your car, you were home free. Before her putative suicide, she'd rented a car at one of those "junker-for-rent" places. After performing radical surgery on her hair and covering it with a wig, she'd donned large sunglasses and disguised her voice for the visit to the rental counter. She produced one of the several fake driver's licenses she'd been able to get through a shady site on the Internet for a grand total of two thousand dollars. The clerk had still looked at her suspiciously, making her heart beat so hard she was afraid it might be visible beneath the tight, trampy-looking jersey she was wearing. But he'd handed her the keys to the car, and she was on her way.

First, she'd hidden her own car deep in the mountains east of Los Angeles, taking the plates off. With the well-paid help of the guy who'd supplied her driver's licenses, she'd transferred the plates to the rental car, which she ditched in the Texas panhandle after picking up another one. Two more cars had brought her to West Virginia, and she'd left the last rental in a glade that seemed to be a car dumping ground. There were four or five cars there already, none of them as new and shiny as the rental car, but she figured it wouldn't take long for it to look as though it belonged there. Then, she'd spent a couple of hours in an old, deserted barn, preparing it for Marti's eventual arrival in accordance with their plan. From there, she'd hiked nearly a full day through the trailless woods to her new home. She'd had a compass, a map she'd drawn herself and a sense of direction that rarely failed her. She also, unfortunately, had bursitis in her hip, and that night, lying on the air mattress in the shanty, she'd longed for a heating pad in the worst way. It had taken several days of rest for her to be able to walk again without hobbling, but now she was fine. Actually, after a few weeks of toting firewood and hiking through the forest in search of game, she felt stronger than she had in years.

Now, Zoe walked into the shanty to get a bowl for the stew, and when she returned to the clearing, the filthy yellow dog was back, sitting in the open space between the fire pit and the woods. He looked from her to the stew pot and back to her again, and she fought a desire to toss the poor creature a bit of the rabbit. Instead, she carefully lifted the pot from the fire and carried it inside the shanty, shutting the door behind her. No need to invite trouble.

She sat on the couch while she ate, trying to picture the June calendar in her mind. If she was figuring her days correctly, Marti's escape should have taken place yesterday or the day before. In Zoe's imagination, the escape was always successful, yet she knew the plan was fraught with difficulty. How the warden would physically get Marti out of Chowchilla was cloudy in her mind, but she trusted that greed would motivate him to operate in a clever and efficient manner. Marti had told her she'd picked the greediest, the least ethical and the most immoral of the wardens to approach with her scheme.

Zoe might no longer have a husband, and she might have lost her daughter to an inept justice system. Her beauty was slipping away from her, and her voice had left long ago. But one thing she still had was money. And she knew from a lifetime of spending, that money could buy anything—or anyone. Marti had always been good at reading people, and she'd read the warden right. He would need enough money to split three ways with two of the other guards, he'd said, and Marti had simply tripled her offer. It was enough money to tempt the pope, Zoe had thought. She was depending on it. Everything had to go according to plan.

It was torture, though, thinking of Marti having to negotiate with prison guards, just as the thought of her being imprisoned for something she had not done was unbearable. Marti in prison! Zoe blamed herself entirely for the fix her daughter was in. She should have hired different lawyers. She'd gone with Snow, Snow and Berenski because they'd always handled everything for her and Max over the years, but criminal law was not their strong suit. They'd let Marti down. Someone said that a car "just like" Marti Garson's Audi was parked in front of Tara Ashton's house the day the actress was killed. Marti didn't even *know* Tara Ashton, much less have any reason to kill her. Tara had been the hot new actress in Hollywood, with a beautifully exotic face, a stunning body, wavy jet-black hair and an undeniable ability to act, setting her apart from other newcomers who were simply gorgeous. Someone else testified that they had seen a woman who looked "just like" Marti Garson leave Ashton's house that afternoon. They swore to this, and Zoe could not tell if they truly believed they had seen Marti, or if someone was perhaps paying them to say so. But why on earth would anyone set Marti up?

There had been no fingerprints at the scene; whoever had committed the murder had worn gloves or wiped everything clean. The prosecutor claimed that Marti had a motive: Tara Ashton had recently been given a part in a movie, a part Zoe had been up for. The part had been *written* for Zoe, for a woman Zoe's age, and then, suddenly, the script was changed to accommodate Ashton. Oh, that had hurt. No one said flat out that Zoe was too old for the part, but who could deny it, when the front page of the tabloids showed a split image of a time-ravaged Zoe next to the fresh, smiling Ashton?

So, the prosecutor built a strong case against Marti, citing her closeness to Zoe and her desire to protect her mother. The argument was, unfortunately, erroneous. She and Marti were not close in the least, and she doubted that Marti had even known the movie role had been handed to Ashton. But Zoe wasn't about to deny that bond with her daughter. She relished the idea of Marti caring that much about her; it was a treasured fantasy. And although she was naturally horrified by the murder, she couldn't help but be touched by the notion of Marti coming to her defense. Yet she knew the explanation for Ashton's murder lay somewhere other than in Marti's love for her mother. Besides, someone had bludgeoned Tara Ashton to death with a hammer, for heaven's sake! Marti was not capable of that sort of violence. But no one seemed interested in looking for another suspect, and that's where Marti's lawyers had gone astray, in Zoe's opinion. They should have dug deeper. Surely Tara Ashton had enemies with more reason to kill her than Marti Garson did.

Marti's face, at the moment the jury's verdict was read, would haunt Zoe for the rest of her life. Marti was twenty-eight, but all Zoe could see in her daughter's huge blue eyes was the baby she'd longed for but didn't know how to mother, the little girl she'd left in the care of nannies as she pursued her career, the teenager she'd shipped off to boarding school. No wonder Marti had eschewed the Hollywood careers that had so consumed her parents in favor of a quieter life behind a computer screen as a programmer.

The jury saw Marti's quiet, reserved demeanor as a facade that hid anger and malice and a fierce, protective love for her mother. A love that only Zoe and Marti knew had never existed.

Zoe shifted her thoughts from the miserable trial back to Marti's escape. Somehow, the warden would have gotten Marti out of Chowchilla, without alarms going off or anyone noticing for hours, at least. And then, because he was anxious to collect the rest of his payment, he would have driven with Marti as fast as he could from California to West Virginia, taking whatever precautions were necessary to avoid being caught. Surely he had changed cars once or twice on the road. He had to be at least as savvy as Zoe had been in this fugitive business.

In a few days, then, Marti would be here with her. Finally, they would be mother and daughter. She could make up to Marti for all the years of neglect, for all the times she had not known how to be a mother and so had chosen not to mother her at all.

They would hide out here for a year or so, until the search for Marti had lost its steam. Then they would somehow get to South

America—or at least, she would make sure that Marti got there—where she could undergo plastic surgery and start a new life. Zoe didn't care what happened to *her* at that point. She just needed to get Marti to safety.

She had everything ready: the compass, map and money Marti would need were hidden in the barn; the trail from the barn to the shanty was marked with scraps of blue cloth. What she wouldn't give for one phone call with her daughter, though, just to know where Marti was now, how soon she could expect to see her! But she would have to settle for knowing that Marti was on her way, and that they would be together any day now. Any day now, she could hold her daughter in her arms.

CHAPTER NINE

Janine felt a need to see the camp in daylight, and so, early Monday morning, she and Joe drove once again into West Virginia. She was behind the wheel this time, and their plan was to drive directly up to the camp, then return slowly, stopping to talk with the waitresses, gas station attendants and store clerks they had been unable to meet with the night before. They would check any alternative routes Alison might have taken, as well. That was, if there was no report of Sophie being found by then. Their cell phones were turned on and ready for that message. Over and over again, Janine heard the words in her head: *"We've found her! She's fine!"*

But neither of their phones rang on the drive to the camp. Joe called the police himself once and learned that there were still no reports of any accidents involving a blue Honda and no sign of Alison's car anywhere along the route.

"How hard do you think they're looking?" Janine asked him, when he hung up the phone. They were only a mile or two from the camp at that point. "Alison has one of the most common cars on the road. Do you think they're stopping every blue Honda they see? Peeking inside any blue Honda parked in a parking lot?"

"You're right," Joe said, and he hit the redial button on his phone. As soon as he had the sergeant on the line again, he started yelling. "*You* guys should be out here checking the restaurants and the gas stations," he shouted into the phone. "It shouldn't be up to the parents to have to take this on."

Janine cringed at the anger in his voice.

"What the hell are we paying taxes for?" Joe continued. "These are *little girls* who are missing. You guys should be moving faster on this." He was quiet for a moment, listening, and Janine could hear the sergeant's deep, calm voice on the phone, although she couldn't make out what he was saying. The cop was handling Joe's temper better than she could, she thought. She knew much of the anger Sergeant Loomis was receiving was truly meant for her.

"Yeah, well, it's not enough," Joe muttered into the phone, his voice quieter now. He looked at his watch. "Fine. All right. We'll be there." He hung up without saying goodbye.

She saw his hand tremble as he rested the phone back on the console.

"They want us and Holly's parents at the police station at three o'clock for a press conference," he said. "They'll have TV cameras there. We're supposed to make some sort of plea for—"

"They think they've been kidnapped, then?"

"Not necessarily. It's just a plea for people to keep an eye out for them."

Janine pulled into the large, gravel parking lot of the camp and turned off the ignition. "Do you think it's weird that Holly's parents aren't out here looking, too?" she asked.

"They have other kids to take care of," Joe said, opening his car door. "And everybody has different ways of coping."

She felt guilty for thinking of Rebecca and Steve Kraft with suspicion. She'd called Rebecca very early that morning to see if she and Steve wanted to drive up to the camp with them, and she had the feeling she'd awakened her. Rebecca had been silent for a moment, as if the thought of making that drive had never crossed her mind.

"No," she'd said. "We'll just let the police do their job and stay here by the phone. I appreciate your effort, though. Please call us right away if you learn anything."

As soon as she stepped out of the car, Janine could hear the boisterous sounds of several hundred happy Girl Scouts. The lot was close to the lake, and the girls laughed and shrieked as they played in the water. Sophie would not have been one of those girls, Janine thought. She wouldn't have been able to swim in the lake because of her catheter. If Janine had been there to clean the tube that protruded from her belly, wrap it in gauze and tape it to her body again, she might have allowed it, but she'd told Sophie not to get it wet at all over the weekend. That and sticking to her diet were Sophie's end of the deal.

As she listened to the mirthful noise from the girls in the lake, Janine wondered if Sophie was capable of making such joyful sounds. Could she shriek that way, with such complete abandon? Janine had never heard her do so, and the thought weighed heavily on her mind. She wanted to know.

They met briefly with the camp director and the counselors in charge of Sophie's cabin, the same people they had met with the night before, along with the sheriff. They were patient and sympathetic with Joe and Janine, and they exhibited real concern over the missing Scouts, but they had not been able to remember any new facts that might help to find them.

"Sophie's a little doll," one of the counselors said, and the other nodded in agreement.

"She's much more mature than the other kids, even though she's so much tinier than they are," the second counselor added. "She knows when it's time to play and when it's time to work, and she does both with equal zeal."

Janine liked that the counselors spoke about Sophie in the present tense, but the words themselves made her cry. She leaned against the wall of the director's cedar-smelling office, and Joe put his arm around her. The intimacy in his touch was unfamiliar after three long years, but she felt the sincerity in the gesture and allowed herself to take comfort from it.

"The last three years of her life have been all work," she said. "I was afraid she wouldn't know how to play anymore."

"Oh, she does," the first counselor assured her.

"Did she shriek at all?" Janine asked.

They looked at her in confusion.

"I mean, the way the girls are doing out in the lake," she explained. "You know, shrieking and yelling and giggling."

"I don't know about shrieking," the second counselor said, "but she definitely had a great time."

"She was amazing about not being able to go in the water," the director said. "She sat on the pier and played ball with the other girls from there. She never complained."

"She's not a complainer," Joe said.

"When I heard she got dialysis, I expected her to have one of those, you know, big veins in her arm," the first counselor said.

"A fistula," Janine said.

"Right. That's what my aunt has. But Sophie told me all about how she gets hooked up to that machine at night through the tube in her stomach. She knew all the terms and everything."

Janine nodded. "We've kept her informed every step of the way."

"You know, Mrs. Donohue—" the second counselor looked Janine squarely in the eye "—I don't know where Sophie is, but I know she's safe. I feel that really strongly."

Janine felt mesmerized by the young counselor's gaze.

"She's sort of psychic." The first counselor nodded toward her co-worker with a laugh. "She does tarot cards and all, and I used to think she was full of it, but I think she's right about Sophie. They just got lost going back or something."

"Thank you," Janine said. "I hope you're right."

* * *

After leaving the director's office, Janine insisted they walk around the camp before returning to the car. The place was so lively with gleeful girls that it was hard to imagine anything ominous resulting from a stay there. Although she knew she was being ridiculous, she found herself searching the face of every little girl they passed, as though she might find Sophie hidden just beneath that child's features. It was both eerie and wonderful to be here, where Sophie had played and laughed most recently, and Janine had an almost visceral sense of her daughter's presence.

"Can you feel her here?" she asked Joe, a bit shyly, since she knew the question would sound absurd to him. "I mean, can you feel that she was here just a day ago? Like there's still a little bit of Sophie's spirit in the air?"

He looked at her oddly. "No, not really," he said.

"That counselor is right about Sophie being safe," Janine said.

"I hope so." Joe pointed toward the path that would take them back to the parking lot.

"No, I mean I *know* she's right." The feeling was so strong, she was smiling. "She's alive, Joe. I can sense it."

"It's best to think positively, I guess," Joe said, and she knew he didn't understand her feeling at all.

Lucas would have. Lucas would have known exactly what she meant.

Back in the car, they studied the map, trying to locate other routes Alison might have taken back to Vienna. They developed a system: once on an alternate route, they peered into the woods as far as their vision allowed, and they stopped at every shop or eatery they could find. Then they backtracked and followed the same routine on a different road. Two people—one a waitress, the other a customer who'd overheard their query at a produce stand—told them they'd heard about the missing girls on the radio that morning. That was encouraging. At least the word was getting out. But the going was slow and otherwise disheartening.

This would be easier from the air, Janine thought, as they walked back to the car from an unproductive stop at a small restaurant. She couldn't question people from a helicopter, but she could cover more territory in more time, and she would be able to see more easily off the beaten track.

They were driving down a narrow road, a highly unlikely route for Alison to have taken, when they came to a fork. Janine stopped the car, not even bothering to pull onto the shoulder, since no one else seemed interested in driving on this road.

"Let's look at the map," she said. "I don't know which way to go."

Joe leaned over and turned off the ignition, but he made no move to look at the map lying on his thighs. Instead he closed his eyes and rested his head against the headrest.

"God," he said, eyes squeezed tightly shut. "Who the hell knows which way she went? I feel like we're getting farther away from finding them with every damn turn we make."

She reached out to lightly touch his arm. "We can't give up," she said, although she certainly empathized with his frustration. "We can't just sit home, twiddling our thumbs." *Nothing could be worse than this,* she thought. *Nothing.* To know that something terrible must have befallen her child, yet have no idea how to help her, or even find her. Or which road to take. A bit of Joe's helpless panic seeped into her, but she shook free of it. If she gave in to it, she would lose her ability to function. To think clearly. And that would get them nowhere.

"You know what I was thinking?" she said.

He rolled his head on the headrest until he was looking at her. "What?"

"That this would be a lot easier in a helicopter. We wouldn't be able to talk to people, but we could at least visualize all the roads. It would take us a much shorter time to check out the roads from above."

He was quiet for a moment, his gaze still on her. "Are you talking about flying it yourself?" he asked finally.

"Yes."

"When's the last time you flew?"

"When I left Omega-Flight. Three years ago." She didn't say *When Sophie got sick,* or, *When you had an affair.* "I bet I could borrow one of their helicopters."

"If you flew, I couldn't be with you," Joe said quietly.

How could she have forgotten his terror of flying?

"Still, Joe?" she asked gently.

"Still and forever," he said. "I'm not even willing to fight it anymore. I had to go to California on business last year and I took the train. Three days there, and three days back."

"I'm sorry." It hurt to see so much fear in such a tough guy. For as long as she'd known him, Joe could barely watch a plane sail across the sky, much less fly in one. The plane crash that had taken his father's life had left scars that would never go away.

"Paula had to go to the conference, too," he said, "and she took the train with me, so it wasn't that terrible."

"That was very nice of her." She was not surprised. She thought that Paula would do just about anything for Joe. "Can I ask you something?" she asked.

"Sure."

"Are you and Paula...?"

"Just friends." He smiled. "I thought you knew that."

She had seen Paula and Joe together numerous times these past three years, mostly at Sophie's bedside or at Joe's house when she went to pick Sophie up there after a visit. She'd seen the way Paula looked at Joe, with a gaze that held admiration and yearning. Why was that look so easy for one woman to read in another, yet men could be so blind to it?

"But you drove down to Florida with her after her mother died," she said.

"She really needed a friend right then."

"But..." she said, hesitantly, then decided to blurt it out. "I always thought she was the woman you had the affair with."

He looked truly surprised. "You're kidding. I had no idea that's what you thought," he said. He shook his head with a half smile. "No, it wasn't Paula. It was someone who worked for us temporarily, and it wasn't an affair, really. I...slept with her once." He looked uncomfortable saying those words to her. "I was screwed up, Janine. I wish it had never happened."

"And all this time I thought it was Paula," she said.

"Paula would never do that to another woman. Her husband cheated on her, which is why she left him."

"So Paula and I have something in common." She instantly regretted her words. They were having a good conversation, and she'd just taken it below the belt. But Joe didn't seem disturbed.

"Yes, you do," he said. "I wish you'd told me you thought it was Paula. I could have saved you from...I don't know, you must have felt awkward around her."

"At first, I did," she said. "But it's been a long time. So, if not Paula, then...is there someone else?"

"Now, you mean? A girlfriend?" He smiled again, this time ruefully. "Lord knows, I've tried," he said. "I've gone out with a few women. They all say..." He shook his head.

"They all say what?" she prodded.

"It's hard to talk about."

"What?"

"They all say I'm still in love with you."

They were the last words she'd expected. "Are you?" she asked.

"Let's just say I would do anything to erase the past and make us a family again." He took her hand in his. "Is there any chance of that?" he asked.

Again, she felt a surge of sympathy toward him. His words,

his obvious honesty and sincerity, were seductive to her, and she allowed herself one brief moment's fantasy of being his wife again. But then she thought of how he would react if she mentioned that, at this very moment, Sophie should be at Dr. Schaefer's office receiving her infusion of Herbalina. And she thought of how, despite his momentary kindness, he held her responsible for Sophie's disappearance, and she knew she could never be that close to him again.

"Now is not the time for this conversation," she said, squeezing his hand. She took the map from his lap and looked out the window at the two roads stretching out in front of them. Neither looked promising.

"Let's go back," Joe said with a sigh. "Let's just go to the police station and get ready for the press conference."

She hesitated, looking down at the map, trying to determine exactly where they were.

"It doesn't mean we're giving up," Joe said. "Just changing our strategy."

She handed the map back to him. "All right," she said.

Joe looked at his watch. "It's after twelve," he said. "We told your parents we'd call before noon. Might as well do it before we start driving again."

She nodded and took her phone from her purse, pressing the memory button for the mansion.

"Hello?" Her mother's voice had that brittle, anxious quality that Janine knew all too well.

"Hi, Mom. We—"

"Let me talk to Joe."

Janine sucked in her breath as though her mother had punched her. "I just wanted to let you know that we haven't found anything," she said quickly.

"Put Joe on," her mother insisted.

Janine shut her eyes. "She won't talk to me," she said, handing him the phone. Her throat was so tight she could barely breathe, and she reached into her shorts pocket for a tissue.

"Hi, Mom," Joe said. "No, no word at all. Any news there?"

She listened as Joe told her mother about the press conference scheduled for that afternoon. When he hung up, he looked at her, and she knew her nose was red from her quiet crying.

"How about I drive back," he suggested.

She shook her head and started the car. She needed something to engage her mind. Yet as she drove, all she could think about were the countless other times she'd done something to elicit the sting of her mother's silent anger.

After she lost the baby on the banks of the Shenandoah, she suddenly noticed babies everywhere. Janine had never paid much attention to them before, not even during the seven and a half months of her pregnancy. But suddenly babies slept in strollers in the shopping malls, reached from carts for forbidden items on the shelves at the grocery store and were carried in sacks against their mother's chests in the bank, where Janine had taken a job to help Joe pay their expenses. Mothers cooed at their little ones, smiled at them, comforted them when they cried, and played peekaboo with them on the counter at the bank. Each time Janine was witness to one of these interactions, she felt the pain of losing her own infant. She had not felt that pain at the time; she had felt nothing, actually, since she had somehow managed to deny to herself that she was about to become a mother. But now she saw, in vivid detail before her, how she had taken that precious life for granted. How could she have gone canoeing that day? How could she have had so little regard for the miracle happening inside her? Her feelings both sobered and depressed her. For a while, she functioned like an automaton, a little Stepford wife, doing everything Joe asked of her, as if complete obedience were her penance for her transgression. Her parents had stopped helping them financially now that there was no baby to consider. She and Joe needed to learn to make it on their own, they said, and, of course, Joe agreed. That was only the beginning of Joe's agreements with her parents.

She was coming to realize that, had it not been for her pregnancy, she and Joe's relationship probably would have died a natural death after high school. They were so dissimilar. He was straight-arrow, goal-oriented, money hungry. He weighed every move before he made it, thinking through every possible consequence. Yet, she did love him, despite his stodginess. He was handsome and kind, and she could talk easily to him—as long as she didn't talk about things that upset him, like her longing for adventure or her boredom with her bank job. She liked that she was helping to put him through school. Once he was out, though, and had made a little money, it would be her turn. She planned to study aviation—although that was one of those things she couldn't talk to him about.

She knew the very day her depression began to lift. She was getting ready for work, watching the early-morning news in their studio apartment, when an ad came on the TV.

"Learn a trade," the announcer said, "and earn money for school at the same time!"

The images on the screen were of young men and women, Army Reservists, dressed in camouflage, crawling on the ground with rifles, pushing buttons on huge computers and...flying planes! Her heart pounded against her ribs as she watched the ad, as if it were beating life back into her body after a long illness, and she longed to rip off her stuffy bank teller clothes and dial the phone number displayed on the screen right that minute. She managed to wait until her afternoon break at the bank before making the call, but within a week, she had signed up for the Army Reserves—without the knowledge of Joe or her parents.

It was another week before she dared to tell Joe what she had done. They were in their apartment, sitting at opposite ends of the sofa, eating their dinner of canned chicken soup and grilled-cheese sandwiches. He had a textbook on his knee, as usual; he was always studying.

"Joe?" she said, when she was halfway through her sandwich.

It was a moment before he looked up, and he kept his finger on his place in the book.

"I did something this week that I'm really excited about," she told him.

"What's that?" He glanced down at the book again, obviously distracted.

"I enlisted in the Army Reserves."

He actually laughed. "You're kidding, right?"

She shook her head. "I saw an ad on TV, and I—"

He withdrew his finger from the book and shut it. "Why would you do anything so stupid?" he asked.

"I don't think it's stupid. I'll be getting training and money for college, so it won't cost us as much for me to—"

"We aren't—" Joe hunted for the words "—we're not army kind of people. Your father even refused to fight in Vietnam, remember? Do you know what he had to go through to get that conscientious objector status? And here you join up? We don't even know anyone in the military."

She looked at him curiously. "When did you get so bigoted?" she asked.

"I'm not bigoted. I'm just being...realistic. I mean, can you really see yourself in a uniform, taking orders? You, of all people?"

"Yes, actually, I can." She felt herself toughening up as she spoke. "And it's only the reserves. I'll just have to be away from home for one weekend each month, although I'll have to be on active duty for a while first, while I'm in Warrant Officer Candidate Development." She spoke very quickly, hoping that by talking rapidly, she could make the long separation seem much shorter. "That's kind of like basic training," she said. "And then I'll go to flight school."

"*Flight* school?"

"Yes." She couldn't stop her grin.

"Oh, Janine, your head's in the clouds."

"I can't *wait* to have my head in the clouds," she said.

"You're going to be surrounded by other guys," he said, and she suddenly saw one of the central reasons for his disapproval. He'd always had a jealous streak.

"That's not why I'm doing it."

"So...when is this supposed to start?" he asked.

She felt a little afraid of what she had to tell him. "I'll leave in September," she replied. "I'll have to go to basic training, like I said, in Fort Rucker. That's in Alabama. That'll take about a year, and—"

"A year!"

"And then I'll stay there for flight school, and then I'll be a Warrant Officer." That sounded so much better than "bank teller"!

"And then what?"

She knew that tight look on his face; he was struggling to hold his anger in.

"Then I'll come home and I'll be able to fly with my reserve unit at Fort Belvoir. Once I'm with the reserve unit, I can have another job. I'll just need to be able to take off one weekend a—"

He threw his book on the coffee table, knocking over his soup. "This is insane!" he said. "I want a *woman* for a wife. Not a soldier." He stomped across the room to the phone.

"Who are you calling?" she asked.

"Your parents. Maybe they can talk some sense into you."

She could feel her strength and resolve slipping away from her, and she was once again the little girl, always under her parents' disapproving thumbs.

Within minutes, her parents had arrived at the apartment, where they attempted to talk Janine out of her "wild plan." They thought she had grown up in the last year, they told her. They thought she was more stable and responsible. She was being unbelievably selfish. She wasn't thinking of Joe or their marriage at all, only of herself and her crazy ideas. Sitting perfectly still, not saying a word, she let them have their say. She was going to do this, even if it cost her the love of her parents. Even if it cost her the love of her husband.

Her mother stopped talking to her that night, and her silence lasted for years. Janine went to Fort Rucker, tucking her family's disdain for her decision in the back of her mind as she learned to fly a helicopter. Her flight instructor called her a "natural pilot," and she knew she had found her passion. Yes, some of the guys badgered her, and others hit on her, but that was not what she was there for. She was in faithful contact with Joe, reassuring him that she would be home soon and how truly happy she was. She told him she couldn't wait to take him up in a helicopter someday. When she finally came home from flight school, she was a happier young woman. And she was, remarkably, a soldier.

As much as she adored flying, Joe loved his chosen career: working with money. He graduated from college soon after her return and took an accounting job with a large, well-respected firm. He was a hard worker, and he became even more serious and sober as he threw himself into his career.

It wasn't until Janine took a job as a helicopter pilot for Omega-Flight, an aircraft leasing company, that she discovered Joe's fear of flying.

She'd received permission from Omega-Flight to take her husband up in the helicopter one weekend, and only then did Joe admit to his fear. She thought back to the few times they had been scheduled to fly somewhere, and how he always decided to drive or take the train instead, making up some excuse about wanting to see the countryside. She had known about his father's accident and chastised herself for her insensitivity. He admitted then how much it upset him that her major passion in life was the one thing he could take no part in. She'd felt sorry for him and held him close to her as he talked about his fear. He rarely let her see vulnerability in him, and it touched her. Yet he was right. Flying was indeed her passion.

Although her mother began talking to her again, she rarely had anything positive to say. What could she and her father tell their friends about her? she asked Janine. How could they admit she was in the reserves, putting on a uniform and playing soldier one weekend a month? Why couldn't she be a normal daughter and wife? They constantly told her about their friends' daughters who had respectable jobs as teachers or nurses.

Now that they were both out of school, Joe had wanted to start a family again, but Janine was not ready to move in that direction. She used her job and her reserve duties as an excuse, but the truth was, she still had nightmares about that chilly October day, when she'd lain on a bed of gold and red leaves, giving birth to a baby who would not live. She would take any sort of physical risk, but she didn't think she could take that emotional risk again.

She lived for the weekends, when she could fly. There was little danger in her reserve duty, and plenty of excitement. But then, the unexpected happened: she was called into active duty in the Persian Gulf. No one, not even Janine herself, had expected she'd be involved in warfare when she joined the reserves. She was prepared, though, proud of her training and excited by the challenge. Her skills as a helicopter pilot would be sorely needed.

She received no support from her parents. The only words they spoke to her during those few days before she was deployed were of the "we told you all along you had no business being in the reserves," and "you made your bed, now you lie in it" variety. They turned their backs on her, both figuratively and literally, refusing even to see her off at the airport.

Joe was only slightly kinder. He said only once that he wished she were not in the reserves, and after that he simply avoided saying anything at all. Although he certainly gave her no overt encouragement, she was grateful to him for keeping his negative thoughts to himself. She knew that was a true challenge for him.

The four months in the Persian Gulf were a growing-up time for her. She flew supplies in and the injured out. Her days were filled with chemicals, explosions, the god-awful smoke and the boredom. She did not see death, but she heard of it, and she was shaken to the point of nightmares by the helicopter accident that took the life of another female pilot.

Returning from Desert Storm, she was a more somber young woman, more keenly aware of the brevity of life, and finally ready to settle down. *Anxious* to settle down. She agreed with Joe that it was time to start a family, and within a couple of weeks after stopping the Pill, she became pregnant. She quit her Omega-Flight job in her fifth month.

To everyone's relief, Janine delivered a full-term, beautiful baby girl, and she and Joe settled into a comfortable family life, interrupted only by Janine's continued monthly duty in the reserves. Her mother, thrilled to be a grandmother at last, began talking to her again. Janine planned to return to work when Sophie started school. She would be out of the reserves by then, and she hoped to take some sort of aviation-related job that would keep her on the ground. Having a child who needed her had done something to her yearning for risk.

The symptoms began shortly after Sophie's third birthday. A little blood in her urine, occasional puffiness around her eyes. She was diagnosed with a rare kidney disease. Her kidneys were still functioning then, but it would only be a matter of time before she needed a transplant or dialysis.

At that time, the news was full of stories of Desert Storm soldiers who were also getting sick with mysterious symptoms, and some of them had produced children with severe deformities and other illnesses. Janine herself felt perfectly healthy, but reading the stories of men and women whose children had been damaged in some way, possibly by the time their parents spent in the Gulf, tapped at her guilt. Was she responsible for Sophie's illness? Was her child paying for Janine's need for adventure and excitement?

Her parents certainly thought so. Janine had overheard her mother telling a neighbor that Sophie was one of those babies who had gotten sick because her mother served in the Gulf War. Janine didn't need them to lay any more guilt on her. She was producing enough of her own.

Joe never directly blamed her for Sophie's illness, but she knew how he felt about her serving in the reserves, and every time he read about a sick child of a Desert Storm soldier, he passed the article to her in silence. That's when she and Joe slipped into the quiet, end stage of their marriage. They related only with regard to Sophie's needs. Her illness consumed them. Joe had an affair, and Janine, in a fit of rage and pain, told him she wanted a divorce. She and Sophie moved into the cottage at Ayr Creek. It had been an unwelcomed move, but they could live there for free, and her parents could help care for Sophie.

"Have I been a good father?" Joe's voice, coming from the passenger seat of the car, startled Janine out of her memories.

She glanced at him. He was staring straight ahead, but she doubted he could see the road for the tears in his eyes. He had been a poor husband, who'd offered her little support in pursuing her dreams, who'd manipulated her with guilt about Sophie's illness, and who'd ultimately betrayed her in the most painful way one partner could betray another. But he had always loved Sophie. He would give his life for his daughter.

"Yes, Joe," she said. "You have been an excellent dad."

CHAPTER TEN

Lucas told the other two gardeners to work in the perennial beds near the woods, while he elected to prune the hedges close to the mansion. The men had looked at him with surprise, since he usually would have delegated the pruning task to them, and he said nothing to explain the change in his instructions. He needed mindless work today, and he also wanted to be close to the mansion. What was going on? Had they heard anything? He'd even worn his cell phone, hoping that Janine would call him with the news that Sophie had been found. He needed that news. He needed it more than anyone could imagine.

Janine had called him very early that morning, while she waited for Joe to pick her up so that they could once again trace the route from the camp. He knew by the gravelly sound of her voice that she had not slept. Neither had he. How did two girls and one adult simply disappear? His best guess was that the leader had taken off with them, for whatever strange and scary purpose. Maybe she just took them someplace for some fun. A pizza dinner and a night in a motel watching television. It didn't seem like a realistic option, but neither did anything else he could think of.

He turned off the electric clippers for a moment to rest his hands. His wrist throbbed beneath the splint, and he hoped he was not doing himself permanent damage. Standing next to the boxwood, he looked toward Janine's cottage. He could picture Sophie running out the front door, laughing, with the energy and joy that had been new to her since she'd been in the study. *Damn,* this wasn't fair. That little girl was just starting to live.

Sophie would have known she needed to get her IV today, but although she acted brave when it came time for that miserable two-hour treatment, she was not above wanting to miss it. He knew that Janine had not told her what would happen to her if she did miss it, not in specific terms, anyway. Sophie would probably delight in the opportunity to skip a session with Herbalina.

He could imagine the conversation in the leader's car.

"Tomorrow I have to get Herbalina," she would have said.

"Who on earth is Herbalina?" the leader would have responded.

"It's not a *who*." Sophie would giggle, her freckled nose wrinkling. "It's medicine. The doctor calls it Herbalina, 'cause it's made out of herbs and plants and things."

"What does it taste like?" Perhaps it would be the other little girl asking that question.

"I've never tasted it." It would be like Sophie to give a little wiseass answer to that question. "I get it in my arm. In a vein."

"That must hurt," the leader might say.

"It does," Sophie would reply. "And I have to sit there for a whole two hours with that needle in my arm." She might show the leader the small mark on her wrist, the site of her last infusion.

"Well," the leader would say slyly. "Why don't you skip seeing ol' Herbalina tomorrow. How about that?" She'd look at the other little girl. "What do you say we kidnap Sophie and take her to King's Dominion for a couple of days instead of—"

Lucas sighed. He turned on the clippers again and ran them along the side of the boxwood. The fantasy wasn't working. No Scout leader could be *that* irresponsible.

He looked up at the sound of the side door falling shut and

saw Donna Snyder walk across the driveway to the three-car garage. Turning off the clippers again, he set them on the ground and walked quickly toward her.

"Mrs. Snyder?" he called.

She stopped to look at him. She was a handsome woman in her late fifties, her blond hair pulled back in a clasp at the nape of her neck. He could easily picture her at the front of a high school history class. She'd probably been an impatient teacher, though; she certainly was impatient with Janine. Even now, her expression was one of irritation at his interruption.

"Is there any news about Sophie?" he asked.

"No," she said. "Janine and her husband are out looking for her."

Her ex-husband, he wanted to correct her. Janine had told him her parents had never truly accepted her divorce from Joe.

"Do they have any idea...any new theories on what might have—"

"No. No one seems to have a clue." She pressed a button on the remote in her hand, and one of the garage doors began to rise. The sunlight caught her eyes as she watched the door's progress. They were rimmed in crimson, and Lucas felt a pulse of sympathy for her.

"This must be very frightening for you," he said.

For a moment, his empathy seemed to alter her demeanor, and the guard she usually held in place when she was around him slipped from her shoulders.

"I wish the police would do more," she said. "They aren't doing much of—" She shook her head. "I guess they just don't know what to do, either. What do you do when a child falls off the face of the earth?" She moved toward the open garage. "And now I have to run to the store because there's nothing in the house. I hate to be away from the phone."

"Let me go for you," he volunteered, and he knew by the expression on her face that she found his offer very strange. "Really," he said. "I'd like to help in some way."

"Why?" she asked. "This isn't your family or your problem."

He thought of telling her he cared about Sophie, but knew that would only feed her paranoia about him. "I'd just like to help," he said again.

"No, that's not necessary." She reached into her purse for her car keys, her guard raised again. "Will you make sure to do the boxwood by the front entrance?" she asked.

"Yes," he said. "And I hope they find her very soon."

He was raking up the boxwood clippings when Joe and Janine pulled into the driveway. It was six o'clock, and he could feel the burn on his face and the back of his neck. He didn't usually work in the full sun for this long and knew he would pay later for having done so.

Janine got out of the driver's side of the car, and even from where he stood, he could see the exhaustion in her face. He hoped she'd been able to focus on her driving better than he had on his gardening. Joe got out of the car and started walking across the driveway toward the mansion, looking straight through Lucas as if he were not there, but Janine waved. She hesitated halfway across the driveway, and he knew she wanted to walk over to him, but Joe turned to her and took her arm, guiding her toward the house.

"Any news?" Lucas called out.

Janine shook her head as she allowed herself to be led inside.

It had been over twenty-four hours, Lucas thought. That milestone seemed significant somehow, and he knew it could mean nothing good.

After he'd finished bagging the clippings, he packed up his tools and drove back to his own house. In the kitchen of the four-room rambler, he took an apple from the fruit bowl and a cooked chicken breast from the refrigerator, then headed out into the woods behind his house.

From his desk chair in the tree house study, he stared out at the woods, laced now with shadow. He had worked far too hard today; the skin on his face was tender to the touch from too much sun. Nausea teased him, and his hand trembled as he bit into the apple. He wanted to call Janine, but thought he'd better wait for her to call him.

Turning on his computer, he tried to focus on his e-mail, but it was impossible. Memories he didn't want bubbled to the surface of his mind. Why fight them? he thought. The present was beginning to feel just as disturbing as the past.

Would the cop show up again or were they through with him? He prayed that was the case. Did Joe and the Snyders still think he might be involved in this whole mess somehow? He wished they would ask him outright. He could honestly tell them that he had nothing to do with Sophie's disappearance.

But that would be the only honest thing about him.

CHAPTER ELEVEN

The inside of the mansion was sticky with heat. In the interest of historical accuracy, air-conditioning had never been installed, and the June humidity was back with a vengeance. Janine, who did not share her parents' passion for all that was historical, especially considering that most rooms in the mansion were never open to the public, felt as though she were being smothered by the air in the parlor. Or maybe it was the atmosphere of discouragement and blame that was sucking the breath from her.

Her mother sat on one of the upholstered chairs, staring out the window. Every so often, she spoke out loud, although in barely more than a whisper. "Where's my *baby?*" It was as though she had been the one who'd given birth to Sophie, the one to sit by her hospital bed when she lay so ill and the one to read to her at night in the little cottage when she was sick and scared. It made Janine feel even guiltier for her role in Sophie's disappearance, as though she'd stolen something from her mother as well as from herself.

Her father played the awkward host, setting out a platter of tortilla chips and salsa for her and Joe, as if they were guests in the house. He was a nice man, her father. A good man who, over the years, often found himself caught in the middle between his rebellious daughter and his cool and angry wife.

"I thought both of you did well at the press conference," he said now, sitting down on the Chippendale sofa.

"What time did you say the police were coming?" Her mother looked at Joe. She hadn't said a word directly to Janine since their arrival, but that was no surprise to any of them.

Joe looked at his watch. "Any minute," he said.

Sergeant Loomis had told them he'd be stopping by tonight to meet the Snyders and catch everyone up on police activity.

"Here comes a car up the driveway," her mother said. "That must be him now." She got to her feet and smoothed the legs of her plaid slacks.

A moment later, Janine opened the door for the sergeant.

"Hello, Mrs. Donohue," the big man said to Janine, as he walked into the parlor. Quickly, he took in the details of the room, and Janine saw the appraisal in his eyes. *These folks have money,* he was thinking. She doubted he knew that her parents were merely the caretakers here, the poor relations of the Campbell clan. They'd had nothing to do with the purchase of the enormous oriental carpet lying on the cherry-and-beech parquet floor or the selection of the veritable gallery of nineteenth-century art on the parlor walls.

Janine introduced him to her parents, then sat on the sofa near her father. "Is there any news?" she asked, knowing very well there was no news and tired of asking the question. If the search had borne fruit, surely the police would have called them.

"No, I'm afraid not." Loomis sat down on the Queen Anne chair, gently, as though afraid he might damage something in this elegant, handsomely aged parlor. "I didn't get a chance to talk with you and Mr. Donohue much after the press conference, and I wanted the chance to meet your...uh, extended family. I just came from the Krafts' house."

"How many people do you have out looking for Sophie?" Janine's mother asked from her seat near the window. Her father offered him the tray of chips and salsa, which he declined with a wave of one big hand.

"Everyone in the department is working on it," he said, pulling a handkerchief from his uniform pocket and mopping his brow. He probably thought their air-conditioning was broken. "And so are the other police departments between here and the camp."

"I still think you need to do more," Joe said. "Janine and I drove all over last night and today, asking people if they'd seen Sophie and checking the side roads. And frankly, we didn't see a lot of cops out. She and I can't cover every possible route they might have taken."

"We're doing everything we can, Mr. Donohue," the sergeant assured him.

"Maybe you should be up in a plane," Janine's father said to Loomis.

"It doesn't make any sense to do an air search at this point," Sergeant Loomis informed him. "To begin with, we don't have any clear idea where to look."

Joe glanced at Janine, and she spoke up. "I'm going up in a helicopter tomorrow," she said, directing the information more to the air than to her parents or the officer.

"Why?" her mother asked, apparently forgetting that she was not speaking to her.

"I need to be able to look down on the area myself," she said. "I have to satisfy myself that I've looked everywhere—and in every way—that I can."

There was silence in the room for a moment. "Are you licensed to fly a helicopter?" Sergeant Loomis asked.

She nodded. "Yes. And I've already made the arrangements." She'd called Omega-Flight from the police station before the press conference, and they'd offered her the use of one of their helicopters. "I'm going up as soon as it's daylight. If Sophie hasn't turned up by then, that is."

"That's ridiculous," her mother said. "If the police say they can't find anything from the air, how do you expect to?"

"I have to try," she said.

"Will you go with her, Joe?" her father asked.

"No, I want to go alone," Janine said quickly, saving Joe from the embarrassment of having to admit he still feared flying.

"I really don't understand you," her mother said.

"Mrs. Donohue," Sergeant Loomis said to Janine. "I think it may be a wasted effort on your part. And are you really up to flying right now? This has been a very stressful—"

"I'll be fine," she insisted, and the tone of her voice put an end to his comments. She didn't dare glance at her mother.

Her father had once told her that, in her youth, her mother had been very much like Janine. She'd had a wild streak, he'd said, and that had cost her the respect—and the money—of her family. Now, she was intolerant of any behavior that reminded her of the girl she used to be.

"I know we talked about the possibility that this might be a kidnap case." Sergeant Loomis looked around at the room once more. "A ransom case. Now that I'm here... I know Joe and Janine don't have a lot of wealth someone might be after, but I'm wondering if someone might know that you—" he nodded at Janine's father "—and your wife are well-off. Can you think of anyone who would know that about you and might have taken your granddaughter with the hope of collecting a ransom for her? You haven't received any calls along that line, have you?" He looked at Joe, then Janine, and they shook their heads. "The kidnappers would most likely tell you not to involve us, but trust me, that would be a mistake."

"No, no calls," said Janine's father. "And we're not actually well-off."

Her mother literally winced at his admission.

"My wife is the last in a long line of Campbells," her father continued, "and we're allowed to live here, but we don't own any of the estate. We don't have any of the Campbell fortune."

"But someone might not realize that," Loomis said. "They might know you live in the Ayr Creek mansion and think you have the money to rescue your granddaughter."

Janine had not considered that. People often thought her parents were wealthy. In reality, they lived on the reduced pensions of two teachers who had taken an early retirement.

"But no one's called," Joe said. "Wouldn't they have called by now?"

"Not if they wanted to get far away before they do."

"Could they be after money from the other girl's family?" Janine's father asked.

"Not likely," Loomis said. "He's a grocery clerk with a slew of kids."

"It sounds like you think Alison might have taken them," Joe said. "The Scout leader."

"Well, on the one hand, that would fit, since everyone knows she drove off with them." Loomis stretched out his long legs, wincing when the chair made a barely perceptible cracking sound. "But we checked her background, and even though people say she's a little...*nutty,* I guess the right word would be...she has no record of doing anything outside the law. She was a straight-A student in college. And the *really* interesting thing is that she's getting married next Saturday."

"What?" Janine said.

"Yeah, not a lot of people knew, apparently. But I've spoken with her roommate, Charlotte, and her fiancé, Garret, and they said it's supposed to be a quiet little ceremony at Meadowlark Gardens. Just a few friends and Garret's family. Alison's mother is in Ohio, and she has a back injury and can't make it. The wedding's been planned for six months or so, and Alison was excited about it. Seems like a funny time to kidnap a couple of kids, doesn't it?"

"I'm so confused," Janine said. "None of this makes any sense."

"I know." Sergeant Loomis had genuine sympathy in his voice. "But it will in time. These things don't stay mysteries forever."

"We don't *have* time, though," Janine said quietly. "Like I told you...like I said at the press conference...Sophie needs..." She felt the eyes of her family on her. Her mother seemed to hate her, her father was disappointed in her, and although Joe certainly shared her frustration, he did not give a hoot if Sophie ever received another IV of Herbalina. "She was supposed to get a medical treatment today," Janine finished.

Her mother scoffed. "She needs treatment, all right, but not that one."

"We know, Mrs. Donohue," Loomis said to Janine. "We're all very aware that Sophie has a life-threatening illness." He turned to her mother. "I know that Joe, here, doesn't agree with the treatment Sophie's getting," he said. "It sounds like you don't either, am I hearing that right?"

"None of us do," Janine's father said. "We think putting Sophie in that study was a mistake. But—"

"You would have rather seen her suffer some more?" Janine said, her voice rising.

"Of course not," her mother said. "But we wanted to give her a chance to *live*. All her doctors, every one of them, said that herbal...stuff...would just give her temporary relief. You gave up on Sophie ever getting better. All you cared about was that she died with a smile on her face."

"Mom," Joe said. "Now's the wrong time for this."

"It's the perfect time," Donna said. "Sophie was always—"

Loomis suddenly stood up, silencing her with the sheer mass of his presence. "Joe's right," he said. "We need unity here, not a lot of tearing each other apart." He spoke in a neutral, peace-keeping tone, and Janine wondered if he'd been trained to do that when family tempers flared. "And we know this is an urgent situation, Janine. What you said at the press conference today will help spread the word. That way, if it's a kidnap situation and the kidnapper gets that information, he or she might decide it's not worth the risk they're taking and get the girl back to safety." He started walking to the door, and everyone else got to their feet.

"I'll be in touch," he said, as Joe opened the door for him. "Meantime, I want you all to be good to each other."

Joe walked with him out the front door, and Janine quickly followed. She didn't dare stay behind with her parents.

Dusk was settling over Ayr Creek as they stood under the portico and watched Loomis walk down the path to the driveway, where his car was parked. The broad front lawn was dotted with fireflies.

Janine brushed a mosquito away from her face. "I'm going to the cottage," she said, once the police car had pulled out of the driveway.

"Would you like me to come with you?" There was hope in Joe's voice.

"No," she said. "I should try to get some sleep if I'm going to fly tomorrow."

"Maybe I'll search from the ground again," he said. "Although—" he shrugged "—I don't know where to begin or where to end anymore."

She leaned forward to hug him, something she hadn't done in years. "We have to keep trying," she said.

He seemed reluctant to let go of her, and she was first to draw away, remembering what he'd said in the car about wishing they could get back together. She didn't want to give him false hope.

"Maybe Paula could go with you tomorrow," she suggested.

He nodded. "I was thinking the same thing. She'd have to take time off from work, but I know she'd want to." He shook his head. "I'm sorry you've had this misperception of her all these years."

"I'm glad to know I was wrong." She turned away from the mansion and headed for the driveway. "Good night," she called over her shoulder. She would leave her parents to Joe.

Once inside her cottage, she immediately sat down on the sofa and reached for the phone.

"Any news?" Lucas asked, when he picked up on his end. He'd obviously been waiting for her call.

"Nothing." She heard the remarkable flatness in her voice. How could she sound so calm, so stoic, when her insides were in turmoil?

"You must be going crazy, Jan."

"I'm leasing a helicopter tomorrow," she told him. "I wanted to know if you'd go up with me."

There was silence on his end of the line. "Won't your parents or Joe know something's up between us if I did that?"

"I don't care if anyone knows, Lucas. I'm tired of this, and I'm sorry I insisted on keeping our relationship secret for this long. It's ridiculous. I've been afraid of what my parents and Joe would say for my entire adult life. *You're* the person I need at my side right now, and I don't care who knows it."

"And that's where I want to be," he said quickly. "It's been hard today and yesterday, not being able to be with you, with all that's going on."

"Come over," she said. "Can you, please?"

"Why don't you come here?"

She loved the tree house, and he knew it. But not tonight.

"I need to stay here," she said. "In case...there's any news."

"Okay. I'll be over in a few minutes."

She hung up the phone and walked into the kitchen, where she opened the refrigerator and stared at its contents. It seemed as though it had been weeks since she'd looked in there, and nothing was appealing. Shutting the door, she wandered down the hall to Sophie's dark room. The door was closed, and when she opened it, Sophie's smell, that delicious scent of the balsam shampoo her daughter loved, greeted her, and she felt weak-kneed. Sophie was still alive in this room. God willing, she was still alive wherever she was.

Picking up the teddy bear from the pillow, she lay down on Sophie's bed and stared at the ceiling. She'd often wondered how parents dealt with the disappearance of their children. How did they survive that period of uncertainty? She was living it, and she still didn't know the answer to that question.

Hugging the stuffed bear to her chest, she raised her head to look out the window.

Lucas, hurry, please.

She wondered how, just eight short months ago, she had seen him as an enemy.

CHAPTER TWELVE

"Mommy, I think I'm going to throw up again," Sophie said, as she and Janine got out of the car in the turnaround of the Ayr Creek driveway. The weather was growing cold. Thanksgiving was just a week away; the trees were bare and the estate was beginning to take on its gray, wintry look.

"Can you walk fast, honey?" Janine asked her. "Can you make it to the bathroom?"

"I don't know." Sophie swallowed hard, her skin pale and damp. She headed down the path toward the cottage, Janine close on her heels.

Lucas was kneeling at the edge of the driveway, wrapping the azaleas in burlap, and Janine put a protective hand on Sophie's shoulder as she always did around him. He'd been working at Ayr Creek for a little over a month by then, and Janine had taken her parents' warning about him to heart. Whether they were right or not about his being a pedophile, they were certainly right about his interest in Sophie. Janine had caught him staring at her when they were outside, and she found herself nervous that he might peer through the cottage windows when he was working in the area.

"Hi, Mrs. Donohue." Lucas stood up from his task. "Hi, Sophie."

"Hi," Janine said, almost under her breath. Her eyes were fixed on the knob of her front door, and with a sinking feeling, she suddenly remembered leaving the key inside the cottage when they left early that morning. She'd separated her car keys from the others in preparation for taking the car to be washed, and in her rush to get out of the house, she'd left the house key behind.

Sophie reached for the door knob.

"It's locked, Sophie," Janine said. "I just remembered I left the key inside. We're locked out."

"Do you have a problem?"

Janine turned to see Lucas leaning on the upright roll of burlap, staring at them. He'd heard her, even though she had been speaking softly and he was a good ten yards away. He had to have been listening very carefully.

"We're locked out," she told him.

"Mommy, I can't wait," Sophie said. "I'm going to throw up."

"Move over here." Janine guided her toward the mulch at the edge of the boxwood.

Lucas turned over the bucket near his feet, emptying it of weeds, and walked briskly to Sophie. He set the bucket in front of her just as she began to retch. Janine put an arm around her daughter, stroking her red hair back from her damp cheek. When Sophie had finished, she stood up, one hand on her stomach, and closed her eyes, leaning against her mother.

"You two are having a bad day," Lucas said.

It was the closest Janine had ever been to him. The soft light of the November sun rested in his pale-gray eyes behind the wire-rimmed glasses, and there was so much genuine sympathy in his gaze and such warmth in his voice, that her guard began to crack. She felt tears burn her eyes.

Lucas reached out as though he were going to touch her arm, then seemed to think better of it and dropped his hand to his side. "Where's the key to the door?" he asked.

"I accidentally locked it inside."

"Are any of the windows open?" He glanced toward the cottage. "How about the back door?"

"I don't think so."

"You and Sophie sit here on the stoop and I'll check it out," he said.

He disappeared around the corner of the cottage and Janine sat down with Sophie on the front step. She put her arm around her tremulous daughter again, and Sophie rested her head against her breast.

"Mommy, I'm too sick," she said.

"I know, sweetie," Janine soothed, pondering Sophie's choice of words. Too sick for what? she wondered. Too sick to be able to run and play and go to school like other seven-year-olds? Too sick to stay out here in the cool weather? Too sick to live much longer? That was what the doctor had told Janine that morning. "She doesn't have much more time," he'd said. "Make her life as full as you're able."

Lucas returned around the other side of the cottage and knelt down in front of them. "You're locked up tight," he said. "Is there a spare key in the mansion?"

"Yes, but my parents are out and they always lock the house when they leave." Was it stupid of her to tell him her parents were not at home? There seemed to be no one around except the three of them, and one of them had demonstrated an unnatural interest in little girls.

"I can get in the back door, but I'll have to break the glass to do it," he said. "I can repair it for you tomorrow, though. I'll just need to get another piece of glass."

Against her cheek, Janine felt the heat rising from Sophie's forehead. "Yes, please, if you could," she said.

She and Sophie waited as he walked around the house again. They heard the sharp crack of breaking glass, followed by the tinkling sound of the shards hitting the linoleum floor of the kitchen. In a moment, the front door opened and Lucas stood in the living room.

"The deed is done," he said. "Come in, and I'll clean up the glass."

Janine helped Sophie to her feet, then reached for the bucket.

"Leave it," Lucas said. "I'll take care of it later."

"Oh, no, I don't want you to have to—"

"Leave it, Janine," he repeated. "It's not a problem. Get Sophie inside here." It was the first time he had called her by her name, and she thought she should be incensed at him for taking that liberty. Instead, she found herself liking that intimacy from him. She wished he would say her name again.

She walked Sophie into the house. "Let's get you to bed," she said, guiding her toward the hallway. She looked at Lucas, who was indeed staring at Sophie, but the look on his face was one of concern, nothing more. She should thank him and see him out the door, but she owed him more than that. "Would you like some lemonade or iced tea?" she offered.

"Just a little cold water would be great." Lucas smiled.

"There's a pitcher in the fridge. Help yourself. I'll be back in a few minutes."

Sophie fell onto her made bed, eyes shut, instantly asleep, and Janine sat next to her for a moment. In the afternoon light from the window, Sophie's eyelids were nearly translucent; Janine could almost see the blue orbs beneath them. The lightly freckled skin on Sophie's face, across her nose and in the gaunt hollows of her cheeks, had that same translucent quality, as though Sophie were slowly becoming invisible, fading away. Janine unfolded the light throw at the foot of the bed and laid it gently over her daughter before leaving the room.

She found Lucas standing in the kitchen, leaning against the old coral-colored tile counter, a glass of water in his hand. "I poured a lemonade for you," he said, nodding toward the glass on the table.

"Thank you." She had not really been in the mood for lemonade, but it suddenly looked delicious, and she took a swallow.

"Do you have a broom?" he asked. "I should get this broken glass off the floor. And I can cover the window with a piece of cardboard and some tape for you, so the cold doesn't pour in tonight."

Janine looked at the glass on the floor and the broken window. He had already done enough. "I'll get it later, thanks," she said. "Let's sit in the living room while you finish your water."

He followed her into the small, square living room.

"I've wondered what it was like in here," he said, as he sat down on the sofa. "This was once the slave quarters, right?"

She nodded as she sat on the leather armchair. "Yes. Twenty people lived in here at one time. Can you imagine what that was like?"

"I did some reading about Ayr Creek before I started working here," he said. "Isn't there supposed to be a ghost in this cottage?"

"Not in the cottage," Janine replied. "She's supposed to be in the woods, searching for her little girl. The woman's name was Orla. Some other slave owner wanted her little girl to work for him, and Angus Campbell, the owner of Ayr Creek, promised Orla he wouldn't split up her family. But one night the little girl disappeared. He'd sold her to the other guy, of course, but he told Orla he had no idea what happened to her. Orla apparently went crazy then, talking to herself and spending every night walking through the woods, hunting for her daughter. You can hear her out there sometimes, keening."

"Do you believe the story?"

"Oh, I believe it, all right," she said. "It's a matter of history. But I certainly don't believe that Orla's ghost is haunting the woods. I've heard the sound that people attribute to her, though, and it *is* weird and eerie, but I'm sure it's just a possum or some other nocturnal animal. You hear it mainly in the summer, late at night, when you're trying to sleep. Sophie gets a bit freaked out by it."

Lucas looked down at his water, swirling it around the inside of his glass.

"Tell me about Sophie," he said. "Her illness...it's very serious, isn't it." It was a statement rather than a question, and once again his voice was so kind that, without any warning, she began to cry. He said nothing as she lowered her head into her hands and let go of the tears she'd been holding in all morning for Sophie's sake. Finally she raised her head.

"I'm sorry," she said.

He shook his head. "Nothing to be sorry for." He brushed a blade of grass from the blue splint on his wrist. "Is it something you can talk about? Can you tell me what her problem is?"

"It's her kidneys. She has a rare disease that usually only affects boys this seriously, but somehow, she was unlucky. She developed it when she was three, and it's just gotten worse."

"Would a transplant help?"

"I gave her one of my kidneys when her symptoms got bad enough, but she rejected it." She bit her lip and looked toward the kitchen. Through the now empty pane of the back door, she could see the woods closing in on the cottage. "She's been through so much. She has dialysis every night, and—"

"Peritoneal?" he asked, surprising her. Most people didn't know that dialysis could be performed at home, using the membrane in the abdomen as the filter for the blood.

"Yes," she said. "We have the machine here in her bedroom."

"How has she done with it?"

"It's not holding her," she answered, and her voice caught in her throat. "This morning her doctor told me there isn't anything else they can do for her. He said flat out that she probably has less than a year left."

Lucas shook his head very slowly. "I'm so sorry," he said. "What terrible news."

"It wasn't really news." Janine sighed. "Just a confirmation of what I've known would happen if she didn't turn around with the latest treatment they've had her on. Now I have to call her father and tell him."

"Is he very close to her?"

"Yes. He's been a much better dad than he ever was a husband." She smiled weakly, regretting instantly that she'd criticized Joe to this stranger.

"Isn't most kidney disease inherited?" he asked.

"Some, yes, but not all. The type she has usually is, but there isn't any of it in my family. We really don't know much about Joe's roots, because he's never had contact with his mother's side of his family—she left him when he was little. His father's dead, but there were no kidney problems on his side that we know of, although we really aren't close to them." She took a swallow of the lemonade, but found it hard to swallow, and she set the glass down on the end table. "Actually, I don't think Sophie inherited it."

"What do you mean?" Lucas asked.

"Do you know about Gulf War Illness?" she asked.

"Well, I know that some of the soldiers who fought in the Persian Gulf think they contracted something while they were there. Is that what you mean?"

"Yes. And some of them are producing children with medical problems."

Lucas looked confused. "I'm not sure I'm following you. Was Sophie's father in the military? Did he fight in Desert Storm?"

She shook her head. "No," she said. "But I did."

He looked surprised. "You're kidding. What branch of the military were you in?"

"Army Reserves," she said. "I flew a helicopter in the Gulf."

"Well." He smiled. "I have to say I'm impressed."

"There's nothing impressive about it," she said. "It was a selfish decision on my part. I wanted to learn to fly, the reserves seemed like an easy way to do it. But it took me away from Joe for long periods of time. And ultimately—" she lowered her voice "—I'm afraid it's going to cost my daughter her life."

"You mean...you think you picked up something over there that caused you to give Sophie her kidney problems?"

"Yes. I don't have any symptoms myself, but I got pregnant with Sophie right after I returned from the Gulf. It fits."

He shook his head, almost violently. "No, it doesn't fit. Those kids have deformities, not renal disease."

"Not just deformities. I've heard of other diseases appearing in the children of Gulf War soldiers."

"But diseases appear in kids no matter what."

She felt herself sink deeper into her chair, deeper into her gloom. "I'd like to believe you, but I don't. I blame myself for what's happening to Sophie. My parents blame me. And so does Joe. He never says as much, but—"

Lucas stood up from the sofa and walked over to her. Sitting down on the leather ottoman in front of her chair, arms folded and resting on his knees, he looked directly into her eyes.

"You are not to blame," he said. His eyes were narrowed and serious, his voice firm with measured words, as if it were very important for her to believe him.

"You don't know," she said.

"I *do* know," he said. "I've done some reading on Gulf War Illness because one of my friends was over there and got sick afterward. I think he really did pick up something there, or else he got it from the anthrax vaccination or those pills they gave them to protect them against nerve agents—"

"Pyridostigmine bromide pills." She remembered those pills and the dizziness she'd experienced after taking them.

"Whatever." Lucas smiled. "So I'm not arguing that the illness is all in their heads. But as I did research for him, I read about the kids being born with medical problems. None of them had renal disease. And here you have some pretty good clues that Sophie might have inherited her illness from her father's side.

A missing mother. Not a heck of a lot of information about his father. So, why are you tormenting yourself over this? You have enough to deal with without taking on that guilt."

His words seemed so logical, yet he didn't understand the core doctrine of the Donohue and Snyder family: whatever Janine did was wrong.

"What about experimental treatments for Sophie?" he asked. "You're not that far from the National Institutes of Health or Johns Hopkins, right?"

"She's in a study at NIH right now," Janine replied. "They're trying a new, miserably toxic medication to block the potassium buildup. That's what she's been on, and that's why she's throwing up all the time. Today, I told the doctor I wanted to take her off it, and he agreed that she's only getting worse on it. I don't want her to spend the last few months of her life sick all the time. Throwing up all the time." She started to cry again, and somehow wasn't surprised when he reached over to touch her arm, lightly, briefly. "I want her to be able to take some pleasure in the time she has left," she said.

"Of course you do," he said. "But don't close your mind to all possibilities. I believe in miracles."

She brushed the tears from her cheek with the back of her hand and smiled at him ruefully. What a surprise he was turning out to be! He was certainly kinder than she'd expected, and far smarter than she ever would have guessed. And he was on her side.

"I have to ask you something," she said.

He raised his eyebrows, waiting.

"This is going to sound...blunt, but I don't think I have the strength right now to figure out a better way to say it."

"Go for it," he urged.

"My parents warned me not to speak to you or to let Sophie near you."

"Why?" He looked truly surprised.

"My father said that when you first came here to look over

the grounds, you showed...well, you seemed inordinately inter-ested in the fact that a little girl lived here. And they've told me that whenever Sophie and I walk past you and they happen to be watching, you stare at her. Is that their imagination?"

He smiled and looked down at his hands. "No, it's not their imagination, but I didn't think I was being that obvious. I had no idea anyone thought I was—" He shook his head. "This is crazy. I could tell your parents didn't like me. They treat me like I'm no better than the manure I spread in the garden. I thought it was some...class thing. The lowly gardener. At least now I know why."

"So why would you stare at her?"

"I have a niece Sophie's age," he said. "My sister's little girl. She lives in northern Pennsylvania, and I only see her on holi-days. I don't have any kids of my own, so she's, in a way, the clos-est thing I have to my own child. I adore her. Spoil her rotten. When your dad told me there was a little girl living at Ayr Creek, I suppose my eyes did light up a bit." He laughed. "I realized quickly, though, that Sophie and I weren't going to get to be bud-dies, because you weren't letting her anywhere near me. I thought you were a pretty cold fish. Now I know why. And I also know you're anything but cold. I've read you completely wrong."

"I guess that makes two of us." She touched her fingertips to his splint. "I apologize."

"Accepted."

"What's wrong with your wrist?" she asked.

"Carpal tunnel."

"Do you wear the splint all the time?"

"Uh-huh. The latest research has shown that if you work and play and sleep in the splints, the better off you'll be."

"Is it from repetitive movement?"

"Oh," he sighed. "I don't know. It's from some gardening task, I suppose."

"Have you ever been married?"

He grinned at her. "Twenty questions, huh?"

She nodded. Suddenly she was very hungry for information about him.

"Yes, I was married for twelve years," he said. "We're still friends. She's a terrific woman."

"Why did you split up?"

"We got married too young." He sat back on the ottoman, letting out a long breath. "We were both twenty. We still had a lot of maturing to do, and when we finally *did* grow up, we discovered that we didn't have a heck of a lot in common. She was a psychologist, and I hung around plants a lot. She wanted a nice colonial home she could decorate, and I wanted to live in a tree."

Janine laughed. "Where does she live?"

"Pennsylvania. She calls from time to time, or I call her. We e-mail. She got married again a couple of years ago, and fortunately her new husband understands our friendship."

"You're very lucky," she said.

"Yes, I am. And what about Sophie's father? Joe, is it? Are you two still friends?"

"Only when it comes to Sophie," she said. It was hard to explain her relationship with Joe. "He's still very close to my parents, since he really has no parents of his own. And they're crazy about him. They still call him my husband. I think they blame me for our divorce, even though he had an affair. They don't know that, though."

"Ouch," Lucas said.

She had told no one, other than her two closest female friends, about Joe's affair. She'd let her parents think her decision to end their marriage was just another one of her impulsive, selfish acts. Joe had begged her not to poison their feelings about him with the truth.

She looked up at the ceiling. "I can't believe I'm telling you so much," she said.

"You don't have to."

"I want to." She went on to tell him about her high school

pregnancy and the shotgun marriage to Joe. She told him about the canoe trip, and her stillborn baby boy.

"All right," he said. "So you showed some poor judgment when you were eighteen, when most kids have poor judgment. You're still blaming yourself for that all these years later?"

"Are you always this supportive of everybody?" she asked.

"Only people who deserve it," he said.

Her gaze was drawn to activity in the driveway, near the mansion. She stood up and, through the bare trees, could see her father's car pull into the garage.

"My parents are home," she said.

Lucas stood up as well. "I'd better get back to work, then," he said. "I'll fix the pane in your door tomorrow. "

She realized she didn't want him to go, but she didn't want her parents to discover him there, either. "Thanks for breaking into the house, and for listening. And for the encouragement," she said, as she walked him to the door. She glanced toward the hallway leading to Sophie's bedroom. "Unfortunately, though, I *don't* believe in miracles."

He stepped onto the front stoop, then turned to look at her, a small smile on his lips. "I'm not talking about religious miracles," he said. "I'm not talking about a sign from heaven. I'm talking about *man-made* miracles. I think human beings can do anything they set their minds to, and somewhere, right now, some scientist is trying to figure out a way to help Sophie and other kids like her. And maybe he—or she—will succeed. All I'm saying is that you need to be open to that possibility. Don't give up hope."

She nodded. "I'll try not to," she said. "Thank you."

She watched him pick up the bucket and walk toward the mansion, where he turned on the hose. Then she walked into Sophie's room to check on her. Sophie was still in a deep sleep, and Janine watched her for a few minutes, making sure she was breathing. How often she was doing that these days! She got up a few times each night, just to make sure Sophie was still with her.

Back in the living room, she curled up in one corner of the sofa, turning so that she could see out the window. She hugged her knees against her chest, watching as Lucas wrapped burlap around one of the shrubs near the driveway. Although he looked no different than he usually did from a distance, she was seeing him with new eyes.

Her knees pressed against her breasts, and the desire that simple sensation awakened in her took her by surprise. She had given up on the sexual part of herself. It had been so long since she'd felt any sexual attraction to a man that she'd talked herself into not wanting it, not needing it. She'd lived these last three years for Sophie. Her body had been nothing more than an instrument for taking care of her daughter.

Now, suddenly, almost guiltily, she felt life returning to that mechanical body. She imagined Lucas here on the sofa with her, the smile in his pale eyes warming her. He would kiss her, hold her. He'd lay her down along the length of the sofa and stretch out next to her, touching her gently, the way he had touched her arm. The fantasy was strong and unbidden and delicious, and it stunned her when she became conscious of it. She was not a fantasizer, not anymore. Dreams only got in the way of coping with reality.

The next day he would come to repair the pane of glass, and she would be sure to be at home when he did. She had the feeling that Lucas could make her dream. He had already given her hope.

CHAPTER THIRTEEN

From where she lay on Sophie's bed, Janine could hear Lucas's car on the gravel driveway. As he pulled into the turnaround near the cottage, his headlights cut through the window to Sophie's room, settling on the Winnie the Pooh lamp on the dresser. Usually, Lucas would have parked out on the street and walked in, so that her parents wouldn't know he was there, but tonight, the rules were changing.

Setting the teddy bear aside, she tried to get up, but found she could not move. Her body was held to the bed by some invisible force. She listened to Lucas's knock on the front door, opening her mouth to speak.

"In here," she said, but it came out only as a whisper. He knocked again, and she heard him let himself in.

"Janine?"

"In Sophie's room," she said, still so softly that she knew he couldn't hear her. But he walked through the small house, and when she heard him in the hall, she raised the volume of her voice a notch or two.

"I'm in here," she said.

He came into the dark room and walked over to the bed. "Move over," he said quietly, and she did. He lay down next to her, taking her in his arms. She clung to him, her breathing quick and shallow against his neck, but she didn't cry. For now at least, she felt wrung dry.

Neither of them spoke for a good ten minutes, as he held her close and stroked her back.

"Do you still believe in miracles?" she asked him finally.

"The man-made variety. Yes."

"We need one now," she said.

"Yes," he agreed. "We do."

"I feel like I'm being punished."

"What for?"

"For enrolling her in Schaefer's study. For sending her off on this weekend camp-out against Joe's advice and wishes. I've ignored what he thinks is best for Sophie during the last couple of months, and now look what happened."

"What happened is that Sophie was well enough to take the sort of risk every other eight-year-old girl takes on a regular basis," he said. "Can't you see that, Jan? Can't you let go of the guilt long enough to see that?"

"Maybe if she'd come back today, I could have. But now...wherever she is..." Janine shuddered. "She must be so scared."

He hugged her close, then released her, resting his hand on her belly. "I can feel your hipbones through your shorts," he said. "When was the last time you ate?"

She tried to think. "I don't know. Yesterday, I guess. I had lunch before I knew she was gone." It seemed so long ago.

"And you've had nothing today?"

"No."

"Come on." He sat up. "Let's feed you."

"I'm not hungry."

"You have to eat something." He put his hands beneath her shoulders and pulled her into a sitting position. "Come on, Jan, seriously. Let's go."

She allowed him to guide her into the kitchen and onto one

of the chairs at the table. Opening the cupboard nearest the window, Lucas peered inside.

She couldn't even think about the boxes and cans of food he was looking at. "I don't think I can—"

"How about soup?" he asked, holding a can of turkey-and-rice soup in his hand. "Are you too hot for that? It would probably be the best thing for your stomach."

"Okay." It was easier to give in than to fight him. She watched as he opened the can and poured its contents into a bowl. While it cooked in the microwave, he took the English muffins from the bread box, pulled one from the package, and put it in the toaster.

"So," she said, watching him, "what have *you* eaten in the last day and a half?"

He smiled. "More than you," he said. "At least I've had enough to sustain life."

He placed the soup and toasted English muffin on the table in front of her, and she ate under his supervision. The soup tasted flat and flavorless; the muffin was impossible to get down, and she left it on the plate.

At ten o'clock, they undressed to their T-shirts and underwear and got into her queen-size bed to watch the news. She was anxious to see the footage of the press conference, and the disappearance of the missing Scouts and their leader was the first story mentioned.

"Two eight-year-old Vienna Girl Scouts and their leader are still missing this evening," the male newscaster said. He was grim faced, but what did he care? He recounted stories like this one every day of the week. Janine suddenly understood what it was like to be on the other side of those news stories. To the public, the disappearance of three people was just one more tragedy; to their families, it marked the collapse of their worlds.

"They were last seen driving away from Camp Kochaben in West Virginia yesterday afternoon," the newscaster continued. "The leader, twenty-five-year-old Alison Dunn, was driving a '97 dark-blue Honda Accord, and was expected to arrive at Meadowlark Gardens in Vienna at three o'clock yesterday afternoon. Police report they have no leads at this time. Ms. Dunn, originally from Ohio, is scheduled to be married this Saturday. The parents of Sophie Donohue and Holly Kraft held a news conference this afternoon, pleading for the safe return of their children."

The camera shifted from the newscaster to the footage of Janine and Joe and the Krafts, who by now had completely lost their cavalier, this-is-no-big-deal facade. The four of them looked tired and frightened. Janine held an eight-by-ten picture of Sophie, Rebecca, an even larger picture of Holly. Joe spoke first.

"If anyone has any information regarding the whereabouts of our children and Alison Dunn, we're begging you to please contact the police," he said.

"My...our daughter has a serious kidney disease," Janine added.

Watching herself now, Janine winced, remembering her slip of the tongue.

"She needs medical treatment immediately," Janine had continued. My God, she looked desperate. "Please, if someone has her, we don't care who you are or why you did this. Just please drop the girls off at a restaurant or a gas station."

Suddenly the camera switched to one of the police officers, someone Janine had not seen on the case until that moment. He appeared to be standing outside the police station, and he squinted from the sun.

"We don't know at this point if we're dealing with a kidnapping situation or what," he said. "All we know is that we've got three missing people to find."

"Is the Scout leader under suspicion?" The question was asked by someone out of camera range.

"We're not ruling anything out right now," the officer said, "but the Scout leader was planning her wedding for this coming weekend, so it seems unlikely she had any premeditated intent to take the girls."

"He's leaving open the possibility of impulsiveness on Alison's part," Lucas said.

The newscaster was once again on the screen, talking about a drug bust in Washington, and Janine hit the mute button. The phone rang, and she jumped, reaching for the receiver on the nightstand so quickly that she knocked it to the floor.

"Hello?" she said, after fumbling to regain the receiver.

"Hi." It was Joe's voice.

"Have you heard anything?" she asked.

"No. I was just watching the news."

"Me, too."

"I've been worried about you," he said. "I know it's late, but can I come over? I just want to be with someone who...who's hurting as much as I am."

Janine looked at Lucas, who was eyeing her from the pillow. The face of the newscaster was reflected in his glasses.

"Joe," she said. "I need to tell you something."

"What?"

"Lucas is here." She rested her hand on Lucas's chest. "Lucas is...he's more than a friend, Joe."

The silence on Joe's end of the line was unbearably long.

"You're seeing him?" he asked finally.

"Yes."

"And he's there right now? This late?"

"Yes."

He sighed, the sound like wind blowing against the phone. "I truly don't understand you."

"I should have been honest about it from the start," she said. "But you and Mom and—"

"When was the start?" he interrupted her.

"November."

"November! You've been seeing this guy since November? You've had Sophie around him?"

"Sophie likes him."

"She's a child," Joe said. "She doesn't know any better. Janine, you've got a good education, you're intelligent... Why would you get involved with a gardener? And a lousy one at that. Your parents told me he doesn't show up half the time for work. They think he has a drinking problem, that he's hungover and can't make it in."

Janine could not help the laugh that escaped her mouth. "He doesn't drink at all," she said. Lucas's eyebrows rose at that. "Not that it's any of your business."

"He's so much younger than you," Joe said.

"Only three years, Joe." Lucas was thirty-two.

"Do your parents know about this?"

"They will tomorrow. Lucas is flying in the helicopter with me." She winced again, fearing she had just struck Joe below the belt.

Joe was silent a moment before speaking again. "They're going to have a fit," he said.

"If you talk to them tonight, please don't say anything about it. Let it come from me."

"It's all yours," he said. "I'd rather not hear what they have to say."

Janine was quiet, imagining her parents' reaction to this news.

"Are you sure he's not...you know, *too* interested in Sophie?" Joe asked.

"I'm absolutely sure."

"Well, look," Joe said. "Whatever's drawn you to him...I'd just like you to think about what I said in the car today. About us. I'm part of your family, whether you like it that way or not. Your parents think of me as their son. Your daughter is my daughter. I screwed up three years ago, I know that. But you've screwed up, too. And we have a daughter who loves both of us, and if...*when* we find her, the best present we could give her would be for you and me to get back together."

"Joe." She shook her head. Where was all of this coming from? "You've never talked about this before. Why now?"

"Because of Sophie. Because she needs us to be united. Because having her gone, spending some time with you, makes me realize what I gave up. I want my family back."

"I'm sorry, Joe," she said. "That's not something I want."

He was quiet again. "You'd rather hang out with your tree house guy?" he asked. "Only little boys play in tree houses."

"I'm going to hang up," she threatened.

"No, don't. I'm sorry. Just going a little nuts here."

She felt sorry for him. He was alone right now, trying to cope with the fact that his daughter was missing, maybe hurt, certainly afraid. "I know," she said softly. "I know this is just as painful for you as it is for me. You can call anytime, okay? Even in the middle of the night if you're upset and need to talk."

"Same here," he said. "Although I guess you have the, uh...Lucas to talk to."

"Lucas is wonderful," she told him, and she felt Lucas's hand on her back, "but he's not Sophie's dad."

"Thanks," Joe said. "Let's talk in the morning."

She hung up the phone and lay down again. "He's talking about us getting back together," she said. "He mentioned it in the car today, too. He said the women he goes out with get annoyed with him because he's still in love with me. I honestly had no idea."

"That's understandable," Lucas said. "He has a funny way of showing he cares, when he and your parents spend so much of their time and energy ganging up on you."

She rolled onto her back. "Well," she said, "the cat's out of the bag, now."

"Finally," he said, and she was grateful to him for putting up with her reluctance to go public with their relationship. She stared at the ceiling. "I'm never going to be able to fall asleep," she said.

"Try." He leaned over to kiss her lightly on the lips. "Let's both try. We're going to need all our resources tomorrow."

* * *

She must have dozed off, because it was a dream that awakened her. In the dream, she and Sophie were at the beach, and nothing in the world was wrong. Sophie was healthy, her body nut-brown and her cheeks rosy. Her red hair, pulled back into a thick ponytail, was much longer than it really was. They were building a sand castle together and talking about eating pancakes for dinner. It was a light and airy dream, and when she woke up and realized that there was no beach, no sand castle, no *Sophie,* she began to cry. She turned away from Lucas, who was sleeping soundly, not wanting to disturb him, and wept into her pillow.

He knew, though. She felt his hand on her back, slowly rubbing along the length of her spine through her T-shirt. He raised his hand to the back of her neck and massaged her there, where the muscles were so tight they hurt.

"I know this is hard," he whispered, his breath against her neck. "Whatever happens, we'll get through it together, Jan."

She rolled over to let him take her in his arms. "I'm so scared," she admitted.

"I know."

"And I know everyone's starting to think that she's dead. That they're all dead. And maybe it seems crazy, but I have this unbelievably strong feeling that she's alive. I feel it in here." She took his hand and held it against her abdomen, just below her rib cage.

"It's not crazy," he said. He reached beneath her T-shirt to rest his hand on her bare skin. "If you felt it in your toes, or your ears, or your knees, *then* you might be crazy," he said. "But as long as you feel it *here,* I'd trust it."

She laughed softly. "Don't tease," she said.

"I'm not teasing, sweetheart." He kissed her softly on the lips. "I love you."

His hand moved to her breast, his touch undemanding and gentle, and when he reached lower to slip his fingers beneath her underpants, she opened her legs to him. Never would she have guessed that she'd be making love tonight, but this was lovemaking borne of need rather than desire. It was soothing rather than passionate, with solace, rather than pleasure, as its goal. And afterward, she buried herself in his arms, and stayed nestled tightly in his embrace until morning.

They were both up before the sun. In the kitchen, Lucas made coffee while Janine called the police station, begging for news that didn't exist. Both of them spun around at the sound of her father barging into the living room, and Janine knew that he had seen Lucas's car in the driveway.

"What's going on?" Frank asked, as she quickly hung up the phone. "What is *he* doing here? Are you all right, Janine?"

"I'm fine, Dad. And Lucas is here because he's a friend."

Her father didn't seem to know what to say to that. He looked even more awkward than he usually did, and she felt sorry for him.

"He was here all night?" he asked finally.

"Yes."

"Janine needed someone with her last night," Lucas said. He had his coffee cup in his hand, and he rested it on the counter as if expecting to have to defend himself physically at any moment.

"Oh, she did, did she?" her father bellowed. "She could have had Joe here, or her mother or myself."

Janine took Lucas's hand in hers. "We've been seeing each other for quite a while, Dad. I didn't want you and Mom to know because—"

"You've *what?* I don't *believe* this," her father said. "Janine, have you completely lost your mind?" He pointed a finger at Lucas. "You! Get out of here and get to work."

"I'm taking today off," Lucas said.

Her father let out an ugly, snorting laugh that was so out of character for him, it made Janine cringe. "You make it sound as though that's an unusual occurrence," he said. "You take off any damn time you feel like it. Why should today be any different?"

"As long as my work gets done, I don't see the problem," Lucas said.

"This is the final straw." Her father's cheeks were that ruddy color he got on those rare occasions when fury replaced his usual stoic anger. "I'm speaking to the Foundation today and getting you fired."

"On what grounds, Daddy?" Janine asked. "That he befriended your thirty-five-year-old daughter?"

"That he is irresponsible, at best. At worst...I don't know what that would be exactly, but I'm sure there's more to...to this man...than you know, Janine. I'd tell you not to be such a fool, but your mother's right. You always were and I guess you always will be."

"Leave my house, Daddy," she said. "Please just go."

Her father laughed again. "Your house? You're staying here out of our good graces, and you know it. This is *my* house, your mother's and mine, and we don't want him—" he motioned toward Lucas "—inside it."

"I've had it." Lucas let go of her hand and took a step toward her father. "First of all, I quit the damn job, okay?" he said. "Does that make you happy? Second of all, Janine needs your love right now, not your criticism, although that seems to be all you and your wife know how to give her. I'm sick of you belittling her. She's been a great mother to Sophie. She's done everything in her power to make Sophie's life as good as it can be, and—"

"Hey!" Her father again pointed one shaky finger at Lucas. Janine had never seen him so livid. "Don't you dare talk to me like that. You're the whole reason Sophie's in that idiotic study. Telling Janine that herbs can work when nothing else can. You're preying on her desperation. I want you to stay away from her."

Janine moved toward her father, grabbing his arm to turn him around and usher him out the kitchen door and through the living room. "I'm a grown woman, Dad," she said, walking him straight out the front door. She was relieved that he didn't resist. He was probably so surprised to find her standing up to him, that he didn't know how to react. "You can't tell me who I can choose for my friends."

He turned to face her once he was outside on the stoop. "Get him out of here, Janine," he ordered. "I mean it. This is my property and I want him off it."

It was not his property, but she didn't want to rub his nose in it. "Daddy...I don't need this right now, okay?" she said. "Lucas is right. I need you to help me now, not harass me. If you can't do that, then...don't come over here again."

She couldn't bring herself to slam the door in his face, but she closed it gently, biting her lip against the threat of tears, and walked back into the kitchen.

Lucas wrapped his arms around her when she came into the room.

"I'm sorry that was so messy," he said.

"He still has it in his mind that you're up to something evil," she said, drawing away from him. "Please don't quit your job over this."

"I think it's a done deal." He poured himself a cup of coffee, and she couldn't help but admire the steadiness in his hand after the scene with her father. Her own hands were shaking.

"Besides." Lucas took a sip of the coffee and smiled at her. "I already have a new job."

"You do?" she asked, surprised. "What?"

"I'm going to help you find Sophie."

CHAPTER FOURTEEN

Zoe used a long fork to transfer the cooked squirrel from the spit onto one of the cheap plastic plates she'd picked up at a Kmart in Ohio. She sat down on a large flat rock near the fire pit, rested the plate on her lap, and began carving the meat from the squirrel's thigh. A strange breakfast, she thought, but she was beginning to like the freedom of eating whatever she wanted, whenever she wanted it. She was beginning to like her freedom, period.

She was just about to raise a bit of meat to her mouth when she heard a sound behind her. The unmistakable rustling of leaves. Could it be Marti? Could she have arrived in West Virginia already? But then she heard voices and knew that more than one person was making their way into her clearing.

Quickly, she set the plate down on the rock and took two steps toward the shanty, where her rifle leaned against the porch. Turning to face the sound, she saw two young people emerge from the woods, bulky packs on their backs. A boy and a girl. Teenagers or early twenties, she thought, as she raised the rifle in front of her face, aiming it directly at them.

They froze when they saw her, both of them automatically lifting their arms over their heads.

"Don't shoot," the boy said.

"Git offa my land!" Zoe shouted, in what she imagined to be an accent appropriate to the backwoods of West Virginia. She kept the rifle in place against her shoulder. It made a great cover for a face that, even with hacked-off hair and no makeup, would still be all too recognizable.

"Okay," the boy said. "We're going. But...we lost the trail somehow."

"Can you tell us how to get back to the trail?" the girl asked.

Trail? Zoe hadn't known there were any trails within miles of her shanty. She'd had to create her own when she hiked in. "Git that way." She moved the rifle toward the east. She didn't know where the trial was, but the road was in that direction. It was miles away, but if they kept walking straight, they'd at least get themselves out of the woods.

"Thanks!" the boy said, far too enthusiastically for the amount of help she'd given them, and he and his companion turned and nearly ran back into the woods.

Shaken by the encounter, Zoe carried her plate into the shanty and sat on the sofa, her gaze fastened to the woods outside her window as she ate the squirrel. Those two kids were the first human beings she'd seen since settling into the shanty. She'd thought she and Marti would be safe here from any intrusion. Thank God she'd had the rifle close by to hide her face and her hillbilly act ready to employ.

Oh, Lord, what if Marti encountered hikers as she made her way out here? She hadn't thought of that. If she was being honest with herself, she knew that crossing paths with a couple of hikers might be the least of Marti's problems. Now that Marti's arrival was getting close, Zoe couldn't stop thinking about everything that could go wrong. There was a chance Marti would get caught during the escape and never make it to West Virginia at all, although the warden was being well paid to make sure that didn't happen. Still, Marti was no seasoned criminal. She did not know how to run from the law, and once the warden was no longer with her and she was on her own in the woods...well, who knew what could happen then.

As she rinsed the plate off under the pump in the yard, though, Zoe's mind turned from Marti to those two lost teenagers again, and she was filled with guilt. They had mothers, too. Worried mothers, no doubt. And here she'd sent them back into the woods without so much as a compass or a glance at a map to help them orient themselves. She considered disguising herself and going after them, making sure they found their way, but she didn't dare. She'd be playing games with her plan if she did that, playing games with Marti's freedom. And that was one thing she would never do.

CHAPTER FIFTEEN

Janine's hands trembled as she held the map, and Lucas wondered about the advisability of her flying the helicopter. He was sitting in the passenger seat, waiting for takeoff, and he didn't know if her tremor was because of anxiety over flying a helicopter after so many years or the result of low blood sugar. He'd been unable to persuade her to eat anything that morning after their run-in with her father.

The door on Janine's side of the helicopter was open, and she was talking with one of Omega-Flight's pilots who was standing on the tarmac. She handed the man the map for a moment, and he handed it back with some instructions Lucas could not hear.

Omega-Flight had given Janine the choice of a number of helicopters. To Lucas's disappointment, she had passed over the cleaner, more luxurious helicopters in favor of one that looked as though it had been built from a giant Erector set. He thought she was taking the worst of the lot because they were offering it to her for free, and she didn't want to take advantage of her old employer. But it turned out that was not her reasoning at all.

"It has a bubble cabin," Janine said, when he asked her why she'd made that selection. "We'll be able to see below us much better. And it's more maneuverable."

Janine closed the door now and looked at him. "Ready?" she asked, and he nodded.

The bird was noisier than he'd expected, but as they lifted into the air, he understood why she had chosen this particular, glass-enclosed helicopter: the entire world was visible to them as they rose above the buildings along the Dulles Toll Road. Despite the seriousness of the situation at hand, Lucas could not help a rush of joyful adrenaline at finding himself suspended in the sky.

"Have you ever been up in one of these before?" Janine asked. She was speaking loudly to be heard above the sound of the blades.

"Once," he replied. "But I don't remember it. I was unconscious." *Damn,* why did he say that? Should have kept his mouth closed. Now he would have to lie to her again. It chipped away at his integrity, lying to a person he loved, and he loved Janine. Loving her had not been part of his plan, but he'd been drawn to her devotion to Sophie, to her sensitivity, and to the strength she didn't even know she possessed. He was closer to her than to anyone else, yet he was lying to her at every turn.

"What do you mean, you were unconscious?" she asked.

"It was a long time ago. I was on a cruise with my wife and I got sick."

"Seasick?"

"Oh, I don't even remember," he said. "It was a combination of things, I guess. I passed out and woke up in a hospital bed. I wouldn't have known I'd been flown there if someone hadn't told me."

"So, you're really a helicopter virgin," Janine said.

"Yes. And given the reason we're up here, I wish I could just stay one."

"I wish you could, too," she said grimly, then handed him the map. "Okay, here's my plan for when we get over West Virginia," she said. "Alison liked to take shortcuts. There was no way Joe and I could cover every possible route in the car yesterday. So I'll just fly over the main route to the camp, then we can branch out from there and cover as many alternate routes and possible wrong turns as we can see."

They were passing over a residential area and Lucas looked down at the lush cover of the trees. It was difficult to see houses beneath the foliage, much less a car. "What are you hoping we can see from up here?" he asked. He'd meant the question to sound compassionate, but having to shout it over the sound of the helicopter sapped it of its gentleness. To be honest, he didn't see the point to this excursion, but he understood Janine's need to do *something,* and he was more than willing to do it with her. He loved that she was not the type to sit and wait while fate took its course. Neither was he.

Janine tensed her lips. "I don't know, exactly. The blue Honda stranded on the side of the road, maybe. A little redheaded girl walking along a deserted lane. I just don't know." She glanced at him. "I have to try, though, Lucas."

"I understand," he said.

Once they began following Route 66, the buildings and homes gave way to rolling meadows and heavily wooded hills. The flight was smooth, the view above the trees spectacular, and Janine seemed to grow more comfortable with the helicopter with each passing minute. Sometimes he had to remind himself that she had flown in the Gulf War. When she allowed herself to be so easily manipulated by Joe and her parents, it was hard to remember that she'd once possessed a cocky, rebellious side. He'd never dared to say this to her, but he thought it was fitting that she lived in Ayr Creek's original slave quarters. She was owned by the people in the mansion, just as those slaves had been. The difference was, the slaves had no choice in the matter. Janine did. Janine's guilt was her real master.

"There's the Shenandoah," Janine said, after they'd been flying about half an hour. Lucas looked down to see the river below them. It was broad and calm at this point, and a couple of cows stood knee-deep in the water near the bank. He wondered if being above that river reminded Janine of the ill-advised canoe trip she'd taken when she was eighteen. He reached over to squeeze the back of her neck, just in case her mind was on that other child she had lost.

After a short time, Janine cut away from 66 and began following Route 55. In a few minutes, they were above the deep woods of the George Washington National Forest.

"Do you see where I marked the camp on the map?" she asked him.

He did, and he helped guide her in that direction. Soon, a lake appeared below the helicopter.

"There's the camp." Janine pointed to the other side of the lake, and they flew above the water, low enough to ripple the surface with the wind from the blades. A few dozen girls were swimming and playing in a roped-off portion of the lake, and Janine actually smiled as she let the helicopter hover above them. The girls looked up at them, round faces tipped to the sky, and waved.

"So," Janine said, as they flew over land again, "let's just make some circles out from the camp. Sort of a spiral, at least for a mile in every direction."

They flew low over the trees, following the path of a narrow road, and Lucas's head quickly began to ache from the effort of trying to see beneath the dense green cover.

"Let's try this road," he suggested, when they had completed their spiral. He held the map toward her, pointing to one of the smaller roads leading away from the camp.

"That's one of the roads Joe and I drove yesterday," Janine said. "We didn't see anything, but we might as well try it again from this vantage point."

The road was very narrow. It looked as though it was rarely used, the paving sloppy and edged with wide bands of gravel. It snaked through the woods for a mile or so before beginning a descent from the mountain. It was easier to see the road then, as it was cut into the side of the mountain and not as obscured by trees. A sheer cliff rose above the road on one side; the land on the other side fell away to deep forest. Suddenly Lucas's gaze was drawn to something in that forest, something dark.

"Janine," he said. "Can you circle around there?" He pointed ahead of them and to the right, where the earth dropped away from the road. There was no guardrail. "I just want to get a closer look."

She turned the helicopter in the direction he pointed.

"A little to the left," he said. "Then stop for a minute so I can—"

He looked through the glass bubble on the lower right side of the helicopter, and his own body began to shake. Below them, carving a space for itself among the young scraggly trees on the steep slope, was an overturned car. He doubted Janine could see it from where she sat.

"Jan." He worked at keeping his voice even and wrapped his hand lightly around her wrist. "There's a car down here. It's turned over. It must have gone off the—"

"Where?" Janine maneuvered the helicopter to try to see what he was looking at, and Lucas wished he knew how to fly this thing so that he could get her away from the area. He didn't want her to see.

"I think we should just make a note of where we are," he said, "and go back to—"

"Oh, my God, my God!" Her hand flew to her mouth, and he knew she had given herself a good view of the overturned car. "Is it a Honda?" she asked.

"I can't tell from up here."

"Maybe I can land on the road."

"No," he said firmly. "First of all, that's too dangerous. Cars wouldn't be able to see you as they come around the bend."

"There are no cars on this road!" she shot back.

"And second, that cliff is too steep. Even if we could land

here, we'd need help to get down there. We should find some other place to—"

"I need to know if it's Alison's car," Janine said. She dropped the hovering helicopter lower, and he gripped the bottom of his seat to brace himself. They were entirely too close to the treetops.

There had been a fire. The saplings and leaves around the car were black, as was the car itself. He could not see the sides of the car, only the underbody. It was the shape and size of a Honda, though, and Lucas knew he was looking at the remains of a horrific accident.

Janine again pressed her hand to her mouth. "This is it, isn't it?" she asked.

"It may be," Lucas said.

"We have to land, Lucas! What if Sophie's still alive in there?"

Lucas's eyes burned as he studied the car. No one could have survived this crash, he thought. Alison must have been driving a bit too fast for the narrow, winding road, or she might simply have hit a patch of loose gravel. Her car had flown off the road at the curve and landed here upside down, maybe crushing everyone inside, killing them instantly, before bursting into flames. He said a silent prayer that was what had happened, that Sophie and the other two would not have suffered.

"Give me the radio," he said. "I'll call the police and let them know what we've found. They can be out here in an hour."

"We might not have an hour!"

"Janine, look at me." He grabbed her wrist hard this time, and she turned toward him. She was weeping freely, and the panic in her eyes, the tremor in her lower lip, broke his heart. He blocked all thought of Sophie being in that demolished car from his mind, or he knew that neither of them would be able to function rationally.

"Now, listen to me," he said. "You have to stay in control of this helicopter. That's your first priority right now, okay? You won't do Sophie any good if you...get in an accident, too. I'll call the police. Sergeant Loomis is it?"

She nodded.

"Then we'll find a safe place for you to land, and we'll come back here and meet the police."

Janine was staring down at the car again, and he turned her face away from the window with his hand.

"How will we get back here?" she asked.

"We'll find a way," he promised. Right now, he just wanted to be back on terra firma.

"Call first," she said. "Call right now."

"All right." He dialed the number for the Fairfax County police, and it was mere seconds before he had Sergeant Loomis on the line. "This is Lucas Trowell," he said. "Janine Donohue and I are in a helicopter above—" he checked the map "—above a little, unmarked road about a mile and a half west of the Scout camp. There's an overturned vehicle below us. It looks like it went off the road and flipped over. It's going to be hard to get to."

In his deep, calming voice, Loomis said he would alert the sheriff in that area. Janine could find a place to land and then someone from the sheriff's office could pick them up to bring them back to the scene of the overturned car.

It was a few more minutes before they received the call from the local sheriff. He directed them to a church parking lot a couple of miles away, where Janine managed to set the helicopter down smoothly. She'd stopped crying, and her trembling had ceased.

She was trying to be strong, Lucas thought, and a stranger might think she was succeeding. He knew better, though. Behind that calm facade, Janine was falling apart. The next few hours would be agonizing for her, and he wished there was some way to spare her from the heartache. He knew that heartache and how it could claw at a person until it ripped them to shreds.

He knew it all too well.

CHAPTER SIXTEEN

"I think you were supposed to turn back there," Paula said.

Joe drove his car onto the shoulder of the road to prepare for a U-turn. This was the fourth or fifth time Paula had needed to correct his sense of direction on this trip, but her voice never lost its patience or concern, even though he'd barked at her in irritation a couple of times. He wondered if Lucas had navigated for Janine. Did she bark at him? Probably not. Janine, under the worst of circumstances, was no barker.

He made the U-turn, then pulled back onto the road.

"I think it's right there." Paula pointed ahead of them, where a narrow road led into the woods.

He turned onto the road, recognizing it as one he and Janine had explored the day before. Could they have driven right past the site of the accident?

He glanced at Paula. "Sorry if I've been hard to deal with for the past hour or so," he apologized.

"Joe." Paula reached over to rub his shoulder. "How could you be any other way right now?"

He had gone into the office for a few hours today, expecting to get a little work done before taking off for West Virginia to continue the ground search, but he'd been unable to concentrate.

He'd kept his small office TV tuned to the local news channel and his phone smack in front of him on his desk, hoping to get a call that would turn this nightmare around. But it was Janine who called him, and she did not give him the news he'd wanted.

He'd stopped in Paula's office to tell her that he was leaving right away for West Virginia, and she asked to come with him. Her offer relieved him; torturous as this drive had been, it would have been even worse if he'd been alone.

He drove slowly, negotiating curve after curve along the narrow road, the gravel spitting out from beneath his tires. Anyone driving too fast along this road wouldn't stand a chance, he thought.

"Maybe the car Janine saw was from an old accident," he said to Paula.

"Maybe," Paula responded.

"I don't know whether to hope it's the Honda or not," he said. "If it is, then...then I guess there's no point in hoping anymore. Janine said the car was smashed and burned."

"We'll have to just wait and see," Paula said. She looked down at his scribbled directions, which rested in her lap. "I think we're very close now. Maybe around the next bend."

They hadn't seen another car on the badly paved road, but their sense of isolation came to an abrupt end as soon as they rounded the next curve. Parked at various angles along the road were two police cars, an ambulance, a fire truck and a tow truck. Joe's heart climbed into his throat as he approached a barrier of orange cones across the road.

A young woman in a sheriff's uniform walked up to the driver's side of his car, and Joe rolled down his window.

"You are...?" the woman asked.

"Joe Donohue."

The woman backed away from the car and moved one of the orange cones to let him through. Joe passed by the barrier and parked on the side of the road farthest from the cliff.

"There's Janine," he said, as he turned off the ignition.

Janine was standing with one of the police officers, and it wasn't until Joe had gotten out of the car that he saw that Lucas Trowell was next to her. He'd wanted to rush up to Janine and pull her into his arms, but the sight of Lucas standing so close to her made him reconsider. What if she rejected his embrace? He had been torturing himself with the fantasized image of Janine and Lucas in bed together since talking with her on the phone the night before.

He and Paula began walking toward the crowd. Joe's legs felt wobbly, and he was afraid to peer over the side of the cliff to see what was holding everyone's attention. He did not like heights, but more than that, he did not want to see the car that may have carried his daughter to her death.

"Joe!" Janine spotted him. She left Lucas's side to run up to him, her arms outstretched, and he was relieved by the warmth of her greeting.

"Are you okay?" he asked, holding her close.

"Not at all," she said, letting go of him. "I'm so scared, Joe."

"I know," he said. "Is there any news? What's the status here?"

"See those two guys?" She pointed toward a couple of young men who were standing at the edge of the cliff. They were wearing what looked like jumpsuits or some sort of uniform.

"Who are they?" he asked.

"They're the emergency rescue guys," she said. "They're going to try to get down to the car."

Joe then noticed that the men had ropes tied around their waists, shackling them to the bumper of the tow truck.

"I wanted to go down with them," Janine continued, "but they won't let me. I can't stand this waiting!"

"Is there any more information on the car?" Paula asked. "Do they know for sure if...?"

Lucas Trowell joined them at that moment, coming to stand next to Janine.

"It's a Honda," Janine said in a low voice, as though it was a secret. "They know that much. And there's only one Honda missing around here."

Lucas shifted closer to her, and although Joe couldn't see for sure, he was fairly certain Lucas had his arm around her back.

"This is rough," Lucas said to Joe and Paula, as if they didn't know. Joe wanted to smack him. It was unnerving to see the Ayr Creek gardener touching Janine. To have him wear that stunned and solemn mask on his face, as though Sophie were his own child, was infuriating.

"Don't you know of any herbs that can fix up a kid who's been in a car wreck?" Joe said, and he heard the ugliness in his voice.

"Hey." Paula punched him lightly on the arm.

Joe shook his head. "Sorry," he said.

"It's all right," Lucas said.

Paula, ever the diplomat, reached her hand toward Lucas. "I'm Paula," she said. "A friend of Joe's."

Lucas shook her hand. "Lucas Trowell," he said.

Joe followed Janine's gaze toward the rescuers, who were just beginning their descent over the side of the cliff.

"I need to see what's happening," she said, moving away from the group toward the cliff's edge.

She had more guts than he did, Joe thought. He did not want to see what was at the bottom of the cliff. But Paula and Lucas began following Janine, and he walked alongside them reluctantly, as though he had no choice.

"Where are the other girl's parents?" Joe asked Lucas, as they walked.

"They're on their way," Lucas said. "The police couldn't reach them until an hour or so ago."

"Stay back, folks," one of the firemen said. He looked hot in his heavy uniform, and he held his arm out to block Janine from getting any closer to the edge of the cliff.

"How far down is it?" Joe asked Lucas.

"Not far at all," Lucas said. "Ten or twelve feet, at the most. But it's steep. A lot of rocks and brush."

"They still don't know for sure if it's Alison's car?" Paula asked.

Lucas nodded slightly, his mouth set in a grim line. "They know," he said. "They checked the license plate number. It's hers. But I don't think Janine realizes that yet. I just wanted to let her hang on to hope a little bit longer."

Well, what a kind fellow you are, Joe thought to himself. "Why the hell were they on this road?" Joe asked. "It goes nowhere."

"It actually comes out on a road that eventually leads to Route 55, so there was a method to her madness," Lucas said. "She liked shortcuts, apparently."

Janine was arguing with the fireman.

"Let me just *stand* here," she said to him. "I won't go any closer to the edge, I promise."

The fireman motioned to Lucas to come stand next to her. He said a few words to both of them once Lucas was near her, probably telling him to keep an eye on Janine, because Lucas locked his hand around her elbow. Joe wished he'd been the one called to Janine's side, but the truth was, he wouldn't have been able to stand that close to the edge.

"What's taking them so long?" he heard Janine ask, and she broke away from Lucas to take another step toward the cliff. Lucas grabbed her arm to hold her back.

A couple of people in uniform—firemen and sheriff's deputies, Joe figured—squatted at the edge of the cliff, talking with the rescuers down below. Joe strained his ears to listen, but could make out little of what they were saying.

"Do you want to get any closer?" Paula asked him. "Do you want to see the car?"

He shook his head, feeling sick and stunned. "I just can't believe this is happening," he said. "I refuse to believe Sophie's been killed in a car wreck. After all her near misses with her kidney problems, and now this."

Paula rested her hand on his arm, much the way Lucas was touching Janine. "Maybe she's alive in there," she said, and Joe could hear tears in her voice. "Let's pray that she is."

He wasn't good at prayer, but he tried now. Paula spoke her prayer out loud, pleading with God to save Sophie, and he repeated the words to himself.

A van came around the bend in the road, pulling to a stop outside the barrier of orange cones, and Joe recognized it as the Suburban belonging to Holly's parents. Rebecca and Steve got out of the van and ran through the cone barrier toward them, but the sheriff blocked their path. He took them aside, talking to them quietly, probably bringing them up-to-date on what was happening.

Just then, the head and shoulders of one of the rescuers appeared over the edge of the cliff. He was leaning back, the rope holding him in place on the side of the cliff as he talked to one of the firemen. They spoke for a moment, while everyone stared in their direction. The fireman finally nodded, then walked over to Joe and the others as the rescuer dropped down the side of the cliff again.

"Gather round," the fireman called, motioning to them to do so.

Rebecca, Steve and the sheriff joined the anxious semicircle around the fireman, and Joe knew from the deep lines across the man's forehead that he had nothing encouraging to tell them.

Joe glanced at Janine. Her eyes were on the fireman, her lower lip clenched between her teeth. She looked as though she was holding her breath.

"I'm afraid the news isn't good," the fireman informed them. "It looks like the car burned up pretty bad on impact. Right now, though, the rescue team can only see two bodies inside."

"Two?" Steve repeated. "There were three of them."

"Right, I know," the fireman said. "And they're trying to find the third. She might have been thrown out of the—"

"Whose bodies have you found?" Joe interrupted him. He couldn't tolerate the slow delivery of information.

"We don't know," the fireman said. "Looks like one adult and one child, but the guys can't really get inside the car yet. They're working on it, but they need to get some tools down there with them."

Joe glanced toward the top of the cliff to see that a few of the emergency workers were lowering equipment to the men below.

"The two in the car appear to have been burned pretty bad." the fireman said.

Burned beyond recognition. The familiar phrase ran through Joe's mind. Never had he imagined it applying to his beautiful daughter.

Rebecca lowered herself to the ground, where she sat, cross-legged and weeping. Steve sat next to her, his arm around her shoulders, speaking to her softly.

The sheriff cleared his throat, readying himself to take over from the fireman. "I think it would be best if you folks went back to Virginia," he said, "and let us—"

"I'm not going anywhere," Janine said. "Not until I know exactly where my daughter is. Please let me go down there and look around."

The sheriff shook his head. "It's too dangerous," he said. "The car's in a precarious position."

"What are they doing down there now?" Joe asked.

"They'll get the bodies out," the fireman said. "Then we'll lift up the car and see if...if the third victim is underneath. If you folks want to stay here, I have to ask that you get over to the other side of the road and away from the cliff. I'll let you know when there's any news."

Reluctantly, they walked to the opposite side of the road and sat down on the gravel, their backs against the brush-covered embankment that edged the road.

Steve stood up almost as soon as he'd sat down. "I'm going to make a run for some drinks. What does everyone want?"

"Vodka," Rebecca said. She sounded serious, but instantly started to laugh, and in less than a second, the laughter turned to tears. She buried her head in her arms.

"Anything for me," Paula said.

"Same here," said Joe.

"Nothing for me," Lucas said, holding up his own nearly full water bottle. He nudged Janine, who was seated next to him, but she shook her head. "Water for Jan," he said.

"No one calls her Jan," Joe muttered under his breath to Paula.

"Apparently Lucas does," Paula said, and he looked at her sharply.

"Whose side are you on?" he asked.

"Nobody's side, hon," she said. "Just...now isn't the time for jealousy. Both you and Janine need support, and it doesn't really matter where it comes from. Okay?"

He felt like a chastised child. Leaning his head against the wall of earth behind him, he shut his eyes.

"It's going to rain," Rebecca said.

Joe opened his eyes again. Sometime in the last few minutes, the sky had grown dark and threatening. In the distance, there was the low rumble of thunder, and the sun was obscured by a thick bank of gray clouds.

"I'm sorry I let her go," Janine said suddenly. She was speaking to him, and he turned to look at her.

"I know," he said. "It's not your fault." He tried hard to sound sincere, although deep in his heart he blamed her. Just as he blamed Schaefer for coming up with the study, and Lucas for talking Janine into enrolling Sophie in it. And he blamed Alison and the Girl Scouts of America. He had to blame *someone.*

It began to rain as Steve returned with their drinks. The sky turned nearly black, and the clouds dropped lower to the earth. Lightning pierced the sky and the firemen and other rescue personnel had to shout to be heard above the beating of the rain on the trees and road.

Janine ignored the bottle of water Steve placed by her side on the gravel. She sat with her arms wrapped around her legs, her head hunched over her knees, and Joe wasn't sure if she was crying or sleeping.

Then the first black bag was lifted over the edge of the cliff. It was hard to tell from this distance, but the bag looked quite large as it was carried to the ambulance. An adult was in there, Joe thought. Alison.

The second bag, though, was considerably smaller, and everyone sitting against the embankment in the rain grew instantly silent. Janine lifted her head from her knees. When she spotted the bag, she suddenly jumped to her feet and ran a few yards away from everyone to be sick in the bushes.

Joe beat Lucas to his feet. "Let me, damn it," he said, and Lucas nodded.

Janine leaned against the embankment, her back to him, and he put his hand on the nape of her neck.

"It's me," he said, not wanting her to think it was Lucas behind her, touching her.

She turned toward him, wiping her mouth with the back of her hand. She leaned into him, into an awkward, pained embrace. Her body shook with her tears.

"How can this be so hard?" she asked him finally. "We almost lost her so many times, and we knew we would lose her for good, soon. It's not as though we weren't prepared for this."

"We *weren't* prepared for this," Joe said. "Not to have her die like this, in an accident, away from us." His voice cracked, and he buried his head in her shoulder. That's what hurt the most: thinking about Sophie dying without either him or Janine there. They had always been there for her. They had never left her alone. Never sent her off on her own this way.

Janine suddenly pulled away from him, a look of determination on her face. "I can't stand this," she said, and she started running down the road toward the ambulance. Joe followed her, the rain beating against his face.

"Let me see her!" Janine shouted at the woman standing near the entrance to the ambulance.

"I'm sorry," the woman said, shaking her head, holding her hands up in front of her to keep Janine away.

"I'd know who it is if you'd just let me see her," Janine pleaded. "I'd know my own daughter."

As Joe reached the ambulance, one of the firemen took Janine by the arm. "We'll know soon enough," he said. He nodded to Joe, communicating without words that he should take Janine away from the ambulance and back to the side of the road.

Janine let herself be led away by him, looking back over her shoulder at the ambulance and the body bag.

"I don't think it was Sophie in there," she said, as Joe led her away. "Sophie's smaller than that. Don't you think?"

"I don't know, Janine." He had no idea. He hadn't really looked at the bag long enough to have formed an opinion.

A squeaking, scraping noise came from the side of the cliff, and he and Janine both turned to follow the sound. A crane attached to the tow truck was lifting the car up from the cliff, the sheriff and rescuers guiding it, shouting instructions to one another. The beating rain made visibility difficult, but it was hard to miss the fact that the car had been nearly flattened in the accident. It must have hit the ground with terrible force.

Janine broke free from him again and ran toward the sheriff, who was standing near the rising car. "Did you find the other child?" Joe heard her shout. "Is she down there?"

One of the rescuers shook his head. "No sign of a third person," he said.

"But there was a third person in the car!" Rebecca called from behind him. Along with Steve and Lucas, she had left the embankment and was approaching the edge of the cliff.

"Do you know that for a fact?" the sheriff asked them. "Did someone see two children get into that car?"

"Yes," Janine said. "Gloria did. The other Scout leader. She said they—Alison and the girls—drove off ahead of them. Besides, there are two children missing. One of them must still be down there. *Please* let me go down and look."

"No, ma'am. As soon as this rain lets up, we'll get down there again and—"

Janine whirled around before he could finish speaking and started running down the road.

"Ma'am!" the sheriff called after her. "Mrs. Donohue!"

Joe started to follow her, but Lucas caught his arm. "Let her go," Lucas said. "She has to see for herself."

"This is not about *your* daughter," Joe said. "Or your wife."

"Janine isn't your wife, either," Lucas said. "She's not yours to control or accuse or criticize any longer."

"You son of a bitch," Joe said, ready and more than willing to punch Lucas in the face, but Paula literally jumped between the two of them.

"Cool it, you guys!" she demanded. "You're not helping. Neither one of you."

"Janine's gone," Rebecca said suddenly, and they turned to see that Janine had disappeared from the side of the road. It looked as if she'd fallen, but no doubt she'd found an area that would let her climb down the cliff safely. She would probably work her way back to the accident site, if no one tried to stop her, and Joe felt more than a little admiration for her—and a great deal of gratitude.

If Sophie was down there, Janine would find her.

CHAPTER SEVENTEEN

No one was bothering her, and that was good. Maybe they were calling to her from above, but the rain kept their voices from reaching her. The teeming rain made the hillside slippery, though, and she had to hold on to tree branches and the trunks of young saplings as she worked her way back toward the crash site. She had to see for herself. Maybe it was Sophie in that child-size body bag, and maybe it was not, but there was one more child who had been in that car, and Janine was determined to find her.

There was no mistaking the crash site. The shrubs and brush were flattened and black, the trees near the site charred. Even with the rain, she could smell the scent of ash and fire. It was a sick smell that burned her nostrils and turned her stomach.

She began to hunt. She was searching for a small, frail child with red hair. In her heart, though, she knew she was more likely to find a tiny, charred body, and she tried to brace herself for that possibility.

She understood, balancing there on the side of the cliff, clutching the rubbery branches of a young maple tree in her fist, why the rescuers had given up for now. There was no sign of life here. She fell to her hands and knees and crawled among the brush and the vines. *Probably poison ivy here,* she thought, as she felt beneath every growing thing, feeling for the form of a child.

But there was no child here. Thirty minutes passed, maybe longer, as she scoured the ground on her hands and knees. The rain had plastered her clothes to her body and her hair to her cheeks by the time she turned her head to see that Lucas was standing above her.

He sat down on the damp, muddy incline and pulled her close to him. Her hands were caked with mud and leaves, and for a fleeting moment, she thought she knew what insanity felt like.

"We need to go, Jan," he said.

She had no strength left to respond.

"They've taken the bodies to the medical examiner's office. They're going to get Sophie and Holly's dental records. Joe gave them Sophie's dentist's name. That's the only way they'll be able to tell who it is that they found. And the sheriff promised that tomorrow, they'll get a team of people out here to search this area for another...child."

She knew he had been about to say "body," and was glad he had caught himself in time. She didn't want to hear that word.

It took them a long time to make their way back up the hill to the road. Rebecca was waiting on the macadam, her arms crossed against her chest, her long hair stringy and wet. She rushed Janine as soon as she saw her.

"I couldn't find anyone," Janine said, winded. She struggled to get her breath. "No Sophie. No Holly. I'm sorry."

"Thank you for trying," Rebecca said, as she wrapped her arms around her.

Janine held her tightly. At least one of them had lost a child today. And within a few hours, either she or Rebecca would have no more reason to hope.

CHAPTER EIGHTEEN

Janine lay beneath the sheet on the double bed, staring blindly at the motel room's fuzzy television. Jay Leno was on, but she'd muted the sound, unable to tolerate the laughter and levity. She watched Jay talking, posturing, nodding. From the bed, she could see her reflection in the mirror above the standard-issue motel dresser. Her expression was drawn, sunken, her mouth downturned. Her eyes were puffy and heavy-lidded. She looked like an old woman.

She was only vaguely aware of the throbbing in her leg. Somehow, while she'd been making her mad foray into the underbrush, she'd cut her thigh. It was a deep, wide laceration she had not even noticed until she was back on the road, when Lucas spotted the blood trailing down her leg, soaking her white sock above her tennis shoe. She'd been unable to stop the bleeding, and everyone had insisted she go to the nearest emergency room. Joe drove her there, while she protested. The wound had required eight stitches to close, and she didn't even wince when the needle pierced her skin. This was nothing compared to what Sophie had endured, she told herself. Nothing.

They had all taken rooms at the motel. Rebecca and Steve were in a room on the second floor. Joe and Paula were on the third floor, sharing a room with two double beds. Janine knew about the beds because Joe had made sure to mention that fact in front of her. As if she cared. Joe was a fool to turn his back on the comfort she knew Paula would be more than happy to offer him

Janine would have loved to share a room with Lucas, whether it had two beds or not, but he was the one who had advised against it.

"Not with Joe here," he'd said. "This is hard enough on him without throwing our relationship in his face."

Jay Leno was bringing out a guest—some perky young woman with long blond hair and a dress that dipped low over her breasts. Her smile was irritating, and Janine clicked off the TV and lowered herself deeper beneath the sheet.

The rain had stopped sometime in the last hour or so, and the only sound now was the tinny, wheezing hum of the feeble air conditioner.

She was afraid to try to sleep, to close her eyes. Sure enough, as soon as she lowered her lids, the images came back to her: the black belly of the overturned car beneath the bubble of the helicopter, the small body bag. *She would have known,* she thought. *She would have been able to tell, if only they'd allowed her to look inside that bag.*

Joe had called her parents. Or, actually, *she* had called them, but her mother had instantly and not surprisingly told her to put Joe on the line. She'd handed the phone to him, and Lucas had chastised her.

"Make her talk to you," he'd said. "Make her act like an adult for once."

But Lucas didn't understand. It was easier to let Joe deal with her parents than it was to face her mother's wrath and her father's disappointment. She'd had a lifetime of that already. Right now, she didn't have the strength for it.

None of them had been prepared to stay the night. They'd gone to a small market in the nearest town to buy toothpaste, toothbrushes and shampoo, and she'd bought a man's cheap white undershirt to sleep in. She was glad she carried her birth control pills in her purse, so she wouldn't miss taking any—although she could hardly imagine ever being in the mood to make love again.

Omega-Flight had been good enough to send someone out to fly the helicopter back to their heliport. She was grateful for all the support they had given her, and she made a mental note to send them a thank-you card when this was all over. Whenever that would be.

The doctor at the emergency room had given her pain pills, explaining that her leg would probably throb tonight. She'd skipped the pills, and even now, lying still in bed, she could barely tell which leg had been injured. *You're numb,* she told herself, and while it was true that her body felt lifeless, her mind could not be stilled. She closed her eyes again, and the image of the small black body bag was with her once more. Groaning with frustration, she threw off the sheet and got out of bed. She took her room key from the dresser and walked out the door onto the outside walkway. Lucas's room was two doors down, and she knocked on it softly, not wanting to wake him if he'd somehow managed to fall asleep.

In a moment, he opened the door. The room was dark, but she could see that he was wearing only his boxers—and, of course, his splint.

"I can't sleep," she said.

"Neither can I." He held the door open for her.

She walked immediately to his bed and slipped beneath the covers, and he locked the door and joined her. He lay on his side, looking into her eyes, stroking her cheek with his hand.

"How is your leg?" he asked.

She shrugged off the question. "It's nothing."

"This is going to be a long night," he told her.

"I want to know, and I don't want to know," she said.

He nodded. His fingers were warm against her cheek.

"Was I wrong to put her in the study, Lucas?" she asked. "I know it's crazy, but Joe is right. If she hadn't been so well, she never would have gone on the trip. And if the wellness was just temporary, then what have I done by—"

"Janine." He gripped her shoulder, hard. "Listen to me. I don't care what Joe says. Or what your parents say. Or even what I say. I care about what *you* say. Please, Jan, trust yourself for once."

She had a sudden memory. She and Sophie were eating dinner a few nights after Sophie's first infusion of Herbalina. Sophie devoured her meat loaf and mashed potatoes, and she'd wanted seconds of cake. Janine had watched her with surprise at first, then with an unaccustomed optimism. Sophie never ate with gusto, not since the illness had become her constant companion. She usually nibbled, pushing food around on her plate, while Janine begged her to take in at least enough calories to get her through the next day. Suddenly, though, Sophie was hungry. And the little girl herself recognized the change.

"Food *tastes* good, Mom," she said. "I don't think I ever really tasted meat loaf before. It must be because of the Herbalina."

She was surprised that Sophie had made the connection between her new appetite and the IV she had weepily endured two days earlier.

"Why do you think it's the Herbalina?" Janine had asked her.

"Dr. Schaefer said my appetite would come back. He said food would taste better to me."

Janine's optimism sank, but only momentarily. Was Sophie's attitude toward her food just a placebo effect, produced by Schaefer's power of suggestion? Yet, Sophie had been on numerous other medications with no positive change in her appetite. And so what if it was the placebo effect? At least Sophie was getting some food inside her for a change.

"If I shut my mind to Joe and my parents, then...I'm glad she was in the study," Janine told Lucas. "If it was Sophie in the car, at least—" she squeezed her eyes shut "—at least she died happy. I mean, these last couple of weeks have been the happiest I've seen her since before she got sick."

Lucas pulled her close to him. It took him a moment to speak, and when he did, Janine could hear the thickness in his voice and knew he was near tears.

"I know," he said. "It's been wonderful to see how she perked up. How she got to play healthy little kid for a while, instead of always having to deal with the side effects of those other meds."

"I wish Joe could see it that way," she said. "And my parents. I think my mother truly hates me."

"Your parents love you," he said. "But they've gotten so used to saying black when you say white, that it's hard for you to ever win with them. And Joe...Joe might come around. He's not so bad. And he's still...besotted with you."

She laughed at his choice of words. "He has a funny way of showing it."

"Well, you know how when you're in love with someone, you feel almost desperate to change them into a person you can relate to more easily."

"I don't want to change you," she said. She leaned back to look at him. "I'm so grateful I have you. I'm so grateful for the way you've treated Sophie and me."

He looked as though he wanted to say something, opening his mouth slightly, then apparently changing his mind with a shake of his head.

"Come here." He pulled her close again, and she rested her head against his chest. "Let's try to sleep," he said. "I'm afraid tomorrow might be another long day."

She shut her eyes, breathing in the scent of his skin. She was uncertain she could handle another day like this one and nearly said that out loud, but caught herself. She knew what Lucas would say. He would say she was strong enough to handle anything. She truly hoped he was right.

CHAPTER NINETEEN

Joe could not sleep. If Paula hadn't been in the room, he would have put on the television, one of the old shows on "Nick at Night" for some mindless entertainment. But Paula was sleeping soundly, and he didn't want to wake her. They had talked for about an hour from their separate beds, and he was grateful for Paula's calm, dispassionate thinking at a time when his own mind was in turmoil.

"There's nothing we can do until we know who was in that car and what might have happened to the other girl," Paula had said. "Until then, worrying won't help."

She had relaxed him, then, with guided imagery, placing him on a beach in Hawaii, and to his surprise, he felt his tight muscles soften with the sound of her voice. There was no one quite like Paula, Joe thought. He had never known anyone so able to remain cool and rational in the face of chaos. The only time he had ever seen her fall apart was the morning she learned of her mother's death, and it had pleased him to be able to comfort her, to give back to her for a change. She had given so much to him over the last few years, as he coped with Sophie's illness and the divorce.

But even after the guided imagery, he still had not been able to fall asleep, and Paula's calming effect was not lasting. He was about to get up and go outside for a walk when there was a knock on the motel door. Quickly, he pulled on his shorts and opened the door.

The man illuminated by the motel light was short and slight and dressed in a sheriff's uniform.

"Are you Joseph Donohue?" he asked.

"Yes."

"May I come in?"

Joe glanced behind him at Paula's bed.

"I'm awake," Paula said as she sat up in the bed.

"Yes," Joe said to the sheriff. "Come in, please." He moved to the side of the room to turn on the floor lamp.

"Have a seat," the sheriff said, as he himself sat down at the small round table near the lamp.

Joe sat on the edge of his bed, his heart pounding. Whatever this man was about to tell him would change his life, of that he was certain.

"We've heard from the medical examiner," the sheriff said. "Your daughter, Sophie, was not the child in the car."

Joe let out his breath. He stared wordlessly at the sheriff, and before he knew what had hit him, he lowered his head into his hands and began to cry.

Paula was at his side instantly. She sat next to him on the bed, her arm around his shoulders.

"Shh, sweetie," she said. And then she took over, as if she realized Joe would not be able to handle this conversation himself. "It was definitely Holly in the car?" she asked the sheriff.

"Yes," the sheriff said. "The dental records allowed the medical examiner to make a firm identification."

"So, what happens now?" she asked.

"First thing in the morning, we'll organize a search party."

"Was there any evidence in the car that would give you a clue what happened to Sophie?" Paula asked.

"Her knapsack and sleeping bag were in the car, in the trunk," the sheriff said. "And we spoke to the other Scout leader, the one who saw the car drive away from the camp with Sophie in it. So, there's every indication she was in the car. The back seat windows were busted out, and we can only conclude that she was able to get out of the car somehow."

Joe looked up at that. "Before or after the fire?" he asked.

The sheriff shook his head. "That we don't know," he said.

"What about blood in the car?" Paula said, talking about blood as easily as she might talk about her garden. "Was there any blood that might indicate she was badly injured when she climbed out of the car?"

"I don't know the answer to that yet," the sheriff said. "We'll be examining the car more carefully this morning."

Joe looked at the sheriff. "Have you told my wife yet?" he asked. "My ex-wife?"

"No, not yet. How about you tell her. I've contacted Alison Dunn's mother in Ohio, and now I have to give the Krafts the news about their daughter." He pulled a piece of paper from his chest pocket. "They're in room 202. One floor down, I guess."

"Oh, God." Joe shut his eyes at the thought of Rebecca and Steve receiving this news. Then he got to his feet. "I'll go tell Janine," he said to Paula.

The sheriff stood up as well. "We're in the process of moving a search-and-rescue trailer up to the road where the accident was," he said. "The plan is for everyone to meet there at 6:30 a.m. That will be the command post, where the searchers will ßget organized."

"All right," Joe said. He let the sheriff out the door, then looked across the room at Paula.

"I'll be back in a while," he said.

Paula nodded. "Good luck, hon."

Janine's room was next to his. He knocked softly on her door, but could hear no sound from inside. He knocked again, loudly this time. "Janine?"

Again, there was no response, and he knew she could not be sleeping that soundly. Not on this night. He looked down the walkway, and his chest tightened with the realization of where she must be. Swallowing his humiliation, he walked toward Lucas's room.

"Is Janine in there?" he called, as he rapped lightly on the door.

From behind the door, there was the rustle of sheets. Quick, whispered words. In a moment, Janine opened the door, but before either of them could speak, the air was pierced by a scream coming from the floor below.

"What was that?" Janine's hand flew to her throat. "What's happening?"

"Let me in," Joe said, as the screaming continued. He pushed past Janine into the room, closing the door behind him, as if he could block out Rebecca's wailing, but the sound still filled the room.

From the corner of his eye, he could see that Lucas was standing in the doorway to the bathroom, dressed in the same khaki shorts and blue T-shirt he'd been wearing during the day. Joe ignored him as he grabbed Janine's hand.

"Holly was the one in the car," he said. "Sophie's still missing."

Janine glanced at Lucas, then lowered herself to the edge of the bed. "Sophie's alive," she said.

"We don't know that," Joe said, "but at least there's still a chance."

"No, she is," Janine insisted firmly. She pressed her hand to her chest. She was wearing a white undershirt, and it was obvious that she had no bra on beneath it. "I can feel it. I *feel* it." She looked at Lucas again, as if for confirmation, and to the man's credit he didn't smile or nod or in any way encourage her. Standing up again, she started for the door. "We have to go back out there," she said. "We need flashlights. Do the police have—"

"We can't go out there, now, Janine." Joe blocked her path. He knew she wasn't thinking clearly. "We're all supposed to meet at the accident scene at six-thirty. There'll be a search party forming then, and—"

"I want to go *now*." She turned toward him, a wild look in her eyes.

"Joe's right, Jan," Lucas said from the doorway by the bathroom. "You wouldn't be able to do anything in the dark, and it's muddy out there. You've got that cut on your—"

He was interrupted by another scream from the floor below.

"I should go to Rebecca," Janine said. She pushed past Joe and was out the door before he could stop her.

Joe glanced at Lucas after she'd left the room. "Next thing you'll know, she'll be out there in the dark, traipsing around those woods."

"Maybe that would be best," Lucas said. "She needs to feel as though she's doing something to find Sophie. She needs to feel as though she has some control."

Joe bristled at Lucas's proprietary tone. "I've known her for twenty-three years," he said. "I think I know what she needs better than you do."

"Then why haven't you ever given it to her?" Lucas asked, then quickly held up his hands in apology. "I'm sorry," he said, shaking his head. "Really, Joe. I'm out of line."

Joe simply stared at him for a moment. Lucas's apology had taken away any excuse he might have had to slam his face into the wall, and he couldn't help but feel a tiny bit disappointed.

"No problem," he said, opening the motel room door. "I'll see you at six-thirty."

CHAPTER TWENTY

Zoe awakened before the sunrise Wednesday morning with her stomach churning. She lay on her air mattress, staring at the rotting wood in the ceiling of the shanty. If everything was going according to plan, today should be Marti's day in the woods. Of course, it might have taken them longer to cross the country than Marti had expected, or they might have been detained somewhere for some reason. Only if absolutely everything had gone right would Marti make it to West Virginia today. What she wouldn't give for a newspaper! What was the press saying about Marti's escape? How close on her trail were the authorities?

She pictured Marti and the warden following the map she had so carefully drawn for them, turning off the highway onto the narrow road, making two more turns until they reached the dirt road that dipped and twisted as it bisected the forest. Marti would be leaning forward in the passenger seat, studying the road, biting her lower lip as she did when she was concentrating hard on something. The break would appear in the woods, and suddenly, the dilapidated, rust-colored barn would be in front of them.

"That's it!" Marti would exclaim, and the warden would pull the car into the overgrown patch of grass around the back of the barn. They would get out of the car, and Marti, truly tasting her freedom now, would run toward the front of the barn and push open one of the broad doors. Inside, she would stop short as she waited for her eyes adjust to the darkness.

"Did you find it yet?" The warden would catch up to her, asking the question before realizing that it was too dark inside to find anything.

Slowly, Marti's eyes would adjust, and the light from the two windows above the loft would gradually illuminate the one empty, long-unused stall at the far end of the building.

"There's the stall," she would say, moving forward.

Maybe the warden would get impatient at this point, and dart toward the stall himself. Would he know where to look? Would he have made Marti tell him over and over again, many times a day, where the money was hidden? Or would Marti have been wise enough to keep that information to herself until he delivered her safely to her destination? Yes, of course she would have been.

So, it would be Marti who would feel along the wall of the stall until she found the boards Zoe had pried loose. She'd reach in and pull out the fat leather bag and hand it to the warden, who would open it, pull out a fistful of bills, and whoop with joy. $500,000! The second and last installment.

Marti would breathe a sigh of relief that Zoe had come through for her. She'd say goodbye to the warden—maybe he'd give her a kiss on the cheek after traveling the breadth of the country with her—and she'd stand in the entrance of the barn, blinking from the sunlight, watching him get into his car and drive away.

Then, Zoe knew, Marti would be afraid. She did not like being alone, and she was no outdoorswoman. Following Zoe's directions, she would walk south along the road, back the way she and the warden had just driven, approximately one mile. Zoe had added this backtracking into the plan to fool the warden, just in case he was caught and pressured to reveal where he had dropped Marti off. Zoe could almost feel the tension mounting inside Marti's body as she searched for the small piece of blue cloth caught in the branches of a tree at the side of the road. Marti would feel both relief and trepidation when she spotted it. Yes, she was on the right trail, but now she would have to enter the very lush, very disorienting forest, with its musty scent riding on the thick, sticky air and the sounds of birds and insects and animals that would be unnatural to her ears.

Zoe had instructed her to follow the trail of blue cloth. Find one piece, then stand and search the forest for the next and walk in that direction. She had made certain that each scrap of cloth was visible from the location of the piece before it. She'd told Marti to remove each piece of cloth as she passed it, so that no one could follow her trail. Marti would have about ten miles to cover in that painstaking fashion. It had taken Zoe most of a day to lay the trail; it would take Marti at least that long to follow it, although sheer terror might quicken her pace. Poor Marti. Zoe hated thinking of her, scared and alone, in the forest.

This would be a long day for Zoe, as well, as she waited for Marti's arrival. If Marti didn't come today, tomorrow would seem even longer. And what if she didn't come tomorrow? Or the next day? What if she never arrived? Zoe would have no way of knowing what had happened to her. So many weak links in the treacherous chain of this plan, so many places where things could go wrong.

She couldn't think that way, she told herself. She got out of bed and walked into the clearing to start the fire for her instant coffee.

She was stoking the fire beneath the pot of water when she heard the sound of crackling twigs directly behind her. Marti! She stood up and spun around, expecting to see her daughter emerge from the woods. At first she could see nothing at all; the woods were too thick for the early morning sun to illuminate anyone inside them.

"Marti?" she called.

Suddenly, a child appeared at the edge of the woods. A small child, no more than six or seven, with red hair and one bare foot. Panicked, Zoe dropped the stick she was holding and ran the few feet to the house, grabbing her rifle where she'd left it leaning against the decrepit front porch. She raised the gun into shooting position, obliterating her face from this strange little intrusion.

"Git back with your folks!" Zoe ordered. "And keep offa my property!"

The little girl had been running toward her, but now she stopped. Her legs and arms were as thin as twigs, her red hair a tousled mess. And through the telescopic sights of the rifle, Zoe could see she was crying. The child's body jerked slightly, as if she were uncertain whether to move forward or to turn back the way she came.

"Where's your ma?" Zoe hollered.

The child raised her hands above her head, the same way the teenagers had done the day before, but it looked as though it took all her strength, and she could not seem to get them straight up in the air. One arm remained bent. She was trembling all over and weeping freely.

"I'm..." Her arms began to fall, as though she were too weak to hold them up any longer. Quickly, she raised them again, as if afraid Zoe would shoot her at any moment. She whimpered, in pain or fear or both, and something in that sound squeezed Zoe's heart so hard that she felt the contraction in the center of her chest.

"I'm lost," the little girl said, her lower lip quivering as she struggled to hold up her arms.

Zoe lowered the rifle to her side. What was she doing, pointing a gun at this baby?

"Oh, sweetheart, I'm sorry." She felt terrible for having frightened her. "Come here," she said, laying the gun on the ground. Her voice was soft, her hillbilly persona abandoned.

The girl hesitated.

"It's all right. I'm sorry I scared you," Zoe said, waving the child toward her with her hands. "I'm not really a mean old lady. Come here, little one."

The girl walked toward her, stumbling a bit, limping badly on her bare left foot. Her face was contorted with her silent weeping, and she fell into Zoe's arms.

The little girl felt bony and frail in Zoe's embrace. *This can't be happening,* she thought. This child was not part of her perfectly laid plans.

"Come with me," Zoe said, and she led the limping child to the porch, sitting her down on the one crooked step. The girl's T-shirt was filthy, the right sleeve nearly torn away from the body of the shirt. Her shorts were ripped, and she smelled of feces and perhaps of vomit. Her bare foot was scratched and bleeding.

"My name is Ann," Zoe lied. "What's yours?"

"Sophie Donohue," the girl said. She lowered her head and the tears started again. "I want my mom."

"Of course you do," Zoe said. She glanced anxiously toward the woods. "And where is she?"

"In Vienna."

Zoe was confused. "Austria?" she asked.

Sophie shook her head. "Vienna, Virginia."

"Oh. And what are you doing out here, honey?"

"I was at Girl Scout camp and..."

"At Girl Scout camp?" Zoe was surprised. "Aren't you way too young to be a Girl Scout?"

"No," Sophie said. "I'm a Brownie. I'm eight. I just look a lot younger."

"Yes, you're a little thing." Sophie could easily pass for a six-year-old, Zoe thought, but then she hadn't had that much experience with little girls. She'd barely seen Marti at the age of eight. That was the year Zoe had taken her singing and dancing routine on the road.

"So," she said, "you were telling me how you got lost."

"I don't know exactly what happened," Sophie said. "We had

an accident, I think. Somehow. I don't know. All of a sudden, I woke up and I was lying against a tree...a down tree...." It seemed hard for her to find the words she needed. "A tree on the ground..."

Zoe nodded her understanding.

"And in front of me was a car on fire. I think I was in the car, and somehow I got out, but I don't remember."

"Who was in the car with you?"

"Alison and Holly. Alison's the leader and we were taking a shortcut. And Holly is my friend."

"And did either of them get out of the car with you?" Zoe glanced again toward the woods.

"I didn't see them. I think they might have been in there. Inside the car." Sophie's face was a wide-eyed mixture of fear and sorrow. "I think they were in the fire. I was afraid to look, and it was so hot. It was hurting my eyes."

Zoe struggled to make sense of Sophie's words. The nearest road was five miles away, of that she was certain. Surely this child hadn't walked five miles alone through the woods. "Where was this, honey?"

"I don't know." She pointed behind her. "Somewhere...I know you're supposed to hug a tree if you get lost in the woods, but I wanted to get away from the fire. And then I couldn't figure out how to get back to the road. I kept turning and turning and—" she lowered her head "—I got so lost."

"How scary," Zoe said. "When did this all happen?"

Sophie shook her head slowly, her red-rimmed eyes unfocused. "I don't know. But I think I've been alone for three nights." She looked toward the woods from which she'd emerged. "I'll never go in the woods again," she said. "I hate them. Every time I fell asleep, I had nightmares."

Zoe caught another whiff of the foul smell emanating from Sophie's clothes. "Did you get sick?"

Sophie nodded. "I think it was some berries I ate. I shouldn't have, but I was so hungry. And then I got diarrhea and...I feel gross."

"And you hurt your arm, I think." Zoe took the small, scratched and dirty arm in both her hands to examine it. "Did you break it, maybe, or...oh, you burned it." There was a long, narrow red burn running the length of Sophie's forearm. She had been closer to that fire than she'd thought.

"Hurts." Sophie carefully removed her arm from Zoe's hands and held it tight against her body.

"Okay, my little friend," Zoe said. "We need to get these dirty clothes off you and clean you up. Let me put a bigger pot of water on the fire. You wait here."

She went inside the shanty, trying to move automatically without stopping to think. If she started to think, she would panic. She was inside some sort of crazy nightmare. Someone would be looking for this little girl. How close were they? What in God's name was she going to do if they showed up? She could slip back into her mountain woman role, holding the gun to her face again, while that someone took the child away. And with any luck, that would be the end of that.

She put the pot of water on the fire, then helped Sophie out of her clothes. In spite of her lack of experience with eight-year-old girls, Zoe was quite certain that Sophie was not typical of children her age. She allowed herself to be undressed with no modesty whatsoever, as though having a stranger lift off her shirt, tug off her filthy underpants was nothing new to her. That's when Zoe noticed the large bandage on the little girl's stomach.

"Why do you have this bandage here?" she asked.

"It's my catheter," Sophie said. "It's taped there so it doesn't flop around."

A catheter. Lord, what had she gotten herself into with this child?

"Ugh, those are gross." Sophie grimaced at the sight of her underpants. "Can we throw them away?"

"Yes," Zoe said. "As a matter of fact, I think we'll bury them."

She tossed the soiled underwear a few yards away from them, then wrapped a green bath towel around the little girl, tucking it in at her chest. "Why do you need a catheter, Sophie?" she asked.

"We hook it up to the dialysis machine," she said.

"So, you have a problem with your kidneys?" Zoe asked.

"Yes, but I'm a lot better than I used to be."

"I'm glad to hear it," Zoe said, her sense of panic mounting. "How often do you need to have dialysis?"

"It used to be every night. Now it's just Sunday and Wednesday nights."

"Today is Wednesday," Zoe said.

"It is? Wow. I missed Sunday night, too. I feel okay, though, I think. I better not drink too much, though."

Oh, this was never going to work. Zoe looked toward the woods again, hoping now that someone *would* appear looking for this child. She would do the mountain mama routine and get the girl out of here.

"The water's probably warm enough for you now," Zoe said. "I'll get you a washcloth, and then you can give yourself a little bath, okay?"

Sophie looked at the door to the shanty. "Can we call my mom first?" she asked.

"Oh, honey," Zoe said, realizing that Sophie had no idea how much of a predicament she was in. "I don't have a phone."

A flicker of fear passed through Sophie's eyes. "Should we go to a neighbor's house and use their phone?"

Zoe shook her head. "I'm afraid I don't have any neighbors either, I live very far from anyone."

"Do you have a car?"

Zoe shook her head again, and tears welled up in Sophie's eyes once more.

"How can I get home?" she asked.

"I'm not sure," Zoe said. "I'll think of something. But listen, honey." She put her hands on Sophie's shoulders. "For now you're safe, and that's what's most important. You'll have a good sponge bath, and then you can sleep for a while. I can tell you're very tired."

Sophie bit her lip, looking toward the shanty door again as if she thought Zoe might have a phone in there and just not know it. "Okay," she said finally.

This was a child accustomed to duress, Zoe thought. Accustomed to things not going her way.

She helped Sophie with her bath, then gave her a bite of rabbit and some canned peas before putting her down for a nap on the air mattress she'd prepared for Marti. The little girl was asleep before Zoe had even left the room.

In the clearing, she washed Sophie's T-shirt and shorts, hanging them over the porch railing to dry. Then she carried the soiled underwear deep into the woods, where she dug a whole and buried them.

Walking back to the shanty, she hoped she would discover that Sophie was gone. Maybe she'd dreamed the little girl's arrival, or maybe the people looking for her had found her and spirited her away. She walked into the shanty, through the living room to the bedroom, hoping, praying.

But Sophie was still there, a fragile little waif in Marti's bed, sleeping free of nightmares for the first time in days.

CHAPTER TWENTY–ONE

At six-twenty, after an hour or two of fitful sleep, Janine and Lucas waited in the motel parking lot, leaning against Joe's car. They had no car with them, since they'd arrived in the area by helicopter, so they would have to ride with Joe and Paula to the command post.

After Joe's visit the night before, Janine had gone to the second floor of the motel to the Krafts' room. The door to the room had been open, and the sheriff was still there, quietly talking with Steve, while Rebecca sat on edge of one of the beds, her head buried in her hands.

Janine had sat down next to her, putting her arm around her.

"I'm so sorry, Rebecca," she said.

Rebecca lifted her head slowly, her face red and damp. "I can't believe it," she said. "I just can't..."

"I know," Janine hugged her gently, as a strange sensation came over her. She knew she was sitting on the bed with Rebecca, but she felt as though she were merely an observer of the scene. She was detached from this woman and her tragedy. There was no longer any possibility of Sophie being the child in that body bag. Somehow, she could not let Rebecca's pain get inside her, and when she spoke, it was by rote, without feeling. "It's completely unfair," she said.

Rebecca leaned away to look at her squarely. "Sophie's probably dead, too," she said. "You know that, don't you? I mean, I really hope she's not, but you'd better get yourself ready to hear that news. Prepare yourself. I wasn't ready for it...for this."

What could she say to that? Janine wanted to respond to Rebecca's cruel remark with one equally as hurtful, but she knew the grief-stricken woman was only speaking out of pain. So she said nothing, just leaned her head against Rebecca's, rocking her gently while she cried, and hating her just a little for suggesting that Sophie had met the same fate as her daughter.

Upstairs, she'd found Lucas in his room, sitting in the dark by the window. "How are they doing?" he asked when she walked in.

"I'm angry that they don't have people out looking for Sophie during the night," she said instead of answering his question. She sat down on his bed, but was up again instantly. "This will be her third night alone out there. She hates the dark."

Lucas nodded. "I remember the night you two were at the tree house and the lights went out."

Janine could not help but smile at the memory. Sophie had panicked in the darkness, which had been truly impenetrable and eerie in the woods behind Lucas's house. But Lucas had lit candles and told Sophie a story about a girl who lived in a tree house who had tried to read a book using only lightning as her source of light. So only a few words here and there were legible to her, and it made for a very funny story. Sophie had giggled. She always thought there was something magical about Lucas.

But Lucas wasn't with Sophie in these West Virginia woods.

"She must be terrified out there," Janine had said, looking out the window into the darkness. Lucas had not replied, and she'd wondered if he thought she was deluding herself. Did he, like

Rebecca, think Sophie was dead? Is that what he was thinking about now, as they waited for Joe and Paula in the parking lot?

"I wish they'd hurry up." She looked up at the door to Joe's motel room.

"I bet he's not pleased at finding you in my room last night," Lucas said.

She hadn't thought about that. Joe must have gone to her room first only to find it empty and then realized she was with Lucas.

"He probably didn't give it a second thought," she said. "He was just thinking about Sophie, like I was."

"I wouldn't be so sure of that," Lucas said, turning at the sound of Joe's motel door opening. They watched as Joe and Paula made their way down the three flights of stairs. Paula was carrying a coffee cup in her hand.

"Morning," Joe said as he neared his car. He clicked the remote button on his key chain, and the locks on the car doors popped open.

Lucas held the back door open for Janine, and she slid across the seat. "Do you remember the way?" she asked Joe once he was in the car.

"I think so," he replied, and he turned the key in the ignition and headed out of the parking lot.

The road was once again blocked off with orange cones, but this time, the barrier was at the entrance to the road, a mile or so from the site of the accident. A uniformed guard let them pass through the barrier when Joe identified himself.

The dawn light dappled the road as they drove along its twists and turns. As they approached the accident site, they began to pass cars and vans parked helter-skelter along the route.

"There's the trailer," Paula said, pointing ahead of them. A white trailer was parked next to the embankment, directly across the road from where the Honda had been found.

Joe maneuvered his car as close to the trailer as he could get, but there were so many other vehicles in the road, that he still had to park a good distance away. Janine was touched and heartened to see dozens of people milling about. Some wore uniforms of one sort or another; others looked like hikers readying for a day on the trail. A few of them had bloodhounds and German shepherds at their sides. Suddenly, she felt less alone.

"I'll go see what's happening," she said, jumping out of the car before Joe had even come to a complete stop. She ran toward the trailer, up the step and through the open door.

Inside, a woman and a man were leaning over a counter, studying a map. Another woman sat at a built-in desk, working on a laptop computer. All three of them looked up when Janine walked in.

"I'm Sophie's mother," she said. "Janine Donohue."

The woman studying the map walked toward her, hand outstretched in greeting, and she squeezed Janine's hand rather than shook it.

"I'm Valerie Boykin," she said. "I'm the search manager in charge of the search for your daughter."

"Great, thank you," Janine said.

Valerie was a tall, big-boned woman with short dark hair. She looked like the sort of take-charge person who could succeed at any task she chose to undertake.

"What do we do first?" Janine asked.

"Is your husband with you?" Valerie looked toward the door of the trailer. "Then I can explain everything to both of you at the same time."

Janine followed her gaze through the door, just as Joe, Paula and Lucas were approaching the steps.

"Here they are now," she said. She made the introductions, and then Valerie took them to one end of the trailer, where uncomfortable seats were built into the walls. They sat down to listen, as she described the form the search would take.

"We've called in search teams from this part of the state, and a few from across the border in Virginia. They've been arriving for the last few hours. They—"

"Valerie?" The man in the trailer called to her, and Valerie looked in his direction.

"Yes?" she asked.

"The guy's here with the portable toilets. Where do you want them?"

"You decide," Valerie said, her voice tinged with annoyance at the interruption. She returned her attention to Janine and the others.

"So, we'll be using a task force approach. That means, we'll combine different types of resources to improve the odds of finding clues. We'll start out with the dogs, breaking the terrain down into a grid so each dog and handler will have their own area to cover. Then, a short distance behind them will be the ground searchers. This way, the dogs don't get confused by the scents of the ground searchers."

"Can we help with the ground search?" Janine asked.

Valerie shook her head. "These people are specially trained. They'll be looking for footprints and other clues."

"I thought we could get out there in the woods and help to look," Joe said.

"You'll have to trust us on this, Joe," Valerie said. "I know it's hard to sit and wait, but that's going to be your job. Oh, and hold on a second." Valerie walked to the other end of the trailer and returned a moment later carrying a large white plastic garbage bag. She held it open in front of Janine.

A charred smell filled Janine's nostrils, but it took her only a second to recognize the burned contents of the bag as Sophie's backpack.

"That's Sophie's!" she said, arms outstretched to receive the plastic bag and its contents.

"Right," Valerie said. "It was in the trunk, so it was not completely destroyed. If you don't mind, take a look through it and pick out a couple of things that might still have Sophie's scent on them."

Janine's hand shook as she struggled to unzip the charred

backpack, still inside the garbage bag. Lifting Sophie's Winnie the Pooh T-shirt from the pack, she raised it to her nose.

"Oh, God." She pressed the shirt to her face again to breathe in her daughter, then handed the shirt to Valerie. "I know this smells mostly like smoke," she said, "but Sophie's smell is just beneath it."

Valerie nodded. "We'll see how the dogs do with it." She took the backpack and garbage bag away from Janine and placed them on the floor of the trailer. "There's one more thing you should know about," she continued. "I don't think this will actually affect our search in any way, but, we just need to be aware of it."

"What's that?" Joe asked.

"You know Zoe? The actress?" Valerie asked.

They nodded, and Janine frowned. Zoe was dead. What could she possibly have to do with Sophie being lost in the woods?

"Well, her daughter—Martina Garson—was convicted of murdering another actress. You might remember—"

"Tara Ashton," Paula said, and Janine remembered the graphic descriptions of the bludgeoning death of the young actress and the well-publicized trial that followed it.

"What does this have to do with Sophie?" she asked.

"Well, about five days ago, Martina Garson escaped from prison in California. She was helped by one of the wardens there, and the authorities figured that the two of them were traveling together. You know, on the run together. Last night, some hikers came across a car on a dirt road about twelve miles from here, as the crow flies. On the other side of this piece of forest." Valerie pointed in the general direction of woods. "Inside the car was a man, shot to death. He's been identified as the warden."

Janine glanced at Lucas, who wore a frown. "What does that mean?" she asked Valerie.

"Well, we're pretty sure it means that Martina Garson shot and killed the warden, for whatever reason. She had definitely been in the car with him. There were beer cans and other paraphernalia with her prints on them. Maybe they had a fight. No one really knows. Maybe she just used him to get across the country and didn't need him anymore. At any rate, the speculation is that she killed him, then took off on foot."

"But that's twelve miles from here," Joe said. "What does that have to do with finding Sophie?"

"Probably very little," Valerie admitted. "But there'll be a search for Garson starting from that dirt road, just like there's one starting from here for Sophie. And, yes, twelve miles is a good distance, but desperate people can cover a lot of miles pretty quickly. The point is, we're going to have to be careful. Garson's considered armed and dangerous. We don't want our searchers to be in jeopardy."

"Is Sophie in any danger from her?" Janine asked.

Valerie chewed on her lower lip for a moment before answering. "Mrs. Donohue," she said. "Janine. Based on the evidence from the Honda... It was completely demolished...."

"I know," Janine said impatiently. "We saw it."

"Well, based on the condition of the Honda and the trauma suffered by the other two victims, it's our best guess that Sophie would have been very severely injured in the crash. I doubt she could have gotten far enough to be in danger from Garson."

"You think she's dead," Janine said, the words more of an accusation than a statement.

"We're operating on the assumption that she's still alive," Valerie said. "But we will have dogs out there who are trained to find the deceased in case—"

"And dogs who are trained to find the living, too, I hope," Janine said. She felt Lucas rest his hand against her back. "I know Sophie's still alive," she said. "I could feel her when I was down there by the car yesterday."

Valerie nodded, although Janine figured the search manager now thought she had a lunatic mother on her hands.

"If she's alive, we will find her," Valerie said. "But you should know that the dogs are going to have some problems today, unfortunately. The rain we had yesterday will make it harder for them to pick up a scent. And more rain is predicted for this afternoon."

"What are the woods like around here?" Paula asked. "Do any people live nearby?"

"No," Valerie said. "The woods are very dense, which can also be a problem for the dogs. There are a few old abandoned buildings...shacks, really, here and there. But no one lives up here anymore."

"What about animals?" Janine asked.

"The usual. Deer. Some bears, but you don't see them much. Hikers have seen an occasional mountain lion, but that's really rare."

"What about using a helicopter?" Janine asked.

"Too dense," Valerie said.

"Val?" A man poked his head inside the door of the trailer, and Valerie waved at him.

"Be right there," she said, then turned back to them. "I have to go. My suggestion to you folks is that you either go back to the motel and get some sleep or—"

"No way," Janine said. Was this woman nuts?

"Then make yourselves at home out there on the road. You can come into the trailer from time to time if you need to get out of the sun or whatever, but it'll get too cramped for all of you to stay in here. We've got some folding chairs you can use if you like."

"Valerie?" the man called again.

"I've got to go," she repeated. "Let me know where you are at all times, and I'll keep you posted on how we're progressing."

She walked away from them, and Janine looked at Lucas.

"Now what?" she said.

"Now we make ourselves at home out on the road, I guess," he answered, getting to his feet.

* * *

They borrowed the folding chairs and set them up near the embankment. Paula drove Joe's car into the nearest town to buy snacks, insect repellent and sunscreen, even though the road would be in the shade for most of the day. Janine protested the purchase of sunscreen.

"We aren't going to be out here that long," she said. She truly believed what she was saying. There were so many searchers coming into the area, and so many dogs, that it seemed impossible to her that Sophie would not be found within minutes.

But the morning wore on, the hours ticking by with no news from Valerie, although searchers regularly stopped into the trailer to talk with her. At one o'clock, Janine's parents arrived. They were solemn and scared, and they doled out the more comfortable chairs they'd brought with them, along with sandwiches and drinks. They'd also brought shopping bags containing new T-shirts and shorts for Janine, Joe and Paula, and not so much as the time of day for Lucas. They parked their chairs close to Joe and Paula, and Janine could hear Joe filling them in on the mechanics of the search.

"We heard about Zoe's daughter on the radio while we were driving out here," Janine's mother said. "She's right in this area."

"Not really," Joe said. "She's at least twelve miles from here."

"Not far enough," her father said.

"Zoe could never accept the fact that her daughter was guilty," her mother continued.

Paula swallowed a bite of her sandwich. "I thought there was reasonable doubt," she said.

"Zoe's life just became so tragic," her mother said.

"Well, she sure got carried away with that plastic surgery," Janine's father added. "She didn't even look like herself anymore."

"But she probably felt as though she had to do it," Paula said. "Her fans expected her to look good all the time."

Janine tried to tune out the inane conversation as she shared her sandwich with Lucas. He looked very tired, and she supposed that her eyes looked just as swollen, her face just as drawn, as his did.

At three o'clock, Valerie finally came out of the trailer to talk to them. She was carrying something in her hand. A cell phone, Janine thought.

"No real news," Valerie said before they could ask. "I just want to get a little more information about Sophie from you."

Janine's father stood up to offer Valerie his chair, but she waved away the gesture, and when she did so, Janine recognized the object in her hand.

"That's Sophie's hiking shoe!" She jumped to her feet.

"That's one of the things I wanted to ask you," Valerie said, handing the shoe to her. It was dirty and soaking wet, but otherwise in good shape. "It's hers?"

"Yes! Absolutely." Janine held the shoe to her chest like a treasure.

"Where did you find it?" Joe asked.

"Only about twenty feet from the accident site," Valerie said. "We haven't been able to find anything else, though."

"You said you wanted some more information about Sophie?" Lucas prompted her.

Valerie nodded. "Well, first of all, let me say that we're very concerned that we haven't found her yet. Given that she's probably injured, and missing at least one of her shoes, we don't see how she could have gotten too far."

"What are you saying?" Joe asked.

"Just that we have to entertain the possibility that she might have...succumbed to her injuries and been found by an animal, and—"

"Don't give up on her," Janine said. "Please."

"No, we're not giving up. We're just exploring all possible explanations for why we haven't found her yet, with this many people looking for her. We rely on statistics to tell us how a lost person might behave," she continued. "A child between the ages of six and twelve will usually try to use the path of least resistance. Unfortunately, there aren't any trails down there, so that makes it tough, both for her and for our searchers."

"Could she have walked on the road instead of through the woods?" Janine's father asked.

"We speculate that Sophie wouldn't have been able to get up to the road from the accident site," Valerie said. "It's just too steep. But we're still searching the roads, just in case she did. We've divided them up for three miles in all directions. But whether she's on the road or in the woods, a healthy child Sophie's age will usually be found within two miles of where they were last seen. It's really, really rare to find them any farther away than that. And Sophie isn't healthy."

"But you'll look farther than that, won't you?" Janine asked.

"Yes, we will, of course, if we don't find her closer in," Valerie said. "We don't give up on trying to find anyone, Janine. Especially not a child."

Joe and Paula, along with Janine's parents, returned to the motel around six o'clock, but Janine and Lucas remained at the command post until eight, when a thunderstorm forced the searchers out of the woods for the night. They drove back to the motel in silence in Joe's car, which he'd left behind for them to use.

Janine didn't have the energy to bother with pretense, so she didn't even stop in her own motel room before going to Lucas's. She lay next to him in his bed, her body limp with exhaustion. Every time she closed her eyes, she saw the white trailer, the searchers in their hiking boots, the well-trained dogs with the anticipatory look in their eyes, and the deep woods that had swallowed Sophie whole.

"I need to go back to Vienna tomorrow," Lucas said suddenly.

They'd talked for a while, but had fallen into a long, discouraged silence, and Janine was as startled by the sound of his voice as she was by the words themselves.

"Why?" she asked.

"Just for the day," he said. His arm was around her shoulders, and he tightened it in comfort. "I have some business I need to attend to. But I wanted to suggest that you go with me, and we—"

"*What* business?" she asked. "What can be more important than being out here right now?"

"It's not more important," Lucas said, "but it's something I have to take care of, and I can't do it from here."

There had always been a secret side to Lucas. Usually, that didn't bother her, but right now she was annoyed.

"Is it related to finding another job?" she asked. How could he even talk about leaving?

Lucas sighed. "No," he said. "There's a project I'm working on with some other people. We're working some things out on-line, and they're waiting for me to get back to them with some information."

"We can get a laptop somewhere," she offered.

Lucas shook his head. "All my material is in the tree house," he said. "I'm sorry, but I'll have to go back. And I thought it would be good if you went with me—"

"I can't leave here." There was anger in her voice, and he hesitated before speaking again.

"There's so little you can do here, sweetheart," he said finally. "The search will go on without you, and my idea was that you could go to Dr. Schaefer's office and get some of the herb stuff...Herbalina...so that if...*when* they find Sophie, it could be immediately administered to her. Also, I'll have to rent a car to go back to Virginia. I can drop it off in Vienna, then we could bring my car...or your car...back. That way, we'd have a car here."

He'd lost her with all the talk about cars. She was still thinking about having Herbalina here, with her, ready for one of the paramedics to infuse into Sophie. She kissed Lucas's cheek. "Thank you," she said.

"For what?"

"For believing that Sophie will be found alive. I felt like I was the only person who still thought that was possible. And for believing in Herbalina."

"I've seen with my own eyes the change it made in her."

"So has Joe," she said. "So have my parents. But that doesn't make any difference to them."

"So," Lucas said. "Will you go with me?"

"Yes," she said, and she pulled herself closer to him, shutting her eyes. She would try to sleep, praying that sleep would be interrupted sometime during the night with the good news she longed to hear.

CHAPTER TWENTY–TWO

Zoe opened her eyes as soon as the birds started singing their tribute to the morning. Light was only beginning to filter into the room, and from her sleeping palette she could see a cardinal in the tree outside the screened window. When she'd first arrived at the shanty, she'd found some old screening half buried in the ground near the outhouse and had nailed it up to the two windows in the bedroom to try to keep the mosquitoes out. Probably pointless, since the other windows in the house had no screens, but it made her feel good to be able to give Marti some space in the house that would be free of insects.

It was a moment before Zoe remembered she was not alone. The memory of the little girl crept so slowly into her mind that when she lifted her head to look at the sleeping palette across the room from hers, she almost expected to see it empty and the child gone, as if she'd imagined her. But there she was, her body so small it barely elevated the lavender sheet above the bed. The little girl was turned on her side, away from Zoe, and her hair lay in red waves on her pillow.

Zoe rested her head on her own pillow again and shut her eyes. What was she going to do with this child? And just how sick was she? When she'd gotten up from her long nap the day before, Sophie had managed to keep her eyes open only long enough for Zoe to wash and bandage her cut—and possibly infected— foot before tumbling back in bed again. She'd slept through dinner, through the evening, through the night, as though making up for the three nights she'd suffered in the woods alone.

She was a sweet girl, a smart girl, and all she wanted was to go home. But Zoe was not sure how to make that happen without putting herself and her own daughter in the gravest jeopardy.

Sometime during the night, she'd come up with a plan: she and Sophie would walk the five miles through the forest to the road, leaving a note for Marti, in case she arrived while Zoe was gone. She would have to fashion some sort of shoe for Sophie's left foot. Even so, that foot was so bruised and damaged by her three days alone, that Zoe wasn't sure how the little girl would manage one mile on the rough forest floor, much less five. But never mind. That was the least of their problems. She would carry the girl if she had to.

So, she would take the girl to the road. It was a little used road, and they might have to wait awhile for someone to come along. As soon as they saw a car, Zoe would hide, and Sophie could wave it down. She'd have to explain all of this to Sophie ahead of time, of course, so Sophie wouldn't give her away. It worried Zoe to let the little girl get into a car with a stranger who might not have her best interest at heart, but there was no other way this could be done.

There was one other problem, though. A big one: Sophie had recognized her.

Over their afternoon snack the day before, Zoe had caught the child staring at her across the firepit.

"You're the most beautiful lady I've ever seen," Sophie had said, and Zoe could not help but be flattered that a child would find her, at sixty years old, befitting of that compliment.

"You look just like Zoe," the girl went on, and Zoe's pleasure gave way to fear.

"I've been told that before," she said, dismayed that, even with her blond hair chopped off to her chin, even with the stripe of gray at her roots and without makeup, she could be recognized by an eight-year-old child. "I don't see the resemblance myself, personally," she said.

"You look *exactly* like her," Sophie said. "Like she looked in that Christmas movie."

"Oh, yes, I remember that movie," Zoe said. She had taken a role in that PG movie at Max's insistence, although she'd balked at playing a grandmother. A stylish pip of a grandmother, to be sure, but a grandma nevertheless.

So, a kind driver who picked Sophie up would take her to the police station or sheriff's office or whatever they had out here, and then Sophie would tell them that a woman who looked exactly like Zoe had taken care of her in the woods. Not such a problem, she thought. People thought Zoe had been dead for months, and even if someone doubted that fact, they'd never guess that she would hole herself up out here in no-man's-land.

"I think you really are Zoe."

Zoe started now at the sound of Sophie's voice. She turned her head to see that the girl had rolled over on her sleeping palette and was staring at her.

"Well," Zoe said, sitting up. "You certainly had a good long sleep. How do you feel this morning?"

"I saw you from the side," Sophie said. "You have that little bump on your nose, just like Zoe."

She thought of arguing, of telling her that any number of people had that little bump on their noses, but she could see by Sophie's face that the child would not be fooled.

"You're right, honey," she said with a sigh. "I am Zoe."

Sophie sat up, a grin on her face. "I knew it!" she said. She was so damn cute when she grinned, that Zoe had to smile herself.

"And I have a favor to ask of you," Zoe said. "A very big favor."

"What?"

"Today I plan to walk with you out to the road and—"

"Through the woods?" Sophie's smile faded.

"Yes. It's a long way. But that's the only way to get you out of here."

"I can't go into the woods again." Sophie's face paled at the thought, her freckles standing out against her skin.

"It's the only way out, Sophie. I can't think of another way."

Sophie said nothing, but the small crease between her eyebrows deepened.

"I will take you to the road. But...this is a little hard to explain...I don't want anyone to ever know that I'm here. It's very important. So I have to ask you not to tell anyone that you saw me here. It has to be our secret, okay?"

"Who should I say gave me this shirt to wear?" Sophie held her arm up in the air, and the rolled-up sleeve of Zoe's blue shirt slipped down to her shoulder.

"You can tell them a lady in the woods helped you. Just not who that lady was. Okay?"

"Why don't you want anyone to know?"

Zoe guessed that Sophie had never heard about her suicide, and there was no point in bringing that up. "It's too hard to explain," she said. "I got very tired of being recognized everywhere I went, so I just wanted to be someplace where I wouldn't see anyone for a while."

"Oh." Sophie nodded, as though she completely understood.

"So here's what we'll do," Zoe said. "I'll make some breakfast for us, and then we'll make some kind of shoe for you to wear, and then we'll start walking."

Sophie looked out the window, where the trees formed a green wall against the rest of the world. To Zoe, those trees were her camouflage, but she tried to see them through Sophie's eyes. How frightening it must have been for her to spend three days alone, able to see nothing but the thick, ghostly forest no matter which way she had turned.

"Please," Sophie said. "Can't you find a phone somewhere and get somebody to come here and get me? I don't want to go into the woods again." Her lower lip was trembling.

Zoe sat up on her air mattress and ran her hands through her hair. "I think you're a very brave girl, Sophie," she said. "Or else you wouldn't have made it for three days all by yourself in the woods. This time, you'll have me with you, honey. You won't be alone. And it will be daylight. You'll be fine."

Sophie looked toward the trees again. "Is there a courage tree out there?"

"A courage tree?" Zoe asked. "What's that?"

"It's a tall tree with big sort of leaves, and it has these flower kind of things on it that fall to the ground. Lucas...that's my mom's boyfriend...says that if you put a flower from the courage tree under your pillow while you sleep, you'll be braver when you wake up."

"Well, I don't know," Zoe said. She thought of the trees she'd seen in the forest. She'd never known much about trees and plants, especially those that grew in the east. "Does it have another name?" she asked.

"I don't know," Sophie said. "I think it's just called a courage tree."

"And does it really work? Putting the flower under your pillow?"

Sophie nodded. "Lucas brings me one the night before I get Herbalina—that's a medicine—and then I'm not afraid to take it. They put it in your veins." She lifted her arm into the air again, and Zoe could see the small, dark bruise near her wrist.

She felt a prickle of fear. The catheter, the dialysis and now this. "Is that medicine—Herbalina—for your kidneys?" she asked.

"Yes."

"How often do you need to get it?"

"Mondays and Thursdays. But I also take a lot of other medicines every day, to help me grow bigger and to keep me from getting too much phosphorus and potassium. I don't have them with me, though. I had enough for camp and that was all."

"Wow," Zoe said. "You sure do know a lot about your medicine."

"My mom teaches me all about it," Sophie said.

"Today is Thursday," Zoe said. "You're supposed to get that Herbalina today, I guess."

"I missed Monday, too," Sophie said, "but I don't feel bad, so maybe I don't need it anymore."

Then again, Zoe thought, maybe she did.

"I tell you what," Zoe said. "You go use the outhouse and wash your face with some water from the pump out front, and I'll see if I can find a courage tree flower for you. Then you can carry it with you when we walk through the woods."

"But I have to sleep on it for it to work."

Zoe felt her patience slipping, ever so slightly. "You can take a little nap, then, before we go," she suggested. A very little nap, she thought. They needed to leave soon if she hoped to get back to the shanty before dark.

Sophie looked dubious. "Okay," she said.

Zoe dressed and walked out to the clearing, where she started the fire and put a pot of water on to boil. Then she walked into the woods. It was a beautiful morning, and she and the birds had the forest to themselves, but there was little time to enjoy her surroundings.

The forest was so dense here that there weren't very many blooming things. She picked one of everything she could find that could possibly be construed as a flower. There were white lacy blooms in the shape of small pom-poms and large, purple flowers that she thought were rhododendrons. Small blue flowers grew like weeds under one particular tree, and in one area, large green-and-salmon-colored seed pods were scattered on the ground. She carried her bounty back to the clearing, hoping she'd managed to find at least one blossom that would sufficiently resemble the flower from Sophie's courage tree.

She found Sophie still in the shanty, still sitting on her sleeping palette.

"I was afraid to go to the outhouse by myself," she admitted.

"Well, maybe one of these will help." Zoe spread her hands out in front of her, the flowers covering her palms and her fingers.

"That's it!" Sophie said, reaching for the green-and-salmon seed pod. She kissed it and put it beneath her pillow, and Zoe smiled. The child really was quite adorable.

"Do you think you'll be able to take a nap right after breakfast?" Zoe asked. "You've already slept so long."

"I think so," Sophie said. "And maybe it will work if I just lie down on it awhile without sleeping."

"Come on," Zoe said. "I'll walk you to the outhouse."

Sophie stepped off the bed, yelping when her bandaged left foot hit the floor. She lifted the foot up instantly, as though she'd stepped on a bee, and Zoe could see that it was swollen, the skin puffy around the gauze. *Damn.* How would she ever be able to walk through the woods with her foot in such terrible shape?

"You and I will have to put our heads together and come up with a creative solution to this problem," Zoe said. "We'll have to be cobblers. Shoemakers."

"I know what a cobbler is." Sophie looked insulted that Zoe had felt it necessary to define the word for her.

"Well, let's figure out the solution over breakfast," she said. "Your clothes are probably dry by now. I'll get them for you, and I'll give you a pair of my underwear to put on. They'll be way too big for you, but better than nothing."

"Do you know where my penknife is?" Sophie asked.

"It was in the pocket of your shorts," Zoe said. "I put it on the front porch."

Zoe walked into the living room, where she picked up a box of instant oatmeal from the shelf she'd formed from crates and rotting wood. Outside, she started a fire in the fire pit, then gathered up Sophie's clothes and her penknife from the porch and carried them back into the bedroom.

Outside again, she cooked the oatmeal over the fire, and after a moment, Sophie hobbled out of the shanty and joined her on the flat rocks. Zoe scooped some of the oatmeal into a bowl and handed it to the little girl, along with a spoon.

"Are your parents divorced, Sophie?" she asked as they ate. "You said Lucas is your mom's boyfriend."

Sophie nodded. "Yup. My mom's boyfriend is Lucas. He lives in a tree house—"

"No!" Zoe said.

"Yes, he really does. He has a regular house in front of it, but he hardly ever uses it. And my dad has a friend named Paula, but she's not an actual girlfriend."

"Do you get along with them? Lucas and Paula?"

Sophie nodded. "Yeah. They're really nice to me."

"And what's your mom like?"

"Oh." Sophie dipped her spoon into the oatmeal. "She's nice, and she takes good care of me when I'm sick. She used to fly a helicopter when I was little, but now she just stays home with me."

A good mom, Zoe thought. Not the sort of mother she had been.

"And your daddy?"

"He's an accountant. He handles money."

Zoe had to smile at her again. She sounded so grown-up. "What grade are you in?" she asked.

"Second. Since I've been getting Herbalina, I've been able to go to school. Before that, this lady—a home teacher—would come and help me do my schoolwork at home."

Sophie must have been very seriously ill, Zoe realized. Perhaps she still was, since she still had that catheter coming out of her stomach. "How long have you been sick?" she asked.

"Since I was three, but I started getting *really* sick when I was five. So, I never got to go to school for more than a couple of weeks, anyway."

"It must have been hard to make friends, then."

"Oh, I had friends in the hospital. And I have friends at Dr. Schaefer's office, and in my Brownie troop." Her face darkened, and tears filled her eyes. "I think Holly is really, truly dead," she said, and Zoe struggled to remember who Holly was.

"You mean the other little girl in the car with you?"

Sophie nodded, swallowing hard. "I don't know how I got out and she didn't. She must've been scared when she was burning up."

Zoe moved next to her, putting an arm around her. "I'm glad you got out, Sophie," she said. "You were very lucky. And very, very brave to survive in the forest. And I'll get you home, honey, by hook or crook."

"What's that mean?"

"It's just an expression."

Sophie set her bowl down. "I'm going to take a nap on the courage tree flower now," she said. "When I get up, we can go, all right?"

"You bet," Zoe said. "Sleep tight."

Sophie started walking toward the shanty, then suddenly stopped. "I never did go to the outhouse," she said. "I completely forgot."

Zoe started to get to her feet. "I'll take you," she said.

"No, I can go by myself." She looked toward the rear of the

shanty, where the outhouse was hidden behind some trees. "So long as you'll be right here."

"I'll be here," Zoe promised.

She sat a while longer on the flat rock, trying to figure out what material she could use to make Sophie a shoe. She had brought three pairs of walking shoes with her and one pair of good hiking boots. Sophie's feet were a lot smaller than hers, of course, but with the swelling and the bandage, and with a little extra stuffing, perhaps one of the walking shoes would work for her.

Zoe was carrying the bowls over to the pump when she heard the sound of crackling twigs in the forest behind her. Dropping the bowls to the ground, she ran to the shanty and grabbed her rifle where it rested against the step. She raised it to her face, her fear mixing with relief, as the rustling sound grew nearer. It would be best if the intruders were searching for Sophie, she thought. She'd do the mountain mama routine, Sophie's rescuers would take her away, and she wouldn't have to make that ten-mile, round-trip trek through the forest. Even better, she wouldn't have to worry about Marti arriving at the shanty to find her gone.

She stood frozen, the rifle pointed in the direction of the sound, and saw a flicker of yellow cloth darting through the trees. Then suddenly, Marti burst out of the woods and began running toward her.

"Marti!" Zoe lowered the rifle to the ground and moved forward to embrace her daughter. "Oh, honey, you made it!" she cried. "You're so thin!" Marti was skin and bones beneath Zoe's hands.

"Oh, God, Mom." Marti clung to her. "I was in the woods all night! I never expected that. It was horrible. I had no flashlight or anything. You should have left me a flashlight."

A flashlight! Of course. Why hadn't she thought of that?

"Well, you're here now," Zoe said. "You're safe." She had just uttered these words to Sophie, who had spent *three* nights alone in the forest without a flashlight. "Why didn't you have the warden drop you off early this morning? Then you could have walked through the woods in daylight."

"I had to do whatever he said, Mom." Marti pulled away from her, eyes downcast, and she waved her hands in the air as she spoke. For the first time, Zoe noticed that she was holding a gun.

"Where did you get the gun?" she asked.

"I managed to take it from him. From Angelo, the warden." Marti sat down on one of the flat rocks. "You tied those blue cloths way too tight, Mom," she said. "It took me forever to untie them all."

"I'm sorry," Zoe said. "I wanted to make sure they didn't come off the branches."

"No way they'd ever come off without someone untying them." Marti rested her head on her hand. She looked truly exhausted, wasting away and pale, as fragile as she'd looked toward the end of the trial.

Zoe noticed the gun again. "What did you mean, you took the gun from the warden?" she asked. "You mean, by force? He got the money, didn't—"

Leaves rustled on the other side of the shanty, and Marti's eyes widened in terror. She stood up quickly, lifting the gun with both hands, like a well-trained cop—or a seasoned criminal—aiming it at the corner of the building just as Sophie appeared. Zoe darted forward to grab Marti's arm.

"Don't shoot her!" she said.

Sophie stood at the edge of the clearing, her bandaged foot off the ground, her arms once again rising in the air, and a look of frozen terror on her face.

"Who the hell is that?" Marti said, lowering the gun in front of her.

"Put the gun down, Marti," Zoe commanded. "All the way down."

Marti set the gun on the ground, and Sophie slowly lowered her hands to her sides.

"Come here, Sophie." Zoe waved the girl toward them, and Sophie edged forward slowly. "Everyone's pointing guns at you these days, aren't they, honey?" she said, working to get a light-hearted tone in her voice, even though her whole body was trembling from Marti's reaction to the unexpected guest. She hugged Sophie with an arm around her narrow, bony shoulders.

"Sophie, this is my daughter, Marti," she said. "Marti, this is Sophie. She got lost in the woods a few days ago and found her way here. I'm planning to walk her up to the road and—"

"You're *what?*" Marti exclaimed.

"Sophie and I have already talked about it. I'll hide and let someone else pick her up to take her to the police," Zoe assured her quickly. "And Sophie understands that I don't want anyone to know she's met me, don't you, Sophie?"

Sophie was staring, riveted, at Marti, but she managed a nod.

"Mother, you cannot do that," Marti said. "They're going to be looking for me. They'll be all over these woods. They probably are already."

"Why would they be looking for you?" Zoe asked. She felt Sophie sidle closer to her. "How would they know to look for you here?"

"They just do," Marti said.

"Listen, Marti." Zoe's anxiety was rising. "You'd better tell me what's going on. You took the gun from the warden, and...I just don't understand. Did something go wrong with the plan?"

Marti laughed. "I'd say that."

"Okay," Zoe said. "Let's just cool our heads about this. Everybody sit down. Pick a rock." She sat down on the nearest flat rock, and Sophie sat down right next to her.

"Not out here in the open," Marti said.

"This is hardly 'the open,'" Zoe countered.

"Mother, you don't get it. We need to go inside."

It would be easier to follow Marti inside the shanty than to fight her. With a sigh, Zoe got to her feet and walked toward the shanty with one protective arm around Sophie, who was hopping along next to her to avoid putting any weight on her swollen foot. Zoe had to help her up the porch stairs. How she was going to get this girl over five miles of forest floor was anyone's guess.

"Oh, my God, you've actually been *living* here?" Marti asked, once they were in the small front room with its sheet-covered sofa, makeshift shelves and filthy walls. "This place is probably crawling with vermin, Mother. There are no screens in the windows."

Zoe laughed, a bit uncomfortably. "Well, yes, that's true," she admitted. "There's not even any glass in the windows, for that matter." She hoped Marti's sour mood was simply a product of her night in the woods and that it would soon lift. "I put some screens up in the bedroom, though."

"Where am I supposed to sit?" Marti looked helplessly around the room.

"The sofa is perfectly clean with that sheet on it," Zoe said, "and that chair is fine." She pointed to the wobbly old wooden chair in the corner. She watched her daughter lower herself gingerly onto the edge of the chair, while she herself sat on the couch. Sophie sat down so close to her that she was practically in Zoe's lap, and Zoe put her arm around her again.

"You're going to have to get used to a little dirt," Zoe said to Marti. "You'll have to adjust to less than perfect living conditions."

Marti looked at her angrily, her eyes filling with tears. "Don't talk to me about adjusting to less than perfect living conditions, Mother," she said. "You have no idea how I've been living. I've been in the slimiest, seediest, most abusive prison on the face of the earth."

Zoe regretted speaking so harshly. She had to remember that Marti had suffered, and suffered unfairly, paying for a crime she didn't commit because Zoe had hired sloppy lawyers to defend her. Marti looked unwell. Her hair was longer than it had been in years. Probably she had not had it cut since the trial. Its pretty blond color had faded, and even her huge blue eyes had lost their sheen.

"I'm sorry, hon," she said. "So, tell me everything. Tell me why you think anyone would be looking for you out here?"

Marti pulled a cigarette from the pack in her shirt pocket and lit it with a purple lighter. Zoe had never allowed her to smoke in the Malibu house, but figured it would be best if she simply bit her tongue about it now.

"I think they'll be looking for me because Angelo told me he was going to tell the police where he dropped me off."

"Why on earth would he do that?" Zoe asked. "He has the money, right? He'll only get himself in—"

"I don't know why." Marti sounded very tired. She rubbed her hands over her face. "I stopped trying to figure him out days ago. That's just what he told me."

"Oh, it sounds like he was shooting off his mouth, don't you think, Mart?"

"No, I don't think, Mom," she said sarcastically. She drew on her cigarette. "I think he's going to tell, and they're going to come looking."

"But then they'd pick him up, too."

"I know it doesn't make sense." Marti waved a dismissive hand in the air, and the ash of her cigarette fell on the floor.

She's going to burn this place down, Zoe thought.

"Maybe he'll call from a pay phone or something," Marti continued. "All I know is that the man hates me and has no scruples whatsoever."

"Well, even if he did call the authorities, he dropped you off by the barn, right?" Zoe asked. "And you walked back a mile to come into the woods, and we're a good ten miles deep into the forest, so it's unlikely—"

"They'll use dogs, Mother. They'll pick up my scent."

Dogs. She hadn't thought of that. "Well, what should we do?" she asked.

"Well, first and foremost, you're not going to leave me here alone and go take her—" she pointed at Sophie "—through the woods to the road."

"I have to," Zoe said. "I don't really have a choice."

"You shouldn't have let her come here."

"I didn't invite her, Marti. She's lost, do you understand? She just found her way here." Beneath her arm, she felt a shiver pass through Sophie's body, and she looked down to see the little girl crying. "It's okay, Sophie. We're going to work this out, honey. She was in an accident and got lost, Marti," Zoe repeated. "You know how you feel after spending one night in the woods? Well, Sophie spent three of them."

Marti looked at Sophie and seemed to soften at that information. "Okay," she said. "All right. But she'll just have to stay with us then. You can't take her—"

"No," Sophie whimpered.

"Marti, I'm going to fix her a shoe and walk her to the road," Zoe said firmly, "and the sooner I get going, the sooner I'll be back."

"Do you honestly expect her not to tell anyone that she met Zoe in the woods?" Marti asked. "And now she knows I'm here. They'll ask her a lot of questions, and—"

"I won't tell!" Sophie promised. "I'll just say a nice lady helped me."

"Right," Marti said. "And they think there's only one 'lady' running around out here in the woods, and that's me. So they'll pump you for information on the lady, and you'll screw up, and—"

"Marti, stop this," Zoe said. "Just calm down. Maybe we shouldn't make a decision about this right this second. I think we all need some time to adjust to what's happening here, okay?" She looked down at Sophie. "Okay, honey? Why don't you go take your nap now, with your courage flower, and when you get up, I'll tell you what we've decided to do. Maybe you should take a nap, too, Marti." She'd have to give up her air mattress to her daughter. She'd create a mattress for herself out of towels and clothing.

"Right." Marti drew on her cigarette again. "Like I could really sleep."

Sophie stood up and limped into the bedroom, closing the creaking door behind her.

"She's limping like crazy," Marti said. "How far is the road?"

"It's a ways," Zoe said. "Five miles. I'll have to make her a crutch or something."

"You'll never get her to walk five miles with her foot like that."

Zoe sighed, afraid that Marti was right. Sophie was not complaining, but it was obvious that she could barely put any of her weight on her left foot.

Marti leaned forward, elbows on knees. "Mother, please. Please! I'm begging you. We can't let her go. We'll all have to stay together. They're going to be looking for me. And—" Marti's voice broke "—I can't go back there, Mother. I just can't," she said, as she lowered her head into her hands. She was crying, her shoulders shaking with the tears, and Zoe could hardly bear the pain that coursed through her own body as she watched her.

"Forget about Sophie for right now," she said, leaning toward Marti from the sofa. "Tell me about *you*. Tell me what it was like for you at Chowchilla. How you got out. Tell me everything."

Marti raised her head again, wiping her face with her hands. Her cigarette had burned down to the filter, and she looked around for a place to stub it out. Zoe handed her one of the Kmart bowls from the shelf near the door.

"It was so bad, Mom," Marti said. "Worse than you can imagine. The food was gross, but that was the least of it. The other women..." She shook her head. "They're *real* criminals. I got thrown in with honest to goodness murderers. And, of course, I'd say I was innocent, that I hadn't done anything, that I was railroaded somehow, and they'd mock me and..." Marti looked out the window, and for a moment, seemed to lose her train of thought. "The lights were on, twenty-four-seven. Do you know how crazy that can make you? The noise...it echoed, all the time. A couple of women killed themselves while I was there, and believe me, I thought about it, too."

"Oh, Marti."

"They raped me," she said. "Every single night, and—"

"*Who* raped you?" Zoe asked, horrified.

"The guards." Marti looked at her, then lowered her eyes. "And there was nothing you could do about it. It's all a big game there. Everyone knows it's going on, and everyone's got a part in it. The prisoners are treated like shit. Like they're not even human. Like they're just put there for the guards' entertainment."

"Marti, I'm so sorry," Zoe said. "Come here and sit next to me." She patted the seat of the sofa next to her.

Marti left her chair and sat down next to her, and Zoe put her arm around her, kissed her temple. It felt alien to touch her daughter that way. There had never been much physical affection between them. But she was determined to change that, and she was relieved that Marti seemed to accept the gesture, that she actually seemed to *want* it.

"I wish I could have prevented you from having to go there," Zoe said. "I felt so helpless."

"It was even worse for me 'cause I'm your daughter," Marti continued, her voice thick. "Like, somehow it made them more important to be able to say they fucked Zoe's daughter."

Zoe winced. "Oh, my darling," she said. "Being my daughter has always been a burden for you. I know that, and I'm sorry."

"Angelo was no better than the rest of them," Marti said. "I picked him because I knew he was the type to take a bribe, which meant he was an asshole to begin with. He made me have sex with him every single night we were on the road, Mom. Two or three times a night."

Zoe's fantasy of the companionable, cooperative warden-prisoner relationship evaporated.

"And he was slimy and disgusting. I'd have to go in the bathroom and puke afterward. Now all I want to do is take a long bath." She glanced around the room. "I suppose there's no tub here, huh?"

Zoe smoothed a stray strand of her daughter's hair back from her forehead. "Just an outhouse," she said, "but we have a pump. I can heat you some water if you'd like to—"

"No!" Marti stood up and walked to the open front door to look into the clearing. "No more fires, for heaven's sake. And we have to figure out what we'll do if anyone shows up here. We need a plan."

"First, let's clear things up about Sophie," Zoe said. "We can't keep her here, Marti. Think about it. Her family must know she's missing, so there are probably people searching for her, too. The sooner we get her up to the road and on her way, the better off we'll be."

"Mom!" Marti spun around to look at her. "She's gonna tell!"

"I don't think she will. I'll talk to her about it some more while we're walking. She's a nice little girl. She just wants to go home. I think she'd keep any secret I asked her to."

"Then you're crazy," she said.

"Listen to me, Mart," Zoe said. "She's sick. I don't know how sick, but she has something wrong with her kidneys. She even has a catheter coming out of her stomach."

"What's that?"

"A tube. It hooks her up to a machine that does the work of her kidneys for her."

Marti shook her head in disbelief. "Who the hell let her loose out here when she's that screwed up?"

"It really doesn't matter," Zoe said. "What matters is that I get her to the road, and that's what I'm going to do. That's final. If we leave right when she wakes up, I should be able to get her up there in a few hours and be back here before it gets dark."

"Fine," Marti said, her cheeks flaming. "If I'm not here when you get back, just assume they found me and took me back to prison for some more rape and battery." She stormed out of the shanty, trying to slam the door behind her, but it only creaked feebly against its old hinges.

Through the window behind the sofa, Zoe watched her run into the forest. She remembered Marti's teenage years, when she'd slam out of the house in a fury over some argument or another. She'd take off for a friend's house or to meet a sympathetic boyfriend on the beach, and Zoe would feel overwhelmed with helplessness—much the way she was feeling now.

This time, though, she knew Marti had nowhere to go.

CHAPTER TWENTY–THREE

"What do you mean, you're leaving?" Joe asked.

He was standing in front of Janine in the parking lot of the motel. It was Thursday morning, and Lucas had gotten a ride into town, where he planned to rent a car. Then he would return to the motel and pick her up.

"Lucas has to go back today, and—"

"So, let him go," Joe said.

She ignored the barb. "I'm going with him to get some of the medicine that Sophie's on, so when we find her, she'll be able to have it administered right away," she said. "We'll be back to-morrow morning."

She had spoken to Valerie Boykin, asking her if a paramedic would be able to administer Herbalina to Sophie. Valerie said they would need a prescription from the doctor to do so, but if they had that, it would be no problem. Yet, although Valerie was kind in her answers, Janine had the feeling that the search man-ager did not believe Sophie would ever get the chance to receive Herbalina—or any other medication, for that matter.

"Why does Lucas have to get back?" Joe asked. "He doesn't have a job."

"There's something important he needs to do." She wanted to

defend Lucas even though she, herself, had trouble understanding his insistence on going back to Vienna.

Her mother was walking down the motel stairs from the second story. "What's going on?" she asked, more to Joe than to Janine. She had circles under her eyes—just like the rest of them. "Have you heard anything?"

"Lucas needs to get back to Vienna, so Janine is going with him," Joe said.

"I hope he isn't hurrying back to his job at Ayr Creek," her mother said. "He realizes he no longer works there, doesn't he?"

"Yes, Mother," Janine said. "He knows."

"I don't think Lucas Trowell can stay in one place more than a few hours," her mother said. "He'd come to work, then he'd leave early. He comes here, then he leaves early. Why are you going with him, Janine? You follow him around like a puppy dog."

"Mom, Sophie's missing," Janine said. "I really don't feel like arguing about this."

"Sophie's missing *here,* in West Virginia, and you're going *home,* to Vienna, to be with your boyfriend," her mother said. "What kind of a mother are you?"

"Janine wants to get some of that herbal...medicine to give Sophie in case they can find her," Joe said. If he thought he was being helpful with that explanation, Janine thought bitterly, he was mistaken.

Her mother made a sound of disgust. "She's going to need dialysis the moment they find her, not herbs."

"Maybe she will," Janine said, "but I want to have Herbalina available for her, anyhow, just in case."

She spotted Lucas pulling into the parking lot in a white Taurus and walked rapidly toward the car without saying goodbye to either her mother or Joe. She was in the passenger seat before he even had a chance to open the door for her.

"Get me out of here," she said, fastening her seatbelt across her chest. "Please."

* * *

Two hours later, she and Lucas pulled into the parking lot of the medical building that housed Dr. Schaefer's office.

"Oh, my God," Janine said as she got out of the car.

"What is it?" Lucas asked her.

"I just realized that today is Thursday. Herbalina day. The kids in the study will be coming into Schaefer's office all day for their IVs."

"Is that a problem?"

"It's just that—" she closed the car door, but didn't move toward the building "—I'll see all these children and mothers that I know, that Sophie and I saw every Monday and Thursday, only this time I won't have Sophie with me."

Lucas walked around the car and pulled her gently into a hug. "Do you want me to go in to get the Herbalina?" he asked. "You could call Schaefer on your cell phone and tell him it's okay to give it to me."

She shook her head and glanced toward the building. "Maybe this is nuts," she stated. "I know Valerie Boykin thinks I'm crazy to bother getting Sophie's medicine. I know she thinks Sophie's dead. I'm afraid everyone who's searching thinks she's dead."

"No, they don't, Jan. You heard Valerie say that they'll go into this with the assumption she's alive."

"They have more dogs who sniff out dead people than those who find live people," she said.

"What makes you say that?"

"I counted."

"Oh, Jan." He hugged her again. "Don't do this to yourself. They're still calling in more search teams. They wouldn't be out there in such force if they didn't think there was a good chance she's alive."

"She *is* alive, Lucas. I know she is."

He nodded. "I trust your intuition," he said. "You and Sophie have a very strong bond, and if you're feeling something that tells you she's alive, then I'm willing to assume she is."

He put his arm around her and began walking with her toward the building. Inside, they took the elevator to Schaefer's office on the fourth floor.

The moment she saw Janine, Gina, Dr. Schaefer's nurse, left the reception desk to come into the empty waiting room.

"Is there any word?" she asked, her hands on Janine's arms.

"Not yet," Janine said.

"We're all praying for her," Gina said. Like Sophie, Gina had red hair, and Janine knew there was more than the usual nurse-patient relationship between Gina and Sophie. "She's a tough little girl," Gina continued. "If any child could survive in the woods, it would be Sophie."

"Thanks," Janine said. She put her hand on Lucas's shoulder. "You remember Lucas Trowell?" she asked. Lucas had come with her the first time Sophie had visited the office, the day before starting the treatment.

"Oh, of course," Gina said. "The courage tree guy."

Lucas smiled. "That's me," he said.

"Shall we sit down out here?" Janine asked. Even though the waiting room was empty, Janine knew Dr. Schaefer had plenty of patients in the large treatment room at the end of the hallway. Parents brought their children from as far away as California to participate in the study.

"No, don't sit," Gina said. "The moms want to see you. They all know. *Everyone* knows. It's been on the news every few minutes." She ushered Janine and Lucas down the hallway before either of them could protest. "You know, one good thing, at least it's summer and not one of the cooler months," she said, as they walked. "It gets so cold in the mountains at night in the spring and fall."

The treatment room was a good size, but it was cramped with eight recliners, against the walls set in a circle. Six of the recliners held small children, and next to each of them sat a parent—five mothers, one father—and every one of the adults jumped to their feet when Janine and Lucas entered the room. Janine was instantly surrounded, accepting their hugs and quiet expressions of concern and curiosity. It was the morning contingent of the kids in the study. Seven, including Sophie, received their IVs in the morning; eight received theirs in the afternoon.

Janine turned, ready to introduce Lucas to the parents, but he had moved away from her. He was sitting at the side of one of the little girls, talking with her, already intent in conversation. Surprised and touched by the scene, Janine returned to her conversation with the parents.

"I'm going to get some Herbalina, so that when they find her, they can administer it right away," she told them.

"Good idea," said Diana, one of the mothers, and the others echoed the sentiment.

"Have they found anything at all?" Gary, the lone father, asked. "Any clues?"

She shook her head. "Just her shoe, but that was pretty close to the crash site."

"We were so relieved to hear she wasn't the girl in the car," Lisa Pitts said, "though I just feel awful for that girl's parents."

Janine nodded, remembering Rebecca's anger and grief from the morning before. She should get in touch with her to see how she was doing, but she couldn't bring herself to make that call. After all, Sophie was still alive. She *was*. And Janine didn't want to hear any more of Rebecca's dire predictions.

Lucas came to stand at her side, and Janine introduced him to her friends.

"Are your kids doing as well on Herbalina as Sophie has?" he asked them.

Janine knew that the study participants had, in every case, improved greatly.

"It's been miraculous," Lisa said.

"Dr. Schaefer's a genius," said Diana.

"Jack only needed four hours of dialysis this week," Gary said, and Janine felt tears sting her eyes. She squeezed Gary's arm. Herbalina was a disease-altering treatment, no matter what Sophie's conventional physicians said. The ability for these children to get by on less dialysis simply had to be proof.

"That's so great," she said. "Sophie was down to two nights a week."

"What about side effects?" Lucas asked the parents. Janine loved his genuine interest. Joe never would have cared.

"Susan's had *major* side effects," said Bonnie Powell. "For example, she suddenly loves to eat, she's on her in-line skates round the clock, and she's happy all the time."

Lucas laughed. "That must be wonderful."

"What's that about Zoe's daughter being on the run near where Sophie is?" Diana asked.

"She escaped from prison," Gary said. "They think she killed the warden who helped her escape, and that she's in the same area as Sophie."

"It's a huge chunk of land," Lucas reminded them, touching Janine's arm in comfort. "If she's out there, she's miles away from where Sophie is."

"Whew, that's a relief," Bonnie said. "After what she did to that actress, I don't like the idea of her being anywhere near Sophie."

"She's not." Janine smiled, taking strength from Lucas's certainty that Martina Garson was no threat to her daughter.

Gina poked her head back in the room. "Dr. Schaefer has some Herbalina for you, Janine," she said. "Come into his office."

Janine looked at Lucas. "Come with me," she said, and he followed her down the hall and into Schaefer's office.

Dr. Schaefer got up from his desk and came forward to give Janine a hug, but he drew back when he noticed Lucas. The doctor had not been in the office during Lucas's previous visit, and

Janine figured that he thought Lucas was Joe. But then she remembered that Joe and Schaefer had met when Joe visited the doctor to lambaste him for putting Sophie in his study. She started to introduce the two men, but Lucas beat her to it.

"I'm Lucas Trowell," he said, reaching out with his hand. "I spoke with you on the phone the other night."

"Yes." Schaefer shook his hand. "I remember." He reached for the small, soft-sided cooler resting on his desk, then turned to Janine. "You need to keep it cool," he said, as he handed her the cooler. "I put the, uh, the prescription in there for you, along with the P.R.E.-5—the Herbalina—so you should be all set."

"Right," Janine said. "Now all we have to do is find Sophie." She thanked the doctor, then started to leave the room, but Lucas didn't budge.

"It sounds like your study's going very well," he said to the doctor.

"Yes, actually, it is." Schaefer smiled that uncertain smile Janine was so used to seeing. No one could ever accuse him of being an arrogant physician. "The results are even better than I'd hoped for," he continued. "I'll be releasing the, uh, two-month data at a press conference in a few days. And we've decided to move the days of the infusion to Tuesdays and Thursdays, to see how the kids do on that schedule. So when they find Sophie, Janine, you'll be bringing her in on Tuesdays rather than Mondays."

"Great." She appreciated his optimism.

"What about lab work?" Lucas asked. "I mean, I know Sophie's doctors thought the improvement would be mostly symptomatic and temporary. Are you actually seeing a change in the blood work?"

Janine felt a bit embarrassed that Lucas was taking up so much of the doctor's time. "He cares a lot about Sophie," she explained apologetically to Schaefer. "That's why he's so interested."

"I understand," Dr. Schaefer said. He answered the question about blood work, but it was still a few more minutes before Janine was able to get Lucas to leave.

Lucas smiled at her once they were in the hallway of the medical building. "Did I ask too many questions?" he asked her.

"No," she said. "I think it's sweet that you care."

Lucas dropped her off at Ayr Creek, pulling the Taurus into the turnaround near the cottage. Janine reached for the handle on the car door, then hesitated.

"Why don't I just wait here for you to finish your work and we can drive back to West Virginia together tonight?" she asked.

He shook his head as he got out of the car. "I can't leave until tomorrow morning," he said. "But we can be on the road at the crack of dawn. I promise."

She got out of the car herself, then walked next to him toward the cottage. "I really don't understand, Lucas," she said. "Is it Joe? Did you just need to get away from him for a while? I know he's been—"

"It has nothing to do with Joe," he interrupted. He stood in front of her cottage door, his eyes squeezed shut, as if deep in thought. "I know you need me right now, Jan," he said. "If I could be in two places at once, I would be."

"If you would just tell me why it's so important for you to stay here in Vienna tonight, I—"

"It's a business thing, and I can't let it go any longer."

"Is it illegal?" she asked, and he laughed.

"No, nothing like that," he said. "And I'll tell you about it when this whole thing with Sophie is over. It's not worth getting into now. For now, just trust me, okay?"

"Okay," she said. She had trusted him completely these past few months. She'd shrugged off her parents' complaints about his missed time at work. She'd never badgered him for an explanation as to why he couldn't see her certain nights of the week.

If one of her girlfriends had come to her, telling her about some guy she liked who was as full of excuses and secretive behavior as Lucas, she would have told that friend to turn tail and run.

But Lucas was not some guy. And she still trusted him. Completely.

CHAPTER TWENTY–FOUR

Joe sat with Paula on the folding chairs outside the trailer. Although the road was shaded, and the June sun had to fight through the trees to reach them, Paula's nose and cheeks were a vibrant pink, and Joe could feel the sting of the sun on his forehead. A few yards away from them, Frank sat on another folding chair, reading a book about the Civil War, and Donna had gone back to the motel for a nap. Paula had bought paperback books for Joe and herself the day before, but she had read only a few pages of hers, and he had not even opened his. There was no way he could concentrate on a novel when his own life felt so much like fiction.

A buzz of radio communication spit from the trailer every minute or so, and Joe took comfort in the knowledge that the woods were alive with people intent on finding Sophie. Searchers came and went from the trailer, some with dogs, some on their own. Cases of bottled water were stacked at the outside corner of the trailer, and buckets of water stood nearby for the dogs. Joe studied each of the searchers' faces, hoping for a smile or a sparkle in an eye, anything that might give him reason to hope. But for the most part, their faces remained unreadable, and they avoided direct eye contact with him.

He wasn't sure how many more days he could tolerate sitting still, helplessly watching while other people tried to find his daughter. He could imagine no more impotent feeling than this. He'd always been in charge of his life; this powerlessness was new and unbearable. And the worst part was that he didn't even have his ex-wife to share the agony with. Janine was so attached to Lucas that she seemed to have forgotten that Joe was Sophie's father.

"I don't understand why Janine went back to Vienna," Frank said suddenly, as if reading Joe's mind.

Joe felt Paula's eyes on him. "To be with Lucas," he said.

Frank shook his head. "I don't understand her. She's putting her own needs above her daughter's."

"She wanted to get her car," Paula said. "To have it here."

"Do you believe that?" Joe asked her.

Paula rested her novel facedown in her lap. "What I *do* believe is that it's Lucas she's getting comfort from right now. *You* blame her, Joe, and you and Donna blame her, too, Frank. You barely even talk to her, for heaven's sake. Lucas is the only person who's giving her any support. Why wouldn't she want to be with him?"

Frank was silenced by Paula's retort, and Joe, although angry with her for it, was stunned by her courage. He was about to respond to her, when there was a sudden bustle of activity on the road to their right. A few of the searchers glanced in their direction as they ran past them into the trailer, and the buzz of the radios was steady and loud.

Joe looked from Paula to Frank and back again. Had someone found Sophie? And had they found her alive?

He got to his feet just as Valerie Boykin came out of the trailer and walked toward them.

Frank got up from his own chair to stand behind Paula's. "Is there some news?" he asked.

"We think one of the dogs picked up her scent," Valerie said.

"One of the dogs who finds live people or...?" Joe couldn't finish the sentence.

"Yes. It's one of the tracking dogs. He might have picked up her scent yesterday, actually, but we weren't sure. Today, he's back on the same trail. So if he's really got Sophie's scent, and we think he does, then she was alive when she left it. He picked it up about a half a mile from the road."

"A half mile!" Frank said.

Joe couldn't find his voice. It seemed unbelievable. His frail little daughter had walked a half mile, by herself, through the woods!

"So," he was finally able to say, "is the dog still following her scent?"

"There's a snag." The pager on Valerie's belt beeped, and she looked down at it for a moment, as though memorizing whatever message she saw in its display, before looking up at Joe again. "The dog reached a creek, and he can't seem to pick up the scent on the other side. We're calling in some of the dogs from the other areas to see if they pick up the same scent and if they might be able to find it on the other side of the creek."

"What would it mean if they can't find it again?" Paula asked.

"Hard to say," Valerie said. "It may mean that she actually walked in the stream for a while, although I don't know why she would do that."

"Maybe she was confused," Frank suggested.

"Or her feet hurt," Joe offered. "Remember, she was missing at least one of her shoes."

"The other probability is that the rain we've had has masked her scent," Valerie informed them. "That's a very realistic possibility."

Valerie's pager beeped again, and this time she excused herself. "I'll let you know the minute we have any more information," she added, as she walked back to the trailer.

"I've got to call Janine," Joe said, walking away from Paula and Frank. "She needs to get back here."

He made the call from the side of the road, away from the activity near the trailer.

"Where are you?" he asked, afraid to hear that she was with Lucas, probably up in his tree house.

"At Ayr Creek," she said. "In the cottage. Is there...has Sophie been found?"

He knew she was bracing herself for the worst. "It's good news," he said quickly. "A little bit of good news, anyhow. One of the tracking dogs—the *live* tracking dogs—picked up her scent today, about a half mile from here."

"Oh, my God!" Janine said.

"Can you imagine she walked a half mile through the woods?" Joe asked.

"Poor baby." Janine's voice was thick. "And she only had one shoe. Oh, Joe."

"I know. It's hard to think about. But it's good news, Janine." He told her about Valerie's plans to bring in the other dogs.

"I've got to come back there tonight," Janine declared.

"Yes," he said, "I think you should."

"Lucas can't come until tomorrow," she said, "so I'll drive myself."

It was fine with Joe if Lucas never returned to the search site, but he didn't like the idea of Janine driving to West Virginia alone at night. Especially not in the emotional state she was in.

"If you told him what happened, wouldn't he leave tonight and drive with you?"

"No," she replied. "He's got to work. It's all right, Joe. I'll be fine."

"*What* work?" Joe asked, annoyed.

Janine hesitated. "I don't know, exactly."

"If he really cared about you, he wouldn't let you drive alone." What the hell did Janine see in this guy?

"Joe. Please. You're being ridiculous."

"Look, I'm coming to Vienna to get you," he said, surprising himself. "I don't want you making that trip alone."

"That's completely unnecessary," she said. "I think you're—"

"I should come home to get some clothes, anyway," he said. "So you just sit tight, and I'll be at the cottage in a few hours. I should be there around—" He looked at his watch. It was four o'clock. He'd need to allow time to stop at his town house in Reston. And he'd need time for a little sleuthing as well. Janine may not care what Lucas found so important to do in the middle of this crisis, but Joe felt the need to know. Something was not right with that man. "I'll be there around nine or nine-thirty. Okay?"

"Yes, fine. If you insist."

He returned to the folding chair next to Paula's. "I'm going to Vienna," he said. "I need to get a change of clothes and pick up Janine. The gardener can't bring her back until tomorrow. He's got something more important to do."

"What's that?"

"I wouldn't know. And Janine doesn't, either. It's another of his big secrets. Doesn't sound like they have much of a relationship, does it, if he won't tell her why he can't come back here tonight?"

"Maybe she knows and she just doesn't think it's any of your business," Paula said.

Joe stiffened. "Is that what you think?" he asked. "That it's none of my business?"

"I think you're obsessed with Lucas Trowell," she said. "I think you are dying to prove him to be a bad guy, so you can woo Janine back for yourself."

"Wrong," he said, annoyed. "I just want to make sure he *isn't* a bad guy. I don't want Janine to get hurt."

"Uh-huh," Paula said, and he knew she didn't believe him. He couldn't blame her. He didn't really believe himself.

"Do you want to go with me?" he asked. "You're missing work, and—"

"I'm not going back to work until Sophie's found," she said. "I've got loads of vacation time. But I *will* go with you to get some clothes and things. Unless—" she shrugged "—unless you wanted to drive back with Janine alone."

"No, no, that's all right." That *had* been his plan, or at least his fantasy. But he could hardly tell Paula she wasn't welcome to go back to Virginia with him.

They drove in silence through the mountains and onto Route 66. His mind was hard at work, and it wasn't until he dropped Paula off at her condo in Reston that he finally spoke.

"I'm going to stop at my place and run a few errands," he said. "Then I'll pick up Janine and come back for you here around nine-thirty or ten."

She eyed him suspiciously. "You've got something up your sleeve," she said. "What is it?"

God, this woman could see through him!

"I don't know, exactly," he said. "But I think I might pay a little visit to the gardener. Without his knowledge."

She shook her head in disapproval. "I don't know what you're up to, but I have a feeling I can't talk you out of it, so I won't even try."

"Good." He smiled at her. "I'll see you later."

CHAPTER TWENTY–FIVE

Janine had to admit she felt alone. She'd been abandoned by Lucas when she needed him most, and she didn't understand why he could not be with her tonight.

She lay on Sophie's bed in the fading daylight, holding the teddy bear to her chest, as she had a few nights earlier. Through the window, she could see fireflies blinking in the half light, moving slowly, as if they were flying through honey.

Lucas has a good reason, she told herself, or else he'd be here with her. But she couldn't help but wonder if she'd misread their relationship. Had she made more of it than actually existed? Right now, she felt as though she didn't truly know him. How close could she be to Lucas if he wouldn't tell her why, on this night of all nights, he couldn't be with her? She'd thought of calling him with the hopeful news that Sophie's scent had been detected by one of the dogs, but suddenly worried that her call would not be welcome. He had important work to do tonight, he'd told her. She didn't dare call.

Just as she began to think of him as dishonest, as someone who had used her, she remembered what he'd been like in Schaefer's office earlier that day. He'd talked to a few of the kids with genuine interest and concern; he'd questioned the parents—and

Schaefer himself—about various aspects of the treatment Sophie and the other children were receiving. He'd been nothing if not sincere. He was a rare man, and she forgave him for deserting her tonight. Whatever his reasons, she knew they were important.

Her mind returned to Sophie. They'd found her scent near a creek, a half mile from the road. That had to mean that her injuries were not all that severe. Otherwise, how could she have walked that far? She must have been afraid, though. She was a stranger to the woods, and by now, she'd endured four nights alone, with the alien noises and unrelenting darkness of the forest.

Baby, hold on. Did Sophie feel deserted? Did she wonder why no one had found her yet? Did she think she'd been forgotten?

Janine rolled onto her side and felt her tears run over her temple onto Sophie's bedspread. And that's when she heard the sound. Lifting her head from the pillow, she listened. The keening was low-pitched and anguished. Orla was out there, walking through the woods surrounding Ayr Creek, searching for the daughter who'd been ripped from her heart in the middle of the night.

And for the first time, Janine knew exactly how she felt.

CHAPTER TWENTY–SIX

The three of them sat on the flat rocks in the clearing, eating cold baked beans and franks straight from the cans. Marti would not allow a fire in case searchers might be able to see the smoke.

Sophie did not have much of an appetite, and Zoe couldn't blame her. The little girl was in pain from the wounds on her foot, and she was also very, very frightened. It was probably beginning to dawn on her that she was not getting out of here any time soon.

Zoe had finally decided against walking Sophie to the road. Her reasons for changing her mind were many. First, Sophie had not awakened from her nap until nearly two o'clock, and there was no way Zoe could get all the way to the road and back again before dark. Second, when Sophie *did* finally wake up, her foot was so inflamed, so obviously infected, that there was no way she could possibly walk on it. Zoe gave her some antibiotics from the stash she'd brought with her, hoping not only that they would help, but that they would have no unforeseen negative effect on Sophie's kidney problems. Who knew what was going on inside the little girl's body?

But the third reason for not taking Sophie to the road was the most compelling: she simply could not put Marti's safety at risk. Yes, Sophie had promised not to give away the identity of the person who'd found her in the woods, and Zoe knew the child was sincere about that. But Marti was right. They would question Sophie until she gave in. She was smart and strong, but she was also sick and scared. No, Zoe could not put Marti in that sort of jeopardy.

When Marti had returned from her angry escape into the forest, Zoe had sat with her on the sofa in the living room, talking quietly, trying to figure out what to do. Both of them had been calmer, then. Both of them ready to reason.

"Please don't take her to the road, Mom," Marti had said. Her voice had been soft, yet pleading, and Zoe'd felt torn apart by the fear that lay just beneath the surface of her daughter's words. "You made this plan for me to get out of prison," Marti said. "This wonderful, elaborate plan. And if you take her, it's going to screw everything up."

"She's a sick little girl, though," Zoe had said. "Seriously sick. I'm afraid she might even die if I don't get her help."

"But how *can* you get her help?" Marti asked. "Be realistic. Her foot is so bad, she has to hop rather than walk. I know your intentions are good, Mom, but if she's not able to walk out of here with you, it's not your fault. It's just one of those things. I mean, it's not like we have a phone or anything so that we can call for help. We'll just have to try to take care of her ourselves, the best we can."

"Except...I could go myself up to the road," Zoe said slowly, thinking the idea through as she spoke. "I could get a ride into the nearest town and let someone know she's here and that she needs help."

Marti simply stared at her. "Tell me you're kidding," she said. "You'd have to let people see you then. They'd know you're not dead. And then they'd find me and take me back to Chowchilla. I'd never get out of there. And you'd probably be in there with me for helping me escape."

"I wouldn't care for myself," Zoe said honestly. "I'm really beyond caring. But *you're* not going back there. I won't let that happen."

"Then you know you can't go and get her help, don't you?"

Zoe nodded. "I know," she said, giving in.

"Thanks, Mom." Marti smiled. She pulled another cigarette out of the pack in her pocket and lit it. Taking a drag on the cigarette, her eyes suddenly filled with tears.

"What is it, Mart?" Zoe asked her.

"I just felt...jealous, or something," she said, staring at the tip of her cigarette. "Watching you with that little kid. You never paid that much attention to me when I was eight."

"I know that, honey," Zoe admitted. "You're right, and I'm sorry."

"Why did you ever have me in the first place?" Marti asked.

Zoe stared out the window at the forest. "I wanted a child," she said. "I was thirty-two, and practically every woman I knew had children. I felt like I was missing something. Your dad was forty-three by then, and he really wasn't interested in becoming a father. He was so attached to his career, and he was also attached to mine, as you know. He never wanted me to get pregnant, because it would take time away from my work." Although she'd been an entertainer since she was small, it was Max who had truly made her into a superstar. She'd been a little bit of everything. Sex kitten. Singer. Dancer. Actress. The one label that had never fit her well, though, had been Mother.

"I don't feel like I ever really knew Dad," Marti said.

"I know," Zoe said. "He was an absent father for you. Just like I was an absent mother."

"Didn't you realize that at the time?" Marti asked. "Didn't you see that you were never there for me?"

Zoe thought about it. She wanted to answer truthfully. This time with Marti was going to be all about honesty. "Yes, I knew that, and I felt guilty about it," she said. "But the truth was, even if I'd had the time to give you, I didn't know how to be a mother to you. I was lousy mother material, and I knew it. That's why I hired nannies for you."

"You were never, ever home," Marti said. Her bitterness was masked, but barely. And she was right. Zoe had been on the road during much of Marti's childhood, and when she *had* actually been at home with her daughter, she'd been honestly uncomfortable with her. Marti had seemed like a stranger to her. Zoe truly had not known her at all.

"That's why I wanted to do this for you, Mart," she said. "I wanted to help you prove your innocence, but the lawyers I hired blew it."

"No kidding." Marti rolled her eyes.

"So, I came up with this plan. I figured neither of us had much left to lose. I'd try to...spring you." She smiled at the expression. "And if we succeeded, great. If we didn't, we were back where we started."

"Mom..." Marti leaned forward. She rested her hand on Zoe's arm and tears filled her eyes again. "I can't go back there, ever, Mom. Please don't let that happen to me."

"I won't, sweetie," she promised, pulling her daughter, her own little girl, into her arms. And she knew that somehow, Sophie would have to heal herself. Zoe was giving up on her, turning her fate over to a force greater than any of them. There was nothing more she could do for the child.

"Hey, look!" Marti said now. She pointed toward the edge of the clearing, and Zoe and Sophie looked up from their beans and franks to see what had attracted her. A huge turtle had lumbered out of the woods, making slow but steady progress across the clearing.

"Is it a turtle or a tortoise?" Marti asked, walking across the clearing to get a better look.

"What's the difference?" Zoe asked.

"I don't have a clue," Marti said.

"It's a snapping turtle," Sophie said with authority.

"How do you know that?" Zoe asked.

Sophie shrugged. She was not a happy little camper this evening. "I just do," she said. She was using her penknife to spread peanut butter on a piece of Melba Toast.

"So," Marti said, as she neared the turtle. "Do they snap?"

"They can break your finger right off," Sophie said.

"Oh, they can, can they," Marti said. She picked up a stick from the edge of the forest and held it in front of the turtle, and Zoe saw her slowly reach into her shorts pocket and pull out a survival knife.

"Oh, don't hurt it, Marti," Zoe said, but she was too late. The turtle stretched out its long neck to bite down on the stick, and with one quick blow, Marti decapitated it.

"Turtle soup for tomorrow night!" she crowed.

"Oh, Marti." Zoe felt shaken, actually sick. She found herself unable to look at the turtle and averted her eyes. Yet *she* had killed animals out here. Why did this feel so different? She looked across the clearing at Sophie, whose face was a mixture of fear and horror.

"Why did you do that?" Sophie asked Marti. "He wouldn't hurt you if you just left him alone."

Marti tossed her knife on the ground and sat down on one of the rocks again. "Because turtle soup is delicious," she said. "That's why."

"And how are you going to make turtle soup without a fire?" Sophie asked. She set down her penknife and got off the rock. Carrying the Melba Toast, she hopped across the clearing toward the shanty.

Marti watched her go. "Sensitive little thing, isn't she?" she said to Zoe.

Zoe cleared her throat. "I have some books in the shanty that will tell you how to clean a turtle."

"We can't have turtle soup," Marti said. "Sophie's right. We'd need a fire."

"So, you killed that turtle for nothing," Zoe said. Anger surged inside her, and she did her best not to let it come out in her voice.

"Don't go getting all sappy on me, all right?" Marti stood up and headed for the shanty. "You and Sophie make quite a team," she called back over her shoulder. "It was just a turtle."

Zoe sat still on the rock after Marti went into the shanty, her can of beans in her hand, her eyes averted from the slaughtered turtle on the other side of the clearing. She was annoyed at herself. *So, it's okay for you to kill animals, but not for Marti to do it?* she asked herself. But then, suddenly, she knew why her hands were shaking, her heart pounding.

She remembered the kitten, the white ball of fluff, that Marti had been given as a birthday gift for her seventh birthday, or maybe her eighth. She'd been thrilled with the kitten, or so it seemed. But one day, the cat disappeared. The nanny found it a few days later, beneath Marti's bed, its neck broken. Marti denied knowing anything about the kitten's death, and Zoe had believed her.

At least, she'd pretended to believe her. Zoe was an actress. She was very, very good at pretending.

CHAPTER TWENTY–SEVEN

Lucas's house was dark. Joe was parked down the block, not certain what he should do next. Lucas's car was in the carport, and Joe's best guess was that he was with another woman up in his tree house. Why else would he desert Janine at a time like this?

Night had finally fallen over Vienna, and Joe got out of his car under the cover of darkness. He heard music coming from the amphitheater at Wolf Trap National Park, followed by rowdy applause and whistles that cut through the still air, and he wondered who was performing there tonight. Not the symphony, obviously.

Moving quietly, he slipped into the woods at the edge of Lucas's property. He had never been to the tree house before, but he knew its approximate location, since he'd seen it from the road in winter when the leaves were off the trees. After a moment or two, he was surrounded by the darkness of the woods and a bit disoriented. Is this how Sophie felt in the woods, night after night? It was unfathomable. He was a thirty-five-year-old man in the safe confines of Vienna, just blocks from traffic, with the civilized sound of music wafting through the trees, and he still felt spooked. How could Sophie survive this?

The reality was that Sophie probably had not survived. When

he was being honest with himself, Joe knew that was the truth. Even if she'd been able to tolerate the emotional anguish of being lost, even if she'd somehow found the courage to make it through four nights alone in the forest, and even if she'd somehow managed to find food that was safe to eat, she could not survive. Her kidneys would not let her. And if Herbalina *was* the miracle drug Janine thought it to be—something he did not for a moment believe—she still would have needed dialysis by now. *Oh, Sophe.* What a cruel way to die. No one deserved to die afraid and alone, least of all his little girl.

Ahead of him, a light flickered through the trees. He walked toward it as quietly as he could and was relieved to see that it was coming from the tree house. The two-tiered house was in darkness except for one brightly lit room, and from where he stood, Joe could clearly see Lucas sitting at a desk in front of a computer monitor. Just the gardener and the machine, no sign of another woman. For this, Lucas had given up a night with Janine? Maybe he was an Internet junkie in need of a fix.

Joe leaned a bit to the left to try to see the screen of the monitor more clearly, and his foot came down on a dead branch as he shifted his weight. It cracked in two, the sound so loud that Lucas turned his head toward the window.

Joe held his breath. Lucas stood up from the computer to look through the window into the darkness, then he disappeared from the room. *He's walking out to the deck,* Joe thought. Any minute, Lucas would turn on an outside light to look for the intruder.

Having no desire to be found spying, Joe turned around and headed swiftly back to the road. *This is, without a doubt, the weirdest thing you've ever done,* he told himself, as he moved through the woods. And he sure as hell didn't want to be caught doing it.

He was perspiring by the time he reached the street and was about to head toward his car, when his gaze was drawn to the two bags of recycling sitting on the curb in front of Lucas's brick rambler. He walked over to the bags and peered inside them.

There were no streetlights on this side of the road, but Joe was still able to see that one of the bags was filled with a week's worth of the *Washington Post*. The second seemed to contain junk mail and magazines. Leaning over, he tore the paper on the second bag, curious to see if its contents might contain any clues to Lucas Trowell.

The paper spilled from the bag onto the curb, one of the magazines falling open, and Joe blinked in horror. The magazine had opened to a picture of a nude child. A girl, Joe thought, although it was hard to tell in the dim light. He moved the magazine with the toe of his shoe, trying to get more light on the picture, but a rustling noise from the woods stopped him. Looking up, he saw a light flickering through the trees. *A flashlight.* Lucas was on his way out here.

Joe backed away from the torn bag of paper and ran toward his car. His hands shook wildly as he climbed into the driver's seat and turned the key in the ignition, and he pressed on the gas, leaving Lucas's neighborhood behind him as quickly as he could.

When he neared Ayr Creek, he pulled to the side of the road, turned off the ignition and rested his head against the back of the car seat. He wanted to wipe the last half hour from his mind. Shame filled him. He was a spy, a voyeur. He was, as Paula had so kindly pointed out to him, obsessed with Lucas Trowell.

Okay, so he'd done the deed. He couldn't take it back. He just needed to let it go.

He started the car again, and by the time he turned into the Ayr Creek driveway, he'd managed to erase most of the escapade from his mind—all except the shadowy image of a naked little girl.

CHAPTER TWENTY–EIGHT

Janine was standing on the tarmac at the small airport, talking with the rental agent, as she waited for Lucas to arrive. She'd called Lucas at five-thirty that morning, when she'd made the decision to rent a helicopter, and asked him to meet her at the airport rather than the motel. It was barely 8:00 a.m. now, and she was early, but she simply could not stay cooped up in her motel room another moment.

She'd had to beg Joe to give her a ride to the airport, since she had no car with her, and she must have hit him at a weak moment, because he didn't put up much of a fight before agreeing to drop her off. She'd also persuaded him to stop by the command post, so that she could leave Herbalina in the trailer's small refrigerator and tell Valerie Boykin her plan. Valerie didn't think a helicopter would do much good, given the dense cover in the area, but Janine could not tolerate another day of sitting and waiting. They wouldn't let her in the woods to look for Sophie, but there was not much they could do about her being in the air.

"I think you're amazing," the rental agent said. His name was Tom. Janine figured he was probably in his forties, although he looked considerably older with his long, gray ponytail.

"You do?" She smiled politely, as she walked around the helicopter. She was anxious to get inside it and up in the air.

"I think if my girl had gone missing, my wife would have buckled under, you know what I mean?" Tom said. "Just hid herself away until they found her. But here you are, out here, ready to fly a helicopter yourself to go lookin' for her."

"I can't stand feeling helpless," she said.

"Well, I think you're something else," Tom said. He offered her a salute and started walking back to the rental office. "You let me know if there's anything else I can do for you," he called over his shoulder.

"I will," she said. "Thanks."

Janine leaned against the side of the helicopter and watched the road for Lucas's car. She'd hesitated before calling Lucas early that morning, still feeling unsure of him after his desertion of her the night before. She'd been relieved when he responded to her call with warmth and willingness, the concern in his voice making her feel foolish for thinking she might have misinterpreted his love for her and Sophie. Their relationship was only seven months old, but those months had been rich with a caring so deep she felt ashamed of herself for doubting it. Lucas was a giver. How could she have forgotten that?

After he'd helped her break into her house, Lucas had become a regular visitor to the cottage at Ayr Creek. At first, she was careful with him around Sophie, but she soon grew to believe that his interest in Sophie was honorable, tied to his feelings for his beloved niece. He treated Sophie almost as though she were an adult, asking her opinion on books and movies and what she'd like for dinner. He taught her riddles. He asked her about her hopes and dreams. A couple of times, he'd had both Sophie and Janine up to his tree house, that world of awe and adventure, and Sophie had lit up at finding herself in the midst of the bare winter trees, able to see all the way to the Filene Center at Wolf Trap, and nearly to Ayr Creek in the opposite direction. Yes, Lucas was a giver, in every meaning of the word.

The true gift he'd given, though, was not to Sophie, but to Janine.

Early one morning, just before Christmas, and a month or so after Lucas had helped her break into the cottage, Janine was awakened before sunrise by a sound that always made her shiver. It was a low-pitched keening, spilling from the woods near the cottage, loud enough to pierce the windows of her bedroom. She'd heard the keening several times before, but only in the warmer months, and each time she heard it, she would lay frozen in her bed, imagining Orla as she traipsed through the forest in search of her daughter. This time, though, Janine felt a longing to know what was truly making that heartrending sound.

She got out of bed, pulling on a chenille robe over her flannel pajamas. Slipping into her sneakers, she walked quietly out the back door of the cottage to the porch. The sound stopped, as though Orla might have seen her emerge from the house and did not want to be discovered. Then she heard a noise from the side of the cottage. Walking around the path, she spotted Lucas carrying a bundled string of Christmas lights in his arms.

He started when he saw her. "You're up early," he said.

"Did you hear that sound?" she asked.

"What sound?"

"The wailing. Crying. Orla."

He looked toward the woods. "Oh, yeah," he said. "It is a bit creepy. But I think you were right when you said it was a possum or something."

She shivered and pulled the robe tighter around herself. "I've never heard it in the winter before," she said.

"Where's Sophie?" Lucas asked. "Still in bed?"

"She's at Joe's for the weekend."

"Ah," Lucas said, adjusting the string of lights in his arms. "I'd like to meet Joe sometime."

That surprised her. "Why?" she asked.

"Just 'cause he's Sophie's dad. And I'm supposing that, like your parents, he doesn't trust me much. I'd like him to know I'm not an ogre."

Or a pedophile, Janine thought. She felt a strong need to keep her friendship with Lucas from her parents and Joe. His visits to her cottage were made on the sly. Neither of them spoke about it, but they both understood the need for discretion. Although she had absolute trust in him, she knew her family would have no faith in her judgment.

"I'm about to make some coffee," she said. "Would you like to come in for a cup?"

"Sure, in a minute. I just want to add these lights to the spruce out front. It looked a little bare to me last night."

Inside the cottage, she quickly changed into jeans and a sweater, then busied herself making the coffee. She felt as though she were about to do something illicit. Not just because her parents would strongly disapprove of her socializing with the gardener, but because this would be the first time she'd been with Lucas alone, without Sophie as a buffer between them. Without Sophie to keep her growing desire for him in check. There had been a few times when she'd felt that desire was mutual, when she'd felt his gaze resting on her as she braided Sophie's hair or made supper for the three of them. She wondered, though, if she might be imagining his interest.

She opened a box of donuts and set them on the table just as Lucas walked in the back door.

They sat in the kitchen, sipping coffee, nibbling donuts and talking, and she wondered if he felt any attraction to her at all. She wished she'd taken a moment to comb her hair, still tousled from sleep, and smoothed some cover-up under her eyes. While she felt the power of being alone with him in the cottage, he seemed intent on talking about Sophie, as he usually did.

"What will she be doing this weekend with Joe?" he asked.

"Not sure," she said, pouring herself another cup of coffee. "Joe said that he and his friend, Paula, might take her to Bull Run tonight to see the Christmas lights. And he usually takes her to an afternoon movie when he has her."

"You know," Lucas said, reaching for a napkin from the holder on the table, "I heard this little blurb on the radio about a study just starting up, and I thought of Sophie. I don't know for sure, but I think she might qualify. It was something to do with kids with end-stage renal disease."

Janine shook her head. "If Sophie was a candidate, her doctor would have told me. He keeps up with all the research that's going on."

"Well, this was something about alternative medicine," Lucas said. "I didn't get all the details, but I did memorize the phone number, just in case it might apply to Sophie."

"Her doc would never go the alternative route."

"Wouldn't it be worth looking into, though?" he asked. "At least checking it out to see what it's all about?"

Janine felt tired. People were always telling her that Sophie should be doing this or doing that to get better. Join a prayer circle, drink water mixed with molasses, take some special, expensive supplement that had cured someone's sister's best friend's father of shingles and tapeworm.

"I don't know," she said.

"You're worn out from all this, aren't you?" Lucas looked sympathetic.

She nodded.

"Well, just to satisfy my own curiosity, would it be okay if I checked into it a little further? I'll get the information and pass it on to you, and you can decide if it's worth anything or not. The study sounded legit and kind of exciting. Really, it did."

"Sure," she said. "Just please don't give me any grief if I don't want to pursue it. Okay?"

"It's a deal," he said.

Without any warning, and without really knowing why, she suddenly began to cry. She turned away from him, raising a tissue to her face, embarrassed by how little control she had over her emotions these days.

He didn't budge from his side of the table.

"What's that all about?" he asked her gently, when her tears began to subside.

For a moment, she couldn't speak. Finally she blew her nose and turned to face him again. "I'm so frustrated," she said. "We've tried so many different treatments, but her need for dialysis keeps increasing. And the medications she's on keep making her sicker and sicker. You've seen it. You know what she's going through. And you—and I—know how this is going to end. Maybe she'll live another six months, maybe a year. It's all I think about. How unfair this is. What did she do to deserve this? When am I going to lose her? How will I bear it?"

He reached across the table and took her hand. It was not the first time he had touched her, but it was the first time she'd felt more than friendship in that touch.

"Janine," he said. "Right now, this weekend, what is Sophie doing?"

She shrugged. "I don't know what you mean," she said, puzzled. "I told you, she's with Joe."

"And you said he'd probably take her to a movie and to see the Christmas lights. *Today* she's alive. *Today* she's having a good time with her dad. And when all you can focus on is what the future holds, you lose today, for both yourself and Sophie. If your life is tied up in worrying about the future, you never enjoy what's possible right now."

She sat back in her chair, the truth of his words washing over her. In the last three years, she'd been ruled by worry. She could not remember a single moment she'd enjoyed in and of itself, without it being tinged by the bittersweet realization that she was, in all likelihood, going to lose her daughter. It was not the first time she'd heard the advice to live for the moment, but it was the first time she felt her spirit rise at the thought.

"Embrace every day," Lucas said.

"Do you do that?"

"I sure try to," he said. "Some days with more success than others."

"Did something happen to you that made you that way?" she asked. "I mean, unless someone's faced adversity, how do they ever get to that realization?"

"Some lucky people get there without suffering, I guess. But yes, I've faced adversity." He fell silent, looking at their hands instead of her face, and although she wanted to know more, she didn't pry.

Instead, she felt a smile cross her face. Sophie was alive *now,* as Lucas had said, and this day was full of precious moments. No matter what tomorrow might bring, Sophie still had today.

"I feel so much better," she said, surprised that such a simple thought could touch her so profoundly.

He raised his eyes to hers again, not speaking, his hand still holding hers. Morning light was beginning to slip into the room, and it seemed concentrated in the translucent gray of his eyes. A dusting of powdered sugar from his donut rested on his lips. Without thinking, she stood up, leaned across the corner of the table and bent down to kiss him.

He grinned at her. "What do you think you're doing?" he asked.

"Living for the moment," she said with a smile. "Seizing the day, and all that."

He stood up and drew her into his arms for another kiss, and she tasted the sugar on his lips, the coffee on his tongue. She thought of all the times she'd imagined making love with him. Without a moment's hesitation, she took him by the hand and led him to her bedroom.

The bed was unmade, the down comforter piled in a heap on the sheet. She pulled off her sweater, then his, and he watched her as though intrigued by what she would do next.

She touched his splint.

"Can we take this off?" she asked.

He shook his head. "No," he said, "but everything else is fair game."

She lifted his undershirt over his head, then reached for the buckle on his belt. He made no move to stop her, but she found herself unable to continue undressing him when he slipped her bra from her shoulders and leaned down to stroke his tongue across her breast. Her legs instantly gave out from under her, and she let him take over, feeling as though she had no choice in the matter. She was going to be made love to by a man who knew how to make the most of every moment.

Afterward, she lay in his arms, awash in a sense of peace that felt alien and new. They had not had intercourse. That had been his call, since she was not taking the Pill, and she had both admired and been grateful for his self-control. Instead, he'd pleasured her with his hands and his mouth, and she'd done the same in return.

"Thank you," she said.

He lifted his head to look at her. "For making love?" he asked.

"No, for the Christmas present. For giving me back my life, and Sophie's. For reminding me what's important."

Lucas's simple counsel had changed the way Janine had lived her life these past few months. She'd found time every day to do something fun with her daughter. She'd rejected any treatment that might give Sophie a few more months of life, only to make those months miserable. And she began arguing with Joe over the best medical care for Sophie. He did not share her new-found appreciation of taking joy in the moment, and he'd looked at her blankly when she tried to explain it to him.

As she spotted Lucas's car turning into the parking lot of the small airport, though, Janine wondered how it could be possible to find any joy in a day like today, when Sophie was lost in the woods, probably sick and undoubtedly terrified.

She walked across the tarmac to meet Lucas. Once out of his car, he hugged her hard. "Still no news?" he asked.

"Nothing," she said.

"Forgive me for last night," he said, holding her, pressing his lips to her temple. "For not being with you. I know it must seem as though I've got my priorities screwed up, but—"

"It's all right," she interrupted. "I know you would have been with me if you could have."

"You are a very understanding woman."

"Forget it," she said, shrugging off the compliment. "Let's just get up in the air."

"Were the dogs able to pick up Sophie's scent again?" he asked, when they were hovering over the site of the accident. It looked so different now than it had only a few days earlier. The car was gone, of course, and the rain had brought new growth with it, the fresh green color masking much of the charred earth.

Janine shook her head. "Not yet," she said. "They figure the rain must have washed away her scent. But I checked at the trailer before going to the airport this morning, and Valerie said they were still trying. They haven't given up."

"Lucky for them," Lucas said. He leaned over to kiss her cheek. "They'd have to face Janine Donohue's wrath if they did."

Flying directly west of the accident site, they were able to locate the creek where Sophie's scent had been found—and lost. Janine flew out from that epicenter in a spiral, much as she and Lucas had done from the Girl Scout camp on Tuesday. It was, as Valerie had predicted, nearly impossible to see beneath the thick cover of trees, but they flew as low as they could, searching beneath the canopy for any movement or swatch of color.

"There's a shack down there," Lucas said after they'd been flying for close to an hour.

The spiral had grown so wide that Janine was about to suggest they give up and go back to the airport. But now she maneuvered the helicopter so that she could look directly down at the dilapidated log cabin. A small fire ring sat in the clearing in front of the shack, but there was no sign of smoke or embers, and the structure looked as though it hadn't been lived in for decades. The fire ring was surrounded by large, flat rocks, and the area around a small, dark crevice on one of the rocks glittered, sending a shard of light into Janine's eyes. *Mica,* she thought. *Or quartz.*

She sighed. "I guess we should turn around," she said, frustrated. "We're way too far from the creek. A good five miles. She couldn't possibly have walked all the way out here."

"Not with a bare foot," Lucas agreed.

Janine turned the helicopter around, and although she continued to scan the terrain below them, she kept picturing the old cabin. The flat rocks. The glittery shard of light. Why was that stuck in her mind? Maybe because she knew that, if Sophie had seen a shack like that one, surely she would have gone inside it for shelter. But that particular cabin was too far from the road, and she and Lucas spotted no other buildings on their flight.

Still, even as she landed the helicopter back at the airport, the image of that log cabin remained firmly planted in her mind.

CHAPTER TWENTY–NINE

From her seat on the sofa, Zoe heard the sound. At first she thought it was thunder in the distance, a storm moving in, and she stopped eating her granola to listen. Sophie sat at the other end of the sofa, her own bowl of cereal cradled in her lap, her swollen foot elevated on a crate, and she heard it, too. Her head jerked to attention, and she turned her face to the window. Only Marti, who stood leaning against the door jamb between the shanty's two rooms, did not seem to notice the sound. She was engrossed in eating cut peaches from the can, having refused Zoe's offer of the granola because the only milk available was powdered.

It wasn't thunder, but some sort of aircraft. Zoe had heard a few planes fly overhead while she'd been living in the shanty, but this was different. This plane was close and getting closer. She looked at Marti again, who had stopped a spoonful of peaches halfway to her mouth, her eyes wide now with fear.

"That's a helicopter!" Sophie practically tossed her cereal bowl on the floor as she jumped to her feet and hobbled toward the door of the shanty.

Instantly, Marti leapt toward her, the can of peaches falling, splattering syrup across the splintery wooden floor. "You can't go out there!" she said, grabbing Sophie's arm.

"Ouch!" Sophie yelped.

"That's her burned arm," Zoe said, and Marti let go of Sophie's left arm but quickly grabbed her right instead.

Sophie tried to wriggle free. "My mom knows how to fly a helicopter," she said. "Maybe that's her!"

The sound of the helicopter was now loud enough to send a chill up Zoe's spine. Through the glassless window, she could see the leaves of the trees flapping madly in the helicopter's wake. Had they left anything outside that would give them away? she wondered. Marti had been right about not having a fire, she thought, and thank God she'd taken the blue tarp off the roof.

"You can't go out there," Marti repeated to Sophie, gripping her arm. "Don't you get it?"

Sophie kicked her hard in the shin with her good right foot.

"Shit!" Marti backed away from the girl, but only momentarily, because Sophie headed for the door once again.

Zoe stood up, ready to stop Sophie herself, but Marti grabbed the girl's shoulders and spun her around to face her. "You little bitch," she said. "This is my *life* you're screwing around with!"

Sophie barely seemed to hear her. She looked toward the window. "It's going away!" she said, struggling to free herself. "Let me go. *Mom!*"

She pulled free of Marti's grasp and ran out the door before either of them could stop her, but she was too late. The sound of the helicopter was growing faint in the distance, and soon all Zoe could hear was Sophie's cries for her mother, and even they were weak and fading and heartbreaking. She knew the little girl was in tears, and she stood up and walked to the door.

"Don't go to her, Mother," Marti said. "Don't reward her for practically sending both of us to jail for the rest of our lives."

Zoe turned to her daughter. "You're a very hard woman, Marti," she said. "I never realized that."

"I had to be," Marti said. "I grew up without any parents to protect me."

Zoe winced at her words, but before she had a chance to respond, Sophie limped back in the shanty, the bandage on her foot spotted with red.

"Your foot's bleeding again, honey," Zoe said. "Sit down and let me take care of it."

Sophie dropped wordlessly to the sofa, raising her foot to the crate again. Her cheeks and nose were red from crying, and she turned her face away from the two of them.

Zoe got to her knees in front of the crate and began unwrapping the bandage. She winced against the pain in her back. How many more nights could she sleep on her lumpy, homemade mattress?

"Get me the peroxide, will you, Mart?" she asked her daughter. "It's in the bedroom in the box by my bed." Sophie's foot looked worse than it had the day before. She wished the antibiotics would start to work.

Marti returned with the bottle of peroxide and a handful of cotton balls. She stood above Zoe, staring down at Sophie's foot.

"You really screwed up your foot, kiddo, running out there like that," she said to Sophie.

Sophie turned her head to look at her. "You are so mean," she said.

"She's not really mean, honey." Zoe dabbed peroxide onto Sophie's foot with the cotton balls. "She's just scared."

"You killed that poor turtle and then didn't even eat it," Sophie said.

They had left the turtle in the clearing the night before. This morning, it was gone, and Zoe figured the dogs had gotten to it.

Marti sat down on the other end of the sofa and lit her lighter. She had no cigarettes left, and playing with the purple lighter had quickly become her new addiction. "Look, Sophie," she said. "Do you understand what's going on here?"

Sophie looked at her suspiciously. "What do you mean?" she asked.

"I mean, if they find *you,* they'll find *me,* and then I'll have to go back to jail. Someday, we'll all be able to leave here, and then maybe you'll be free to go, but that's a long way in the future."

Sophie stared at her foot as Zoe wrapped it with fresh gauze. "Why were you in jail?" she asked.

Zoe tore off a piece of surgical tape and glanced at her daughter, wondering how she would answer.

"They think I killed someone," Marti said.

"Did you?" Sophie looked up at her now.

"No. But the evidence made it look like I did. So I'm supposed to be in jail for the rest of my life." She sighed. "Do you know what it's like in jail?"

"Not really."

"Well," Marti said, "imagine being trapped someplace you can never, ever get out of. And people there hurt you. The wardens, who are there to make sure you don't get out, hurt you all the time. And the other prisoners hurt you. Everyone hates everyone else. You have no choice what you eat, and it's all garbage, anyway." She flicked her lighter again and stared at the flame. "You have no freedom to go any place," she said. "You have to do whatever they tell you to do, or you'll end up in solitary, locked up all by yourself, day and night, with no lights and...man, you just go crazy."

Sophie cast a sideways glance at Marti, then studied her foot again. "I think I know a little bit what jail must be like," she said. "Some kids I know say that dialysis is like being in jail." She shrugged. "I guess it is, in a way. Every single night, before I got Herbalina, my mom hooked me up to a machine by my bed. She used the tube in my stomach, and I'd be attached to the machine all night long. It was hard to roll over, and hard to get up to go to the bathroom. In the morning, she had to leave some extra water in my stomach, and I always looked fat. All day long, I had to measure everything I drank, even things like ice cream and Jell-O, 'cause they're really liquids, and if I had too much liquid, I'd get really sick. I couldn't eat stuff that my friends ate, like bananas or French fries." She looked again at Marti. *"You* got put in jail when you didn't do anything wrong, and *I* had to get dialysis when I didn't do anything wrong, either. Sometimes bad things just happen to people."

"Shit happens, huh?" Marti said. She stood up and stretched. "I am so bored! I'm going to read for a while in the bedroom."

She doesn't get it, Zoe thought as Marti left the room. *Or maybe she gets it and she just doesn't care.* She was finished with her bandaging job. She stood up and, on a whim, leaned over to kiss the top of Sophie's head. This child was so brave.

As she put away the peroxide and threw out the blood-stained bandage, tears burned her eyes. Sophie was in jail once again, she thought. Only this time, she and Marti were the jailers who were keeping her there.

CHAPTER THIRTY

"I feel terrible saying this," Joe said, as he turned onto Route 66. "But I'm beginning to wish that Sophie had been killed in the car accident, too."

There. He'd finally said those words out loud. The thought had been eating away at him for a couple of days, but he'd been holding it inside, still trying to pretend to the rest of the world that he thought Sophie could be found alive. He couldn't imagine saying those words to anyone other than Paula.

From the passenger seat of his car, Paula reached over to rub his shoulder.

"I know, hon," she said. "But I'm still hoping that somehow...by some miracle..." She shook her head, and he knew she was as frustrated as he was.

It had been another long, disheartening day of sitting helplessly by the trailer, staring into the woods that had taken his daughter from him. It seemed to him that every dog from the search-and-rescue teams had been called to the creek to try to pick up Sophie's scent. Valerie told him that some of the dogs seemed to find the scent for a moment or two, only to lose it again. Even the cadaver-seeking dogs were brought into the area, but no one was upset when they, too, seemed unable to pick up a scent.

Now he and Paula were headed back to Vienna. All of them—
Janine and Lucas, Donna and Frank—were on their way home,
because tomorrow was Holly Kraft's funeral. And although Joe
fought the feeling as hard as he could, he could not help but think
that perhaps Holly's parents had been the lucky ones. They
knew where Holly was. They knew that the end for her had been
swift. They knew she was no longer suffering.

"I can't believe it's been five days already," he said.

"It seems like five weeks to me," Paula said.

"Did you hear them say something about ending the search
on Sunday?" Joe thought he had overheard Valerie mention
something to that effect, but he had not wanted it to be the truth
and so had not pressed her.

"I think that's what Valerie said," Paula said.

"And then we'll never know what really happened."

"They'll still be looking tomorrow, hon," she said.

"She could be anywhere," Joe said. "And when I look at that
topographical map in the trailer...I'm overwhelmed by how
much land is out there. How much territory there is to cover."

Joe's cell phone rang, and he grabbed it from the console.
He doubted he would ever be able to answer a phone dispas-
sionately again.

"Hello?" he said, as he opened the mouthpiece.

"Is this Joe Donohue?" It was a woman's voice, and he
thought immediately of Valerie Boykin. He steeled himself for
what she might tell him.

"Yes," he answered. He was aware of Paula leaning closer to
him, as if trying to hear what the caller had to say.

"This is Catherine Maitland, from Monticello," the woman
said. "I understand you needed some information on one of our
former employees."

"Oh, yes." Joe had nearly forgotten about the call he'd made
to Monticello that morning. It seemed so long ago.

"The name they gave me was Lucas Trowell," she said. "T-r-o-w-e-l-l. Is that correct?"

"Yes."

"Well, I think there's been a mistake," she said. "We have no record of anyone by that name working here."

"He wouldn't be working there now," Joe said. "He's a former employee."

"We have no record of him *ever* working here," she said.

This was not what Joe had expected. He thought he might hear that Lucas had been an irresponsible worker at Monticello, as he was at Ayr Creek. He even thought he might hear something regarding Lucas's abnormal interest in young girls. But he had certainly not expected to hear that Lucas had never worked there.

"Uh, he would have worked there in the late nineties," Joe said. "He was a gardener. A horticulturist."

"I've been the human resources director here for fifteen years," the woman told him. "I could tell you the names of all of the gardeners, landscape architects, et cetera, who worked here during that time. Lucas Trowell is not one of them."

"But someone there gave him a glowing reference when he was applying for his job at the Ayr Creek estate in northern Virginia," Joe said.

The woman was quiet for a moment. "Are you sure he didn't work at Mount Vernon or one of the other historical properties?" she asked.

"I'm sure." Joe felt his jaw tighten, and his head was beginning to ache. He let go of the steering wheel for a moment to rub his temple. "Listen," he said. "Thanks for your help."

"I don't think I was really much help," the woman said.

"Yes, actually, you were."

He closed the phone and laid it back on the console, then glanced at Paula. She was studying him intently.

"Well?" she asked. "What was that all about?"

Joe tightened his hands on the steering wheel. "Something's rotten in the tree house," he said.

"What are you talking about?"

"Well, it appears that Lucas never worked at Monticello."

"What made you think he had?" Paula asked.

"He told the Ayr Creek Foundation that he'd worked there. Frank told me that they gave him a very high recommendation."

"I don't understand. Who were you just talking to?"

"The woman who's the head of the human resources office at Monticello. She said no one by that name has ever worked there."

"Why would she call you about it?"

"Because I called her. I wanted to find out the real scoop on what sort of employee he'd been. There's something not right about that guy." He looked at her again. "I spied on him a bit last night." This seemed to be his evening for confessions.

"You *what?*"

"I wanted to know why, if he cares about Janine so damn much, he refused to go back to West Virginia with her last night. So, I went to his house. I expected to find him with another woman."

"And?"

"I could see him inside the tree house, working at the computer."

"Ooh." Paula's voice was teasing. "How very incriminating."

"Right. And who knows, maybe I was too early—or too late— to catch him with another woman. But then I looked through his recycling at the curb and I—"

"Joe!"

"Don't give me a hard time, okay?" He was in no mood for Paula's moralizing.

Paula sighed. "So, what did you find in his recycling?" she asked.

"Kiddy porn."

"Oh, God. Ugh!" Her hand flew to her mouth. "Are you kidding?"

"I wish I were," he said, although the truth was, he was beginning to take a sadistic delight in getting the goods on Lucas Trowell.

"You mean, you found magazines or what?"

"I only saw one. It fell open to a picture of a nude child. A girl. That's all I needed to see. I called Monticello, because I wanted to know if he'd left there of his own accord, or if maybe he was actually fired. I never expected to find out that he hadn't worked there at all. I have to tell Janine." He would call her the second he got home.

Paula was quiet a moment. "I don't think you should tell her," she said.

He looked at her in surprise. "Don't you think she has a right to know?" he asked. "Wouldn't you want to know that the guy you're sleeping with is a liar at best, and a pedophile at worst?"

"Right now, though, Lucas isn't hurting anyone," Paula said. As always, she was the voice of reason. "And Janine gets a lot of comfort from him. Even if he *is* everything you say, now is not the time to dump all of that on her. You'd be ripping her support system right out from under her."

Joe scowled. "I don't want her with him any longer. Sleeping with him any longer." He shuddered. "It makes me sick to think about her being with someone like him."

"Joe..." Paula adjusted her seat belt to turn toward him. "You know I love you, hon, right?"

He nodded.

"Sometimes you can be pretty selfish."

It wasn't the first time someone had told him that, but he didn't like to hear those words from Paula. He could always count on her to tell him the truth, and this was one truth he didn't feel like hearing.

"So, if I tell Janine that her boyfriend might be a criminal, I'm being selfish?"

"If you told her right now, then, yes. I'd say you were."

He didn't get it. Her rationale made no sense to him. But he trusted her in a way he trusted no one else.

"All right," he agreed. "I'll hold off until this whole mess blows over."

Paula smiled as she leaned over to kiss his cheek. "That's my boy," she said. "You're not so bad, after all."

CHAPTER THIRTY–ONE

Lucas did not know where to look. He sat next to Janine in a pew near the center of the chapel, clutching her hand to comfort her, although he needed the comfort every bit as much as she did. Possibly more. Two rows ahead of them, Joe and Paula sat next to Donna and Frank. Joe had acknowledged Janine with an embrace and a kiss on the cheek, but Donna and Frank had ignored their daughter, and Lucas hoped that he was not entirely the cause of their cruelty. It was not like him to ignore their wrath— *anyone's* wrath—without addressing it, putting it on the table, trying to fix it. But Lucas was not himself these days

The small chapel in Vienna was filled with people, both adults and children, and the sorrow in their faces was nearly too much for him. A large photograph of Holly Kraft rested on an easel near the pulpit, and he'd looked at the picture without meaning to, his gaze slipping in that direction before he'd realized what he was doing. He'd only looked for a moment, but that had been enough for the little girl's smile to burn itself into his brain, and he wished he could think of another image to take its place.

He kept his eyes averted from the front pew, where Rebecca and Steve were sitting with the rest of their children. He couldn't look at the minister, either, nor could he give any attention to

Holly's other relatives, who, one after another, came up to the microphone at the front of the chapel to talk about Holly's life and her spirit and her future cut short. Some of them attempted to tell funny stories about Holly, and had it been an adult being eulogized, the anecdotes might have provided some relief, some gentle reminiscence. But there was nothing funny to be said about a child struck down before she'd truly had a chance to live.

Before today, Lucas had been to only one other funeral for a child, and that had been one too many. He'd made a promise to himself that he would never attend another funeral like it. Yet, there was no way he could turn Janine down when she asked him to come with her today. Now, he tried to focus on her, to forget about himself. He glued his gaze to her hand where it rested locked in his own. Her nails were short and a bit ragged after a week's worth of neglect. Her skin was lightly tanned, and he was keenly aware of the yellowish cast his own skin had next to hers. The sight gave him a jolt; he had not realized that his skin had taken on that unhealthy hue. Seeing it made him feel panicky, and he must have squeezed Janine's hand involuntarily, because she looked at him briefly before facing the front of the chapel again.

He'd shift his focus to Joe, Lucas decided. He would shut out the rest of the chapel, and sure enough, the harder he stared at the back of Joe's head, the blurrier, the blacker the edges of his vision became. Joe's dark hair looked as though it would never turn gray or grow thin. His neck was tan above the collar of his shirt, and his shoulders were broad. Lucas did not need to see Joe's eyes to remember how they looked; the moment he'd first met Joe, those eyes had held him fast with their familiarity. It was as if he'd known Joe all his life.

Paula had her arm around Joe, and her thumb stroked his back just below the shoulder seam of his jacket. She was so obviously in love with him. And Joe was so obviously in love with Janine.

The soft, yearning sound of a violin began wafting down from the balcony above their heads. The music was poignant, excruciating in its subtlety, and Lucas wanted to run from the chapel, just as he'd wanted to escape from that last funeral. He could run out of the chapel and keep on running, until his mind was numb to the pain.

But he did as he had done before: he remained seated, holding the hand of the woman he loved, praying for this long exercise in remembering to come to an end.

CHAPTER THIRTY–TWO

Zoe wasn't certain if Sophie was truly sick or simply depressed, but the little girl hadn't gotten out of bed at all that morning. At noon, Zoe finally went into the bedroom to check on her. Carrying the wobbly chair from the living room into the bedroom, she sat on it next to Sophie's sleeping palette. Sophie was lying on her back. Her eyes were open, and the skin around them looked swollen, as though she'd been crying for hours.

"Are you all right?" Zoe asked.

Sophie rocked her head back and forth on the pillow. "I'm getting sick," she said.

"What kind of sick?" Zoe asked. "Is it your kidney problem?"

Sophie nodded. "I can tell. I feel like I used to feel when I didn't get enough dialysis. Before Herbalina." She held up one of her arms. "My hand is puffy," she said.

It *was* puffy, and Zoe knew that her little stash of antibiotics would never be able to touch what was wrong with this child. She realized, then, that the swollen look of Sophie's eyes was not from tears so much as from the disease. Sophie had not been crying at all. Instead, she was stoic and resigned to her fate, and that broke Zoe's heart in two.

She found Marti in the clearing, sitting on one of the rocks, flicking her cigarette lighter on and off as she stared into the flame. She turned toward Zoe as she approached.

"Why, oh, why didn't I think to buy about a hundred cartons of cigarettes before I came out here?" Marti asked.

"You would have had to carry them through the woods," Zoe said, as she sat down on another rock. Sophie's penknife lay open next to her, and Zoe closed it and slipped it into her shorts pocket.

"That's true." Marti nodded.

"I need to talk to you about Sophie, Mart," Zoe said. "I have to find a way to get her some medical—"

"Mother—"

"I *have* to, Marti. Let's talk about this, all right? Let's find a solution instead of simply saying we can't do it. She's very, very ill. I think I should go and get help for her."

"And then what?"

"And then we'll have to face the music, whatever that may be." She made it sound easy; she knew it would be anything but. "I promise you, honey, I will find the best criminal lawyers in the land this time. We'll appeal. We'll get you off."

"I have to tell you something." Marti stared into the flame of her lighter again.

"What?"

Marti glanced at her, then returned her gaze to the lighter. "I killed Angelo," she said. "I killed the warden."

"Marti...I don't understand." She didn't want to.

"I had to do it. I got him the money from the barn, and once he had it, his attitude completely changed. Up until then, we'd agreed that he would drive off and leave me there. But all of a sudden, he changed his tune. He was going to kill me, Mom." She looked at Zoe, those long-lashed blue eyes as innocent as a child's. "He was afraid that, if I got caught, I'd talk, and they'd come looking for him. I think he planned to kill me and bury me in the woods someplace."

"Did he tell you this?" Zoe asked.

"No, but he got real nervous after he had the money, and I noticed he had his gun out of the glove compartment, where he usually kept it. I figured out what he was going to do. I should have realized it earlier. He would never just let me go once he had the money. So I grabbed the gun before he could. I shot him before he could shoot me."

Zoe swallowed the bile rising in her throat. Marti's delivery of the details was flat and cool, and that was as frightening to her as the information itself. It reminded her of the conversation she'd just had with Sophie, when the little girl had spoken about her illness with such stoicism. Was Zoe the only person in these woods capable of emotion right now? Or did Marti and Sophie know something she did not about coping with feelings that were too raw, too dangerous, to be brought into the light of day?

"So..." Zoe tried to think this through. "They would have found the warden dead and figured you did it."

"Bingo."

No wonder Marti had seemed so distant, so disturbed and so desperate since arriving at the shanty. She *had* murdered someone. Had she shot him in the chest? In the head? Zoe couldn't bear to think about it. She thought of the ease with which Marti had dispatched the turtle.

"What happened to the money?" she asked.

"I took it," Marti said. "I put it back in the barn, so we'll know where it is if we want to get it before we go to South America."

"Oh," Zoe said. It upset her to know that Marti could have been so calculating and calm after murdering the warden that she'd thought to put the money back in its hiding place.

"So." Marti slapped her hands down on her thighs. "Now you know. Now I *do* have murder on my hands. You wouldn't be able to get me off, Mom, even if we could get a jury to believe me about Tara Ashton."

"But it was really self-defense," Zoe said, although she wasn't quite sure. "You had no choice."

"Thanks for believing that, Mom." Marti smiled and got to her feet. "But I'm afraid you're the only person in the world who would."

Zoe watched her daughter walk around the shanty toward the outhouse. Marti was being brave, she thought. Here, she'd been carrying the weight of the murder around with her for the past few days. She was probably having nightmares, flashbacks to the incident, and she'd kept them all to herself. But Zoe knew she was imagining how she, herself, would react to having placed a bullet into the body of another human being. She was not certain Marti would react the same way.

She remembered a time, long ago, when Marti was in boarding school. Zoe had received a call from the school, telling her that Marti had stabbed another student with a Swiss Army knife. Zoe had driven up to the Santa Barbara school, refusing to believe her daughter had been capable of such an act. Sure enough, by the time she reached the school, the other student had recanted the accusations, saying she had accidentally stabbed herself while using the knife to carve a jack-o'-lantern. Zoe had left the school in relief, and she'd been able to ignore the fact that, as she was being questioned by the authorities, Marti's demeanor had been almost scary in its calm detachment. And that Zoe's personal checking account had plummeted by several thousand dollars right around the time of the stabbing.

She hadn't thought of that incident in many years. She hadn't wanted to. It had been easier to ignore it, to forget about it. But now, as she waited for Marti's return from the outhouse, she feared that she might have *two* sick people on her hands: one with an illness of the body, the other with an ailment of the mind and heart.

CHAPTER THIRTY–THREE

Janine and Lucas drove to West Virginia late Saturday night. Joe, Paula and her parents planned to arrive the following day, but Janine was anxious to get back. The funeral had been painful and emotional, but she'd found herself growing quietly excited as she sat in the grief-filled chapel, the image of the log cabin she and Lucas had spotted from the helicopter planted firmly in her mind. It teased her while the minister spoke. She could see the deserted clearing. The fire pit. The crevice in the rock. The hint of quartz.

It had not been quartz. Not mica. The glittery shard of light had not come from something *in* the rock at all, but rather from something *on* the rock.

That thought came to her as Holly's relatives took to the pulpit, one by one, to talk about the little girl they'd lost. Janine heard nothing they said. Instead, she pictured the flat rocks, and in her mind, the small, dark crevice in one of them turned into the penknife Lucas had given Sophie; the shard of light was the glint of its blade. The image grew stronger and sharper in her mind as the service continued, and she could barely wait to escape from the chapel to tell Valerie Boykin her theory.

Once they had left the funeral, she used the cell phone in Lucas's car to call the search manager.

"I think I saw Sophie's penknife on a rock near a log cabin, about five miles from the road," she said when she had Valerie on the phone.

Valerie took the information in, wordlessly, and Janine knew the search manager was humoring her. Valerie was about to give up. Janine could hear it in the silence.

"Please," Janine begged. "Just have someone go out there and check."

"I know how much you want Sophie to be found alive, Janine," Valerie finally said. "We all do. But she couldn't have walked that far. You know that, don't you? And you're not even sure of the location of the cabin."

Janine had pleaded a while longer, then decided her only recourse was to get to the site early in the morning and make her plea in person. Lucas had agreed to go with her, but only reluctantly. He seemed a little distant, and she feared that he, too, was giving up.

They arrived at the trailer early Sunday morning to find it and its tow truck standing alone on the road. There had been no orange cones forming a barricade across the road when they'd turned onto it minutes earlier. There were no sheriff's cars, no vehicles belonging to the searchers. The only other sign of the activity that had consumed the area during the past week was the blue portable toilet standing next to the embankment.

"Where is everyone?" she asked Lucas as she parked near the trailer.

Lucas didn't respond, and she feared she knew the answer. They had called off the search. To the rest of the world, Sophie's short life was now a closed book.

Valerie Boykin looked up from the desk in the trailer when Janine and Lucas stepped inside. Slowly, she got to her feet.

Nothing needed to be done quickly, now, Janine thought. The emergency was over, at least in Valerie's eyes.

"I've been waiting for you," Valerie said.

"Where is everyone?" Janine repeated.

"We've decided to call off the search, Janine," Valerie said with real sympathy in her voice. "I'm so sorry we couldn't have done a better job for you. But with no sign of Sophie, and with the dogs completely unable to pick up her scent again—if it was ever her scent they found in the first place—there seems to be—"

"You can't just stop looking," Janine said. "You have to check that log cabin."

"The medical consultants have told us that, given Sophie's condition, she couldn't possibly have survived this long out there," Valerie said.

"That would be true if she hadn't been taking Herbalina," Janine said. "But she could—"

"The doctors don't believe that a herbal treatment could possibly make that much difference to her." Valerie put her hand on Janine's shoulder. "I'm so sorry. I know this is hard to hear." Valerie looked at Lucas as if asking him for some support, but Lucas only excused himself and went outside to use the portable toilet.

"Well," Janine said, "I guess now I'll be allowed to search for myself, right?" Anger clipped her words. "The mother is allowed to look for her daughter only when everyone else has given her up for dead."

"Janine," Valerie said, "I can understand—"

"She's not dead, damn it!" Janine pounded her fist on the counter. "I know she's not."

She stomped out of the trailer and stood in the middle of the road, arms folded across her chest as she waited for Lucas. She'd been there for a few minutes when Valerie appeared at her side.

"Are you really planning to search yourself?" Valerie asked her.

"You better believe it," Janine said.

"Well, then, take this with you." Valerie handed her a small device, and Janine recognized it as a GPS, one of the tools the searchers had used to keep from getting lost. "We don't want to have to come back here looking for you, too," Valerie added.

"I don't know how it works." Janine looked at the gadget in her hand.

"It's easy to use," Valerie said. "I'll give you a little tutorial, and you can borrow one of the maps. Then you'll always know where you are. Okay?"

Janine nodded. "Thanks."

"Come inside when Lucas gets out of the john," Valerie said. "I'll show you how it works."

It was another minute before Lucas joined her on the road, and she held the small black device up to show him. "Valerie gave me a GPS," she said. "Will you look for Sophie with me?"

He did not show the sort of enthusiasm she'd been expecting. "You mean, now?" he asked.

She nodded. "Please, Lucas. Every minute counts."

He looked into the woods, then touched her arm. "How will you know which way to go, Jan? The dogs couldn't find her. I'm not sure—"

"We'll go in the general direction of the cabin we saw," she said. He still looked dubious.

"I have to try, Lucas," she added. "I couldn't live with myself if I didn't."

It took him a moment to look at her again, and he nodded. "All right," he said. "I'll help you today, but I have to go back to Vienna tonight."

"You don't believe she's alive, either, do you?" she asked.

He took off his glasses and rubbed his eyes, and she noticed how tired he looked. How beaten. "What I do believe is that you need to look for her," he said. "That you won't rest until you've searched every possible inch of this forest for her, and that's okay. And I'll help you. But I'll have to be on the road by four. All right?"

"All right," she said, although she knew that he, like Valerie, was only humoring her. He thought this was a fruitless mission. Maybe it was, but she wouldn't know that until she'd searched the woods herself.

Inside the trailer, Valerie showed them how to use the GPS, then Janine leaned over the map on the counter.

"The cabin we saw was somewhere up in here," Janine said, pointing to an area on the map. "Did they search up that far?"

"Like I told you yesterday, Janine, that's over five miles from here," Valerie replied. "We cut off the search at three miles in every direction. It's extremely doubtful she could have gotten any farther than that."

"You don't know her," Janine said. "And I told you I saw her penknife lying on one of the rocks near the cabin."

"You *think* you did," Valerie said. "It would be very hard to see anything that small from the helicopter. Our minds can play some mean tricks on us."

"Jan," Lucas said, "I think Valerie's right. I think even if Sophie hadn't lost a shoe and even if she'd been in the best shape, she couldn't have made it that far. I know that cabin's been on your mind, but I think it's just because it was one of the few things we could see from the air, so that's where you can imagine her being. But I—"

"I need a target, Lucas," Janine interrupted him. "I need a goal. Something we can walk toward. I think we should start at the creek where the dogs picked up her scent, and then head from there toward that cabin. It's as good as any other direction. And if Sophie had seen that cabin, she would have gone to it."

"It's very far," Lucas said again.

Janine looked at Valerie. "Is the Herbalina still in the fridge?" she asked.

"Yes." Valerie walked toward the small refrigerator at the rear of the trailer. She took the soft-sided cooler out of the lower compartment, then reached into the freezer for some Blue Ice. She handed the ice and the cooler to Janine.

"Thanks." Janine opened the cooler and placed the Blue Ice inside it, then slipped the strap of the cooler over her shoulder. She looked at Lucas.

"Ready?" she asked.

"As I'll ever be."

They said goodbye to Valerie, then began walking down the road, heading for the part of the cliff where the descent into the woods was less steep.

As they entered the woods, Janine could hear a truck engine cough to life and knew that Valerie and the trailer were leaving. How did the woman feel after an unsuccessful search? Janine wondered. Would images of Sophie haunt her dreams, or could she simply put this week behind her and move on to the next search with the hope that it would have a happier ending?

She and Lucas didn't speak as they hiked toward the stream. This area had been searched over and over again, and so they didn't bother looking for clues as they walked. Janine was certain that Sophie was farther out than any of the searchers had imagined. They didn't know what a fighter her daughter could be.

She felt some disappointment in Lucas. Not just that he was anxious to get out of the woods and go home to Vienna tonight, but that he'd given her so little support with Valerie. Whether he was willing to admit it to her or not, she knew he thought Sophie was dead. He was lagging behind her as they walked, and she could hear him breathing hard. At this rate, he'd never make it all the way to the cabin. His heart was not in this. Maybe she should have simply sent him to the motel and had him come back to pick her up later.

They were only a hundred yards or so into the woods when Lucas suddenly stopped walking.

Janine turned to look at him. "What?" she asked. "Did you see something?"

Lucas shook his head. He drew in a long and labored breath, scaring her, and she walked back to him quickly.

"I'm sorry," he said. "I'm not feeling well. I'm going to have to go back."

Holding on to his arm, she studied his face. In the shadow of the trees, his skin took on an unhealthy yellowish cast. His face was damp; perspiration ran from his forehead into his eyes.

"What's the matter?" she asked.

He shook his head. "I need to sit down." He looked around as if searching for a chair.

"There's a tree stump just ahead," she told him. "Can you make it over there?"

He shook his head again. "I'll just sit right here," he said, lowering himself to the forest floor.

"Does your chest hurt?" she asked, wondering if he were having a heart attack.

He shook his head.

"Where's your water bottle?" she asked.

"It's not with me."

"Maybe that's your problem," Janine said. "You're dehydrated. Here." She reached over her shoulder to pull her own water bottle from her backpack and held it out to him.

He brushed it away with his hand. "No," he said. "I don't want any."

She lowered herself in front of him. There was a deep crease between his eyebrows.

"Are you in pain?" she asked.

"Muscles are cramping," he said. "And I'm just...weak. Nauseated."

"Would you please drink some water?" She held the bottle out to him again. "You're probably dizzy because—"

"I don't *want* it," he said with some genuine anger, and Janine drew away from him.

She stood up and shrugged herself out of her backpack. Inside it, she found a handkerchief. Squeezing water from her bottle onto the cloth, she ran it over his hot, damp forehead and the back of his neck. He shut his eyes as she dampened the cloth again and wrapped it around his right wrist. Reaching for the splint on his left wrist, she began unfastening the Velcro.

Instantly, Lucas opened his eyes and grabbed her hand. The handkerchief fell to the ground.

"I won't hurt your wrist," Janine said. "You're arm is so hot. You're perspiring.... You're soaked under the splint. Let me take it off and put some cool water on you."

He stared at her a moment, the look in his eyes blank and a bit scary. Slowly, his eyes fell shut, and Janine reached for the Velcro again.

"Janine..." His voice trailed off, and she knew he was too weak and tired to fight her.

Carefully, she unfastened the splint, not wanting to manipulate his wrist in any way. He was always so protective of it. She removed the splint, rested Lucas's hand on his knee, then picked up the handkerchief from the ground and wet it again with water from her bottle. Lifting his hand, she gently turned it to place the handkerchief on the inside of his wrist.

She sucked in her breath at what she saw: the inside of Lucas's forearm bulged with the unmistakable surgical crossing of an artery and a vein.

"You have a *fistula*," she said, her mind instantly on fire.

He nodded, his eyes still closed, and suddenly she understood the cause of his yellow skin, his camel-like ability to go without water, the muscle cramps, the weakness.

"Oh, Lucas, my God!" she said. "Why didn't you tell me? Why on earth did you keep this from me?"

"I need to get to a dialysis center," he said.

"Yes," she said, standing up again. "Do you think you can make it back to the car?" She glanced in the direction of the road. They had not come that far.

"I think so," he said. He leaned on her heavily as he got to his feet, and she wrapped her arm around him as they walked to the car. There were so many questions she wanted to ask him, but they would have to wait. Right now, he would need all of his energy and concentration to get through the woods and up the cliff to the car.

Climbing the cliff was slow and painful, and Lucas was severely winded by the time they reached the road, his breathing loud and ragged.

"You sit on the edge of the cliff, here," she said, helping him lower himself to the ground. "I'll bring the car over to you."

She raced down the road to her car, then drove toward him, parking as close to him as she could. He practically fell into the passenger seat, and she buckled the seat belt around him before getting in behind the steering wheel.

"Do you know where the nearest dialysis center is?" she asked.

"Take me back to Fairfax."

"I don't think you should wait that long," she said.

He rolled his head to look at her. "They're going to admit me, Janine," he said. "I don't want to be stuck in a hospital way out here."

"Okay," she agreed. If he worsened on the trip back to Virginia, she could find a hospital along the way.

They rode in silence until she was on 55. Then she reached across the console to rest her hand on his knee. She was truly angry with him. He'd lied to her, but now was not the time to dump her anger on him.

"What's wrong with your kidneys?" she asked.

"Same as Sophie," he said. "It didn't hit me until I was in my late twenties, though."

"So, that's why you were so interested in Sophie."

"Initially, yes."

"What about Herbalina?" she asked. "Have you wondered if it might help you?"

He was quiet for a moment, and she thought he might have

drifted off...or worse. She glanced worriedly in his direction and saw that he was licking his dry lips.

"I actually spoke to Schaefer about it," he admitted. "Apparently it doesn't work on adults. Maybe with a little tweaking, he said. But...not yet."

"What about a transplant?"

"I'm on the list," he said. "Have been for a few years."

"Oh, Lucas, why?" she asked. "Why didn't you tell me? You know I would have been there for you."

"You had enough on your plate."

"When is the last time you got dialysis?"

"Thursday."

"That's why you had to go back to Vienna Thursday night," she said. "Damn it, Lucas, I wish you had told me! This is so crazy. How many times a week do you need it?"

"Four," he said.

"Four! And you haven't had it since Thursday? Lucas, what are you—" She suddenly realized exactly what he had done. "You've been screwing up your dialysis schedule to be with me," she said. "Haven't you?"

"I haven't been as faithful about it as I should have been," he admitted. "I skipped a couple of sessions. Didn't stay long enough when I did go."

"Oh, Lucas," she said. "I just wish you'd told me." Gripping the steering wheel, she pressed the gas pedal lower to the floor, knowing at least as well as he did the risk he had taken with his life.

CHAPTER THIRTY–FOUR

Lucas didn't want Janine with him in the dialysis room, but as the nurse pushed him past the other beds in the wheelchair, he didn't have the strength or the breath or the heart to tell her not to follow.

He hadn't wanted her to know about this, ever. Certainly, he hadn't wanted her to find out the way she had. He knew she was angry with him, as well as confused by his secretiveness and hurt by his reluctance to trust her with information about a condition that was so much a part of him—and, ironically, a part of her, as well.

There were a few other patients in the room, and he knew one or two of them, but he had no energy to return their waves as he was wheeled across the floor. He transferred from the chair to the adjustable bed, leaning back against the raised mattress, and held out his arm for Sherry, the nurse who had dialyzed him many times before.

Janine sat down in the chair at the side of his bed. "Is he going to be all right?" she asked Sherry.

"Once we get this fluid out of him," Sherry said, then turned to Lucas. "I need to give you your Epogen injection first," she told him, and he nodded, offering her his other arm.

"My hands and feet are tingling," he said, knowing that Sherry would understand the meaning of those symptoms. So, of course, did Janine.

"His potassium's too high," Janine said.

"Yeah, well, I'm not surprised," said Sherry. "Let's get some blood work on you, my friend, and see what's cooking."

He felt Janine's eyes on him as Sherry gave him the Epogen injection and drew his blood for the lab work. Poor Jan. Her hair was a mess, her face wan and worried, a streak of dirt across one cheek. She'd been pulled through an emotional wringer these past seven days, and he wasn't making it any easier on her now.

When Sherry had finished drawing his blood and freed his right arm, he reached over the edge of the bed to take Janine's hand.

"Sorry," he said.

"What for?" she asked.

"For keeping this from you, and for pulling you out of the woods today. And for giving you something else to worry about when you already have enough to deal with."

Janine bit her lip. Her gaze moved to his arm, where Sherry was inserting the needles into the fistula.

"I felt like I could trust you," she said. "I felt as if I could tell you anything. And all the while, you were keeping this huge secret from me. I was a fool for missing all the clues, especially today. Your face is swollen, and your legs. And here I was trying to get you to drink."

"You were thinking about Sophie," he said. "I'd given you no reason to suspect there was anything wrong with me."

"That's Lucas for you," Sherry said, pressing a button on the dialysis machine.

Lucas recognized that chiding tone in Sherry's voice.

"What are we going to do with you, Luke?" she asked. "You've been playing with fire lately. Missing treatments. Coming in days late for your appointments. Not staying for your full treatment. You can't get away with that. You're not new to this stuff. You know better."

"He's been trying to help me," Janine said, holding his hand more tightly.

"You're not going to be much help to your friend here if you're dead," Sherry said bluntly.

"Yes, Mom," Lucas replied, but he knew she was right. In all his years on dialysis, he had never treated his disease as irresponsibly as he had lately. He'd certainly been through times of stress before, but he'd always taken great pains to keep his body as healthy as he possibly could.

"I'm calling your doc," Sherry said. "We need to admit you for a day or two. Get you stabilized and back on track."

He nodded, resigned. He'd expected them to admit him. At another time, he might have been relieved to turn over responsibility for his recalcitrant body to someone else for a while. Not now, though. The timing was very poor. He had so much work to do. Work Janine knew nothing about. Work that, if he died, would never get done, and that, he knew, would be a tragedy. For that reason alone, he should have taken better care of himself.

Sherry left the dialysis room to call his doctor, and Lucas looked at Janine.

"I don't want you to stay," he said. He was so tired. All he wanted to do now was sleep.

"I want to stay," she said, tightening her hand around his. "I can't believe that you've been dealing with this alone, Lucas. You've been trying to help me, when you should have been worrying about yourself."

"I'm serious," he said. "I just want to sleep during the dialysis. You go home."

She turned away from him, and he could practically see the wheels spinning inside her head. He knew what she was thinking.

"I don't think you should go back to West Virginia alone," he said.

"I won't go today," she said. "I want to be near you. But I'm not giving up on Sophie. I can't explain it, Lucas, but I know she's out there."

There was something in her eyes he had not noticed before. Determination, yes, but more than that. Her eyes had an almost maniacal sheen that made him afraid for her.

"Jan," he said, "look at me. Look at what's happened to me by skipping dialysis, by eating more haphazardly than usual, by not taking all my medications faithfully. And now realize...I know it's hard, but please, Jan, try to face the facts. Sophie still needs dialysis. You know she wasn't yet to the point where she could get by with Herbalina alone. And she's missed two Herbalina treatments now. Plus, she's had no food since the crash, except maybe whatever she could find growing wild in the forest."

She looked away from him again. The crazy sheen in her eyes had turned to tears, ready to spill over her cheeks at any moment.

"I know it's terrible to think about," he said. "I know it's excruciating, but—"

"And I can't think about it." She stood up. "All right. You win. I'm going home."

There was no anger in her voice, but he knew he'd hurt her by ripping the hope from her heart.

"Please call me if you need anything," she said. "I'll check back later to see if they admitted you."

"Okay," he said. "Thank you for bringing me here."

She leaned over to kiss him on the lips. "I love you," she said. "Get better, please. I can't lose you, too."

He watched her leave, the soft-sided cooler containing the Herbalina the last thing he saw as she walked out the door.

He wondered if he should call her later, if he should reveal everything to her. He could tell her that he, too, knew the pain of losing a child. But he knew he would not make that call. She had learned enough of his deception for one day.

CHAPTER THIRTY–FIVE

Janine had experienced moments of anguish and despair over the last few years with Sophie, but nothing compared to the way she was feeling now. Sitting on the sofa in her cottage, she watched old videotapes of her daughter. In her mind, the videos were divided into those featuring the relatively healthy Sophie, before she was five, and those starring the sick Sophie, beginning just before the failed transplant. Sophie may have been dancing or skating or mugging for the camera in each period of her life, but Janine could see the difference in her daughter's face. The healthy Sophie hadn't a care in the world. Her smile was genuine, unafraid, trusting of the world. The sick Sophie often wore a smile, as well, but it was a brave smile, a smile to mask the fear and discomfort. A smile designed to reassure her mother.

Lucas was in a couple of the most recent videos. One of Janine's favorite tapes had been made in the tree house just a few weeks earlier, when the Herbalina was beginning to work its magic. A happy, unpained smile was on Sophie's lips as she helped Lucas sweep off the deck of the tree house. Lucas used a large push broom, while Sophie swept with a smaller kitchen broom. There were giggles and laughter and lots of affectionate looks passing between them. Lots of love. Watching the film, Janine fought the tears filling her eyes. Was she going to lose both of them? she wondered. Both Sophie and Lucas?

Lucas's nurse, Sherry, had caught up with Janine before she left the dialysis unit.

"He's told me about you," Sherry said. "I know all about your daughter. I just wanted to tell you how sorry I am. This must be a very hard time for you."

"Yes, it is, thanks," Janine had said.

"Lucas seems to care a lot about your daughter and you," Sherry had continued. "He's a smart guy, but he's been taking too many chances with his health lately. I'm not sure what's going on with him."

"He's been helping me," Janine said.

"Right. And I get the impression you had no idea he was sick."

Janine shook her head. "I didn't know."

"Well, now that you *do* know, please try to look after him a bit," Sherry said. "His body can't continue this way. If he hadn't gotten in here when he did, I don't know how long he would have lasted before he suffered respiratory arrest or had a heart attack. He could easily have died. He still could, if we don't get his potassium and phosphorous back in balance."

"I know," Janine said. She thought of how disappointed she had been in Lucas for remaining in Vienna that night she'd wanted him with her in West Virginia. How many other nights should he have ignored her wishes and come to the hospital for dialysis? "I wish he had told me what was going on with him," she said.

"He plays his cards close to the vest, that's for sure," Sherry said. "I'd known him for months before he told me about his daughter."

"You mean *my* daughter," Janine corrected her.

"No, no," Sherry said. "I meant *his* daughter. The one who died."

"I..." Janine struggled to think clearly. "Could you have him mixed up with someone else?" she asked. "He has a niece Sophie's age, but she's still living...at least as far as I know."

Sherry looked surprised, then wrinkled her nose. "You mean, you don't know about his daughter?" she asked.

"He told me he didn't have any children."

Sherry let out her breath. "Yikes," she said. "I think I just put my foot in it."

"What are you talking about?" Janine asked.

"Well, it's certainly not my place to tell you," Sherry said, "and I never would've said anything if I thought you—"

"Tell me," Janine demanded. Her patience was ready to snap. "I can't take any more of these secrets."

Sherry looked toward the dialysis room, then turned to face Janine again. "Well, he had a daughter with the same disease," she said. "It's usually hereditary, as I'm sure you know, since your own daughter had it."

"*Has* it," Janine corrected her. She wasn't yet ready to speak about Sophie in the past tense.

"And it usually affects boys," Sherry continued, "but there's all sorts of variations on it, as you probably know. So, anyway, his daughter also had it, and she died when she was ten."

Janine shook her head, incredulous. "That's simply impossible," she said. "He would have told me."

"He didn't even tell you that he was sick himself," Sherry said gently. "For some reason he hasn't wanted you to know all of this. I probably never should have said anything."

Janine looked toward the door of the dialysis unit. She was tempted to march back in there and confront him, make him explain why he had kept so much from her, but she knew this was not the time to press him.

"I'm glad you told me," she said.

"Maybe that's why he was willing to jeopardize his own health to help you find your little girl," Sherry suggested. "You know, a way of making up for his own loss, somehow."

She'd driven home after the encounter with Sherry, numb and confused. She'd stopped at the mansion to speak briefly with her parents, telling them about Lucas's illness and how, all those times he'd left work early, he'd been going to dialysis. She realized instantly that she should not have told them. They had no sympathy for him. He should have been honest with them, they said. He shouldn't have taken a job that was too taxing to his health.

Then they changed the subject to Sophie.

"We want to start planning the memorial service for her," her father said.

"We thought there should be balloons," her mother said. "You know, in Sophie's favorite colors. I thought that would have been a nice touch at Holly Kraft's funeral, especially since there were children—"

"You don't plan a memorial service for someone who might still be alive," Janine said. She stormed out of the house, slamming the door behind her. Everyone, even Lucas, was ready and willing to bury Sophie.

Inside the cottage, she'd put on the videotapes. She needed to see Sophie alive.

The next tape had been made during one of Sophie's hospitalizations, when she was five years old. She was trying to learn an Irish jig from a clown, her hospital gown hanging loose around her small body as she hopped awkwardly from foot to foot, and the image brought a wistful smile to Janine's lips.

Gravel crunched in the Ayr Creek driveway, and Janine paused the videotape. Standing up, she pulled aside the curtain to look outside. Joe's car was headed toward the cottage, and she watched as he pulled into the turnaround.

"You're here," he said, surprised, when she met him at the door.

"Yes."

"I was coming over to see your parents," he said, "but when I saw your car in the turnaround, I thought I'd see if you were home."

"Come in," she said, standing back to let him into the cottage.

Joe glanced at the television, at the still image of Sophie and the clown.

"Damn," he said, his voice quiet. He shoved his hands into his pockets and shut his eyes.

"Sit down," she said.

He drew in a long breath as he opened his eyes and took a seat on the sofa.

"I'm relieved to see you here, Janine," he said. "To see that you're not still hunting for Sophie."

"I haven't given up, if that's what you mean," she said, sitting at the other end of the sofa. "I had to come back because Lucas was with me, and he got sick."

"What's wrong with him?"

She shook her head. "You're not going to believe this. He has end-stage renal disease."

"What?"

"I know. It's crazy. I guess he kept it from me because he didn't want me to have to worry about him when I already had Sophie to worry about."

"So...what happened? I mean, what sort of symptoms was he having?"

"He's on dialysis," she said. "That's why he had to come back here the other night. It's also why he missed some work when he was the Ayr Creek gardener. So, he was having the sort of symptoms you'd expect from someone who wasn't being careful about getting the right amount of dialysis. He was very tired and weak and short of breath. His face and hands and feet were swollen. He's in dialysis right now, and they're probably going to admit him to the hospital to get him stabilized."

"I just can't believe this," Joe said. "Do you think that's why he's been so interested in Sophie?"

"Of course," she said. "Or, at least, that's part of it."

"What's the rest of it?"

"He had a daughter with kidney disease, too, Joe. She died when she was ten."

He looked at her blankly. "Have you known that all along?" he asked.

She shook her head. "I only found out tonight, and not from Lucas, either. His nurse let it slip."

Joe looked at the still image on the television screen. "Janine..." he began, but his voice trailed off.

"What?" she prompted.

He shook his head. "Nothing," he said. "I need to get some answers from Lucas, that's all. This is getting weirder and weirder."

"What is?" she asked. "Answers about what?"

"Don't you think it's strange that he wound up working at Ayr Creek, where there just happens to be a little girl with the same disease his daughter had?"

"Maybe that's why he took the job," she said. "Remember, my father said that Lucas seemed uninterested in working at Ayr Creek until he mentioned that Sophie lived here, a little girl with kidney disease. I think Ayr Creek probably seemed like a step down from Monticello for him, but when he heard about Sophie being here, he couldn't resist."

"Well, maybe," Joe said, but he didn't seem at all convinced. He looked at the TV again. "Do you think I could borrow some of these videos?" he asked. "I'd love the chance to look at them sometime when I'm in...a little better control."

"Of course." She leaned forward to pick up three of the tapes from the coffee table. "I've already gone through these," she said, handing them to him.

"Thanks." He rested the boxes in his lap, running his fingers over the smooth cover of the one on top. "Are you serious about going back to the woods to look for Sophie again?" he asked.

"Absolutely. She's out there, Joe. I mean, I realize that from a logical perspective, she may not have been able to survive, but I still want to find her. And the truth is...I still have a feeling she's okay."

"I'd offer to go with you, but I—"

"No, thanks," she said. "I have no problem going alone. I got a GPS from Valerie and a map and my cell phone."

"I don't think your cell will work in the woods, though."

She feared he was right about that. "I'll be fine," she said.

"Won't you be afraid, being out there alone?"

She smiled. She had thought this through. "No," she said. "If Sophie could do it, I certainly can. It probably makes no sense to you, but I feel close to her out there. And being alone, without Lucas or anyone, will make me feel that much closer to her. To what she experienced." Her eyes burned, and she blinked back the tears. "I'm just torn about leaving Lucas," she continued. "I thought he was going to die, Joe. I really did. And I just couldn't bear..." She stopped speaking, knowing that it was unkind of her to let Joe see just how powerful her feelings were for Lucas.

"You really love him, don't you?" he asked.

She nodded. "I'm sorry," she said. "I know it's not what you wanted. What you've been hoping for. But I do love him."

"It just bothers me that he lies to you."

"I think he had good reasons," she said. "At least, I think his reasoning seemed good enough to him."

Joe looked at the floor a moment, then his nostrils flared slightly with the intake of breath. "I'm not so sure that's all he's lied to you about."

"What do you mean?"

He shook his head as though he regretted his words, and got to his feet. "Nothing in particular," he said. "Just...use your head with him and not only your heart. Promise me that?"

She thought of pushing him to tell her more, but tonight, she really didn't want to know.

"Okay," she agreed, standing up to walk him to the door. "I promise."

After Joe left, she leaned against the door and shut her eyes. Tomorrow, before she headed back to West Virginia to continue her solo search for Sophie, she would talk with Lucas. She wanted to know why he had felt the need to keep so much from her. For tonight, though, she would have to suffer with the mystery.

CHAPTER THIRTY–SIX

Although it was very early in the morning when Zoe opened her eyes, sunlight already peeked through the cracks in the bedroom ceiling, and she could tell it was going to be a beautiful day. Yet, that realization did nothing to lift her mood. She'd gone to bed feeling as low as she'd ever felt; this morning, she felt even lower.

What the heck had happened to her life? A few years ago, she'd been married to a fine and loving man, she'd had a career that was the envy of most entertainers. It had been on the downhill slope, to be sure, but she'd still had fans who would pay any amount to see her sing or dance or act, and the critics loved her movies, even if the general taste of the public had shifted. She'd lived in beautiful surroundings, and when she'd been able to put her fears about her career on hold, her life had seemed exciting and full.

Now look at yourself, she thought. No husband, no career, no house on the beach. She had to use a damn *outhouse,* for heaven's sake. She'd actually enjoyed the isolation and the challenges at first, back when she'd had the shanty and the woods and all of West Virginia to herself, but now she felt trapped in those same woods with her daughter, whom she loved, despite the fact that she was beginning to think of her as unlovable. And she felt painfully responsible for an eight-year-old girl, a child she could not help without gravely harming her own child—as well as herself.

"Good morning."

Lifting her head from her leaf-stuffed pillowcase, she saw Marti sitting sideways on her sleeping palette, her back against the wall. She was reading one of the paperbacks Zoe had brought with her to the shanty.

"Good morning." She returned the greeting, then looked across the small room at Sophie's bed. Sophie was facing her, her eyes open, a look of resignation on her face. The skin around her eyes was noticeably puffy, even in the dim, early morning light.

"How do you feel today, Sophie?" she asked

Sophie didn't respond right away. The only sign that she was alive at all was the slow blinking of her eyelids.

"Sophie?" she repeated. "How are you?"

"I think I'm going to die soon," Sophie said finally. Her voice possessed an eerie calm.

"Well, aren't we dramatic this morning," Marti said.

"Why do you say that, Sophie?" Zoe asked, alarmed.

"'Cause I know," Sophie said. "I mean, I've known for a long time that I might die. I'm not really scared or anything."

"You're not going to die, honey," Zoe said. It seemed the right thing to say. But Sophie was not fooled by platitudes.

"You don't understand about kidney disease," she said. "I can't live without dialysis."

"How long will it take you to die if you don't get it?" Marti asked.

"Marti!" Zoe was appalled at her daughter's insensitivity. Worse, she had the uncomfortable feeling that, if Sophie *could* say how long it would take her to die, Marti would start counting the days.

"Well, she's talking about it like it's no big deal," Marti said.

"I don't know how long it will take," Sophie said. "I've never done it before."

Zoe had to smile at the smart-ass tone of the little girl's answer.

"How can I help, honey?" She raised herself up on one elbow, a twig or something from her makeshift pillow cracking beneath her weight. "You told me it's important for you to watch what you eat. What would be best for you?"

"Protein," Sophie said. "Meat. Chicken."

"Well, I can probably find a rabbit or a squirrel that I could kill with my rifle, and we could have that for dinner if you like."

"You forgot we can't have a fire," Marti said.

"I don't want you to kill anything," Sophie said.

"Kill one of those mangy dogs, why don't you?" Marti suggested.

Zoe ignored her. "There's a kind of fish that I've caught here that's pretty tasty," she said, remembering the mild flavor of the dark-scaled fish. "How about I try to catch one of them? Fish is good protein."

"Okay, I guess," Sophie said.

"Well, I hope you both like sushi," Marti said.

"Marti, we're going to have a fire," Zoe said, startling both of them with her impatience. "I am going to feed this child. If we hear a plane or something overhead, we can pour water on the fire and get inside, okay?"

"It sounds like you've already made up your mind, Mother," Marti said.

Zoe got out of bed and walked across the room to Sophie's palette.

"Let me take a look at your foot, honey," she said, lifting the covers from Sophie's feet.

Sophie lay still as Zoe carefully unwrapped the bandage. The swelling had gone down a bit; the wound didn't look nearly as angry and raw, and she felt enormous relief.

"It's much better, Sophie," she said. And Sophie raised her head to look at her foot herself. "The antibiotics are working."

Sophie dropped her head to her pillow again. "If only they could fix the rest of me," she said.

"I know, honey," Zoe said, standing up. "I wish they could, too."

She sat on a rock near the stream, her bucket and net at the ready, watching for one of those dark-scaled fish to swim by. Usually, they were plentiful. Today, when she really needed them, they seemed to have disappeared from the stream. And the lack of them was giving her way too much time to think.

She thought of Marti's reluctance to have a fire. Those two words, *Marti* and *fire,* elicited discomfort in her, and she was afraid she knew why. For many years, those words had been joined together in her mind, although she'd tried hard to fight the cerebral link she'd formed between them. How old had Marti been when the fire occurred? Eleven? Maybe only ten?

Zoe and Max had been called back from New York, where they'd been filming a movie, because there'd been a fire in the Malibu house. The nanny's room had been destroyed, positively gutted, and at first everyone thought that the young woman had fallen asleep with a lit cigarette in her hand. But after the fire investigators searched more deeply into the cause of the fire, they determined that it had been set, deliberately, sometime in the middle of the night. It had started with a gasoline-soaked rag, which had been tucked in the corner of the room and ignited in some way. And a gasoline-soaked rag would not simply appear in the nanny's room, unless someone had placed it there.

Max tried to make a case for the nanny having done it herself. She was depressed, he argued. She drank a little.

From her hospital bed, her arms burned, the nanny pleaded ignorance, but Zoe and Max ignored her protests and made a public show of firing her. The incident was in the headlines for a few days, and Zoe doubted the poor woman had ever been able to find work again. But it had been critical to keep the spotlight off the person whom the fire investigators saw as the real culprit: Marti.

Marti denied having had anything to do with the fire, however, and there was no real proof that she'd been involved, so it was easy for Zoe to discount the investigators' theories. Oh, my, how good she'd been at denial in those days! Don't ask, don't tell. That might have been the mantra of the Garson-Pauling household. Neither she nor Max ever wanted to ask Marti if or why she had done something wrong, because then they would have had to deal with the answers. It was far easier to let things slide. And let them slide, they did.

When Marti was being evaluated for entry into boarding school, the counselor had a long talk with Zoe.

Did Marti ever wet the bed? the counselor had asked.

"Yes, until she was twelve," Zoe had admitted. Max had spanked Marti for her bed-wetting, which he viewed as pure belligerence on her part.

"Aha," the counselor had replied, jotting something down in her records, and Zoe thought she'd better watch how she answered the questions from then on.

"Did Marti like to play with fire?" the counselor asked. "Did she like to strike matches? Was she fascinated by flames?"

"No," Zoe said. She blocked the fire in the nanny's room completely from her mind. It was amazing how easily she could do that.

"Any cruelty to animals?" the counselor asked.

Zoe thought of the kitten, but there had never been any proof that Marti'd had anything to do with the demise of that little ball of fur.

"No," she'd said. "Why are you asking me such strange questions?"

"Oh, we ask all our parents these questions," the counselor explained. "You see, there's a triad of behaviors that predicts some possibly disturbed or violent behavior in later life," she said. "Bed-wetting in late childhood, fire-setting and cruelty to animals. So it's just something we like to rule out, as a matter of course, when we're interviewing a candidate for the school. We don't see much of it here, of course. It's mostly something you see in kids who've been neglected or abused."

"Oh," Zoe had said.

She'd managed to finish the interview and make it all the way out to the street before getting violently sick to her stomach.

It was a moment before Zoe realized that one of the dark fish was right in front of her in the stream, practically taunting her as it dodged between the rocks. Reaching forward with the net, she scooped it up easily and dropped it into the bucket. Another fish just like the first one nearly swam into her net, and there was yet another right behind that one. There must be a whole school of them, she thought, and she caught a few more before deciding she had enough to make a good dinner for the three of them.

And she would make it over a fire. She would study Marti's face across the flames and wish to God that she had her daughter's childhood to do over. She would give Marti all the time and love in the world, all she had deserved and been deprived of. But she didn't have the past to live over. She only had the present, and she would do everything in her power to keep Marti from returning to prison. Marti needed help; she was willing to admit that now. But it was not the sort of help prison could provide for her.

Sophie was sitting on the front step when Zoe got back from the stream. She looked a bit better than she had that morning, although maybe it was just because she was sitting up and her face did not look quite so swollen.

"I caught our dinner," Zoe said. "Let me get a knife from inside and I'll clean the fish out here with you."

"Zoe?" Sophie looked up at her. "I want to go home."

Zoe placed the bucket on the ground, then sat next to her on the step.

"I know you do, honey," she said. "I wish I knew how to make that happen."

"I want to see my mom," Sophie said.

Zoe looked over her shoulder. "Where's Marti?" she asked, almost in a whisper.

"Inside. Reading."

Zoe glanced toward the open living room window, then returned her attention to Sophie, as she struggled to find the words that would help the little girl understand her predicament.

"Your mother took very good care of you, didn't she?" she asked, finally.

Sophie nodded. "Yes."

"And I need to take very good care of my daughter, too," she said. "I'm afraid, Sophie. I'm worried about you, that's true, but I'm even more afraid for Marti." She lowered her voice, uncertain if Marti was in the living room or the bedroom. "She's...not very well. Her mind isn't right. I didn't realize that. Or else, I just didn't admit it to myself. But I can't let her go back to prison. I know that must be hard for you to understand, but prison would be the worst place for her. She would never get well there. And she would only suffer."

Sophie chewed on her lip and looked ahead of her, toward the clearing. "If *my* mom was Marti's mom," she said, "and if she was here with us, she'd find a way to get help for both of us. My mom would figure it out." She got up from the step and hobbled around the side of the shanty toward the outhouse.

Zoe watched her go, then stared down at the fish, crowded together in the water-filled bucket. Was Sophie right? she wondered. Might another mother be able to come up with a solution to this dilemma? If she could, she'd be a much better, a much braver mother than Zoe could ever hope to be.

CHAPTER THIRTY–SEVEN

Joe pulled into the hospital parking lot just before noon. In a few hours, Janine would be on her way back to West Virginia to continue what he was certain was a futile search for Sophie. He didn't know how to stop her, or how to comfort her, and it hurt him to realize that Lucas would probably know how to do both. That pain paled in comparison, though, to his certainty that Sophie was dead. His daughter—*their* daughter—was gone, and Janine, the person he needed as his partner in grief, could not grieve with him. She was too busy holding on to the slim hope that somehow Sophie had survived her ordeal.

All night long, Joe had thought about how he should handle the situation with Lucas. So, he had kidney disease. And *maybe* he'd had a daughter who had died of the same malady, but frankly, Joe had his doubts about that. Still, those facts could not explain why Lucas had lied about working at Monticello, nor did they explain why he had that kiddy porn in his recycling bag.

The only thing he could think of to do was to confront Lucas. He would tell him what he knew and get his response. And if Joe's suspicions were correct about the man, he would demand a promise from him to leave Janine alone.

Lucas's room was directly across the hall from the nurses' station, and as Joe walked toward it, he was able to see straight into the room through the open door. He stopped walking when he spotted a man and a woman locked in an embrace, silhouetted against the large window. Was it a double room? he wondered. Was that Lucas's roommate embracing his wife?

He started walking again, entering the room and turning toward the first bed, expecting to see Lucas lying in it, but the bed was empty. At the sound of Joe's entry, the woman looked over the man's shoulder to see who was intruding on their privacy.

She dropped her arms from around the man's neck. "I'll be back later, babe," she said, drawing away from him, and only then did Joe realize it had been Lucas in her embrace. Lucas was holding the woman's hand, but he let go of it when he spotted Joe.

The woman walked toward the door, smiling at Joe as she passed him, and he saw that she was pregnant, at least six or seven months so. Anger rose inside him as she left the room. True, he wanted Lucas to be proven a cad, but not to this degree, and not at Janine's expense.

"What the hell is your story?" he asked Lucas, once the woman was out of earshot.

Lucas sat down in the chair next to his bed. He was attached by an IV to a bag of clear liquid, which hung from a pole above the bed, and he moved the pole out of the way so he could see Joe more easily.

"Come over here, Joe," he said. He motioned toward the chair near the end of the bed. "Have a seat."

With a few long strides, Joe crossed the room and sat down. He stared at Lucas, who was dressed in a flimsy blue-and-white hospital gown, and who still looked pale and a bit bloated from his near call with death. But he felt no sympathy for the man sitting across from him.

"What's your game?" he asked.

"That was my ex-wife," Lucas said.

"And is that your baby she's carrying?"

Lucas smiled. "No. We've been divorced for several years. She's remarried. When she heard I was in the hospital, she came down from Pennsylvania to see me. We're still friends."

Joe no longer knew what to believe when it came to Lucas Trowell. He leaned forward, elbows on his knees.

"Look, Lucas," he said. "I don't know what I'm dealing with here. I know you've got something to hide. You somehow turn up working at Ayr Creek, with the same disease as my daughter, and as I'm sure you know, it's not the world's most common illness. I know you never worked at Monticello." He thought he saw Lucas flinch at that revelation. "And, I admit this was way out of line of me, but I went by your house the other day, and I saw a magazine in your recycling bin that had a picture of a nude little girl in it. So, since you insist on hanging around my wife—my ex-wife—and since you spent so damn much time with my daughter, I think I have the right to know exactly who you are and what you're up to." Joe heard the sudden break in his voice; he hadn't expected the rush of emotion that accompanied his words. The thought of Lucas being anywhere near Sophie was unbearable.

Lucas licked his lips and leaned back in the chair, eyes closed, and for a moment, Joe thought he was simply going to sleep. But finally, he spoke.

"I'm not a pedophile, if that's what you're thinking," he said, opening his eyes again. "I don't know what magazine you could possibly be talking about. The Monticello thing—" Lucas looked out the window "—that's a little harder to explain, but trust me, I have my reasons for tampering with the truth there."

"I *don't* trust you," Joe said, standing up in disgust. "You've lied left and right to Janine, who's completely honest and...unsuspecting. You lied to Donna and Frank, and apparently to the Ayr Creek Foundation that hired you. You have zero integrity. What gives you the right to 'tamper with the truth,' as you call it? Where do you get off?"

"Look, Joe." Lucas's voice sounded quiet and controlled after Joe's outburst. "Sit down again, please."

Joe was tempted to walk out of the room, but something in Lucas's solemn demeanor compelled him to take his seat again.

"I didn't want to tell you this," Lucas said, "at least not now, but it looks like you need to know, or else there's going to be a major misunderstanding between us."

"Tell me what?" Joe asked. His gut was churning.

"I developed kidney disease when I was in my teens," Lucas said. "I started dialysis about ten years ago, when my kidneys completely failed on me. I was married then...to Sandra, the woman you just saw in here. We had a daughter named Jordan, who inherited this disease from me, but she had it much worse. Her kidneys failed when she was just six. Her mom gave her a kidney, just like Janine did for Sophie, and Jordy did pretty well with it at first, but then she rejected it."

"Same as Sophie," Joe said.

"Right. So she was back on dialysis again." Lucas shook his head, and there was some anger in his eyes. "What a lousy way for a kid to have to live, you know? Needles and machines and the restrictive diet and all." He looked out the window again, lost for a moment in his own memories. "Anyhow," he finally continued, "she ultimately died. She was ten. She had an infection that went systemic. Killed her in a couple of days."

Joe wondered if Lucas was telling tales again, but the fact that his daughter now had a name, *Jordan,* somehow made her real. It made her very much like Sophie. Besides, Joe recognized the pain in Lucas's face. He saw that pain each time he looked in the mirror.

"I'm sorry," he said, starting to believe Lucas was telling the truth.

"Thanks," Lucas said. He drew in a long breath. "Well, I was actually a botany professor at Penn State back then," he said. "And...well, I'll get to that in a minute." He looked perplexed and offered Joe a half smile. "It's hard to know what to tell you next. I knew I had inherited my illness from my mother's side of the family," he said. "I asked her who else in the family had kidney disease. She mentioned a couple of my cousins, along with an uncle and her father. And then she told me that she'd always worried about a son she'd deserted when she was very young."

Joe held his breath. What the hell was he saying?

"I'm talking about you," Lucas said.

Joe stood up. "That's crazy," he said.

"You and I are brothers, Joe."

Joe didn't know whether to believe him or not. Too many lies had come from this man's lips, and this one was too far-fetched for him to swallow.

"I don't blame you for looking so shocked." Lucas nearly smiled. "I was, too. She was always such a good mother, such a moral person. It seemed completely out of char—"

"Why didn't she ever try to find me?" Joe asked. He'd never said those words out loud before, but they'd played on his mind every day for over thirty years. "She knew where I was."

"She was ashamed, and it was very difficult for her to talk about," Lucas said. "She told me she got married when she was eighteen and that she was a heavy drinker and used drugs. She didn't get along with her husband and she felt saddled by her baby. By you."

"So, she left," Joe said, sitting down again. "I was a year old."

"Yes, that's right. She moved to the Philadelphia area and eventually got herself straightened out. She met my father there, and they got married and had me. My father knew about the baby she'd left behind, but he was the only person who did, until she told me. I felt a need to find you, to meet you, to see if you had inherited this disease or..." His voice trailed off, then he shook his head. "Whew. I guess I have to tell you everything. I guess—"

He stopped talking as a nurse walked into the room. Joe waited out the silence impatiently, as the nurse checked Lucas's IV bag, then left the room again.

"We don't look a bit alike," Joe said. He was still clinging to denial.

Lucas smiled. "If you could see our mother, you'd know that we're brothers," he said. "You have her eyes."

"Does Janine know any of this?"

"No," Lucas said. "And please, Joe, the rest of what I have to tell you needs to stay between us. I know you don't like me, but I'll have to trust you with this. Please. I think you'll understand when I tell you. Okay?"

Joe was uncertain how to answer him. "I guess that depends on what it is you're going to say," he said. He felt no brotherly love toward Lucas.

"Fair enough," Lucas said. He eyed the glass of water on his night table, and Joe recognized the same look of thirsty longing that Sophie often wore when she'd already had her allotment of water for the hour.

"When Jordan got sick," Lucas said, "I began doing some research on my own time. I was very interested in herbs and other plants that were thought to have medicinal qualities, and I did a lot of reading about those that were thought to help people with kidney problems."

"So that's why you thought Schaefer might have been on to something with his Herbalina," Joe said.

Lucas smiled again. "No, that's not quite it. I actually began taking some of the herbs myself. I noticed no improvement, or at least, very little. But then I began giving some of them to Jordan. There was a definite improvement in her condition. She was able to go longer between her dialysis treatments. I kept playing around with the formula, finally coming up with the idea of using it as an IV infusion, but Sandra wouldn't let me do that to Jordan. That scared her, understandably. Jordan died while we were still arguing about it, but her death was completely unrelated. Still, it broke up our marriage." Lucas looked down at his arm, where the IV was attached. He touched the tape holding the needle in place gently, absently, then looked at Joe again. "Sandra always wanted a family," he said. "Now she's found herself a guy who won't pass on any deadly disease to her children."

Joe winced. "That must hurt," he said, surprising himself with his sympathy.

"Well, it did at first, but not now," Lucas said. "Now I'm just happy for her."

"So...I'm not following you about the herbs," Joe said.

Lucas nodded. "I knew I was on to something with them," he said. "I also knew that no one would listen to a botany professor's theory on using herbs in treating end-stage kidney disease. So I did some research into physicians who might take my work seriously and who would be willing to take the risk of...posing as the head of the study, when I was actually the one doing the research behind the scenes."

"Are you saying that Schaefer's study is really *your* study?" Joe asked, incredulous.

"Yes. Schaefer agreed to head up the study after I told him about the results I'd had with Jordan. He doesn't really get it, though, but that doesn't matter, as long as he's got me working behind the scenes. Herbalina's working, Joe, whether you want to believe that or not. I don't care if Schaefer gets the credit for it. I just want to help those kids who are suffering like Jordan and Sophie did."

Joe shook his head. "You are even more of a crook than I thought you were," he said angrily. "You lied every which way about the study and you took those children—those little lives—and cut them off from treatment that was proven to work and put them on—"

"The formula we're using still needs a lot of work." Lucas ignored his outburst. "And I'd like to find out why it doesn't work with adults and how I might be able to change it to make that happen. But my time's running out. I should be getting dialysis four times a week now, for four or five hours each time. It's getting harder for me to find a way to earn a living with that sort of interruption in my work, and it eats away at my research time, as well. The formula needs tweaking, but I'm having trouble putting enough time into it these days to do what needs to be done."

Joe shook his head again. "This is just... My mind is boggled, Lucas," he said.

"Back to you and Sophie for a minute," Lucas said. "I really wanted to find out if you might have had any children with kidney disease. So, when I found out that you did, I had to figure out a way to get Sophie into the study. I wanted my niece to have a chance at getting P.R.E.-5. That's Herbalina." Lucas looked a bit uncomfortable. "I knew how to garden," he said, "but I certainly didn't have the background to get the job at Ayr Creek. So I had a friend fake the Monticello reference for me."

"Man, you are just... You don't quit, do you? You develop some secret formula, and that gives you permission to break all the rules."

"I know it must seem that way to you, Joe," Lucas said. "And maybe you're right. Maybe I do think that what I'm doing is important enough to allow me to break a rule or two. But the fact is, I got Schaefer to believe in P.R.E.-5. Actually, he and I had planned to do the study under both our names, using his first to give it credibility. But when I found out about Sophie...well, she wouldn't have been allowed in the study if I had been one of the researchers, since she'd be a relative."

"You are absolutely crazy."

"Maybe. Maybe not." Lucas grinned. "I think you're in for a surprise. Schaefer's having a press conference this afternoon to announce the two-month results of the study. The results are excellent, across the board. Better than even I had expected."

"I won't believe it until I hear someone other than Schaefer— or you—say that the stuff has some merit."

"I think you should watch the press conference then." Lucas still wore his grin.

"Will it be on the news?" Joe asked.

"Should be. Definitely."

"Even if the herbal stuff is the miracle you think it is, I'm still bothered by the way you used Janine," Joe said. "I realize that you're not above using anyone if it means advancing your research, or whatever. But you played with her emotions in order to get Sophie into your study."

"No," Lucas said. "I fell in love with Janine. For real."

Joe rubbed his chin with his hand. He wasn't sure whether to believe Lucas on that point or not. He wasn't even sure that he wanted it to be the truth. "And how do you explain the porn you had in your recycling?" he asked.

"I don't know what you could be talking about," Lucas said. "I just had old mail and newspapers in the recycling. Oh!" He looked as though he remembered something. "Medical journals, maybe? There might have been medical journals in there. Pediatric journals. Could that be what you saw?"

Yes, it certainly could have been. Instantly, the image of the nude child returned to him, and only then did Joe recall that the photograph had been in black and white and rather clinical in its pose.

"I don't know," he said, unwilling to give up his anger toward Lucas so easily.

"Your skepticism is completely understandable, Joe," Lucas said. "I was never playing with a full deck."

Joe looked at him. "My mother," he said. "I'd like to hear more about her."

Lucas smiled. "She'd like to hear more about you, too," he said. "She—"

"Joe?"

Both men turned toward the door at the sound of Janine's voice. Joe stood up.

"Hi, Janine," he said, getting to his feet. "I just stopped in to thank Lucas for helping us search for Sophie."

"Oh," she said, but she wore a suspicious expression on her face, and he was certain she didn't believe him. Then she looked at Lucas, and Joe saw the concern in her eyes, the affection, the sort of loving gaze that she'd never had for him.

He started toward the hallway, touching her arm as he passed her. In the doorway, he turned around to look at them. Janine was standing next to Lucas's chair, and she waved, but it wasn't Janine he'd turned around to see. He'd just needed to take one more look at the man who claimed to be his brother.

CHAPTER THIRTY–EIGHT

"You're so quiet today," Paula said. "And you've barely touched your dinner."

Joe was at her town house, sitting next to her on the sofa, watching the six o'clock news in the hope that it would cover Schaefer's press conference. He looked guiltily at the TV tray in front of him, at the steak Paula had grilled especially for him; she would never eat red meat, herself. But he had no appetite, no interest in food. And no ability to think about anything but his conversation with Lucas that afternoon.

"Sorry," he said. "I'm not very hungry right now."

"Do you want to try a different channel?" Paula asked.

"No," he said. "This is fine." He cut a chunk from the steak. It was perfectly cooked, medium rare, and he raised it to his mouth only to stop it halfway, as the newscaster began to speak again.

"And there's hope on the horizon for children with kidney failure," the man said, a lilt in his voice, as though he actually cared. "That story next."

Joe rested his fork on the side of his plate and reached for the remote to turn up the volume. He'd told Paula that Schaefer was going to have a press conference this afternoon, but he'd said nothing about his conversation with Lucas. He had to sit with that news himself awhile before he could talk about it with anyone else. That secret conversation still felt as though he'd dreamed it.

"What do you think he's going to say?" Paula asked.

"I'm not sure," Joe said. "And with Sophie gone, I'm not even sure what to hope for."

Footage began of the press conference, which had been held at Children's Hospital. Schaefer was at the podium, with several men and one woman sitting at long tables on either side of him.

Schaefer spoke in his vaguely Boston accent as he described the study. A film was shown of several of his young patients receiving Herbalina—which he called by the more scientific name Joe had heard Lucas use that afternoon: P.R.E.-5. Except for the fact that they were hooked up to IVs, the children looked hale and hearty, and they joked with their parents, with Schaefer and with the camera crew.

"We certainly had hope this treatment would...uh, work, but it has far exceeded our expectations," the little man said in the halting style Joe remembered from the one antagonistic conversation he'd had with him before Sophie began the study. "Of the seventeen patients starting P.R.E.-5 treatment just, uh, two months ago, normal kidney function has been restored in two of them, and all the others have significantly reduced their dependence on dialysis."

A pediatric nephrologist from Children's Hospital took the podium, and Joe recognized him as one of the many physicians who had, at one time or another, consulted on Sophie's medical treatment. He was one of the doctors, as a matter of fact, who had tried to dissuade Janine from enrolling Sophie in the study.

"I will be the first to admit that I had no faith in this unorthodox treatment," the doctor said. "But as of this time, having examined fifteen of Dr. Schaefer's patients, I have to say that their improvement is not only astonishing, but it also seems to be accompanied by very few, if any, side effects. It's time that we took a more serious look at P.R.E.-5, and move this ground-breaking research to a larger scale."

Other speakers took to the podium, but the message was the same in every case: amazement that P.R.E.-5 was working, admiration for the unassuming little man they thought to be its creator, and a readiness to move forward with the next stage of the research.

Joe was literally shaking by the time the footage was over. His body felt out of his control, and somehow Paula knew. She hit the mute button on the remote, knelt next to him on the sofa, and wrapped her arms around him.

He let his head fall against her shoulder. "It was going to work," he said through his tears. "Sophie really was getting better. She would have been all right. She would have..." He shook his head, unable to speak any longer. Lucas had been telling him the truth. His tangled web of lies had been woven for a noble purpose. And he'd risked everything to be able to have Sophie in the study of a treatment he believed in.

"God," Joe said, "the grief I gave Janine over this!"

Paula held him tightly, as if to stop his shaking. "You didn't know," she said. "Who could have? You operated on the best information available. You took the recommendations of Sophie's doctors. What more could you do, Joey?"

"You yourself thought I should give the herbal stuff more credit," he said.

"Oh, I don't know, Joe," Paula said. "I can truly understand why you would think that strange little guy had no idea what he was talking about."

"He doesn't."

She leaned away from him. "But you just said—"

Joe loosened her arms from around him and shifted away from her so that he could look into her eyes. "You wondered why I've been so quiet today," he began.

"Yes."

"Well, I had a long visit with Lucas this morning."

She looked puzzled. "And...?"

"And it turns out that *Lucas* is the brains behind the study."

"Lucas? What do you mean?"

"Yes, ma'am." Joe stood up and ran his hands through his hair. "Lucas is the brains. And he would have been Sophie's savior, too. Just like he's been Janine's advocate against me, and against her parents. Against us blockheads. And my big contribution was to stand in Janine's way and make her life miserable. You said it yourself. She got her support from Lucas. She got jack from me." He groaned, pressing his hands to his temples. "I can't believe all the things I've misinterpreted!"

"I'm lost," Paula said. "What are you talking about?" She sat on the sofa, staring up at him, the expression on her face one of both confusion and worry.

He sat down next to her again. "You know that Lucas has renal failure," he said.

"Yes, and I still think that's a weird coincidence that he—"

"He's not actually a gardener."

"What do you mean?"

"He's a botany professor," Joe said, "and I guess he played around with some herbs and came up with Herbalina, which he thought would help pediatric patients. He knew no one would pay attention to him if he wanted to head the research, so he found Schaefer to do it for him. Schaefer's just a front."

"But isn't that a bizarre coincidence, that Lucas happened to take the Ayr Creek job, with Sophie living in the cottage there?"

"It was no coincidence," Joe said. He drew in a long breath, then let everything Lucas had told him that morning spill out of him. He described the loss of Lucas's own daughter, his discovery that he had a half brother named Joe, and his manipulation of every law in the books to get Sophie into the study. By the time he'd finished talking, Paula was crying.

"Why are *you* crying?" he asked.

"Because I hurt for you."

He squeezed her shoulder. "Thank you."

"And I love you."

He looked at her, surprised by the emotion, the ardor in her voice. "I love you, too," he said.

"No, Joe. I mean I *love* you," she said. "Not just as a friend, which I know is how *you* mean it."

He studied her face—the fine lines around her eyes, the freckle on her left nostril, the one lock of dark hair that never stayed in place above her ear. She was dear to him. But it was true that he had never thought of her as anything more than a very close friend.

"You know you're very special to me, don't you?" he asked, knowing those words were a weak response to her admission.

"Yes, I do. And I've watched you yearn for Janine," she said. "It's hurt me, because I wanted it to be me you were yearning for."

"I've always been honest with you," he said. "I mean, I never gave you reason to—"

"No, you've made it clear we were just friends. But that hasn't stopped me from wanting more. Or from loving you."

Joe shook his head. "I'm not even sure I know what love is anymore," he said, frustrated.

"You do."

"How do you know?"

"Because you showed it to me when my mom died," she said. "You came over to be with me in the middle of the night. You skipped work and your golf game and dropped everything for me. You drove down to Florida with me, so I wouldn't have to make the trip alone, and you worried about me when I didn't eat. I felt very, truly...loved. So, I don't believe you when you say you don't know what love is. I think you are positively over-flowing with it, Joey. For Sophie. For Janine. And even for me."

He thought back to the moment Paula had called him to tell him that her mother had died. He'd felt her pain across the phone line, felt it deep in his bones, deep enough that it had brought tears to his eyes. He would have done anything in his power to save her from that hurt.

"Come here, Paula," he said, pulling her close to him again. He held her tightly, feeling himself fill with gratitude and admiration for her, and he wondered if she just might be right about him, after all.

CHAPTER THIRTY–NINE

"We're all so sorry about Sophie," the nurse said when Joe checked in at the reception desk in Schaefer's office Tuesday morning. She had red hair, the same shade as Sophie's, and he couldn't stop staring at it.

"Thanks," he said. "And thanks for squeezing me in today."

"No problem. I know Dr. Schaefer would want to extend his condolences to you in person." She peered over her shoulder to look down a long hallway. "I can take you back right now," she said. "The kids are getting their Herbalina IVs, and he's in his office."

He followed her through the waiting room door and down the hall, remembering the only other time he'd set foot in this office. He'd left yelling then, cursing this fool of a doctor for taking advantage of Janine and making a guinea pig out of Sophie. God, he'd been a pompous ass.

But Dr. Schaefer did not seem one to hold grudges. He stood up and reached across his desk to shake Joe's hand, and the smile he wore was kind and sympathetic.

"Mr. Donohue," he began. Motioning to one of the chairs in the room with his small, wiry hand. "Please, uh, have a seat."

Joe took a seat on the other side of Schaefer's broad walnut desk.

"I'm sorry about Sophie," Schaefer said. "It's an incredible tragedy. Just when she was getting well."

Joe nodded. "And I know now that she *was* getting well."

"Yes." Schaefer nodded. "I spoke with Lucas. He called from the hospital and told me that you know everything."

"I was...shocked," Joe said. "I still am."

"You understand the need to keep what you know to yourself, don't you?" Schaefer looked worried.

"Yes, I do." Joe shifted in his seat. He'd come to this meeting with several questions on his mind, questions that had kept him awake most of the night, and he was anxious to get to them. "Do you think Sophie would have been cured if she'd been able to continue with the...P.R.E.-5?" he asked.

"I'm not sure about cured." Schaefer played with the silver fountain pen on his desk, rolling it an inch to the left, an inch to the right. "But I believe we could have gotten her disease under very good control. And I believe that Lucas was on to something, and if he'd only had the chance, he could have played around with his formula, or maybe with the way it was, uh, administered, and in time, he would have come up with both a cure for the kids and a way to make it work with adults. That's where he was headed."

"Well, he can still do that, right?" Joe asked. "You're talking in the past tense."

Schaefer shook his head. "Did he tell you how sick he is?"

"He needs frequent dialysis. An eventual transplant, I suppose?"

"They took him off the transplant list."

"Why would they do that? Because he's too sick?" He remembered that Sophie needed to be in otherwise good health before they would allow her to receive Janine's kidney.

"No. He's stabilizing. Physically, he'd be able to tolerate a transplant. But they took him off the list because he's, uh, handled his treatment very irresponsibly of late. He's missed dialysis treatments, he's rushed through them. Taken too many risks with his life, when other candidates follow their treatment to the letter."

"Why did he do that?"

Schaefer chuckled softly to himself, and Joe felt slightly mocked. "First, because he put so many hours into trying to find a cure for pediatric renal failure while pretending to be a gardener," he said with more than a touch of sarcasm. "But more recently, because he's put so many hours into trying to find your daughter."

Joe felt chastened. "He should have taken care of himself first," he said. "He won't be much good to anyone else if he's not able to do the research."

Schaefer fingered the pen on his desk, and it was a moment before he spoke again. "Do you know what it's like to put the needs of other people ahead of your own, Mr. Donohue?" he asked.

Joe narrowed his eyes at the verbal barb. "Yes, I do," he said, his anger rising. "I was a good father to Sophie, damn it."

"I don't doubt that, and I'm sorry." Schaefer looked suddenly contrite. "I'm stepping over the, uh, the line here," he stammered. "It's just that Lucas Trowell is a humanitarian who loved your daughter and your ex-wife, and who hasn't allowed himself much happiness in his own life because he cares too much about everyone else. So, I'm impatient with any criticism of him right now. And I have the National Institutes of Health breathing down my neck because they're hot to take the P.R.E.-5 study to a higher level, and—"

"Can *you* do it?" Joe asked, leaning forward in his chair. "I mean, do you understand enough about the...the formula or whatever to be able to manage the research without Lucas?"

Schaefer shook his head. "I understand the current formula," he said. "I understand how it works. But I don't have a clue about the theory behind it. I don't know how to manipulate it...to, uh, *tweak* it, as Lucas would say. And I'm worried that Lucas will never be well enough to continue doing the research behind the scenes. So I'm in a bind, and you're hearing my frustration."

"I understand." Joe stood up, still stinging a bit from the doctor's attack on his character. He'd come to this meeting with a number of questions, but one primary purpose: to know if Schaefer could continue the study without Lucas's help. Now he had the answer.

The red-haired nurse saw him walking down the hall after leaving Schaefer's office.

"Mr. Donohue!" she said, rushing toward him. "I wanted to catch you before you left. A few of the kids are getting their IVs right now, and their parents wanted to see you."

"I don't really have time." Joe kept walking. He was not up to meeting a bunch of sick kids and their parents.

"Please. They begged me to bring you back to the Herbalina room."

He made a show of looking at his watch, although there was nowhere he truly needed to be.

"Okay," he said. "Just for a minute."

She guided him down the hallway once again. The large room at the end of the hall reminded him a bit of a dialysis treatment room, but there were none of the cumbersome dialysis machines, only IV bags on poles, and four kids sitting in recliners. Three women and one man rose to their feet as he entered the room.

"Joe!" one of the women said, as though she knew him. She took his hand, squeezing it between both of hers. "We feel so terrible."

"Sophie was such a delight," another woman said. "We all miss her so much."

"She was doing so well on Herbalina," the first woman said. "It's so unfair."

The man shook Joe's hand. "I'm Jack's dad," he said, nodding toward the small boy in the recliner. "We got to be sort of a family here. I know you didn't think much of the study, from what Janine said, but I hope you realize now that she was making the right choice for Sophie."

Joe nodded. "I know."

"That was Sophie's chair." One of the women pointed to the recliner nearest the window. A few stuffed animals were propped up against the back of the seat. "All the kids brought stuffed animals in, you know, for Sophie when she came back. I guess we'll eventually donate them to the hospital or something, but for now we like having them there as a reminder of her."

Joe could only nod again; he seemed to have lost his voice. He could picture Sophie in that chair, hooked up to an IV the way these other kids were, bravely enduring yet another affront to her fragile and unreliable body.

He looked around him at the three boys and one girl. A couple of the boys smiled at him. Another read a magazine, while the little girl colored in a coloring book. Joe knew they were all smaller than their ages would suggest, but they had rosy cheeks and sparkling eyes.

And thanks to Lucas Trowell, they had every reason to hope.

CHAPTER FORTY

Joe needed to be alone.

After leaving Schaefer's office, he drove directly home. Downstairs in his family room, he mixed himself a drink, even though it was still early in the day and he was not much of a drinker. Right now, though, he felt the need.

The stack of videos Janine had given him was on the coffee table, and he picked one up at random and inserted it into the VCR, then slouched down on the sofa and hit the play button on the remote. The image on the television was of a clinical-looking room, the walls lined with recliners, and it took him only a moment to recognize the setting as the room he had visited an hour earlier: Schaefer's Herbalina room. But in this film, the chairs were empty, the room still. Then, suddenly, he heard voices, and the camera moved in the direction of the long, empty hallway.

The red-haired nurse appeared in the hallway, leading Janine, Lucas and Sophie toward the Herbalina room. Janine held Sophie's hand, and Lucas had one hand on Janine's elbow. In his other hand, the one with the splint, he was carrying a plastic grocery bag.

"See the camera, Sophie?" the nurse said, pointing straight ahead of her. "You're one of our first patients, so we're making a little movie about you."

The camera closed in on Sophie.

Sophie.

Oh, God. So tiny and pale. She looked puffy and sick; Joe had almost forgotten how sick she had looked before starting Herbalina. She was clutching Janine's hand hard, and the frightened look in her huge eyes seemed to be asking, *What new torture do I have to endure now?*

"You don't need to be afraid, Sophie." Janine seemed well aware of her daughter's trepidation. "You're just visiting here today, and Gina will explain everything that they'll do here. Then we can come back tomorrow for your first treatment."

"And there will be other kids here then, right?" Lucas asked the nurse...as if he didn't know.

"That's right. There will be six other children here tomorrow. So you'll all be able to talk and laugh together, and we can play some cartoons on that screen over there."

The camera followed Sophie's gaze to the large screen TV in the corner of the room, but the sight of it did nothing to alter her suspicious expression.

"Why don't you pick out the chair you'd like to sit in tomorrow?" Gina suggested. "We'll reserve it for you, then, and it can be your chair when you come every time."

"How many times?" Sophie asked.

"Every Monday and Thursday," Janine said. "Twice a week."

"I don't want to come here that much," Sophie said. She was still holding Janine's hand, clinging to her. "Please, Mom," she begged.

"Sophie." Lucas sat down on one of the recliners so that he was at her height. "They have something here called Herbalina," he said, "and your mom and the doctor who works here think that it can help you feel much, much better. You wouldn't need to have your dialysis nearly as much. You could probably go to school again, right?" Lucas looked at the nurse for confirmation, and Joe thought about how ludicrous that was. But Lucas was doing a good job of playing ignorant for the sake of the ruse.

"Yes, he's right, Sophie," Gina said. "We think Herbalina's going to change your life. Now, which chair would you like?"

Sophie looked from chair to chair, then pointed to the one next to where Lucas was sitting.

"Hop on up," Gina said, and Sophie reluctantly let go of Janine's hand to climb into the huge chair. She looked so fragile, so heartbreakingly small and vulnerable in that big chair, that Joe had to pause the tape for a minute to bring his emotions under control.

"Now you will be able to either sit up like that or recline a bit, whichever makes you most comfortable," Gina said, once Joe started the tape again. "Then I'll put a little needle into the vein in your arm and—"

"No!" Sophie hugged her arm against her body.

"You've had needles like that before, honey," Janine said. "You know they're not that bad."

"No," Sophie repeated. "No more needles."

"Herbalina is a liquid," Gina said. "It looks like water. It comes in a plastic bag. In order to get it from the bag into your body, we need to put it through a tube and get it into your vein with a needle. It will only hurt for the tiniest of seconds."

"Mommy..." Sophie reached for Janine, the helpless look on her face tearing at Joe's heart. He felt for Janine, as well, knowing how much it hurt her to put Sophie through yet another form of torture. It must have been especially hard with Herbalina, when she was facing such an unknown treatment and outcome—plus the wrath of her parents and ex-husband.

"Sophie," Lucas said, "I have something for you."

Sophie turned to him. There was unabashed trust in her eyes, and Joe knew that Janine was not the only Donohue female to have fallen in love with the gardener.

Lucas reached into the grocery bag he was carrying and pulled out some sort of plant. He rested it on Sophie's lap, and Joe leaned closer to the TV to try to get a better look at the green-

and-peach-colored blossom. It looked like the seed pod from a tulip poplar, but he couldn't be sure.

"What is it?" Sophie asked.

"This is a flower from the courage tree," Lucas said, with some reverence in his voice. "It's very special and very magical."

"What kind of magic?"

"Well, if you put a flower from the courage tree beneath your pillow when you go to sleep at night, you wake up feeling brave in the morning."

Joe waited for Sophie to scoff at Lucas's claim. She was too smart for that, he thought. A born skeptic. She'd questioned the existence of Santa Claus at the age of four, and never bought into the tooth fairy.

But Sophie stroked the peach-and-green seed pod with her fingertips. "Does it really work?" she asked.

"It always works for me," Lucas said. "Works like a charm, as a matter of fact. Will you try it tonight?"

Sophie looked at the seed pod again. "Okay," she agreed.

"Hooray, Sophie!" Gina clapped her hands together.

"I'm so glad, honey," Janine said.

Sophie offered the smallest possible grin she could manage, then wrinkled her nose. "Can I get out of this chair now?" she asked.

A few minutes later, Joe turned off the tape, but he remained seated on the sofa, staring at the dark television screen, still seeing the images there. He saw the love in Janine's face for Lucas and the amazing strength she seemed to draw from him. He saw Lucas's ploy to get Sophie to take the medicine he had created, that he knew would make her well. Medicine that could make any number of children well.

He'd blamed Sophie's illness on Janine. He'd blamed it on her selfish enlistment in the reserves, her tour of duty in the Gulf War. He'd never for a moment thought that *he* might be to blame—that something in his genes might have caused her to be sick, that something in his stubborn, self-righteous nature might have interfered with her getting well. He owed Janine. He owed her much more than a simple apology.

Getting up from the sofa, he walked upstairs and out the front door. He turned in the direction of the trail that ran through the woods surrounding the town homes. He knew there were tulip poplars along that trail. He needed to find a courage tree of his own.

CHAPTER FORTY–ONE

It had rained during the night, and there were puddles of rain-
water in both the bedroom and the living room. Zoe tore one of
her many sheets into rags, and she and Marti spent most of the
morning plugging the leaks in the ceiling of the living room. They
would have to do the bedroom later; Sophie was still sleeping.

They'd worked in silence, taking turns balancing on the wobbly chair to reach the cracks between the boards of the ceiling.
Marti was still angry over the night before, when Zoe had built
a fire to cook the fish. Sophie, although admitting to not gener-
ally liking the taste of fish, devoured two of the flaky fillets, but
Marti had stalked off into the woods with a can of cold ravioli.
She'd returned hours later, after the sun had gone down. Still
sulking, she had sat in the living room in the dark, flicking her
lighter on and off, while Zoe read in the bedroom. Pretended to
read, actually. She could hear the sound of Marti's cigarette
lighter, and with each *flick,* her fear for her daughter intensified.

Once she had blown out the candle in her lantern and shut her
eyes, she'd found herself unable to sleep. Sophie's breathing was
loud and labored, but that was not all that was keeping Zoe
awake. Her thoughts were on the telltale triad of behaviors about
which the boarding school counselor had spoken so many years

before. Whether or not that counselor had truly been in the habit of asking those provocative questions of all parents, she had clearly seen something in Marti that Zoe had tried hard to ignore. One more time, Zoe had failed her daughter by denying that Marti had any problems. If anything *had* been wrong with Marti, Zoe had hoped the boarding school could fix it, quietly. The world should never know that Zoe Pauling and Max Garson had a troubled daughter. If Zoe had admitted to her daughter's problems and obtained help for her, would she be all right now? Would she be a happy, normal, productive young woman? Would she still have been capable of murdering the warden? Would she have been capable of murdering anyone?

It was her turn on the rickety old chair, and Marti held it steady for her as she raised a piece of the lavender sheet toward one of the cracks. Steeling herself, Zoe took in a breath, ready to ask the question that had plagued her during the night and was still dogging her this morning.

"There's something I need to ask you, Marti," Zoe said, as her fingers pushed the sheet into the crack. "And I want you to be completely honest with me."

"About what?"

Zoe hesitated, but only for a moment. "Did you kill Tara Ashton?" she asked. She kept her eyes on the ceiling, pressing the sheet into the crevice with greater force than was necessary.

Marti did not answer, and all Zoe could hear was the sound of Sophie's breathing through the bedroom door. She looked down at her daughter.

"Did you?" she repeated.

Marti was holding onto the back of the chair. She looked up at her mother with those beautiful, dark-lashed eyes.

"Yes," she said

As carefully as she could, Zoe stepped off the chair and sat down on its edge. She felt as if she were choking, and it took her a moment to find her breath.

"Why?" She tried to keep her voice even and gentle. "What compelled you to do that? I thought you didn't even know her, Marti."

"I didn't." Marti sat down on the sofa, avoiding Zoe's gaze. "I told the jury the truth when I said I didn't know her. I met her ten, maybe twenty minutes before I...before it happened."

"I—I don't understand this," Zoe said.

Marti's eyes filled with surprising tears. Zoe had rarely seen her daughter cry, not even during the trial. "Mom...I don't want to tell you why I did it. I didn't want you to ever know."

"Tell me," Zoe said.

"She called me." Marti glanced out the window toward the forest. "Tara Ashton. She called me a couple of weeks after Daddy died."

"Why would she call you?"

"She said she needed to see me. That it was extremely important. I didn't have a clue what she wanted, but I went over there anyhow. She sounded so insistent."

Marti had been to Tara Ashton's house, after all. Zoe thought back to the witnesses who had said they'd seen Marti's car there, seen her exit the building. Zoe had thought they were mistaken, at best. Liars, at worst. She'd been wrong.

"She let me in," Marti said. "She was all smiles and...oh, you know what she looked like. Just beautiful and...so damn sure of herself." Marti looked teary-eyed again, and Zoe felt confused.

"Were you jealous of her?" she asked. "Was that it?"

"Jealous of that bitch?" Marti laughed. "No way."

"Well, then...what happened?"

Marti looked uncomfortable. She shifted her weight on the sofa, raising her feet to the sheet-covered cushions, then lowering them to the floor again. "We sat in her living room," she said finally. "She gave me a glass of ginger ale. *Ginger ale*. I thought that was weird." Marti wrinkled her nose at her mother. "Who drinks ginger ale? And then she told me that—" Marti looked up at the ceiling and let out her breath. "Oh, Mom," she said. "I just don't want to tell you."

"Tell me *what,* Marti?" Zoe was bracing herself. She had no idea where Marti's admission was headed, but she knew it was going to sting.

"She told me that she was pregnant, and that Dad was the baby's father."

Zoe caught her breath, then let it out in a laugh. "Well, that's ridiculous," she said.

"I thought it was, too," Marti said hurriedly. "But then she told me that Dad had helped her get the part that you were supposed to get in that movie. She said he got them to write it for a younger woman so she could have it."

Zoe could barely breathe. She remembered Max coming home from his office one day, telling her that he'd argued with the writer. He'd described how he'd pleaded with the man to keep the character in the script just the way she was—perfect for Zoe—but the writer had wanted to rewrite the part for Tara Ashton. Max had looked genuinely pained over the turn of events. Suddenly, Zoe wondered exactly whose idea it had been to rewrite that role.

"I still don't believe it," she said.

"Mom, I do." Marti leaned forward. "She was going to get DNA testing done on the baby. She had a lock of Dad's hair...she actually showed it to me."

Zoe laughed again, less heartily this time. "He hardly had any hair," she said.

"I know that. But she had this piece of it, and it looked like his, you know, a little curly, the way his hair was in the back, and she said she was going to use it to get DNA testing done, and that it would be all over the papers and all, unless..."

"Unless what?"

"Unless she got some of Dad's inheritance."

"Dad's inheritance?" Zoe shook her head. "Honey, I just don't believe..."

"Mom, you never believe anything, you know that?" Marti stood up, her arms waving. "You never believed I did anything wrong, when I was fucking up left and right. You don't believe Dad could have done anything wrong, when half of Hollywood knew he was screwing around on you. You don't even believe that little kid in there is going to die." She pointed toward the bedroom door.

Zoe shut her eyes. All she could see behind her closed eyelids was the softly curled gray hair above the nape of Max's neck.

"Mom, it was like I had no choice," Marti continued. "She was going to hurt you one way or another. I *hated* her for that, for what she was planning to put you through, especially right after Dad died. Either she was going to go directly to you to tell you about her and Dad, and you would have had to give her money—and she wanted a lot of it—to keep it quiet. Or she was going to plaster the news all over the universe. That's what she told me. Either way, you were going to get hurt, and I just..." Marti shook her head and sat down on the sofa again. "She'd been hanging pictures," she said. "She had a hammer there, on the coffee table. I—"

"I'm sure you didn't actually mean to do it," Zoe said. "You probably just impulsively picked up the hammer and..."

"Oh, I meant to do it, Mom," Marti corrected her. "I meant to wipe that smug grin off her face. I picked up the hammer and...man, I just let her have it."

Zoe fell silent. For a long moment, neither of them spoke. Then, finally, Zoe braved yet another haunting question.

"Did you...did you feel any regret, Marti?" she asked. "I mean, didn't it bother you to kill her? To know that you took someone's life?"

"If she'd been a decent person, then I would have felt bad about it," Marti said. "Just like I would have felt bad about Angelo, if he hadn't been such scum. Tara was scum, too. She deserved exactly what she got."

What could she say? How did you respond to your child when she let you see the evil inside her? Recriminations would not help, of that she was certain. And anyway, she was just as responsible as Marti for what had happened.

She leaned toward her daughter. "Marti," she began, "first of all, thank you for telling me this."

Marti looked away from her, studying the corner of the living room floor. "Second, honey, you need help," Zoe continued, her voice far calmer than she felt. "Do you see that? You've always been...troubled. It's my fault, I know that, and you're right. I didn't want to see it. I never got you help when you needed it. But I want to help you, now."

"Don't get any crazy ideas, Mom," Marti said. "I'm not turning myself in or anything like that. They'll put me back in prison. You know that."

"That's the last thing I want," Zoe said. "I wouldn't let them put you back in prison. I know that's not what you need, darling."

"But that's what will happen, Mom. If you turn me in, they'll put me away for life."

A rasping sound came from behind the bedroom door, followed by silence, and Zoe listened, afraid, until she heard Sophie's breathing begin again.

"Sophie's so ill, Marti," she said. "I think we have to—"

"Mom, if you're thinking about getting help for her again, just forget it," Marti said. "I've killed two people." She spoke slowly, deliberately, as though she feared her mother had lost the ability to understand her. "One more isn't going to make much of a difference at this point. Especially one who's half dead already." Marti stood up, and fear filled Zoe's heart.

"Don't you dare touch that girl," she said.

"Don't worry," Marti said, as she walked out the front door of the shanty. "I wouldn't dream of hurting your precious little baby."

* * *

Sophie got up later that afternoon. She shuffled into the living room on her swollen feet, and Zoe looked up from where she was lying on the sofa.

"How are you feeling, little one?" Zoe asked. Her throat was dry, and she had trouble getting the words out.

"Not so good." Sophie sat down at the end of the sofa, and Zoe moved her feet to make room for her. She'd been lying there all afternoon, ever since the discussion with Marti that had rocked her hold on the universe. Nothing had been as it seemed in her world. Marti had not been the daughter she'd presented to the public with pride, and her marriage had been no better than any other Hollywood union. Of course, there had been rumors about Max's tomcatting over the years, but she'd ignored them. There was always talk like that about people in power, about people with fame. If you didn't ignore the rumors, they would eat away at you. But she'd ignored so much. It was far easier to deny that anything was wrong.

"I'm so afraid, Sophie," Zoe said, her gaze resting on the little girl's puffy face.

"What are you afraid of?" Sophie asked

Zoe shook her head. "I'm afraid for you, and for Marti. I'm a little afraid *of* Marti, actually. She's...she's just..."

"She's crazy, I think," Sophie finished the sentence for her, and Zoe had to nod in agreement.

"And I want to get help for you, darling. I do. I wish I could. But if I did that, I'd be sending my own daughter to..." She shook her head. "They'd lock her away for the rest of her life," she said. "Maybe worse. They won't see what I see...the troubled little girl inside her. They'll just see someone who—who has done some terrible things. It's always that way. They put people in prison instead of trying to help them."

Sophie looked out the window. "I think I have to go to the outhouse," she said, standing up.

She hasn't heard a word I've said, Zoe thought to herself, as she watched Sophie hobble out the front door of the shanty. Just as well. Those words were truly not meant for the ears of a child.

She must have drifted off, because the next thing she knew, Marti was standing over her.

"Where's Sophie?" Marti asked. "She's not in the bedroom."

Zoe sat up on the sofa, her head foggy. "She—" Zoe struggled to remember. "She went to the outhouse, but that was a while ago, I think." She stood up quickly, heading for the door. "I hope she's all right out there."

She and Marti rushed around the side of the shanty to the outhouse. It was empty. There was no sign of Sophie anywhere.

"That little bitch must be trying to get away," Marti said. She ran back to the front of the shanty, and by the time Zoe caught up with her, she was emerging from the cabin with her gun in her hand.

"Where are you going?" Zoe asked.

"I'm going to find her," Marti said.

"You don't need to take a gun with you." Zoe reached for the weapon, but Marti quickly turned away from her and headed for the woods.

"I'm just going to scare her with it," she called over her shoulder.

Zoe ran after her, but Marti swung around, pointing the gun in her direction. "Leave me alone, Mother," she said. "I mean it."

Frightened, Zoe set out in the opposite direction, hoping that she would be first to stumble across Sophie. The little girl could not have gotten very far, not in the shape she was in.

She searched for nearly an hour, her nerves on edge as she listened for Marti's gun to be fired. But there were no gunshots, and no Sophie.

She reached the shanty before Marti had returned, and when she looked into the bedroom, she spotted Sophie sound asleep on her sleeping palette. Her breathing was loud and gravelly, but at least she was still alive.

Lying down on her own palette, with its lumpy mattress of towels and clothing, she vowed to stay awake all night. She would not let Marti harm this little child.

CHAPTER FORTY–TWO

Janine was turned around. Even with the GPS, she felt uncertain of her bearings, although she'd tried to follow her progress on the map. If these woods got any thicker, she would not be able to make her way through them. She had a new appreciation for hiking trails—and for the people who cut them. But she felt no fear at being alone in the forest, amazing even to herself. She knew it was because she felt so bonded with Sophie in these woods. She could *feel* Sophie out here, the way she had at the camp.

This was her second day alone in the forest. She'd been out here the previous afternoon, trying in vain to find the old log cabin and returning to the motel just before dark. She was not having any more luck today, but she knew the cabin had to be around here somewhere. She'd passed another cabin an hour or so ago, and at first she'd thought she'd reached her goal. She'd been apprehensive as she'd neared the old shack, and she'd understood the source of her anxiety: if Sophie was not inside the cabin, Janine's last hope would be dashed. She'd felt relief when she saw that the shack was actually caving in on itself, that it was barely more than an old stack of boards and could not possibly have been the log cabin she and Lucas had seen from the air. That was fine. The longer it took her to find that log cabin, the longer she could cling to hope. She knew her thinking was irrational, even a little bit crazy, but that was how she felt: half, maybe two-thirds, out of her mind.

Shortly after stumbling across the shack, she'd found herself near the peak of a small hill, and she'd taken the opportunity to call Lucas. It had been impossible to get through to him on the cell phone while she'd been deep in the woods, but in the more open air at the top of the hill, she reached him easily. He was still in the hospital, he said, getting chewed out for not taking better care of himself. He sounded cheerful, though, and she remembered all the times he'd put on that happy voice to boost Sophie's spirits. He was doing it for *her* now, but she was not as easily cheered as Sophie had been. And, as it turned out, he could not keep up the act for long.

"Janine," he said, after he'd been quiet for a moment, "I think you should come home."

"Do you need me?" she asked.

"Of course I need you, but that's not it. It's just...it's time to let go, Jan."

She felt a stab of betrayal. "But I haven't found her yet," she said.

"It's been too long," he said. "I'm getting worried about you."

"I'm close," she said. "I think the cabin must be nearby."

She heard him sigh as he gave up the fight. "Take care of yourself, okay?"

"I will," she said. "You, too."

She'd hung up the phone and continued her trek, walking in what she hoped was the direction of the log cabin.

Now she was turned around and aware of how the light in the forest was beginning to fade. She looked at her watch: five o'clock. She would have to head back to the road soon if she hoped to get out of the woods before dark. Just a little farther, she told herself.

She had walked another ten yards or so when she heard something in the brush to her right and stopped to listen.

Quiet. Everything was still. Then the rustling sound came again. She'd heard any number of squirrels and birds and rabbits and other small animals scratching in the undergrowth during her afternoon in the woods, but this was different.

"Sophie?" she said, her voice softer than she'd intended. "Sophie?" she called again, louder this time.

The rustling subsided, then began again, and she walked slowly in its direction, stopping short as she spotted the source of the sound: a dog was digging wildly in the earth, leaves and twigs flying out from behind his front paws. Broad-headed and bony-shouldered, his yellow coat mangy and matted, the dog turned his head toward her and bared white teeth.

Janine froze. She looked away from the mongrel, afraid to antagonize him further, and she let her breath out when the dog suddenly turned and trotted off in the opposite direction. Her gaze was drawn to the bare earth where he had been digging. There was something there, something pale in color, something that didn't belong in nature.

She nearly tiptoed toward the exposed earth, afraid of what she might find buried there.

It was the edge of a piece of cloth. Janine lowered herself to her knees and brushed the earth away from it, then let out a gasp as she recognized Sophie's flowered underpants. She pulled them from the earth. They were soiled; Sophie had been sick. She dug farther, her hands quickly growing raw from the vines and brush and soil as she searched for more of Sophie's clothes, more clues.

Finally, she sat back on her heels in frustration, looking down at her filthy hands.

Okay, why would Sophie's underpants be here? She tried to clear her head, to think straight. *Would Sophie have buried them herself? Could someone have kidnapped her, after all, harmed her, killed her, and buried her clothes helter-skelter through the forest?*

Whatever the answer to this puzzle, she needed to get the searchers out here again. She turned on her cell phone, but there was no signal this deep in the woods. She tried to remember the location of that peak from which she'd called Lucas, but she knew it was far behind her, and she was no longer sure of the direction.

She got to her feet and began moving around the forest, trying her phone in different areas. With every step, the forest seemed to grow duskier, and she knew she had to leave now or face a night alone in the woods. But she was so close to Sophie. She could feel it. As close as she'd been in eleven days. She would not leave her now.

Still trying her phone every few minutes, she continued to search, losing herself in the darkness and not caring, until it was too dark to move with any sureness or safety. Then she lowered herself to the ground, ready to share the night in the forest with her daughter.

CHAPTER FORTY–THREE

It was the early edge of dawn when Zoe awakened. She couldn't have said why, but she slipped her arms beneath her pillow as she rolled over on the sleeping pallette, and she felt something cool against her fingertips. The strange sensation made her jump. What *was* that?

Sitting up, she lifted the pillow. She was not sure what the object was at first; the light was so dim in the room. But then she looked more closely to see that it was a seed pod from the courage tree.

So, that's where Sophie had been the afternoon before. Zoe's heart ached with the realization that Sophie thought she could give her courage. The little girl did not know how difficult a task that was.

What was it Sophie had told her a few days earlier? That her mother would be able to figure out a way to save both her and Marti? At least, Zoe thought, Sophie's mother would probably try.

Picking the bloom up in her hands, she looked over at the child. Sophie's face was still badly swollen, and her raspy, labored breathing was the only sound in the room. On the third pallette, Marti was sound asleep, her hand falling over the side of the bed to the floor, her fingers locked around the handle of her gun.

Zoe put the seed pod down on top of her pillow and quietly slipped on her shoes. Then she walked carefully over to Sophie's bed, leaning over the little girl.

"Sophie," she whispered.

Sophie started, and Zoe held a finger to her lips. "Get up quietly, honey," she said. "We're getting out of here."

CHAPTER FORTY–FOUR

Today was the day.

Janine awakened, stiff from sleeping upright against a birch tree, with that thought in her mind. She stretched carefully, rolling her head around on her neck to work out the stiffness. The forest was misty, filled with the musky morning scent of earth and trees, and sunlight was just beginning to sift through the canopy.

Today she would find Sophie, one way or another. It would be over.

She got to her feet and took a long swallow from her water bottle. After relieving herself in the brush, she tried her cell phone again, but there was still no signal. She needed to talk to the sheriff. She needed to talk to Lucas.

Clicking on her GPS, she tried to pinpoint her location on the map. She was five miles from the road, deep in the heart of the forest. There was a creek nearby, she saw by the map. If she were building a cabin, she would want it to be near water, she thought, and she set out in that direction.

After only a few dozen yards, her feet began to ache and burn, and she stopped walking to give them a rest. She could only imagine how much Sophie's feet had hurt from walking through the woods, especially given the fact that she'd had only one shoe, and that thought started her moving again.

She was near the creek, according to the information on the GPS, when she heard a crackling, crashing sound from the woods to her left.

Let it be a deer and not a bear, she thought, standing still.

It was neither. Janine saw flashes of color through the trees, but it was a moment before the flashes grew together to form a person. A woman? Yes, it was a woman, dressed in tan shorts, a red top. And she was carrying something on her back. A child. A red-haired child!

"Sophie!" Janine started toward them, moving as swiftly as was possible through the thick undergrowth.

The woman kept walking, her step quick but labored under her burden.

"Sophie!" Janine called again, and the woman turned to glance at her, although she never stopped walking. Janine could see Sophie's head resting against the stranger's back. One of her feet was bandaged, and it bounced against the woman's thigh as she walked.

"What are you doing with her?" Janine yelled as she neared them.

The woman seemed to pick up her pace, and Janine scrambled after her.

"Wait!" she cried, and the woman finally came to a stop.

Janine caught up to them, and Sophie lifted her head from the woman's back. She was very ill, her color a sickly yellow, her face puffy with fluid.

"Oh, baby," Janine said.

"Mom." Sophie reached one swollen arm toward her. There seemed to be no fear in her at being carried by the woman. Or else, she was far beyond caring.

Janine held her daughter's puffy face between her hands. "Oh, Sophe," she said. "Oh, Sophe."

"She's sick," the woman said. "We have to get her out of here."

Janine reached for Sophie. "Let me have her," she demanded. "I'm her mother."

"I've got a good hold on her for now," the woman said. "We'll take turns. It's a long way out of here, and I'm not really sure which way to go."

Janine had no idea who this woman was or how she came to have Sophie on her back, but she was not an enemy, of that she felt certain. Perhaps she was a searcher who'd remained behind, out here on her own.

"I have a GPS," Janine said, "but I also have a cell phone. Let me call for—"

"We have to get out of here *now*." The woman looked over her shoulder, and Janine knew that something more than Sophie's illness was spurring her on.

"This way," Janine said, pointing. Still holding tight to the soft-sided cooler, she dropped her backpack on the ground to free herself to run, as the woman took off ahead of her. She was not a young woman, yet she seemed hugely strong and agile, and it took Janine a few seconds to catch up to her again.

She had so many questions, yet it was not the time to ask them. They no longer seemed important, anyway. She just took her lead from the woman and raced along next to her, checking the GPS from time to time, her vision blurred from her tears. Sophie was alive!

Branches snapped against her face, and she feared that either she or the woman would twist an ankle on a tree root or fallen branch if they kept up this pace.

"Can we stop for a minute?" she asked after a while. "I want to try my phone to see if I can get a signal."

The woman looked behind them again. "All right," she said, coming to a stop, breathing hard. "Let me put Sophie down for a minute."

Janine helped her lower Sophie to the ground. She had never

felt her daughter's body in this condition, with her skin so taut and discolored over the puffiness.

"Can you sit up, honey?" she asked her.

Sophie barely seemed to hear her, but she offered Janine a smile all the same.

The woman sat down next to Sophie, still breathing hard. Her shirt clung to her back with sweat, and she watched while Janine tried the phone.

"Still no signal," Janine said, staring at the display. "Look. Let me find some higher ground." She thought again of the hilltop she'd reached the day before, but was still unsure how to get there. "You can stay here with Sophie, and I—"

"No." The woman grabbed her arm. "I think we're in some danger here."

"From what?" Janine asked. "From who?"

"We just are. We need to keep moving. Can you carry Sophie for a while?"

"All right."

The woman helped her lift Sophie into her arms, and for just a moment, Janine couldn't take a step forward. Instead, she buried her head against the hot, damp skin of her daughter's neck to breathe in the earthy scent of her hair and scalp.

"Come on." The woman tugged at her arm, and they set off again.

They had gone another half mile when she knew she wouldn't be able to carry Sophie one more step.

"We have to stop here," she said, lowering Sophie to the ground again. She checked the GPS. "Please. Stay with her," she said. "Let me find the highest point around here and see if I can call out from there."

The woman did not even look at her. She dropped to the ground next to Sophie, putting one arm around the little girl's shoulders. "Okay," she said. "Hurry back, though. Please."

Checking the GPS, Janine walked ahead a bit and to the north, where she began climbing up a hill, slipping on rocks and grabbing the branches of trees to keep her balance. She tried the cell phone every few yards, finally catching a signal when she neared the crest of the hill. Pulling a scrap of paper from her shorts pocket, she dialed the number for the sheriff's office.

She barely had the breath to speak into the phone. "This is Janine Donohue," she said. "I've found my daughter. We're in the woods, and we need to get her out of here right away. She needs immediate medical attention. She can't walk, and she'll need a helicopter."

The sheriff was silent for a moment. Maybe he still thought she was crazy. "Do you know where you are?" he asked.

She gave him the coordinates for the area where she'd left Sophie and the woman.

"We'll get right out there," the sheriff assured her.

She hung up the phone without saying goodbye, already making her way back down the rise. She needed to be with her daughter.

CHAPTER FORTY–FIVE

Zoe leaned back against a fallen tree, watching Sophie's mother as she sat cross-legged on the forest floor, holding her ill—perhaps her dying—child in her arms.

"What's your name?" Zoe asked her.

Sophie's mother raised her cheek from where it had been resting against her daughter's head.

"Janine," she said. She looked into the woods, in the direction of the road, still two or three miles away from them. "Please let them come soon," she prayed aloud.

It had been nearly a half hour since Janine had returned from making her call. She'd told Zoe that help was on the way, and then the two women had settled into a silence made necessary by Janine's fervent attention to her daughter.

Zoe had not been able to stop herself from listening for the crackle of leaves that would indicate that Marti had followed—and found—them. But aside from the hum of insects and birdsong, Sophie's labored breathing had been the only sound in the forest.

"Where did you find her?" Janine asked now. "Are you one of the searchers?"

Zoe was not certain how to answer. "I was living out here in a shanty," she said. "Sophie showed up there a few days ago."

"Didn't you know she was lost?" Janine asked. "Why didn't you call the sheriff's office?"

"I have no phone," Zoe said. "And I didn't know how much of an emergency this was. How sick she was." She hated herself for making excuses. If Sophie died, she would have no one to blame but herself.

Janine lowered her cheek to Sophie's head again and closed her eyes. She rocked her daughter slowly, holding one of her small, bloated hands in her own, and Zoe fell back into a guilty silence.

Two men and one woman, all dressed in EMT uniforms, arrived after another half hour had passed. None of them looked at Zoe with any unusual interest, and she guessed she had made a more successful transition from actress to mountain woman than she had thought.

They'd brought a stretcher with them, and they strapped Sophie onto it, her tiny body asleep, her breathing still uneven and rasping.

"I have medication she needs with me," Janine said, pulling the strap of a small case from her shoulder. "Can one of you start an IV?"

"Can't do it here," the woman said. "Let's get her to the chopper. They can run an IV there."

They raced through the forest as quickly as they were able, the stretcher making the going rougher and slower than it would have otherwise been. Finally, they reached a road, but it was high above them, and it took the effort of everyone to push and pull the stretcher and Sophie up the short cliff.

The road was filled with vehicles—sheriff's cars, a fire truck and an ambulance—and people in a variety of uniforms rushed toward the stretcher as it rose above the cliff. It was disorienting, seeing all those people, all that activity, after spending a couple of months alone in the woods, and Zoe hung back at the edge of the cliff.

"We'll just carry her to the chopper," one of the rescuers said, waving away the medic from the ambulance.

Zoe turned to see a helicopter sitting at the edge of the dirt road, precariously balanced on an outcropping of land that looked like it might be used as a place to turn around or as a scenic overlook. She felt frozen in place. Where should she go? Should she turn herself in to the sheriff right now? But before she could decide, Janine surprised her by grabbing her arm, and Zoe willingly ran with her toward the helicopter.

"Are you a paramedic?" Janine asked the young woman who helped them climb inside the helicopter.

The woman nodded. She'd pulled a stethoscope from around her neck and was listening to Sophie's chest. "She has kidney failure, right?" she asked.

Janine nodded. "Yes, and I have medication with me that needs to be administered to her intravenously." She opened the soft-sided case and pulled out a plastic bag filled with liquid.

"What is it?" the paramedic asked.

"It's called P.R.E.-5," Janine said. "She's taking it as part of a study." She reached into the bottom of the case and drew out a page from a prescription pad, handing it to the paramedic, who scanned it quickly.

"Okay," the young woman said. "Let's get her hooked up."

Zoe watched as they found a vein in Sophie's puffy arm and inserted the IV.

Once the infusion was running and the helicopter was in the air, she looked across the stretcher at Janine.

"Will this work quickly?" she asked.

Janine shook her head. "Right now, she needs dialysis. I'm just hoping this can give her a chance."

"It's Herbalina, right?" Zoe asked.

Janine looked surprised. "How did you know? Did Sophie tell you about it?"

Zoe nodded.

Janine smiled at her, then cocked her head to the side, and Zoe knew that the younger woman was seeing her—*truly* seeing her—for the first time. Janine's eyes widened.

"My God, you're Zoe," she said.

Zoe leaned across the stretcher to touch Janine's wrist. "Right now," she said, "I'm just a mom like you, trying the only way I know how to save my daughter."

CHAPTER FORTY–SIX

Sophie was going to sleep through the dialysis, that much was clear. Janine sat at her bedside in the hospital in Martinsburg, West Virginia, praying that she would survive the myriad problems her failed kidneys had brought upon her. She was hooked up to a respirator and attached to monitors of all sorts. The attending physician said it was a miracle that she was alive at all, and he became an instant believer in the power of Herbalina.

She gave him Dr. Schaefer's number so that they could discuss the treatment for Sophie's condition. And once she was certain that Sophie was getting the best care possible, she went into the lounge outside the intensive care unit to call Joe.

There was no answer at his home phone, and no answer on his cell phone, either. If he had the cell turned off, she knew he was probably in the middle of a tennis game with Paula, and it both amazed and irked her that he could play tennis with Sophie still missing. But then, he thought Sophie was dead and that there was nothing more he could do. She left a message for him, then called information for Paula's number. But, of course, there was no answer at Paula's house, either. Paula had left her cell phone number in her answering machine message, though, and Janine jotted it down.

Then she called Lucas at Fairfax Hospital.

"He's in surgery," the nurse who answered the phone told her.

"Surgery!" Janine said, alarmed. "What for?"

"They found a transplant for him," the nurse said. "He's getting a kidney."

"Oh, my God, how wonderful!" Janine said. She asked several more questions, trying to determine how long Lucas had been in surgery, when he was expected to be in the recovery room, but the nurse could offer her few answers.

She tried Joe's number again, and when there was no answer, she dialed the number for Paula's cell phone. She was surprised at how quickly Paula answered the call.

"Paula, this is Janine," she said. "Is Joe with you?"

Paula hesitated. "No," she said. "Where are you?"

"I'm in West Virginia. I found her, Paula."

"Janine! Oh, God, Janine, is she...?"

"She's alive, but very sick. She's in the hospital here in Martinsburg."

"Where did you find her?" Paula asked, then added quickly, "Oh, Janine, you never gave up. You were right!"

"It's a long story," Janine said. She thought about seeing the dog in the woods, and about her first vision of Zoe carrying Sophie on her back. She thought of Zoe turning herself in to the police once they had reached the hospital, offering to lead them to her daughter, Marti, begging them to get Marti help rather than simply returning her to prison. Too much had happened. Way too much to tell Paula right now. "Do you know where I can find Joe?" she asked.

Paula hesitated again. "I'm not sure," she said. "If I hear from him, I'll tell him to call you though, all right?"

"Yes, please. He should get here as soon as he can."

"I...all right," she said. "I'll tell him. And, Janine? Please keep me informed on Sophie's condition."

"All right," she said. "I will."

CHAPTER FORTY–SEVEN

Joe had no idea where he was. He tried to open his eyes, but the bright light forced them shut again, and he heard himself groan. His entire world was centered on the dull ache in his side.

"How do you feel, Joey?"

He turned his head toward the voice and forced his eyes to truly open. Paula was sitting next to his bed, stroking the hair back from his forehead. Then, slowly, he began to remember where he was—as well as his reason for being there.

"It's over?" he asked. His mouth was painfully dry. He tried to lick his lips, but his tongue offered no moisture.

"Yes," she said. "And you did very well. Lucas is still in surgery, but so far, things are going smoothly."

He nodded. He vaguely remembered having this conversation with her already, and guessed that this was not the first time he'd gained consciousness. This *was* the first time he felt truly awake, however.

"I have some other news, Joe," she said. "Some wonderful news."

"Tell me." He could see that she was smiling.

"I heard from Janine," she said. "She found Sophie. She's sick and in the intensive care unit at a hospital in West Virginia, but she's alive."

He was dreaming. He had to be. He tried to sit up, but the pain cut straight through him.

Paula put her hand on his shoulder to hold him down.

"Whoa," she said. "They'll have you up soon enough. They told me you'll be walking in the morning."

"Where did she find her?" he asked.

"I don't know the details, but...Joe, I need to tell her where *you* are. She's trying to find you to tell you about Sophie."

He pictured Janine at Sophie's hospital bed, alone. How many times had the two of them shared that vigil?

"I have to get there," he said.

"I spoke with your doctor. You're not going anywhere for at least three days, and even then, you're just going home to rest."

"I want to see Sophie." His voice sounded childlike to his ears, and that was the way he felt—like a child who wanted something desperately. "I need to get out of here," he said.

"I know you do," Paula said. "And you'll be able to soon. But not yet. Right now, though, I need to know what to say to Janine. I want to tell her the truth, Joe. I think it's the only way to make her understand why you can't be there."

"No," he said. "There's no way you can tell her the truth without telling her that Lucas and I are brothers, and that would lead to other questions, and...no one else can know. Lucas shouldn't have told me all that he did, and I shouldn't have told you."

"I'm glad you did," she said, and he knew he'd *had* to tell Paula, that he was incapable of keeping secrets from her.

"But I want Janine to know what you did," Paula said. "To know that you saved Lucas's life. That you're the most incredible man on earth. That you sacrificed—"

"Paula," he said, interrupting her.

"What?"

He took her hand and lifted it to his lips. "I don't need her to know any of those things," he said. "It's not Janine's opinion that matters to me anymore."

CHAPTER FORTY–EIGHT

They finally let Janine into Lucas's hospital room. She walked in quietly, not wanting to wake him if he was still asleep. He lay in the bed, hooked up to a couple of monitors and an IV, and he looked pale and pained, but his eyes were open, and he smiled when he saw her.

"Hello," he said. "You found me."

She leaned over to kiss his temple. "Not only did I find *you*," she said. "I also found Sophie."

His mouth fell open.

"She's safe," she added hurriedly. "She's going to be all right."

He didn't seem to know what to say. "Have I died and gone to heaven?" he asked. "Or is this just a dream?"

"Neither." She pulled a chair close to his bed and sat down. "It's a very long and quite amazing story," she said, knowing there was too much to tell him just then. "She was staying in the log cabin."

"The one we saw from the—"

"Right."

"You had a feeling," he said.

"Yeah, I did."

"Where is she?"

"She's here in the pediatric unit. They transferred her here this morning from a hospital in West Virginia."

"I can't wait to see her," Lucas said. He shook his head in disbelief. "This is too wonderful."

She saw his eyes begin to tear, and she handed him a tissue from the box on the nightstand. It was a moment before he could speak again.

"Oh, Jan," he said, "I'm so glad for you. And for Joe."

"Joe doesn't know yet," Janine said. "I can't reach him. Paula said he went off on some retreat or something, and he doesn't even have his cell phone with him. Isn't that weird?"

Lucas smiled. "A retreat, huh?" he asked.

She nodded. "Doesn't really sound like Joe, does it?"

Lucas's smile turned to a grin. "Oh, Joe might surprise you," he said. Then he reached out his arm, wrapping his hand around her wrist, tugging her toward him.

"Come closer to me, sweetheart," he said. "I have so much I want to tell you."

EPILOGUE

One year later

The waiting room in the hospital was chilly, and Janine slipped into the sweater she'd brought with her.

"Why do they have the air-conditioning turned up so cold?" her mother asked. "Don't they know there are sick people in a hospital?" She was sitting a few seats away from Janine, a magazine in her hands, but Janine knew she hadn't turned a page for at least the past hour. Her father was just as distracted. He had one of his Civil War books with him, but his eyes were glued to the double doors at one end of the waiting room rather than to the pages in front of him.

"I don't know, Mom," Janine said. "Would you like to borrow my sweater?"

"No, thanks," her mother said. "I'll get another cup of tea if we don't hear anything soon."

Sophie suddenly ran into the waiting room from the corridor, a few steps ahead of Lucas, who was walking more carefully, balancing two cups of coffee in his hands. Sophie carried a can of Coke, and she plunked down in the seat next to Janine.

"No news *yet?*" she asked, and Janine was reminded of all the times that question had been on everyone's lips a year earlier, when Sophie had been lost in the woods.

"Not yet," Janine said, as she took one of the cups of coffee from Lucas. She smiled up at him. "Thanks," she said.

"Donna? Frank?" Lucas asked her parents. "Are you sure I can't get you anything?"

"Nothing, thank you," her father said.

"Nothing, unless you can get some warm air into this room." Her mother was still a complainer, and Janine guessed she always would be, but she treated Lucas—and Janine—with kindness these days. It was Joe who had brought about that change in her parents. He'd pointed out that they would no longer have their granddaughter had it not been for Lucas's secretiveness and Janine's rebellious tenacity. Somehow, Joe's words had made a difference.

Sophie shivered, from either the cool air, the Coke or the excitement, and Janine rubbed her daughter's bare arms.

"Here," she said. "Let's put your sweater on you." She pulled Sophie's purple sweater from the back of her chair and handed it to her.

Sophie rested her Coke on an end table, then stood up to put on the sweater. Lucas stood above her, helping her with his free hand.

"I never knew it took babies so long to get born," Sophie said, sitting down again. "How long did it take for me?"

"About twelve hours," Janine said.

"Wow." Sophie's eyes were wide. "Sorry, Mom."

Janine laughed. "You were worth every minute," she said.

"It's funny to be in the waiting room for a change, instead of in there." Sophie nodded toward the double doors.

"It's wonderful, actually," Lucas said. He sat down in the chair on the other side of Janine.

"You can say that again." Her father closed his Civil War book and rested it on his lap, apparently giving up the facade of reading.

Sophie had needed only one hospitalization since recovering

from her traumatic misadventure in the woods the summer before. The outpatient surgery had occurred three months ago, when they'd removed the catheter from her stomach. It was no longer needed. Sophie was in the second phase of the Herbalina study, and she had not needed dialysis at all for over six months.

On the other side of the waiting room, a woman sat engrossed in one of the tabloid newspapers, and from where Janine sat, she could read the bold headline. *Zoe Spotted In Cancun!* Janine had to smile. For once, she wished the tabloids were reporting the truth.

Marti Garson had spent this last year in a psychiatric hospital, and it was doubtful she would ever be released. After the helicopter had dropped Janine, Sophie and Zoe off at the hospital in Martinsburg, Zoe had turned herself in to the police. Janine had heard her agree to lead them to the log cabin and her daughter, as she pleaded with them to help Marti, rather than send her back to prison.

Janine had lost track of Zoe then, as she focused on the needs of her own very sick daughter, and it wasn't until the next day when the news was full of the bizarre story that her attention was once again drawn to Zoe and her plight.

No one really seemed certain what had happened as Zoe and the authorities approached the cabin. The official report was that Marti had panicked, barricading herself inside the cabin, threatening to kill everyone, including herself. According to the sheriff's office, she began shooting wildly through the cabin windows, and one of her bullets had struck and killed her mother.

But there was another tale, one Janine preferred: Zoe had once again faked her own demise and was living in blissful isolation, away from public scrutiny and, yes, the barbs of the tabloids, somewhere in the mountains of West Virginia. Or perhaps, Janine wondered now, in Cancun. That was the explanation she would forever choose to believe.

Joe suddenly stepped through the double doors, wearing blue scrubs and a wide grin. His eyes were on Sophie.

"You have a little brother!" he said.

"Yippee!" Sophie ran to him for a hug.

"Wonderful news!" Her mother clapped her hands together.

"Congratulations!" Her father stood up to shake Joe's hand, and Lucas put his arm around his brother's shoulders.

"How's Paula?" Janine asked.

"Great," Joe said. He couldn't lose his grin if he tried, Janine thought, and she stood up to kiss his cheek.

"Daddy?" Sophie looked up at Joe.

"Yes, Sophe?"

"Is he all right?" she asked. There was worry in her face.

Joe squeezed her shoulder. "They're going to test him when they get him to the nursery," he said. He and Paula had opted against amniocentesis to determine if their baby carried the gene for the kidney disease Sophie and Lucas shared. It wouldn't have made any difference to them if he did. They knew there was treatment available for him.

"We can walk over to the nursery now, if you like," Joe said to all of them. "You'll be able to see him, then, Sophie."

They left their coffee cups, soda cans and magazines behind them as they followed Joe through the corridor to the nursery. Lining up in front of the long nursery window, they watched as a nurse wheeled a plastic bassinet toward them. The name *Donohue* was on a card at the foot of the bassinet, and a dark-haired, sleeping angel of a baby boy lay bundled inside it.

"Look at all that hair!" Janine's mother said.

The baby definitely had Paula's black hair, Janine thought, but she was certain his nose and lips were Sophie's.

Sophie stood in front of Joe. "He's so little!" she said. "Can I hold him, Dad?"

"Very soon," Joe said.

There were a few more comments about the baby's good color, his tiny fists, his peaceful slumber. Then, for a moment, no one spoke.

Joe finally broke the silence. "We're naming him Luke," he said, his gaze still on his new son.

The name was no surprise to Janine; Paula had told her weeks ago that if the baby was a boy, they would name him after Lucas. But Lucas hadn't known, and Janine felt the emotion in his grip on her hand.

She and Sophie had moved in with Lucas in February, when the remodeling on his rambler had been completed. They'd built a second story, adding bedrooms that looked into the trees. The green-and-salmon-colored seed pods on the tulip poplars were now in bloom, and Janine could see them through the bedroom windows each morning when she awakened. There was a second tulip poplar outside Sophie's bedroom window, as well.

The night before Sophie had the surgery to remove the catheter, Lucas and Janine had gone into her room to tell her good-night. They'd expected her to be a bit anxious over the procedure she'd be having the next day, and Lucas had fretted over the fact that the seed pods were not yet out on the tulip poplars and he had nothing to offer Sophie to tuck under her pillow.

As Janine stood in the doorway, Lucas sat on the edge of Sophie's bed and told her that she no longer needed a bloom from the courage tree beneath her pillow, since she now lived in a house virtually surrounded by the trees.

"I don't believe in the courage tree anymore," Sophie had said, and Janine had felt the tiniest jolt of disappointment at her daughter's words.

"You don't?" Lucas asked.

"No," Sophie said. "There's no such thing as magic. The courage tree just makes you *think* you're getting courage from it, but really, the courage is inside you all the time."

Lucas had smiled and leaned forward to kiss her forehead. "What a wise, wise girl you are," he'd said.

None of them liked to remember the previous June, when their lives had been filled with fear and worry and too many secrets.

Only Sophie seemed to have emerged unscathed from the experience. The annual Scouting trip to Camp Kochaben was coming up again in a couple of weeks, and to everyone's surprise, Sophie wanted to go. She talked about getting a new sleeping bag and being able to swim in the lake this time, as though no one would hesitate about her making the trip. Joe had given his permission, but Janine had held back.

Now, as she watched her daughter, her entire family, looking through the nursery window to embrace this new life, she knew she had to let Sophie go. And she vowed to reach deep enough inside herself to find the courage that had been there all the time.